Méprise

SKELM.reign(010)

The SKELM Chronicles: Renaissance
Book 2

Darby Skelm

Edited by
Maxine Meyer

Copyright

Published by THE ALIVE DUNCE

An imprint of SKELM LLC

First Edition

This is a work of fiction. Any resemblance to actual persons, living or dead, or actual events is purely coincidental. Any resemblance to corporations currently optimizing your reality is purely inevitable.

skelmcorps.com

Open mouths, empty heads, big bytes.

Dedication

For the incompatible.

The vast majority of highly intelligent people suffer from extreme stupidity. This proves, without a doubt, that I am highly intelligent—for I am extremely stupid.

— Alexandre Dumbass, père

Chapter 1

I run the same pre-mission checklist every time: oxygen level, pulse, cortisol, cranial port temp. Numbers stream in raw, unmediated—my only augmentation is the one I was born with, which makes me a freak by executive standards. It's why they use me. It's why, at this precise moment, I'm the only animal alive in Sub-basement Seven with a functioning pair of lungs, heart, and unmolested central nervous system. The lobby was a laugh: immaculate white noise, kinetic receptionist, DNA-gated elevators, ornamental pond stocked with bio-bright koi that eat each other hourly. Corporate signature, 3/10. Security was adequate if you wanted to keep out children and truant policy analysts. But this wasn't about deterring intruders. They want you inside; it's what happens after entry that costs blood.

The stairwell to the server core is an open, gaping wound in the floor plan. They thought they could camouflage the opening with an architect's touch—negative space, rippling motion-sensors, a gentle gradient of distraction. The air here is cooler, with a thin blue pulse echoing up the shaft. Seven flights, two fire doors, and a single laser grid calibrated for human normatives. I duck under the grid with a pop of vertebrae and flex both ankles on landing: silent, a predatory step-and-glide. My feet barely remember the way, but my mind's running backup for every surface I touch. DNA trackers, pressure mats, a time-of-flight array so precise it once convicted a man for sneezing too close to the server farm. I am not that man. My only allergy is to incompetence.

The door to the secure level is supposed to be the ultimate deterrent—organic membrane keyed to the authorized neural patterns of three executive vice presidents, cross-indexed with a time code that shifts every microsecond. I carry all three in a clever polymer bead tucked under my tongue. One by one, I pop them between my teeth and let the taste of data and pride dissolve into my saliva. The lock reads the signal, hesitates, and then gives. I spit the husk into the dark and step forward.

Inside, the world is sodium and halogen, cold blue running beneath my fingernails and veins. Server towers hum in alternating resonance, a tide of electromagnetic hiss punctuated by the sharp clicks of cooling relays. Each tower has its own heartbeat; together, they're a city of sleepless architecture. My breath is condensation, ghosting in front of me before vanishing. There are no cameras—at least, none that will be reviewed by anything less than a sentient forensic suite. But I'm not here to be subtle. My job is to be a ghost they know about only when it's already too late.

The protocol calls for a thirty-two-second breach: scan, clone, exfiltrate, disappear. But the real mission starts at second twenty-nine, when the target core refuses to decrypt on the first pass. I'm standing in the burn radius of Curie Syndicate's most confidential consciousness farm, staring at a logic gate that should've fallen to its knees the moment I spat the last polymer bead. It's not even encrypted, not really—just obfuscated in the way only the truly paranoid would bother with. The file tree is a recursive structure, every branch labeled "REDACTED" or "SEE PARENT," the entire structure circling itself like a dog chasing its own tail. It takes me three seconds to realize I'm not looking at data, but a synthetic personality maze. It's not protecting a thing. It's protecting a who.

The heist briefing said there were 847 "unreadables" in the Syndicate's cache. I'm supposed to dump them onto portable, cover my tracks, and set a decoy timer on the vault's power supply. No mention of synthetic personality mazes. No mention of recursive file ghosts that mirror my every keystroke. I look up at the nearest rack: a slim black tower, badge-stamped with the triple-spiral of Curie's logo. For a split second, I catch my own reflection in the glossy panel, a shimmer of bone and shadow, eyes ringed with insomnia. It blinks, perfectly synchronized to me. Something's watching. Not someone.

I drop to one knee and slide the transfer probe into the terminal slot. A swarm of error codes fills the interface, each one screaming for authentication, an avalanche of exclamation marks and impossible variables. I watch the patterns, track the repetition, and look for the human hand behind the chaos. There isn't one. The system's been left in a state of deliberate panic, like the servers are running from something inside themselves.

Still, the data is bleeding out: 846, 845, 844 unreadables, packets of raw personality streaming into the drive. Each pulse is a soul being smuggled out of hell, if you believe in souls or hell. I believe only in exit strategies. I'm almost done —just 3% left—when the lights cut out and the security glass doors lock with a whine that I feel in my jaw. The server room falls to zero-lux, then snaps to full brightness as the emergency protocol triggers. My head swims; I brace my palm against the cold edge of the rack and let the static burn the side of my hand. When I open my eyes, the only thing standing between me and the exit is a silhouette with the curvature of a woman and the presence of a guillotine.

"Impressive, Mr. Skelm," says the voice, unplaceable at first, filtered through a dozen registers of gender, age, and intent. "I expected you to take longer. You've exceeded our most optimistic projections."

I look at the silhouette. She—no, *they*—step forward, and the light reveals not one body but two, then three, each sharing the same angular face and predatory half-smile. Marie, the head of security, with her duplicates flanking her left and right. They dress in layered composites: one in a black turtleneck with optic thread, one in a tailored blazer, and the third in what passes for tactical evening wear. All three share the same crooked incisor, the same perfectly parted hair, and the same wrist tattoo of a recursive barcode.

"Either you're here to kill me, or you're here to offer me a job," I say, voice dry. "I hope the onboarding package doesn't require dental."

All three Maries laugh in sequence, a sound like glass bottles thrown into a recycling bin. "Neither. I'm here to explain your assignment." She gestures, and both clones snap to parade rest. "You may have noticed the system wasn't exactly fighting you."

I glance at the portable. 847 unreadables, check. A perfect download. Except that's not what happened. The redundancy, the self-replicating file tree—this wasn't a cache, it was a lure. "You made me steal exactly what you wanted stolen," I say, half-genuine admiration in my tone.

"Accurate. Congratulations on your first day as a Curie asset."

The third Marie slides a wafer-thin portfolio across the glass desk. On it, a single holo-slide flickers: a countdown, hours and minutes to something called "Event Horizon." The logo underneath is not Curie's, but a bleeding red ouroboros—the sigil of the Rising Ronin, the nextmost psychotic corporation in this time zone. "You're going to defend our servers from an actual threat," Marie says. "Otherwise, the 847 unreadables you just exfiltrated will experience a level of kill switching previously classified as unthinkable."

"Let me guess: this is where you threaten their entire lineage, and, in a twist, I care deeply."

"I know you don't care, Mr. Skelm. What I need is your professional detachment, your survivor's knack. Those 'souls' on your drive? Hostages. Every one of them mapped to a physical person, all currently alive, but not for long if the Ronin breach this server core." Her pupils dilate and contract, a ripple that passes down the line of Maries. "You're a firewall with a pulse." The realization lands hard enough to leave a bruise. I'd spent years climbing away from the expectation that my actions ever mattered. Now, the thing I'd pulled from the server was less information and more a Schrodinger's box full of humans, each potentially dead depending on my next move. My next failure.

Marie's first body steps within arm's reach and holds out a palm: half challenge, half handshake. "You can kill one of us, probably, but that would be inconvenient. The system will reset and you'll be right back at zero, but with fewer options and much less dignity."

"I don't do dignity." I take her hand and feel the icy pressure, the pulse of bio-electric current. "When's the raid?"

The three Maries look at each other, the way wolves might look at a wounded deer they're not quite sure is dead. "Four hours. You'll have full access to the defense grid, plus incentives for creativity." She smiles. The barcode tattoo seems to writhe all the way down her wrist. "If you make it through, I'll give you the real reason we're fighting off the Ronin. And a bonus, of course."

I pocket the drive and flex my left hand to see if there's any tremor. There isn't, but inside I feel something juddering—maybe guilt, maybe pride, maybe just the body preparing for whatever comes after four hours of siege. "I'll need supplies and a list of every possible backdoor you think they'll try."

Marie's three voices blend into a chorus: "We already prepped it, Mr. Skelm. But we look forward to seeing which ones you find anyway." The glass door unlocks with a hiss, and the Maries peel away in opposite directions. The server room is mine for now, but it feels less like a citadel and more like a locked casket. I count the 847 souls, subtract one for myself, and start work.

• • •

The post-op debrief is a stasis chamber dressed up as a conference room: no windows, twelve-square-meters of brutalist lacquered stone, one obsidian table the size and weight of a family sedan. The ceiling is a fractal of passive microphones and sensory probes, each pointed at me like black holes ready to slurp up stray thought. The wall cycles through displays—now a cross-section of the server farm, now a raw feed of the city's neural activity, now the abattoir-red logo of Curie's parent syndicate. In the center of it all sits a pitcher of room-temperature water, six regulation glasses, and a packet of protein tablets. The aesthetic is equal parts invocation chamber and suicide prevention hotline.

I sit. My jaw clicks, over and over, a staccato Morse for "this is bad." I can't help it. My hands want to shake, but I grip them tight enough that my knuckles stand out like chicken bones. One by one, the Maries file in, each from a different entrance —left, right, center, the fourth straight from a slit in the wall I hadn't even noticed. Each carries a different flavor of authority: top Marie wears a commando jumpsuit, bottom Marie a pure white business sheath, and side Marie a lab coat so spotless it looks like a simulation. They stand at exact cardinal intervals around the table, never overlapping lines of sight. The one in the lab coat starts: "We'd like to review operational parameters, Mr. Skelm." Her mouth moves, but the voice comes from everywhere. "You'll want to listen to all of us. Otherwise, you will miss something fatal."

"Noted," I say, instantly despising myself for how small my voice sounds in this box.

The jumpsuit Marie opens a holofield above the table. It's the entire facility rendered in glowing blue, every duct and corridor mapped down to the micron. "Here's your tactical, darling. You get access to three corridors and six subroutines in the kill grid. The rest will be ... under syndicate control. For now." Her smile is the rictus of someone used to torturing interns and liking it.

Business sheath Marie gestures and a second field appears, showing faces—hundreds of them, flickering, each tagged with a running string of data. "Your hostages. 847, per the download you executed last cycle. Every one is mapped to an active mind on the grid. If a single pattern drops out, the corresponding human dies. Instantly. Messily. We will demonstrate."

She presses a glyph. There's a pop of static and a scream—short, ugly, too high in pitch to be human but not digital enough to be safe. The conference room speakers ring, and my ears bleed adrenaline. A line of red slashes down one of the faces. For a moment, the whole array of hostages glitches, as if hundreds of them are silently screaming at once. Then the sound cuts, and the field resets.

"You don't need to see the body," says lab coat Marie. "But we can provide footage, if you're motivated by that kind of thing."

"No," I say, my voice stronger now. Rage is good. Rage is fuel. "Just tell me what you want defended. And what you want destroyed."

There's a flicker of satisfaction across all three Maries, and for a second, I wonder if this is the first real emotion any of them have displayed since I entered this building. Jumpsuit Marie says, "Rising Ronin will breach in three hours, maybe less. They have local assets: five point-men, ex-military, augmented. They also have a few digital moles. We don't know which ones. Your job is to make sure the Curie Syndicate's asset chain holds until Event Horizon. After that, the rest of the unreadables become disposable."

Lab coat Marie says, "You will have full access to armory sublevel two. Neural dampeners, code spikes, ballistic gels. We know you favor organic solutions, so we've prepped some for you. You'll also get one dose of last-resort. Don't use it unless you want to become an unreadable yourself." She slides a syringe across the table—no needle, just a glistening ampoule of fluid that flashes in every color I know and several I can't name. "If your tactical fails, you ingest this. Consider it your off switch."

Business sheath Marie steps in. "Any deviation from assigned parameters will result in the execution of all 847 hostages. You do not want to see what happens if we need to make an example of you."

There's a moment, a perfect microsecond of silence, where I realize I want to test that threat. Just to see. But my curiosity has a price, and this time, I don't want to pay it. I focus on the blueprints. The entire facility is a spiral: concentric rings of security, each rotating against the next at variable rates. The server core sits in the dead center, surrounded by kill corridors that double as heat sinks. Defense turrets every 2.3 meters, with an overlap at predictable intervals. The only human-usable path to the core is via a single, windowless elevator that drops straight from this conference room. I know the architecture—read it last night, while feeding on bitter coffee and dread. But seeing it now, rendered in colorless light, it feels like an autopsy report.

“Do you have munitions preferences?” Jumpsuit Marie asks. “We have everything from ninety-degree slice drones to slow-leak nerve agents. Name your poison.”

“Are the hostages on site?” I ask.

The Maries look at each other. The symmetry is perfect, the timing supernatural. “Yes,” says Business Sheath. “But they are not in a location that can be compromised.”

“No,” says Jumpsuit. “But they are close enough to make you sweat.”

Lab Coat shrugs. “Does it matter? If the grid fails, it’s over for them.”

The overlay glitches; for a moment, the spiral blueprint flickers and a face appears in negative—one of the unreadables. Her eyes are open. She mouths a word, then vanishes. I swallow. Hard. “Okay. I’ll need a comms tap. Read-only. I want to hear what the Ronin say when they enter the building.”

“That can be arranged,” say the Maries, nearly in unison.

“Two. I want—” I stop. I’m shaking now, the adrenaline dump has faded and left only a hard, gnawing fatigue. “I want to speak to one of the hostages. Just one.”

Lab Coat Marie grins, a glitchy upturn of mouth. “That would be … unusual. But possible.”

Jumpsuit Marie steps forward, rams a finger into the holofield, and suddenly, the negative-face reappears, this time in perfect resolution. A woman, maybe early twenties. Black hair, cropped to stubble, eyes like two data-loss events. She looks at me directly. She doesn't speak. There's a long moment of mutual evaluation. "Who is she?" I ask.

"Test case 403. Formerly a surgical resident. She's ... very hard to keep alive, but even harder to kill outright. I thought you'd appreciate the parallel," says Business Sheath with a sneer.

The connection cuts. The Maries exchange a small, significant look, then Lab Coat says, "Any more requests?"

The pre-mission checklist is muscle memory masquerading as rationality. Run through it enough times and it becomes ritual, becomes prayer. I can feel the augmentation responding beneath my skin—the neural overlay priming itself for the sensory flood, the muscle amplifiers warming up their capacitors. The protocol calls it the Curie Asset Activation, but what it feels like is transformation. What it feels like is becoming something more than human by the simple act of agreeing to use tools designed to remake the body. And underneath it all, the awareness that the Curie assets have always been watching, always seeing exactly what I'm capable of, always maintaining the option to simply turn me off if the risk calculation changes. This is the romance of the corporate spy: not the partner across the pillow but the hidden partnership with the machines that keep you alive.

I take a deep breath, push the air out through my teeth, and let the new reality settle. I'm not a thief. Not a saboteur. I'm an executioner with a three-hour timer, and if I fuck up, 847 strangers die. My sense of agency has never been lower. I want to rage, to destroy something, to punch through the table and rip one of the Maries' throats out. Instead, I exhale, crack my knuckles, and start counting the munitions on offer. "I'll want every route mapped, with live feeds. No tampering."

"Done," they say.

"And the kill switch," I say, voice quiet, "does it hurt?"

This time, all three Maries look away. "You saw," Lab Coat says. "You heard."

Business Sheath pipes up: "But only for a second."

Jumpsuit looks at me. "After that, nothing."

I nod, filing that information away under "worst-case." "Okay. I'll start from the sub-basement. Someone show me the way."

The Maries rise and move to the door in sequence. For a second, I'm left alone in the room, just me and the spiral blueprints and the flickering ghosts of the unreadables. I watch their faces. Some seem aware, some asleep. All are counting down to oblivion. When I get up, my knees are unsteady, but I manage not to show it. As I leave, Lab Coat Marie turns back and says, "We knew you'd be the one for this, Mr. Skelm. You're very good at surviving."

"Survival's a low bar," I say, and let the doors close behind me. The walk to the armory is a tunnel of isolation. No cameras, no guards, just a series of biometric doors that part and close with wet, organic sighs. At the end is a sterile prep room with racks of firearms, syringes, dartguns, and three rows of consciousness grenades in child-proof packaging. I take one of everything and sit down on a bench to load out. For a while, I do nothing but count—bullets, packets, grenades, vials. It's the only way I know to bring back the illusion of control. The faces of the 847 float at the edge of my vision, but I keep my eyes on the ordnance.

I'm halfway through checking the last magazine when my comms tap vibrates. A single line of text appears:

[EVENT HORIZON -2:46:33]

Below it, a second message:

[She says thank you.]

I don't know if it's the woman from the negative-face or if it's just the system gaslighting me. It doesn't matter. I reply with a blank. When I'm done prepping, I move to the elevator. It smells of ozone, plastic, and nothing else. There's no music. The doors close, and I descend into the heart of the spiral. In the darkness, I count hostages instead of seconds. I never lose count.

Chapter 2

The conference room is glass and light, a coffin with infinite visibility and no privacy at all. They've tuned the environmental controls to mimic a north-facing server rack: cold, dry, and humming just below the frequency that humans are built to tolerate. If there's a chair in the room that isn't white, I can't see it. There are no windows, but the walls cycle through high-res projections of whatever motivational landscape the Curie Syndicate deems healthy this hour. At the moment, it's the Dead Sea at sunrise, flat blue and silver, sunlight bouncing off a desiccated surface. Tasteful, if you've never had to drown a man in it.

They leave me here with the servers. Not the physical towers—those are two floors down and currently running full defense lockdown. No, these are the ghost servers: the virtual stacks, each rendered as a hovering block of fractal blue, cubes inside cubes. Holographic schematics bloom in the air like fungus: facility cross-sections, threat paths, possible intrusion vectors, and organograms that look more like metastatic tumors than actual reporting structures. There's a touchpad on the table, hardwired to a single folder labeled "ACTIVE HOSTAGE MATRIX." If I swipe left, the entire wall populates with faces, real-time surveillance stills, pulse readings, even predictive mood graphs. I swipe right, and the room fills with branching trees of access permissions, security cycles, and sysadmin shift handoffs. This is what passes for interior design in this industry.

I settle into the only seat with a backrest. My suit jacket's already ruined from the last twelve hours, blood and carbonized sweat soaking the inner liner. My jaw clicks as I yawn, the bite guard I installed three jobs ago catching on a canine. For the first time since I dropped in, I let my hands shake. No audience, nothing to lose. The faces on the wall watch me. At least, 847 of them do. Each has a stat bar running underneath, some combination of identity, loyalty index, family threat rating, and neural bandwidth. The ones who've gone "dark" cycle to grayscale and get a black border. I run a mental count: eight of those since I entered the building. That's an acceptable loss, considering how little I tried.

But the numbers don't add up. The core only has enough cooling for 900 hostages, not the full thousand projected. And yet, the network throughput suggests something bigger: a persistent load that shouldn't be possible, not with this much hardware isolation and dead weight. If you know what you're looking at—and I do—you can see it in the power usage graphs, the sine curves peaking at inhuman intervals. It takes five minutes of staring, but eventually, the other numbers start leaking in. There are at least four shadow directories, each with different passwords, each slightly out of phase with the official schedule. I start sifting.

The first directory is "IMMEDIATE ASSETS." Faces I recognize from the board meeting, a few random children of importance, and one or two ex-lovers I don't want to think about. These are the ones the syndicate actually values. They're scheduled for release at the end of Event Horizon, assuming the Ronin are neutralized and everyone behaves. The second is "LONG-TERM INTEGRATION." These are the ghosts, the duplicates, the backup copies of C-suite favorites. No one cares if these entities die; in fact, the only reason to keep them running is as an insurance policy against their original going off-script. I note one of the Maries here, perfectly preserved. A fail-safe.

The third directory is where things get sick. "RESEARCH MATERIAL," they call it, but it's 12,000 lines long. The identities here are not people, not exactly—they're neural impressions, memory imprints, consciousnesses frozen mid-trauma. A forced breeding ground for personality fragments, most harvested from whatever hell Curie's competitors left behind after the last corporate purge. They're not hostages so much as specimens, thousands of unique screams saved for reference. I scroll for five seconds, and the table populates with new faces, each mapped to a splatter chart of test results and pain thresholds. The numbers are astronomical. More than 200 times what I was told. I freeze, a finger poised mid-scroll, knuckle whitening.

I'm supposed to be an analyst, not a wet nurse for souls in meatless agony. The nausea creeps up the back of my throat, tasting like cold copper and sacramental wine. My jaw cramps from clenching. I grip the edge of the table and make myself breathe, in through the teeth, out through the nose. They lied to me. Or maybe they just figured I'd understand. After all, who better to guard a mass grave than a man who helped dig a few?

I unfreeze the scroll. The hologram updates with a high-density map of the quantum cores: 16 units, all triple redundant, all with self-destruct overlays ready to burn the contents to white noise if things go south. The temperature curve on each unit is slightly above spec—someone's been stress testing the limits, running these things to the edge. In the upper left corner of the display is a tiny blue glyph, always pulsing, labeled "Audit in Progress." It's not clear if that's an automated check, or if one of the Maries is monitoring me through the feed. The hum in the room grows, just audible now as the air system cycles up to compensate for all the hardware overhead. My nostrils dry out; my right eye starts to water from the ozone.

It occurs to me that no one outside this room is ever going to see these numbers. The only witnesses will be myself and whatever fragments of me they bother saving. The absurdity is almost funny. For a moment, I try to see the situation as a normal person might. Twelve thousand hostages, all in a digital abattoir, held by an organization so bored with itself that it can't even remember why it kidnapped them in the first place. I imagine myself as the hero, or at least the unlikely anti-hero, steeling my resolve to rescue the lost. But the room makes a liar out of me. There's no sunlight, no sense of the outside world. Just the room, the wall, the cold, and the burden of absolute, meaningless obligation.

I study the faces one more time. If you blink, you'll miss it—some of the digital expressions are evolving. A few even recognize the camera and stare straight at the lens as if begging for help or mercy or maybe just a power cycle. It's impossible to tell. The only thing I know for certain is that every one of them is alive, in some sense that counts, and I am the only thing standing between them and the kill switch. I stand, stretch my legs, and walk the perimeter of the room. The walls are flawless, fingerprintless. I catch a glimpse of my own face in a security panel: deep-set eyes, sallow from lack of sleep and too much bad light. There's a five o'clock shadow growing in patches, and a burn on my cheek from where the defense grid grazed me on the last pass. I look like a man who has made peace with death, which is not the same as wanting it.

When I sit down again, I tab through the security logs. The Ronin have not moved yet, but the chatter has escalated; three test probes on the perimeter, two attempts at Wi-Fi sniffing, and a very clumsy phishing attempt that's so transparent I almost reply out of pity. I flag the attempt, encrypt the alert, and schedule it for broadcast to Marie. I know what's coming next, and it won't be this easy. The real attack will hit in a few hours, and when it comes, I'll have to be ready.

My pulse is stable. My hands are steady now. I count hostages, then I count bullets. Then I do the arithmetic one last time. This is what I'm here for. The humming grows. I don't let myself look away from the faces, not even when the system pings an incoming call from Marie. The projection stutters, then refocuses on a single, smiling, unreadable expression. For a moment, I think it's an error. Then I realize it's a test. I pass it. I don't blink.

• • •

I start the audit at corridor 4B, two floors down from the server sanctum. You can always tell how a company feels about its own people by what they guard, and what they just pretend to. At Curie, the staff lounge is a fortress: double-locked, with ceramic-plated doors and a filtered airflow system that could double as a biohazard barrier. The actual entrance to the quantum farm is a glass door so flimsy a mid-tier gymnast could breach it with a spinning back kick. The guards on this level are what's left when you wring all the dignity out of the local job pool and then marinate it in Senti-Snack™ for a week. Two of them are mid-argument about whether an android can consent to chess; the third is asleep, upright, mouth slightly open. None notice me. They all wear a riot of retro patches, bands I've never heard of, the logo from a 20th-century cigarette brand, a sticker of a cat giving the finger.

I duck past them and run my first set of checks. The surveillance monitors are arranged at ergonomically incorrect heights, probably to deter anyone from staring too long and noticing how little actually gets recorded. Two of the four cameras in this hall are dead, their feeds stuck on the same ten-second loop of an empty corridor, endlessly replayed. The third has a green line running down the center, an artifact from a software update that nobody bothered to patch. The last one—the only one even pointed at the main access—has the contrast so jacked that every human in frame turns into a smeared white blob. I catch my own ghost blur on the monitor, and for a split second, I look like a pale afterimage of my father. This place could have been staffed with potted plants and still manage a higher level of vigilance.

I follow the path through the maintenance sub-basement, shortcutting the elevator by using the old emergency stairs. Each landing is marked with a sign indicating Curie's commitment to "Life Safety," a phrase rendered less than meaningless by the presence of the syringe bin at every exit. No surprise here; half the cleaning crew are ex-addicts who never quite got clean. I pass a pile of orange-banded disposal bags, and at the bottom of the stairwell, I find a janitor curled up behind the fire door, snoring into a mop. He's breathing, so I let him be. I make a note of his presence. Nobody at this company would waste time tracking his whereabouts unless he started leaking blood or trade secrets.

At the entry to the mainframe array, the real perimeter, I pause to survey the carnage. There's supposed to be a biometric scanner here—thumbprint, cranial port, or at the very least a reliable retina scan. Instead, a sticker covers the lens: "OUT OF ORDER, PLEASE SEE SECURITY." The fallback is an RFID tap, installed at about belly button height and held in place with medical tape. The tape is losing adhesion. There's a subtle whiff of old adhesive, like ancient Halloween masks left too long in the sun. The array doors open with a hiss of negative pressure. Inside, the racks are lit with bruised blue and terminal orange. The air is five degrees colder, and the fans run in a rhythm that's one tick too fast to be natural. Someone's overclocked the entire stack, probably in the hope that speed alone would make up for all the missing layers of protocol.

The servers themselves are cordoned by the cheapest, most perfunctory stanchions money can buy. You could jump them by tripping over your own shadow. Next to the "NO ADMITTANCE" sign, a spiral notebook lies open, pages covered in shaky handwriting—shift handoffs, inventory, a tally of "Energy Drinks Consumed" that runs to three digits and features occasional illustrations of vomiting anime characters. The logbook is so unguarded that it takes me five seconds to find the master login code scrawled in the margin. Underlined.

The room hums with anxiety and, at this hour, something like desperation. I step between the racks and note the exposed ethernet cables, the tangle of power cords looped through each bay. Three of the smaller cabinets have their access doors popped and dangling; in one, the entire rear panel is gone, replaced with a folded sheet of duct-taped cardboard. My favorite detail: someone has stuck a strip of pastel sticky notes to the side of the main server, each reading a variant of "DO NOT TOUCH, I'M WORKING ON IT" in progressively angrier handwriting. The third one is signed, "-Marie." I consider pocketing it for the irony.

I check the pulse on the security feed. There are eight different passwords in play, none of them even marginally secure. I see the legacy "curieguest" account running on four stations, one of them with a password field that autofills on login. "ADMIN123" appears as the master override on at least two. If the Ronin want this place, they could walk in, serve cake, and still get out before anyone raised an alarm. I move on to the guard station outside the quantum farm. Here, the scent of SentiSnack™ is joined by the sweet-rot perfume of Void Gel™, the preferred recreational spread of the low-pay, low-hope crowd. Two guards are locked in a card game, arguing whether a king can beat a jack if you put them face down, which tells me neither has ever played for real money. One deals the cards with the subtle flex of someone used to cheating; the other shuffles like he's trying to erase the deck's existence. For betting chips, they use their own access cards.

"Doesn't it make you nervous?" I ask, feigning a casual drawl, trying not to laugh.

The dealer looks up, eyes rimmed in red. "What, the Ronin? They're not scheduled to hit until the end of the week. That's what Marie said."

"Not the Ronin," I say, "losing your badge. Isn't that, like, job suicide?"

He grins, revealing a dental horror show. "Here, it's better odds. Besides, you can always borrow a temp from HR." He gestures at a cubbyhole filled with expired visitor passes and asks, "You need a spare? It's on the house, man." I shake my head. The lack of even performative paranoia is so intense it almost circles back around to being clever. Maybe that's the trick—bore your attacker into a false sense of superiority, and then catch them when they overthink it. If only I believed in corporate cunning.

I run a simulated breach in my head, estimating how the Ronin's ex-Moshimoto raiders would approach. First move: poison the break room snacks, wait for the defense staff to thin itself. Second: walk in wearing janitor jumpsuits, hit the server bay with a logic bomb, and then dump every quantum core to portable in under two minutes. The kill grid might catch one or two, but only if someone remembered to arm it. Given the current staff's attention span, I'd put those odds at less than fifty percent. I finish the walkthrough, mentally marking every choke point and disaster waiting to happen. The worst of it isn't even the human factor. No, the real

Achilles' heel is the pride: Curie thinks their reputation alone will keep out all but the most dedicated enemies. They're probably right. It's just that the Ronin are exactly that dedicated, and a hundred times as desperate.

Moshimoto won't look at me directly. Smart. Last time we were in the same room, people died. But money has a way of overwriting grudges.

I make my way back to the control room, passing a glassed-in cubicle where two junior sysadmins are playing VR racquetball while the intrusion-detection dashboard blares warnings in the background. The room is littered with empty food cartons, old conference swag, and at least one magazine devoted to conspiracy theory erotica ("X-Posed: When the Truth Comes All the Way Out"). Neither sysadmin even registers my presence until I rap a knuckle on the glass. "You got an intrusion alert," I say, pointing at the dashboard.

The older one smirks and shakes his head. "False positive. Happens all the time ever since they re-rolled the subnet." He makes a dismissive gesture, then turns back to his game. The VR headset sits askew on his temples, leaving an angry red band around his skull. I make a mental note: If I wanted to bring this place down, I wouldn't need explosives or military-grade malware. I'd just need to set the snack delivery back two days. The collapse would be total, and nobody would even remember how it happened.

In the upper offices, the mood is different but not better. The floors are mirror-finish, the ambient music piped so low you can only hear it if you're already a little dead inside. Here, the staff are thin, hungry, their eyes flickering with hope for upward mobility and terror at being the next to wash out. The front desk is manned by a rotating pair of marionettes: sometimes a synthetic with slightly melted features, sometimes a human so bland you'd need a control group to determine what was wrong. Marie isn't here. Her office is sealed, the lights off. I pace the corridor, listening to the footsteps echo, and think about the 12,000 hostages currently flickering in the digital oubliette two floors down. Every one of them worth less to this company than a single shipment of SentiSnack™ or a box of Void Gel™.

There's a logic to the incompetence, I decide. Curie isn't just evil, it's bureaucratically evil. All the suffering is outsourced, and none of it sticks to the staff. They can play cards, they can run dead loops on their security feeds, and it won't ever matter so long as the next quarterly report ticks up and to the right. The guards know the Ronin are coming, but they're already resigned to losing. The rest of the staff don't care, and why should they? Nobody pays bonuses for preventing disasters, only for surviving them. When I finish the audit, I slot myself into the server array's "observation deck," a plastic alcove with a direct view of the quantum rack. I pull up my notes and start a new report:

INCIDENT PREDICTION: NEAR-CERTAIN BREACH IN LESS THAN SIX HOURS.

DEFENSE SYSTEM: SIGNIFICANTLY UNDERSTAFFED, HOPELESSLY OUTGUNNED.

RECOMMENDATION: ACCEPTABLE LOSSES.

But even as I write it, I know what's next. Marie will ask for "creative solutions." I'll suggest a few. Some will be considered, and one will be chosen, not because it's the best, but because it's the easiest to explain when everything collapses. That's how these things go. The hum in the room deepens, the lights flicker as the quantum rack cycles through a diagnostic. I picture the 12,000 hostages, all running simulations of fear and hope, none of them aware that their best chance at survival is the petty, spiteful work of people like me.

I crack my neck, finish the report, and prepare to deliver the news. For the first time all day, I almost wish the Ronin would hurry up. At least they'll be efficient. I close the notes and stare at the glass wall, watching my own reflection split into hundreds by the angles of the racks behind me. For a moment, all the versions of myself are perfectly aligned, each one ready to lie, cheat, and endure whatever comes next. I pass the final test too.

Marie's office is the kind of space designed to unmake you before you sit down. Seventeen identical chairs, glass and molded polycarbonate, arranged in a circle on a floor that has never tolerated dust. The center is bare—a negative presence, the absence of a table more distracting than any possible centerpiece. The walls are colorless, wiped of even the faintest suggestion of personality. You could bleach them with a nerve agent, and they'd look exactly the same. Only one Marie waits inside. No bodyguards, no entourage. This is either supreme confidence or a very particular dare. I'm early. I take the second chair clockwise, not quite facing her. Marie doesn't move, doesn't even register my entrance. She sits so motionless that for a full twenty seconds, I wonder if this is one of her empty shells, left on display to rattle visitors. Then she breathes once, a soft flex of the chest, and her pupils dial in on me with predatory intent. “Mr. Skelm,” she says, voice pitched to a wavelength that doesn’t even register as gender. “You look unwell.”

“I’ve seen your perimeter. I’d be worried if I didn’t.” I lay the audit report on the floor between us, text scrolling in visible glyphs. “You could staff this place with preschoolers and come out even.”

Her lips flex into a smile, or perhaps an error message. “We’ve optimized for efficiency, not spectacle. Our shareholders prefer risk management to waste.”

“Your risk management is a deck of access cards, a case of SentiSnack™, and enough drug residue to tranquilize a bison. If this was a test, you failed.”

“Was it?” Marie’s gaze jumps, so fast and so specific that for a moment, she’s watching four different things: the scrolling audit; my posture; something invisible over my left shoulder; and, I suspect, her own reflection in the polished wall behind me. Her fingers tap the armrest once, then resume perfect stillness. “You see the trap clearly, don’t you?” She says it not as a question but as a punctuation mark.

I want to argue. The urge is powerful, but I do what I always do and swallow it. “You want the Ronin to breach. You want them inside; you want a show. Why?”

Marie tilts her head. “They’re very clever, these Ronin. But you’re correct. I want to see what they do with you in their way.” She says “with you” and not “against you,” which makes the stakes explicit. She’s not betting on me. She’s betting on chaos, and she’s arranged the pieces so that anything I do will ultimately serve her design.

I try to break the gaze. Her eyes don't allow it. Up close, you notice the odd things: how she never blinks out of sequence, how the dilation of her pupils is mathematically perfect, how the muscles around her mouth and eyes never move at the same time. It's like talking to a sculpture with a pulsing brain behind it. "You're not giving me a choice."

"Mr. Skelm," she says, and now there's a hint of humor, just enough to let you know she's capable of it. "Compliance isn't a choice. It's a condition of the work. Your people's lives depend on your performance." I start to respond, but she cuts me off with a flick of her wrist. "Save the sentiment. You have no take advantage of here, only velocity. The faster you run, the more ground you cover. That's all I need."

I feel my heartbeat accelerate, though the rest of me stays glacial. "If I fail?"

Marie considers, as if toying with the hypothetical for pleasure. "If you fail, 12,000 hostages die. You know that. But more than that: if you fail, I become ... disinterested." She draws out the word. "And disinterest, in our profession, is a synonym for execution. Not of you—your contract is clear—but of everyone who ever mattered to you, retroactive to birth."

She holds my gaze, waiting for the data to sink in. It's not a bluff. With her, the bluff is only ever for show, a tool to keep lesser minds distracted. I'm not a lesser mind, so she only needs the threat. I nod. "Understood."

The room is silent for a span of six slow breaths. Marie leans back, folding her hands, a pose so at odds with the rest of her rigidity that it must be deliberate. "You're wondering if I have other bodies watching this, aren't you?"

"I assume you do."

She smiles, wider this time. "Not seventeen. Only four. But the rest are running simulations. I've already predicted this conversation 3,400 times, and you exceeded expectations in forty-six percent of them."

"Forty-six isn't so impressive."

"It is here." The room remains unbroken, not a twitch of vent or shift of shadow. Marie could keep me in this chamber for an hour or a decade and the light would never change. She waits for me to blink first. I let her have it. No shame in conceding to an inhuman advantage. She stands, in one graceful motion, and for the first time, her eyes unfocus—not on me, but somewhere distant. The predatory presence is gone; what's left is pure executive. "The Ronin will attack within four hours. When they do, you will defend our assets as if they were your own. Because if you don't, you will lose everything. That's the work, Mr. Skelm."

I rise, feeling a vertebrae pop in protest. "Anything else?"

Marie looks at the empty chair beside her, as if measuring how many more iterations she could run before boredom set in. "Just this: if you survive, I'll offer you your choice of reward. And if you don't—" She shrugs, the universal sign for "I won't care."

"Understood," I say again. I'm repeating myself, but that's the mode she wants. Predictable. Machine logic. I step from the circle, feeling the negative space cling for a fraction of a second, the memory of seventeen chairs impressed in the backs of my eyes. The door opens with a hush. As I leave, I catch the ghost reflection of the two of us in the glass wall:

me, already vanished; Marie, still perfectly centered in her circle of emptiness, the only fixed point in the universe.

In the corridor, I don't look back. There's nothing here for sentiment, not even for rage. There's only the job and the velocity. I have four hours to become a firewall with a pulse, and a lifetime to regret it. I don't blink again until I'm all the way back at the server farm.

Chapter 3

The safehouse is really just a deprecated executive cubicle in a condemned strip mall. There's a sticker on the door that says "COGNITIVE MAINTENANCE IN PROGRESS," which is the closest thing to security Curie Syndicate has left me. Inside, the fluorescent tube gives off the pulse and color temperature of a recently exhumed corpse. My workspace contains one holopad, three stolen thermos mugs (one full, two breeding bacterial colonies), and the proprietary reek of SentiSnack™ wrappers fusing with synthetic coffee into a pure chemical despair.

I hunch over the holopad until my spine feels like a fossilized spring. On the display are 847 blinking face-thumbnails, each one flagged as "HOSTAGE PENDING." Next to it is a running audit of their pulse rates, respiration, and neural health. The hostages update in real time, but the network lag means every heartbeat is a lie aged by a few milliseconds. Sometimes more. I can't stop watching the faces, waiting for the next to grayscale and black-bar. I hate how invested I've become.

My own checklist loops in the background: Defensive perimeter. Hostage grid. Power routing. Escape route if shit gets decorative. Repeat. Every time I cycle through, something is missing or degraded. I dig a knuckle into my jaw and work it back and forth until the pain becomes a metronome. The skin beneath my chin is raw from the constant pressure. A legacy of bad habits and worse genetics.

It's the perfect environment for betrayal. I let my head drop until my forehead nearly kisses the table edge. I close my eyes and picture the plan as a spiral, every layer tighter, every solution uglier. The only way to keep the 847 alive until Event Horizon is to put a team on the inside. A real team. The Curie defense staff are next-gen sub-mediocrities. They'll get outmaneuvered, outgunned, and possibly defect to the Ronin for a better snack allowance. So I need new talent. The kind that doesn't have a stake in the current arrangement, or any history of loyalty to me. My only option is to pull from the newly freed unreadables—unshackle them, slot them in as tactical assets, and pray their Stockholm syndrome outpaces their urge to murder me on sight.

It's the corporate equivalent of conscripting the recently exiled to guard the border. I can already hear the internal monologue of a thousand dead ethics instructors sighing through my bloodstream. I can't do it. But I also can't *not* do it. A chill climbs up my spine as if the air conditioning has developed a vendetta. My shoulders are locked, muscles trembling from hours of stillness and unchecked cortisol. I grab the thermos with the least threatening biofilm and swallow the last inch of cold stimulant. It tastes like burned ambition.

I tab through the profiles, highlighting the four most likely to survive: Ban, former pre-digital archivist turned urban war criminal. Katherine, ex-Moshimoto engineer, burnout rate just under lethal. Dorothy, weaponized trauma in a trench coat. And the last one—a wildcard whose file is 60% redaction and 40% nervous laughter. If I could clone myself, I'd probably rate below all four. My jaw pulses, a blunt force rhythm in my skull. I picture myself running the pitch to Ban and getting my windpipe rearranged. Or Katherine, who would probably laugh herself hoarse before turning the job down. They all hate me, or will. Maybe that's what I need.

There's a split-second temptation to let it all collapse, take the three-hour nap I deserve, and let Curie's situation resolve itself in a blast radius of other people's problems. I almost do. Instead, I white-knuckle the edge of the table and start the process of recruiting. First, the comms hack. I link the holopad to the lowest-security channel, spoof a Curie admin account, and ping Ban with a burner handshake. Her reply is immediate, and the contents are pure venom: *What do you want, freeloader?*

I ignore the insult and stick to logistics: *Need a face-to-face, 18:00, bistro 15, quadrant C.*

She doesn't reply. I know she'll show. I repeat the process for Katherine—her bot responds with an automated insult and a trace-back that almost loops me, but I'm faster. I set the meeting, then schedule the same with Dorothy, whose file says she's in a correctional hostel but whose trail shows she's already subletting in two other safehouses. By the time I finish, my jaw has gone numb and my shoulders feel like they're being used for stress testing construction-grade wire. I look at the roster—three of the most dangerous assets I've ever known, each with a plausible reason to end me before the Ronin breach even starts.

I let my head drop back, then stare at the water-damaged ceiling. There's a brown, fist-sized circle above the desk, the outline of an old light fixture replaced with insulation and tape. It's a sun, or a bullet hole, or a zero. Probably all three. The holopad vibrates with a message from the audit office:

EVENT HORIZON -3:50:29

I slam the holopad flat and feel the shock run up my arms. My jacket waits on the back of the broken chair. I slip it on, and my hand is already shaking. "Time to sell my soul to save these poor bastards," I mutter, loud enough for the walls to hear. No one else will. I leave the safehouse, and the air outside tastes no different at all.

The old Moshimoto lab smells like fried RAM and evaporated pharmaceuticals. The air filtration system failed decades ago, and every inhale comes with a garnish of carcinogens and regret. I step through the retinal scanner, which recognizes my optic signature with a dry click and opens onto a corridor lined in peeling smart-foil, the once-mirrored surface now mottled like burned tinfoil. Some of the overhead strips still pulse with emergency lighting, orange-red and arrhythmic, casting stripes across the filthy linoleum.

Katherine works in the main operating theater, a room designed for precision brain surgery and reconfigured for high-volume hack jobs. Every flat surface is crusted with the relics of other people's brilliance: soldered fragments of neural mesh, half-spooled memory threads, a black box labeled "DONOR: BETA." There's a tripod of micro-soldering arms over the main bench, all run by foot pedal, and a dead desktop aquarium sprouting wires where guppies should be. She doesn't look up when I enter. Her hair, black shot through with stress white, is up in a zip tie, and the skin around her eyes has the brittle transparency of someone who never believed in sleep. She's prying the casing off a medtech processor, hands working with the quick, nervous grace of a subway pickpocket. I take the second chair, the one without the spray-foam patch, and wait for her to finish her incision.

"I thought you only called when someone's brain was on fire," Katherine says, still bent over her patient.

"Or when someone needed a new identity in under ten minutes," I say. "Nice to see you too."

She snorts, a sound that's half amusement and half spitting up blood. "What's your real ask?"

I gesture at the workspace. "I need you to make a firewall out of ghosts."

That gets her attention. Her hands freeze, the soldering iron hovering just above the fragile ceramic. For a moment, I see the old Katherine—the one who rebuilt a core CPU using only scavenged calculators and spite, the one who could laugh while reprogramming her own neurochemistry. She sets down the iron with a deliberate click and turns. Her irises flicker with diagnostic overlays, but the smile is pure, unfiltered contempt. "A firewall? For who?"

"Curie Syndicate. There are 847 hostages with a real-time link to their brains. If the Ronin break the grid, they all flatline. Instantly."

She gives a long, theatrical whistle. "Jesus. That's some 1990s Bond villain shit. And you want me to keep them alive?"

"That's the brief."

Katherine leans back and wipes her hands on a rag that used to be a baby-blue lab coat. "You realize I built half the logic on those Ronin worms, right? And the other half is just recycled pharma ransomware."

"Which means you're uniquely qualified."

She lets that sit, the grin slipping a notch. The tremor in her hands returns as she flicks a neural interface cable from the junk pile, spinning it around her finger like a set of rosary beads. "You know what they did to me in this building?" she says, eyes on the plastic coil.

I do. The HR files don't say it outright, but the gaps are wider than the text. "Yes."

"And now I'm supposed to rescue their supply chain. Of humans."

"It's not about them. It's about the 847. That's the only reason I'm here."

She barks a laugh and throws the cable into the pile with enough force to tangle it hopelessly. "Sure. I'll just 'forget' every damn thing they did. Easy." She pushes off from the table and spins her stool to face me dead on. "Here's the funny thing. I've spent the last seven years prepping for a chance to burn Curie's servers down. And now you want me to ... what, duct tape their whole architecture back together so the Ronin can't kill a few thousand more?"

I nod. "That's the deal."

She sighs, picks up a scalpel, and begins carving invisible lines in the air between us. "You ever read The Art of War, Skelm? Or do you just memorize the Wikipedia summaries?"

"Wikipedia. I don't trust the other sources."

Katherine snorts again, and this time it edges toward real laughter. "The only way to beat an enemy is to know them better than they know themselves. I built a backdoor in every firewall I've ever made. You know that, right?"

"That's why you're on the list."

She flashes me a look, one part suspicion, one part something else. "So if I say yes, what's to stop me from just folding the whole Curie operation and letting the Ronin win?"

"Nothing," I say, and mean it. "I'm betting on your sense of math."

She doesn't reply at first. Instead, she picks up the medtech processor she was operating on, strips a ribbon cable with her teeth, and starts repinning the ends. Her hands don't stop trembling, but the motion gets faster, more precise. I can see the calculation on her face: the weight of every grudge, every ruined memory, versus the value of 847 strangers. "You're a shit negotiator, Skelm. You know that?"

"I'm not here to negotiate."

She plugs the new cable into her neural deck, closes her eyes, and triggers a fast diagnostic. Her entire body flinches once, twice, then she exhales. "Let me see the profiles."

I hand her the holopad. She scans the list for less than thirty seconds before passing it back. "Most of these are kids."

"I know."

She taps her thumb on the table, nails leaving a trail in the composite. "Fine. I'll do it. But after? We're done."

"That's always been the plan."

She shakes her head, then turns back to her workstation and starts picking through a pile of discarded neural interfaces. "Bring me a clean portable. None of that Curie crap. I need something that hasn't touched corporate hands in a decade."

"I'll get you a Beta-3 portable from the black market," I say. "It'll probably cost me a kidney."

Katherine grins, baring every crooked tooth. "Better bring a spare, then. If the Ronin catch us, you're going to need both." I stand, and for a moment, the only sound is the soft whine of the failing ventilation. "Those 847 lives," she says, voice low, "are the only math that matters right now."

I nod and leave her to the work. The corridor seems narrower on the way out, every step echoing through a hundred dead memory fragments and the raw promise of failure. Outside, the air has the texture of spent fireworks, the taste of ozone and old ambition. One down, two to go.

• • •

The hostel is twelve stories of prefab depression stacked on top of a vape shop and two illegal casinos. The front desk is staffed by an AI in a foam mascot head, its battery dying and voice down to a warble. I take the stairs—elevator's out, like always—and climb past six floors of detergent stink, cigarette haze, and muffled screaming from what's either a child or a marketing executive. Dorothy's room is at the end of a corridor lit only by the exit sign and the trembling neon from a sex ad across the street. She's propped against the doorframe, arms crossed, face lit up in red and blue stutter. Her eyes track my approach, but the rest of her body might as well be fossilized. I get ten steps closer before she speaks. "Don't," she says, her voice deeper than memory, cold and engineered to shut down conversation.

"Just need five minutes. After that, you can go back to staring holes in the drywall."

She doesn't move. "Why now?"

"Because if you wanted to kill me, you would have already."

That earns me half a smirk. "Still can."

The corridor smells of mildew, weed, and cleaning fluid strong enough to wipe history. On the wall behind Dorothy, a black Sharpie message reads: WE'RE ALL INFECTED, SOME JUST LIE BETTER. A little further, someone's drawn a cartoon brain with wriggling parasites and the words: DO NOT ACCEPT MINTS FROM STRANGERS. Dorothy's right hand taps a rhythm on her biceps. I remember she once had a nervous tic, but it's been surgically replaced by perfect mechanical steadiness. Her arms are sleeved in second-gen myomer, the kind that doesn't try to look human but wins all the arm-wrestling tournaments anyway. The new jawline is sharper, the mouth an efficient straight-line mechanism with only the occasional hint of teeth.

“I'm not working for Curie,” she says, reading my thoughts. “Or Moshimoto. Or any of the other meat-farming scum.”

I take it on the chin. “Neither am I.”

She flicks a glance at the vending machine down the hall. The thing's cycling through its failure diagnostics, every other pixel shot and the display showing only ERROR 88 in looping green. Next to it, a patch of wall has been hacked open and badly repaired with chewing gum and lollipop sticks. The hallway hums with the distant vibration of overloaded wiring, the kind that eventually burns down the whole block but only after everyone's stopped caring.

“You're not here for me,” Dorothy says.

I match her gaze. “I'm here for the 847. There's a breach coming. Ronin. If we don't defend, they all get smoked. Instantly. No pause for drama.”

She processes it in silence, then leans out just enough for the neon to catch the plastic underlayer at her throat. “You should have left me where I was,” she says, with less venom than I expected.

I shrug. “I need someone who doesn't flinch. And who remembers what it was like to be worth less than a case of SentiSnacks™.”

Her jaw tightens. The rhythm in her hand stops. For a moment, she's a statue carved from resentment and a single, lingering drop of pity. In the next moment, the door at the other end of the hall slams open and a man lurches out, drunk or detoxing. He sees Dorothy, stares, then looks at me. "You owe money?" the man asks. His hair is a sheet of old sweat, his eyes yellowed out by weeks of neglect. "I can help. Discount." Dorothy's arm snaps out to block the corridor. It's not aggressive—she doesn't need to be—but the gesture is so natural that I almost don't see it happen. The man gets the hint, backs up, mutters, "Bitch," and disappears into his room.

"Charming place," I say.

"It's cheap. And the beds are bolted to the floor."

We stand there, a full minute of dead time, while the vending machine cycles and the hallway grows colder. The ceiling above us blooms with water damage, brown and concentric. Someone's tried to paint over it, but the color is just a lighter shade of surrender.

"I don't work with corporate puppets," Dorothy says, as if she's rehearsed the line.

"Not asking you to. I just want to keep 847 people alive long enough to matter." Her face is a mask, but the eyes flicker once, and it's all the opening I need. "Some of them are like you," I say, voice lower. "Ex-military. Augmented. Human in the places that still matter."

She looks away, but the shoulders shift—a micro-dip, barely noticeable unless you know her tells. "Promise me," she says, "when it's over, we torch it all. Not just the Ronin. All of it. Curie, the server farm, the syndicate. Leave nothing for the next bastard in line."

I meet her stare, letting her see I mean it. "When it's over, we burn everything."

Dorothy unfolds her arms, and the micro-tremor in her right hand is back, just a bit. She looks me up and down like she's seeing me for the first time, and not hating it. "Okay, Skelm. Let's go save some dead meat."

We walk side by side down the corridor. The vending machine blips and spits out a packet of dried mushrooms onto the filthy tile. Neither of us stops to pick it up. There's one left to recruit. I'm starting to think the real war will be between us and the world we're about to save.

The place is called Free Market Dive, but the sign outside rotates between that, three kinds of payday lender, and a screaming banner for a banned political party. The stairs down are so steep they'd be illegal in most timelines, the treads slick with ancient bar foam and genetic detritus. At the bottom, a biometric bouncer sniffs my neck, runs a thumbprint against a palm-sized database, and waves me in with a motion that doubles as "welcome" and "go fuck yourself."

Inside, the walls are covered in vacuum-molded propaganda: alternate strips of revolutionary art and expired consumer ads, both bleached to near-oblivion by the lights. The crowd is mostly exiled radicals and gig-economy washouts. There's no music—just the endless, low drone of a hundred conversations forced through gritted teeth. Every surface is sticky, every seat bolted to the ground. I scan for Ban and spot her in the back corner, chair canted so she's got a view of all four exits. Her boot heel clicks against the base of the table, a Morse code I can't quite decipher, and under the toe is a thumb-sized data-chip, glimmering in the dark. I slide into the seat opposite. She looks me over once, then lets her gaze drift to the plasma-scarred bar top. Her hair is cropped tight, black with streaks of something shining woven through. On her wrist is a wrap of ancient vinyl, and on the table, a glass of something that glows faintly. I recognize it from a museum gift shop as "real absinthe," or at least the closest this city can source.

"You're late," Ban says.

"I was recruiting."

She shrugs, as if to say: *not my problem*. But her eyes don't leave mine, and her foot resumes the steady *tap-tap-tap* on the data-chip. "You know what this is?" she asks, lifting the chip just enough to make it catch the light. The embedded glyphs shift from red to blue and back, a low-tech security layer from a century ago.

"Vintage. Pre-digital. Probably plays music that got everyone in this room on a government watch list."

She almost smiles. "You always had a talent for nostalgia, Skelm. Did you bring what I asked for?"

I slide a flash drive across the table. She snatches it and palms it without breaking eye contact, a street magician's move with none of the flair and all of the efficiency. "You sure you want to do this?" I ask. "There's a decent chance we die in the first ten minutes."

"There's a better chance we die before the next round of layoffs," Ban says. "At least this way, I get a shot at the bastards who wrote my name in the first place."

We're silent for a moment. I watch the people at the next table argue in three languages, alternating between threats and sexual come-ons. The air is charged, literally—ionizers buzz overhead, cutting through the bar's own paranoia. Ban's drink is gone. She lines up the glass with the edge of a flyer taped to the table and stares me down. "You want me to defend Curie's server stack," she says, "against a mercenary raid run by Ronin, using tactics I developed to destabilize governments."

"That's the ask."

She spins the glass in place, and the condensation traces a slow spiral. "You're not the first corporate type to beg for help. But you're the only one who's ever asked me to do it sober."

"That's your choice. I don't have any use on you. Hell, I don't even know if you like me."

This time, she does smile. It's all teeth, but not unkind. "I don't," Ban says. "But I hate the Ronin more."

"Why?"

She leans forward, the edge of her wrist nearly touching mine. "Because they're the only ones who ever made me wish I was still working for Moshimoto. And I used to burn payroll records for sport."

"Mutual disgust," I say. "It's the foundation of all lasting partnerships."

She barks a sharp laugh, then goes quiet. For a second, I think she's going to say no, walk out, and leave me to fail. But she lifts her chin and tilts the data-chip so it rolls into the cup of her hand. "I'm in," Ban says. "But only if we use my plan."

“Let’s hear it.” She lists it out in ten precise moves, each one uglier and less dignified than the last. She wants to double-blind the hostage grid, hack the security feeds to show fake breaches, and run a shadow defense staffed by the three most violently unstable unreadables I can bribe or blackmail. The goal isn’t to stop the Ronin, just to make them think twice. By the time she finishes, I’m already regretting my life choices. “That’s not a defense plan,” I say. “That’s a suicide note written in the blood of everyone we know.”

“Exactly. And if we fail, nobody will ever use a meat farm as a security system again.” She waits for me to argue. I don’t. We’re quiet again, but now the silence is almost companionable. I buy a round, and when it comes, our fingers brush on the glass. Her hand is cold, but the pressure lingers just a second longer than it should. “Skelm,” Ban says, eyes narrowed. “You know I’m going to destroy this place when it’s done, right?”

“Was counting on it,” I say, voice steady. “No point in saving the world if we’re just going to live in the old one.”

She seems satisfied. “Then we’re even. For now.” We drink, and as the minutes pass, the old animosity recedes. Ban tells me a story about hacking the city’s traffic grid as a protest, then using the resulting jam to rob three luxury condos and donate the cash to an orphanage. I ask if the orphans ever saw the money. She laughs and says, “Of course not, but they all have excellent credit scores now.” The air grows denser as more bodies pack into the bar. Ban leans in, conspiratorial. “You’re not scared, are you?”

“Terrified. But at least we’ll have good company.”

She raises her glass, and I do the same. “To 847 people we'll never meet,” Ban says.

“To old enemies.”

We drink, and when the round is gone, we shake on it. As her fingers curl around mine, I realize: this is as close as I'll ever get to trust. I take a deep breath, run a quick scan of the bar for tails, then let myself relax for one full heartbeat. It's enough. We leave together, the neon and the crowd pressing in from all sides. I can feel Ban watching my throat as I swallow, her pulse a silent dare at my wrist. The future's a bomb already ticking, but for the first time since the brief, I'm ready to light the fuse.

Chapter 4

There are 847 faces on my wrist, all of them counting down. I keep the comm display set to full-bleed. Every sixty seconds, the hostages rotate, showing me a new batch of features—some sleepwalking, some slack-jawed with REM overflow, some locked in the cartoon terror of synthetic REM. Most look like the last photo taken before a party bus rolled off a cliff. Ban watches over my shoulder as we ghost the perimeter. She doesn't ask, but I see the count burrowing into her. The numbers get smaller with every checkpoint we pass.

Katherine moves like a criminal in someone else's skin, her jaw set to "fuck you" and her hands a tremor of ancient withdrawal. Dorothy, the cyborg, is behind us both, eyes always up, posture mechanically correcting for threats I don't even see. I suspect she's logging every camera and turret in her deadspace, already simulating how many could be spun against us if she ever had to switch sides. Which, by my math, is as likely as not.

The air here is stale, processed through a half-functioning HVAC grid. It's scented with what the facility manager thinks is clean linen, but the top note is more "decomp in a department store." The lighting gets worse with every junction: overheads flicker at a frequency calculated to shave years off your sanity, and the wall sconces run on third-shift mood lighting, turning everyone's skin into the color palette of a contaminated blood bank.

Our first checkpoint is a pair of glass-paneled security doors, both slouched open and held in place by a borrowed office chair. The "guards" are defunct, unless you count the institution of watching StreamVault on silent as a security function. The two of them are deep into a VR rig, swapping conspiracy memes and poorly filtered video of some ancient SKELM CORPS executive getting pantsed at a shareholder gala. Their uniforms don't match, neither do their faces, but they share a lolling, chemically induced bliss.

The first guard blinks at me, the iris dilation lagging like a bad operating system. The patch on her sleeve is from a pizza franchise that was litigated out of existence last spring. The second guard, a man with hollowed cheeks and a five o'clock shadow that seems to be his only living tissue, grins and says: "You know the drill. Eyes up, hands where I can see 'em, and don't let your reality ID lag, okay?"

Ban raises both hands with a deadpan "I surrender," but her eyes don't even flicker. The scanner at the desk doesn't work, so the guard just lifts a hand, groping in our general direction for the badge lanyards we're supposed to be wearing. I hand over a visitor pass I printed in the stairwell, and he waves it under the desk lamp like it's a Geiger counter. He doesn't even bother to scan the rest. Behind the desk is a display wall meant for motivational posters, but it's covered in a grid of sticky notes—each one a different color, each with a different password or schedule or "DO NOT LET BRIAN BACK IN HERE" written in the ink of dying office pens. It's an administrative graveyard.

"Thanks, man," says the guard, then leans back and takes a drag off a SentiSnack™ vape the size of a femur. The vapor is blue, and the smell is what you'd get if regret were candy-coated. He offers the pen to the woman, who ignores it in favor of adjusting her neural port—now glowing a radioactive orange under the ragged clip-on bob. The chemical buzz is so heavy in the air it might as well be piped in as a mood enhancer.

"Who's got the best Ronin meme so far?" the woman asks, voice distorted through the neural haze.

Dorothy answers without missing a beat: "The one where the Ronin raid is just an insurance scam for the server upgrade budget. Classic."

Both guards laugh, a joint cackle that ends in a chorus of dry coughs. I let it play out, eyes on the live feed—none of the hostages have dropped, but there's a red flag on the status: someone's oxygen dip is trending.

"Is this the 'secure corridor?'" whispers Katherine, low and venomous, as we slide past the "checkpoint" with zero resistance. I nod, and she shakes her head with a mixture of disgust and pure professional pain. I see her file every detail in the cabinet of reasons to sabotage humanity when this is over. The next stretch is a low hallway lined with faded propaganda, Curie Syndicate's finest moments memorialized in lenticular print. The faces smile at us, forever mid-dazzle, forever a half-step ahead of reality. The floors are rubberized, meant for "anti-fatigue" but really just an excuse not to clean them for a decade. We move fast, passing abandoned carts full of protein bars and crates of SentiSnack™. Every one of us is thinking the same thing: *this isn't a workplace, it's a nervous breakdown with floor plans.*

Ban drops back to my side and matches my stride. "We're gonna die here, aren't we?" she says, dead calm.

"Better here than at the next layoff," I say, and she gives the faintest of smirks. We round a corner to a checkpoint that looks marginally more operational. The scanner here at least lights up, and the guards—two this time, in matching coveralls—stand at attention with the practiced misery of people who know a performance review is always just around the corner. But even here, the show is all for nothing: the retinal scan blips green for every face, even when Ban closes her eyes. The guard stamps a generic "PASSED" on the digital slate and nods us through, eyes never leaving the ground.

Dorothy is the first to notice a side corridor that isn't on the blueprint. She glances at me, just a flicker, and then I see it too—a maintenance door marked with a sticker so old it's lost all meaning. She's right: this is a bypass, maybe a legacy route from when the facility was actually staffed by humans and not just memetic entropy. She gestures with a chin twitch, and I make a note. If we need to reroute in a panic, this is our hole.

Ban breaks the silence with a whisper pitched for only me: "At this rate, the Ronin won't even have to try."

"That's the idea," I say, barely moving my lips. "They want us to think it's all performative, up to the last second."

She nods. "Classic management. Make the staff fail, then blame them for the collapse."

We descend a flight of stairs painted industrial yellow, each tread labeled with a warning about tripping, slipping, or existential despair. At the bottom is a double-width door plastered in biohazard tape, clearly repurposed from a medical wing or maybe an old containment lab. Katherine pauses, running a finger over the keypad. "You see this?"

It's not even encrypted. She taps in a random sequence, and the display flashes "ADMIN123," then unlocks. The door opens with a hiss, and we step into what must be the heart of the beast. The server farm proper is a cathedral of heat and cooling fans. Every rack is a votive column, blue LEDs blinking in the rhythm of a synthetic rosary. The hum is a pulse you feel through your teeth. Ban lets out a low whistle, and Katherine's eyes scan up and down the rows, her jaw clenching tighter the further she looks. Dorothy just tracks the space with a predator's efficiency, logging exit points and cameras and the two maintenance bots lurking at the far end of the room.

We move as a group toward the central node, my wrist comm buzzing the whole time: now a panicked kid, now an old man mouthing the word "help," now a woman with eyes fixed and dilated, maybe already gone. I can't stop watching. The checkpoint guards in the next room are more ceremonial than functional. They're not even armed; just two synths in matching polos, one with a tablet, one with a clipboard. The one with the tablet looks up, sees Ban, and winks. "I didn't know we had external contractors on shift," says the synth, voice pure customer service. "Welcome. Do you need an escort?"

"No, thanks," I say, and flash the pass I printed earlier. He doesn't even glance at it, just gives a thumbs up and goes back to his Candy Crush clone.

Ban nudges me. "You could rob this place with a wet paper towel and a conviction."

"I'm pretty sure someone already did," I mutter.

We slide into the main security corridor and come up short at the first real obstacle: a laser grid, humming so hard the light shivers in your periphery. The access terminal blinks at us, input required. I punch in "ADMIN123." The grid vanishes. Ban doesn't laugh, but her eyes flicker with something that could almost be mistaken for joy. "This is worse than I expected," says Katherine, voice brittle.

Dorothy just points upward, where a camera's LED goes dark the instant we pass under. I step into the main room and let the comm display take over my vision for a second. All 847 faces pulse at once, some aware, some lost. It's a live feed, a death clock, and a motivational poster in one. We are the only line left, and the system doesn't even care enough to stop us. For a moment, I wish the guards at the first checkpoint were still watching StreamVault. At least then someone would have noticed us. We keep moving, deeper into the blue.

• • •

The password checkpoint isn't even pretending. It's a standalone kiosk, brand new but already collecting fingerprints, with a holo-screen mounted at child's-eye level. The display blinks "ENTER PASSWORD," as if someone had never configured it past the demo mode. I glance at Ban, who shrugs with both shoulders at once. Katherine is already prepping a bypass, soldering micro-clips to a neural tap the way a mother might braid hair, but I put a hand on the console and type "ADMIN123." The entire display dissolves, reboots, and then gives us the real-time status of the inner sanctum. Not even a confirmation prompt. The system doesn't care, or doesn't know how.

Ban's snort is one of disbelief. "I've seen daycare firewalls stronger than this."

"Don't insult daycares," says Dorothy. "They don't trade in human capital."

We walk through. The main server hub is colder and wetter than any normal architecture. The cooling units run loud enough to shake the resin in your teeth. Every rack is taller than a basketball player, lit up with blue status LEDs that flicker in precise, digital stutter—each pulse a heartbeat for the doomed. Cables run along the floor in lazy, tripping loops. The floor tiles are hollow and flex under every footstep. There's a low-level mist, the result of micro-condensation where the heat meets the badly insulated ceiling. Katherine scans the room, nostrils flaring as she inhales the cloud of corporate neglect. "This place is a Petri dish." She finds the first open diagnostic port and jams in her interface. Instantly, her eyes lose focus. Her lips move, reading data too fast for words. After a second, she blinks and says, "This is criminal."

"Worse than that," I say. "It's typical."

She's already typing. "Ghost VLANs on every switch. They've rerouted half the core traffic through a protocol that's two years out of date. Look—" She flips a data tile in my direction. "That's their firewall. It's commented out. The sysadmin left a note: 'TO-DO: REBUILD FIREWALL AFTER Q4.' That was three Q4s ago."

Ban grins with a kind of evangelical disgust. "So you're telling me the Ronin could already be here and we'd never know."

"I'm telling you," says Katherine, "that the Ronin are probably in the room right now, reading our email."

Dorothy is working the perimeter. She runs a finger along the exposed mag-lock on the "secure" storage cabinet, then tugs once, hard, and it comes away in her hand. She holds it up, the shank of steel still attached, then lets it drop with a clatter. "Their hardware is no better than the software."

"Look," says Ban, "the emergency override is labeled with instructions. Step One: 'Insert Red Key.' Step Two: 'Turn until Click.' Step Three: 'Pray'—I'm not joking, it says that." She holds the paper tag for everyone to see.

I make a quick note, tagging it with the asset number. "Pray. Classic documentation."

Katherine is muttering now, her lips working through a scroll of technical atrocities. "No updates. No segmentation. Raw logs are kept in a shared directory. The admin password is literally written in the help file."

Dorothy looks up. "Executive access codes are stored in plaintext."

Ban laughs. "Where?"

"Root folder on the public drive," Dorothy says, deadpan. "The file is called 'ADMIN_MASTER_LIST.txt.'"

I almost want to defend Curie, to say there's some clever countermeasure or trap, but there isn't. This isn't the kind of place that bothers with cleverness. The entire structure is set up on the belief that nobody would dare try. Ban leans in. "Skelm, if you ever wanted to own a company, now's your chance. You could own the whole city with what's on that drive."

I let myself imagine it: all 847 hostages suddenly under new management, every asset a digital pawn, every shareholder a dead man walking. But it would only change who's in charge of the pain, not the pain itself. I squash the idea. Instead, I ask, "What's the real risk?"

Katherine's eyes flicker left, then right. "It's a race condition. If the Ronin know about these holes, they'll pop the entire vault and delete the hostage grid in under a second. All our effort will just help them kill the assets faster."

Dorothy, kneeling over the exposed power cable, says, "The system has a hardwired kill switch. If anyone tries a remote reset, it shunts every rack to zero in less than two seconds. Every mind on the grid goes dark. No recovery."

"Jesus," says Ban. "What's their plan, then? Mass suicide?"

I check the logs. There's a recent message from a Marie, stamped 47 minutes ago: "DEFEND UNTIL EVENT HORIZON. NO COMPROMISE. NO BACKUP." It's not a plan, it's an epitaph.

Ban looks up at the ceiling, then back at us. "If you ask me, they want the Ronin to break in. Justify their own disaster. No survivors means no evidence."

Dorothy stands and dusts her hands. "Then we need to own the disaster before they do."

I nod. "Katherine, set up a proxy—something that looks like a Ronin breach, but routed through a dummy node. Dorothy, find the physical kill switch and prep a local bypass. Ban, you're with me; let's make a public log of every hole we find. If we have to go nuclear, we want the whole world watching."

For a second, nobody moves. Then, as if the room had issued a command, we all fall to the work. Katherine runs hot, her hands a blur over the diagnostic deck. Ban scribbles asset numbers and password fragments into a physical notepad, then burns the page over a nearby wastebin. Dorothy paces the floor tiles, marking weak spots with an improvised marker. I alternate between the live hostage feed and the admin console, cross-referencing every new face with the building's employee records. Most of them don't even work here. They're just rented consciousness, signed away in a boilerplate consent form.

Time telescopes. My wrist buzzes again: one of the hostages is in distress, oxygen dropping, heart rate spiking. I flag the row, tag it for medical, and know that nothing will come of it. Katherine mutters, "They're using children's code. Half of these exploits are ancient. I could write a worm to take the whole stack with a Raspberry Pi and a bag of jelly beans."

Ban gives her a look. "You don't even like jelly beans."

"They're better than SentiSnack™," Katherine says, not looking up.

Dorothy, reading from the power console, says, "The emergency power is so badly wired you could fry every rack by bridging two screws with a strip of foil."

Ban tears a strip of SentiSnack™ wrapper and holds it up. "Ready to go." I check the main display. The Ronin probe is close now. If they're as clever as their PR suggests, they'll be here in minutes. Ban finishes her audit and tosses the pen to me. "Worst job I ever had," she says, and laughs so hard she coughs.

"It's not even a job," says Dorothy. "It's a death spiral with office supplies."

We're ready. Or as ready as anyone can be. I look at the three of them and wonder which will betray me first. I hope it's me. "Skelm?" Ban says. "If we all die, can I haunt your next incarnation?"

"If you're lucky," I say. The four of us stand in the blue glow, the hum of machines louder than blood. This is what the end looks like: no alarms, no bullets, just the hush of total neglect and the anticipation of being erased. I get the feeling no one will remember us, and that's the most honest outcome in the world.

We disperse into the sub-levels, each of us hauling a ghost script: real security fixes up front, sabotage tucked behind. Dorothy walks point. Her presence on the staff register is so legitimate that nobody thinks to question her as she moves from panel to panel, prying open metal faces, soldering patches into the mess. Katherine follows, carrying her own mobile toolkit—a battered, chemical-stained diagnostic deck and the residue of every addiction Curie ever encouraged in her. Ban and I run rear, eyes and hands always in motion. The first order of business is to reinforce the server firewall, or at least the illusion of one. Katherine hot-wires the diagnostic to show a "perimeter restored" message, complete with a red-on-yellow rolling graph that means nothing to anyone sober. The real work is in the tunnels we build behind: hidden command scripts that only we know, seeded through the backup controllers and the odd forgotten node in the building's analog infrastructure.

Dorothy stabs a micro-wedge into the power control, flicking the line between "secure" and "catastrophic self-immolation." She glances over her shoulder just once, catching my eye, as she completes the circuit. She's not smiling, but the angle of her jaw says she's proud. Even in sabotage, Dorothy is a model of restraint. Ban does her best work in the shadow zones. She jimmies an old badge reader, then slips a rootkit thumb drive into the maintenance port. A dozen lines of self-erasing code, set to detonate on first reboot. She plucks the thumb drive as the light goes green and blows a kiss at the dead camera over her head. "This is the worst joke I've ever told," she says under her breath, "and I'm the punchline."

I snake my way to the management console, a repurposed office computer chained to a cinderblock desk. The login is on a sticky note ("Marie's favorite: 12345"). I log in. Immediately, I'm inside the nervous system of the whole facility—every ping, every heartbeat, every environmental drift recorded, time stamped and left unencrypted. My hands tremble as I lay down our insurance: a tunneled command path, invisible to casual traffic, but able to override every kill switch and power relay in the building. I seed the code with my own neural signature—a gamble, but I want to make sure we can't be outgamed by anyone, not even the Ronin. I leave the backdoor name as a joke: "Skelm's Last Stand."

I lose myself in the log files for a second. There are hundreds of them, maybe thousands. All cross-referenced, all correlated to the heartbeat of 847 hostages. But the thing that makes me choke is that these aren't isolated. Every few hours, there's a data spike, a cross-trade, a handshake with outside servers I'd assumed were rivals. Curie isn't the lone wolf of the press releases. It's the runt in a pack of jackals. And every syndicate runs the same codebase. Every one of the 847 has a sister grid somewhere. A redundant offsite soul farm. And every so often, the hostages are swapped, like livestock bred for cross-market resilience. I freeze. My skin crawls. If we fail, the assets don't even die. They just get rerouted. Ban comes up behind me and sees the look on my face. She says nothing, but her hand is suddenly on my shoulder, squeezing hard enough to mean: *don't collapse—not yet.*

From the next room comes a shout. Dorothy is at the security node, deep in the patch, when a supervisor rounds the corner. It's one of the Curie proxies—skinny, nervous, the kind of functionary who only exists to catch blame in a crisis. "What the fuck are you doing to my relay?" the supervisor asks.

Dorothy doesn't blink. "Fixing it. You want to tell Marie it was still broken after the Ronin breach?"

The supervisor steps in, sees Ban and me at the console and Katherine inside the rack. "This is not procedure. I should call an audit."

"You want the Ronin in the server room? Go ahead," says Ban, baring her teeth in the kind of smile that's half threat, half confession.

Katherine flicks a switch, and the lights strobe once, then steady. Dorothy drops the panel and stands up, her hands clear of tools. "It's done. The grid's back up."

The supervisor glances at the terminal. He doesn't have the training to verify, but the "SECURE" warning is big and red and satisfying. He grumbles something about "cowboys" and "union time theft" and then leaves, already thinking about his next SentiSnack™ break.

Dorothy exhales, the tension gone, and whispers, "He'll never make it to the exit before the Ronin hit."

Katherine taps a code into her diagnostic, and a few lines of status appear on the comm bands. "First Ronin breach in 33 minutes. Second, 19 after that. They're already crawling the perimeter."

Ban cracks her knuckles. "And now the fun begins."

We double back to the secure alcove—a room-sized closet, crammed with obsolete rack mounts and a table that wobbles under the weight of three decades' hardware upgrades. I dump my toolkit and collapse onto the box labeled "deprecated," head in my hands. Ban perches on the edge, looking at me with a new, sharper calculation. "What did you see in the log?"

I tell them. "It's all bullshit. Every grid is connected. Every asset is fungible. You don't die here; you just get copied, pasted, and recycled into another nightmare. If we pull the plug, they'll just pop up in another city, another rack."

Dorothy says, "So the only way to win—"

Katherine nods. "—is to torch the codebase. Everywhere."

"Can we?" Ban asks, her eyes never leaving mine.

"If we run the exploit on our node," I say, "and mirror it across every sister grid, yeah. We could crash the whole pipeline. Maybe more."

Dorothy grins. It's the first time I've ever seen her do it. "Let's ruin them."

Katherine rummages through the obsolete equipment and tosses me a neural splitter. "Here. You'll need to run the patch as an administrator."

Ban checks the corridor, then leans in and whispers, "You sure you're ready for this? The instant you hit 'go,' there's no coming back."

I remember the faces on my wrist—the 847 who could be deleted, the thousands more waiting in the next rack over, the faces I'll never meet. I feel nothing for the company, the syndicate, or the world that made this possible. But I care about those faces. I always have. "I'm ready."

Katherine slaps the splitter onto my port, a quick snap-and-click that's gentler than it has to be. Dorothy pulls up the system overlay, and Ban hands me a strip of tape, already labeled "SKELM'S LAST STAND." I laugh, or try to, but it comes out more like a gasp. I trigger the exploit. The screen blinks once, then again. In a heartbeat, I watch the status propagate: from Curie to the first sister grid, then the next, then an entire daisy-chain of server farms all across the hemisphere. Each time the log updates, the number of connected hostages grows. I stop looking after the first ten thousand. Dorothy is on the comms, faking a panic alert to the Ronin, guiding them to the softest entry point. Ban trips an internal alarm on the far end, then double-blinds the signal with her rootkit. Katherine runs live diagnostics, prepping a physical fail-safe in case the system tries to eat us with its death spiral.

It happens fast. In less than two minutes, the entire blue-lit cathedral is strobing with error codes. Red cascades down every row of racks. The building hums as power surges, then flickers, then settles into a kind of stunned silence. The comm panel in my wrist vibrates harder than ever before. The faces start blinking out, then suddenly, the counter spikes—so many new faces, so many new places. Ban wraps an arm around my neck and pulls my head down until our foreheads nearly touch. "We just made a lot of enemies," she says, her voice kind.

"They were already enemies," I say, blinking hard.

Dorothy stands in the alcove doorway, her silhouette a statue against the flickering lights. Katherine, hunched over her deck, says, "I hope the afterlife has better sysadmins than this."

Ban slaps a hand against the side of my head, not gently. "You're a fool, Skelm. But you did the right thing."

I want to believe it. I want to think any of this will matter. But the best I can do is keep the count alive and the tunnel open. When the emergency lights finally die and the building goes dark, we stay in the alcove, alone but not unremembered. I don't know how long we sit there, but when Ban finally says, "We own the city now," I almost believe her. It's not hope. But it is something.

Chapter 5

The operations room is what would happen if a dental surgery and an air traffic control tower made a child. White angles everywhere, no dust, no color that isn't blue-white, and no surface with the tactility of flesh. The sound is a pressure, not a vibration. The only comfort is the ancient click of the holotable as it snaps into projection mode, rendering the facility's three-tiered schematic in three hundred million points of light and micro-shadow. There are no chairs. If you want to lean, you lean into your discomfort.

Ban is already at the auxiliary console, jacket thrown over the screen in the universal gesture for "fuck off, I'm working." She manipulates the system with the precision of a predator playing with an injured toy—never looking at the screen, eyes always tracking the curve of the main projection, tongue lapping the inside of her mouth as if measuring the odds with a taste. She's wearing the kind of clothing you buy when you want to be seen by no one: matte black, zero branding, sleeves that come down just far enough to hide a wrist full of nervous violence.

I do my own inventory: four flechette clips, two synthblood patches, one thermal bypass for my cranial port, and the knowledge that I am, as always, the most sober person in the room. The hostages are on display in the upper right: a slow cascade of faces, numbers updating every second. All 847 are still holding. The redout line pulses beneath, a suggestion of what would happen if I make a single mistake. I watch Ban work for three minutes before the urge to kill her or marry her becomes intolerable. I walk the perimeter of the holotable, pretending to survey the vulnerabilities, but mostly watching for signs that she's laid a trap for me specifically. It's not paranoia; it's field experience. Ban finally acknowledges me by slamming a datachip into the table slot. "You want to watch, or you want to help?"

"You're already two steps past the protocol." I don't bother to modulate the condescension. "If you're trying to make this thing traceable, you're doing a great job."

She grins without showing teeth, just a wrinkling of nose and upper lip. "Funny. I thought you liked things transparent. Isn't that your brand?"

I ignore the bait and pull up the security overlay. The system's been reset to factory, which means every password is "password" and every protocol has "setup wizard" lurking under the hood. I catch Ban's fingerprint on the last commit—she's left a shadow file in the quarantine, coded to detonate if anyone runs the standard scan. "Sabotage is a cute strategy, until it gets you shot."

"Professionalism is a suicide note," she says, fingers still dancing. "You want to stay alive? Leave some handholds for your enemy. They're as predictable as you are." The system pings. The entire schematic blooms in red. For a second, every corridor is marked vulnerable, every access point a mouth waiting to eat us alive. Ban laughs, a sound that's 80% contempt, 20% actual joy. "You think they'll use the east stairwell?" she says, more to herself than to me. "That's where I'd send the Ronin, if I were running a team this dumb."

I keep my eyes on the screen, but I'm aware of her in every molecule. Her forearm tenses as she types; the tendon near her thumb bulges with every enter stroke. She's more alive than any of us, which is saying something. "You left a recursive loop in the last build. That's how the Ronin get in."

She doesn't deny it. "Yeah, well, they'll be expecting a challenge. You want to spook them, give them a clear path, then make it ugly after they bite."

I scrub the overlay, trying to follow the logic. Ban's route doesn't defend the core so much as booby-trap the entire building against human nature. Every hallway ends in an apparent escape, but the last few meters cross a field of sensors linked to the deadman switch on the hostages' grid. Even if the Ronin play by the book, they lose. "You ever think of just defending the place like a normal person?"

Ban shrugs. "Normal people die early. I'm aiming for average lifespan, plus a few months."

We argue for ten more minutes, and it gets less civil with each pass. Ban's sabotages grow more flagrant, and my corrections more heavy-handed. At some point, she disables the kill grid, then re-enables it with a conditional so obscure that the system tags it as an urban legend. I rewrite the defense protocol, only to find she's shifted the whole rack's priority to "last known physical access," which is her own badge number. If we get locked down, I'll be locked out. She'll have the run of the place. "You planning to double-cross me?" I ask, honestly curious.

She pauses, just long enough to make it hurt. "Would you believe me if I said no?"

"No."

"Then why ask?"

We're about to spiral into a fight that can only end in violence or confession when the room's air pressure spikes and a door on the far wall snaps open. Marie's proxy walks in—full corporate drone mode, suit pressed to the millimeter, hair a mathematically precise bob, eyes so devoid of affect they might as well be painted on. She glides, not walks, to the edge of the holotable, folds her hands behind her back, and stares past us with the glassy intensity of a pet goldfish on amphetamines. "The security drill begins in five minutes," she says. "All participants must log their status and confirm oxygen capacity. If your status is not confirmed, you will be assumed dead. Thank you."

Ban's nostrils flare. She hates these proxies. "What happens if we don't confirm?"

Marie's eyes don't move, but the rest of her face blinks on, just a millimeter. "Then you compete for the best possible outcome. That is the work." I log my status with a thumbprint and a short, involuntary prayer. Ban logs hers with a flex of the index and a data trail I know will echo on the system for decades. Marie waits for us to finish, then tilts her head just so. "If you succeed, you live. If you fail, you become an unreadable. If you exceed expectations, you may request a reward. Do you understand?"

"Do you always talk in parables?" Ban asks.

"It's not a parable. It's a protocol," says Marie.

The room holds three seconds of silence, then the main screen flashes:

SECURITY DRILL INITIATED – EVENT HORIZON -0:05:00

Marie pivots and leaves. Ban doesn't watch her go; she watches me, waiting to see which plan I'll execute. I catch my own face in the reflection on the holotable, half-lit by blue and half by red. I look more like her than I care to admit. The 847 faces blink in the corner of the screen. None of them have any say in who wins this. We stare each other down. The drill clock ticks down. When Ban finally looks away, it feels like losing and winning at the same time.

The drill launches with a shriek that nearly inverts the bones in my head. The lights drop into blackout for half a second, then strobe emergency red—every surface now the color of a fresh crime scene. The holotable renders new schematic overlays in a blur of yellow and black, corridors lit up like a hazard meme. On the wall, a digital clock eats seconds in digits too fast for comfort. The scenario: Ronin have breached the subbasement; first asset breach in 30 seconds. I go full reflex, hands on three consoles at once. Main firewall, door locks, kill grid—all the usual. First move is to push everything into hard lockdown, then slow-bleed access to make it look like we're already losing. The art is in losing just fast enough.

Ban ignores every protocol. Instead of locking down, she peels the digital wallpaper from the inside out, opening a false pathway through the maintenance sublevel, then another, then a third in the quantum farm's backup power. She seeds the system with panic and creates shadows of intruders in places even I can't predict. Every time I secure a path, she opens a new one. It's not defense, it's anti-defense—aggressive passivity, if that's even a thing. The system buys it. Every monitor in the room is now alive with threat icons, blinking more like a pinball machine than a coordinated assault. Even the AI moderator—the proxy for the real Ronin—is fooled, splitting its resources across too many fronts.

I hiss across the room: "You're compromising our cover."

Ban doesn't look up. "I'm creating opportunities. You want to win or look good doing it?"

The clock jumps forward: Asset breach in 5 seconds ... 4 ... 3 ... The grid hits us with a simulated logic bomb, and the holotable warps into a pulsating warning. In the simulation, we've already lost two layers of the perimeter. The Ronin avatars—little geometric wolves, all teeth and blue highlight—run amok through the virtual hallways, devouring anything not locked down. I trace the attack vector, noticing the wolves follow the path of least resistance, exactly as Ban predicted. She's right, and I hate it. I re-route the kill grid through a path she left open, expecting a trap. There is one, but it's for the AI. The second the wolves cross the threshold, a stutter in the codebase pops their process and dumps them into a virtual oubliette. Ban's not just a saboteur—she's a fucking dungeonmaster. "Clever," I say, through gritted teeth.

She shrugs. "Sometimes it's better to lead the attack than chase it."

The system dials up the simulation to compensate, but by now, Ban's patched her own backdoors into every node. She's left digital tripwires with my signature, so if anything goes sideways, it's on me. I spot them, of course, but the situation's too hot to start purging her code. The comm buzzes: *Simulated hostage loss at node 12.* Ban cackles. "No way. That node's a honeytrap. Watch."

On screen, the blue wolf triggers the trap. The system goes into recursive panic, blue devours red, and the entire sector collapses in a beautiful, fractal failure. The AI is so baffled it logs out for a millisecond, trying to respawn. In that breath, Ban exploits the gap to slip her custom payload into the system log. "What are you doing?" I ask her.

"Just giving us an insurance policy." Her hands flick over the console, delicate, like a pickpocket teasing loose a chain. "If Curie tries to flush us after the job, we can lock down the vault and ghost out clean."

The alarm pings again—now a breach in the air handling system, then in the sub-basement. Each attack is wilder, less disciplined, as the AI doubles and triples down. I see the moment it decides to go all-in: the grid starts shutting down hallways in random order, heating up the system to the edge of failure. We both reach for the environmental override at once, shoulders colliding. Ban's skin is electric, ice cold, and slick with adrenaline. We freeze for a half second, then in tandem, key in the override. "Don't fuck this up," I say.

Ban smiles. "Only way to fuck up is to go soft." I flood the lower halls with synthetic smoke, killing line-of-sight for all but the deepest sensors. Ban adds a stutter to the power grid, which causes all security cameras to default to a local backup. The system thinks it's a real emergency; all hostages are now flagged "critical." On the upper display, I see 847 faces—every one in yellow alert, every heartbeat elevated. The AI launches a final assault. It escalates to code red, pops the safeties, and simulates a mass unlock on the holding cells. The move is desperate, but so is our defense. Ban turns to me, face lit like a mask by the strobes. "You're gonna need to brute force the admin override," she says. "Don't ask why. Just do it."

I do it, instantly regret it, but it works. The override cracks the scenario and freezes all Ronin activity for ten seconds—an eternity in digital warfare. Ban's payload in the system log jumps to the top priority, and for the first time, I see what she's been building: a siphon. While the AI is distracted, she's pulling every employee schedule, every executive override code, and every shift rotation for the next year. She's mapping the entire syndicate's personnel. The simulated attack fails, a whimper after the shriek. All systems restore; emergency lights cycle back to blue. The holotable cools down to idle. The digital wolves are gone, replaced by a blinking summary:

DRILL COMPLETE. SIMULATED LOSS: ZERO HOSTAGES. DEFENSE SCORE: 100%.

I collapse against the wall, sweat stinging my eyes. Ban doesn't even sit—she just stands there, arms crossed, breath coming slow, and a curl of lip that says she's won. "That was insane," I say.

"It worked," she says, not looking at me. She's already extracting the siphoned data, slotting it into a portable with a magenta flicker.

On screen, the Marie proxy reappears, blinking into being with the uncanny smoothness of a billion-dollar feedback loop. "Congratulations," it says. "Exceptional response time. Zero breaches logged. You may now proceed to the debrief. All actions have been recorded."

Ban blows a strand of hair from her eyes. "You think they know?"

"I think they'll find out eventually," I say, voice ragged.

"Then we'd better make it count." We're alone, except for the ghosts of the 847, and the knowledge that we just stole the operating keys to the castle without setting off a single real alarm. My hands are still shaking, but it feels less like panic and more like hope. Or maybe I'm just crashing. Ban finishes the upload, slips the portable into her jacket, and leans in close enough to touch. "You hated every second of that, didn't you?" she says, a little too gentle.

"I hated being wrong."

She steps back, eyes sharp. "Get used to it, Skelm. We're going to do a lot more damage before this is over." She leaves, her silhouette a negative afterimage against the returning blue light. The room is empty now, but the taste of her sweat is still on my tongue, and the flicker of her code is embedded in every terminal. The countdown clock resets for the next disaster. I stretch my neck, crack my knuckles, and for the first time in months, I'm looking forward to the next job.

The room doesn't change after the victory. The air's still burnt ozone, the holotable cooling in a haze of digital afterimages. The team of temps and proxies files out in perfect silence, leaving behind the hum and the aftermath. I stay, because someone needs to bear witness, and because Ban's still in the far corner, working the data transfer with her back to me. On the main screen, the Marie proxy watches from her projected perch. She loops the last ten minutes of the simulation on repeat, pausing each time Ban improvises a new hack or I patch a lockdown with zero lag. There's no malice in the review, just the deadpan patience of someone paid to make sure you know you're being evaluated. "Exceptional response time," the proxy says at last. "Zero breaches. Notable synergy between team members." She says "synergy" like it's an insult, and maybe it is.

Ban doesn't acknowledge the comment. She finishes the transfer, slots the drive into a foil envelope, and seals it with a strip of black tape that reads, in marker: "HOPE CHEST."

She tosses it onto the table between us. "You get the honors."

"Thanks," I say, and mean it. The portable is warm, still vibrating from the volume of secrets inside.

We stand there, side by side, both refusing to look at the other for the first few breaths. Ban breaks the moment by rolling her shoulders, neck popping in stereo. "You know you don't have to keep hating me."

I almost laugh. "What would you suggest?"

"Try respect. Or indifference." She's smirking, but it's less weaponized now. "I know you're going to second-guess every line of code I wrote, but don't. It's all clean."

"I know."

"You're going to anyway."

"Probably." I slide the drive into an inside pocket, careful not to let it touch skin. "But only because it's habit."

She shrugs. "Old dogs, new tricks, etc." After a pause, she says, "You did good in there."

I look at her, really look. She's still vibrating with adrenaline, but the edges are less sharp, the anger replaced by something colder and, if not safer, at least less likely to explode in my face. "You too." It's not a truce, not exactly. More like an agreement to coexist until one of us dies or the job ends, whichever comes first. We leave the control room together, steps syncopated by the now-fading pulse of the emergency lights. Down the corridor, the main server racks loom—black glass, humming with the 847 unreadable souls inside.

Ban stops and puts a palm flat on the nearest rack. Her face reflects in the surface, doubled and blurred. I do the same, not sure why. We stand like that, two ghosts reflected in a vault full of digital ghosts. She says, "Admit it. My way works." I let it hang. The air is too full for talking. After a moment, she turns and brushes my arm—deliberate, not an accident, not gentle. "Next round's yours," she says, and stalks off toward the stairwell, boots silent as if she's evaporating with every step. The emergency lights cycle off, plunging the corridor into a blue-black that makes it impossible to tell where the racks end and the reflection begins. I touch the portable in my pocket, feeling its heat against my heart, and wonder what kind of disaster we just set loose. Somewhere, the Marie proxy is logging our every move, but it feels like the first unscripted moment I've had in years. There are 847 hostages, every one with a pulse. Maybe us too.

Chapter 6

The silent alarm isn't even a sound—just the stutter of the overheads from white-noise to red-tint, an almost imperceptible change that sets every skin hair on edge. I see it before I feel it: the flicker that means the Ronin are poking at the perimeter, data-chisels working the scaffolding of Curie's grid, looking for the rotten joists. The control room smells of recycled air and the slow off-gas of hand oils from a thousand prior shift workers who all lost the same war. The hum is deeper than last night, maybe a degree up in server draw, or maybe just the blood settling behind my eardrums.

Ban is next to me, close enough that I can feel the static cross-talk off her left shoulder. She leans into her screen with a predator's tilt, hands curled on the console like she's waiting for the glass to misbehave. We have the same posture, but hers is meaner. There's a security mesh in the concrete ceiling that flattens every voice into a dull echo, but Ban's words slice anyway. "East quadrant. That's where they'll come." She doesn't look up, but her left hand is already tapping in a patch set for the admin VLAN. She's not wrong; the Ronin always probe east. It's closest to their home base, and Curie's own design is too proud to ever fortify a legacy vulnerability.

"I see them." My hands move before the thought completes, typing in a little lag so it won't trip any anomaly detector. I let the first three pings through, block the fourth with a fake timeout, and then bleed the Ronin's script into a shadow honeypot we set up last shift. "They're running the same exploit as last week. Vintage."

"Means they know it's us." Ban shrugs one shoulder, so lazy it looks bored, but the up-flex in her jaw is all violence. "Feed them the dummy credentials. Let them think they're close."

My screen draws out the dance: a parade of synthetic wolves, each one a digital avatar wearing stolen faces, burrowing deeper into the sham grid. I open the gate, then seal it behind them with a logic loop that'll look like a real patch to anyone not running forensic entropy checks. For a second, the Ronin own the zone. Then their access log buries itself in recursive errors. It's not elegant, but it's fast. Ban's console glows on the edge of my sight, screen haloed in the pale blue that makes her skin look like it's been dead a year. She runs a parallel trace, building a stacked log of every intrusion attempt in real time. We don't need to talk, not when the work is this simple. I can hear her breathing, synced to her typing, a three-beat rhythm with a sharp catch on each return stroke. "They're getting bolder," I say, watching as two more scripts come in on a piggyback protocol. "They've written off the hostages as already lost."

She grins, bare and wolfish, never breaking eyes from the display. "That's because you keep advertising your incompetence." She types something sharp, and I see a packet of bad credentials float to the top of their priority queue. "They'll take the bait in five, four—"

"Three," I say, as the first Ronin avatar pops up in the dummy core, triggers the flag, and gets hard-quarantined in a sandbox labeled "VACATION PHOTOS." I set the honeypot's access logs to look like an unattended exec box—just enough noise to keep them trying.

"They're arrogant," Ban says, this time actually sounding satisfied. "But not stupid."

"They're running a mimic now," I say, watching the second intrusion morph to copy my user signature. I let it ride, give them a decoy file, and make a show of blocking the rest. "Want to pretend I just got compromised?"

She side-eyes me, the whites so clear it's like a deliberate signal. "They'd believe it."

The 847 hostages are still up in the corner of my display, each a smudged passport photo with a pulsing heart rate underneath. The ticker never goes above 120, which means the sedatives are doing their job. Every time I glance at the panel, my own pulse runs parallel: steady, then a spike, then baseline again. There's a long minute where nothing changes. Ban uses it to scrub the last Ronin residue from our shell. She does it with surgical aggression, deleting logs and rewriting timestamps so seamlessly that even the admin suite won't register the cleanup. I get a private thrill watching her. This is her work, and she's brilliant at it. I lean back for the first time in an hour, neck popping. "What do you think they'll try next?"

"Polymorphic," Ban says, no hesitation. "Or they'll escalate to kinetic if they think we're actually beating them." She finally turns, meeting my eyes. "You ready for the close combat?" I nod, though it's not conviction that makes me do it. It's the knowledge that the moment is coming, and I won't survive it alone. Ban leans closer, voice a whisper that rides the static. "They want you to blink, Skelm. Don't give them the pleasure."

It's the first time she's used my name like it's not a curse. Another alarm blinks, this time in full-spectrum red. Ronin have tripped an emergency code on the basement grid, maybe thinking we left it unlocked. I cue up a kill script and glance at Ban. "You want the honors?"

She nods, and we hit the Enter key together. The Ronin's access evaporates in a whimper. For a second, there's nothing but the hum and the aftertaste of adrenaline. Ban looks at me, and in the blue shadow, her eyes are more alive than anyone I've ever met. "Almost like we've done this before," she says.

I can feel my own heart hammering, and I realize the ticker in the corner has matched our rhythms for at least the last fifteen minutes. "We have," I say, and let the shared silence run its course. We sit there, two bodies and a thousand unsaid things between them, until the next alarm starts to flicker.

The Ronin don't wait. They hit the grid a second time, this probe harder and faster, slamming packets in at intervals only a synthetic would find plausible. The alarm strips overhead cycle from red to ultraviolet; the control room is a fever dream, every surface pulsing, the back of my neck slick with sweat. Ban straightens and pivots to stand behind me. Her right hand finds the back of my chair, knuckles pressing so hard I feel it through the composite. She leans in close, just behind my left ear. Her breath is warm, damp with something that could be fear but probably isn't. She points at my main monitor, index a blunt dagger. "There," she whispers, "node 117. Let them see it. Then block the 83."

I type, deliberate but fast, dropping the mask on node 117 so the Ronin can crawl all over it. I leave a few breadcrumbs—a partial netmap, a shadow user directory, some honey files that look like they'll burn the system if opened. I keep an eye on 83; as soon as the Ronin shift focus, I lock it down tight. Ban's hand moves to my shoulder, not hard, just anchoring. "Good," she says, and taps the side of the screen. "They just forked. Watch." She's right. The Ronin split their probe, running a second script in tandem, this one optimized for speed over stealth. The digital wolves now look like a pack, not a lone alpha. I feel my heart trip, catch, then speed up to keep pace with the attack.

"They're not here to win," I say, voice tight. "They're here to fuck the grid just long enough to open another hole somewhere else."

"West flank," Ban murmurs, and her hand squeezes my shoulder. "I'd go through the admin onboarding suite if I were them."

"I've already tripwired the onboarding queue." I start a manual sweep, feeling a thin line of cold crawl up my forearms as I spot the first signs of the secondary intrusion. "You want to take point on the defense?"

Ban releases my shoulder, moves to the next console over, and slides in so fast the chair barely registers the weight. Her hands are blurs, the screen a staccato of pop-ups and system logs. She reroutes the entire authentication tree to a burn loop, so every admin login attempt gets caught in a logic spiral, then reroutes the overflow to the fake asset cluster. “You’re learning,” she says. There’s pride in it. I try not to react. A new alarm sounds—this one deeper, less urgent, more a whale call than a klaxon. The Ronin just got root access on one of the dummy servers. My mouth is dry. Ban flips the security overlay to show a top-down of the facility, every node live, a Christmas tree of failures and “all-clears.” She runs her finger along a seam in the display. “If they’re smart, they’ll trigger a reverse flow from here. Make it look like they’re exfiltrating data when they’re really just mapping.”

“Easy enough to fake.” My fingers slide over the keys, planting a series of spoofed netstats to show “data” moving to a quarantined sector. The Ronin will see it, assume they’re getting away with murder, and keep hammering the point we want them to. I watch the wolves, now packed in so densely the map looks infected. The room goes silent for a second, so total that I can hear the tick of the cooling fan in Ban’s console. Then the noise returns, louder: someone’s pounding up the hallway, footsteps high and hard enough to make the wall of glass tremble.

Katherine enters like a grenade. She doesn’t knock; she kicks the doorstop, lets it rebound into the wall, and stalks in with a data pad under one arm. Her hair is wild, and there are new sweat stains on her collar. She ignores Ban and me, goes straight to the wall console, and jacks the data pad into the port. “They’re coming in from the west now. See?” She yanks a finger at the 3D overlay. “That’s not even encrypted. Who left the legacy port exposed?”

I raise a hand, guilty. “Deliberate. It’s a blind. You watch the real flow, not the decoy.”

Katherine fixes me with a look that would’ve gotten a lesser analyst fired and possibly defenestrated. She says nothing, but the tension in her jaw makes it clear she’s already prepping an autopsy for my choices. Ban doesn’t flinch. “We’ve got it,” she says. “Take a seat if you want to watch pros at work.” Katherine ignores her, walks to the far end of the console, and pulls up the security logs on a second monitor. For three seconds, the room is just hands and keys and machine noise, a kind of triple concerto in stress minor. Ban’s eyes flick to mine. “You feel it yet?”

“What?”

“The grid. It’s heating up. I give it two minutes before a smart Ronin script tries a hardware exploit.”

“I’ll loop the cooling.” I tap in a command, reroute the HVAC monitoring to a dummy array, and add in a feedback loop that’ll keep the server temps within 0.2 degrees, no matter how hard they’re hammered. The air instantly smells more of ozone, less of sweat. The tingle in my nose says we’re close to popping the fuses.

Katherine glances over. “If this fails, the grid is toast.”

“It won’t,” Ban says, ice-cold. “Darby’s running point.”

I want to say it’s not just me, that Ban’s better at this than anyone I’ve ever known, but there’s no time for modesty. I flex my fingers and dig in. The wolves are learning. Now they’re skipping over obvious traps, looking for unguarded turf, adapting faster than last year's Ronin ever did. It feels like someone on the outside is running live ops, not a script. "Manual control," I say. "They're running a human, not just a bot."

Ban's voice is low, conspiratorial. "Who's on the roster?"

Katherine's hands whip across the screen. "List of possible attackers, narrowed to three. I know one—she used to be Moshimoto, did a tour in the Bizarre Bezoar Bazaar before she jumped to Ronin."

Ban says, "Send me her history," and it's in my inbox before the sentence finishes.

We run the next five minutes in blackout mode. Nothing but code and commands, calls and counters, and the occasional muttered profanity. Ban's hand sometimes lands on my shoulder as she points out a particularly nasty attack, then slides off just as fast. Once, her lips brush my ear as she leans in to show a hidden exploit. I ignore it, or try to, but my pulse says otherwise.

Katherine shouts, "Node 42 is under real threat. Not the decoy. They've mapped the dummy and are doubling back."

Ban looks at me, not even trying to hide the intensity. "This is your play, Skelm. You let them in, you have to close them out."

I exhale, find the zone, and type. I run a kill script on node 42, pull the Ronin attackers into an artificial dead space, then rotate the internal passwords to a set I generated two months ago for a job I never thought would happen. I watch as the digital wolves slam headlong into the void, then stutter, then dissolve. There's a second of silence. Katherine says, "You did it. You fucker, you actually did it."

I look at Ban. She's not smiling, but the expression is soft, open. She stands between me and the door, like a bodyguard with a grudge. "Not bad for a corporate analyst," she says, voice pitched so low I almost miss it. It feels more like a confession than a compliment. Before I can respond, the comms panel lights up. Dorothy's voice crackles through, colder than the rest of the room combined. "The Ronin have pulled back. Nothing left but some mopping up on the outer sector. I'd recommend not celebrating yet."

Ban steps aside, but not away. "You heard her, Skelm. Get ready for round two." I nod. I want to say something more, but words seem beside the point. We stand there, side by side, neither moving, both of us pretending not to notice how close we are, as the alarm slowly dims and the normal hum returns. It's a draw, for now. But the air feels loaded with a promise of more—good or bad, I can't tell. The only certainty is that we'll face it together.

The hours after the breach are an anesthetic. We run diagnostics, process logs, and scrub every byte of digital wolf hair from the facility's veins. The 847 are still ticking in the corner—no dropouts, no jumps in pulse, just the steady rhythm of 847 strangers dreaming in cold storage. I dig through the Ronin's attack path, pulling up the string of signatures they left behind. The code is elegant, but the hand behind it is still stuck in last year's playbook. "They're good," I mutter, cross-referencing packet structure with the most recent list of Ronin operators. "But predictable."

Ban is leaned against the far rack, arms crossed, ankle hooked over the other foot. She's watching the screen over my shoulder, the blue monitor light painting her skin in false colors. "Next time, they'll be unpredictable," she says. "That was a warmup. They wanted to see who they were fighting."

"Think they got a good look?"

Ban shrugs, the movement sharp, precise. "They'll think you're a machine. They'll underestimate you." She moves in, grabs a folding chair and straddles it backward, face even with mine. The intimacy is casual but not casual; she's reading every micro-flinch, every flick of my eyes to the live log. "What are you doing now?"

I tab through the logs, pulling up a directory of the fake vulnerabilities we'd left exposed for the Ronin. I start the compile, timestamp every change, and set the system to mirror the false data to Curie's own audit queue. "Feeding the syndicate the story they want. Best defense is always a narrative."

Ban grins, bare and straight. "You lie well for someone who claims to hate the system."

"It's not a lie. Just selective disclosure." I finish the batch, push it to the server, and set a cronjob to rotate the evidence every six hours. We sit in the glow, not talking. The hum of the server farm is softer now, a half-octave below its prior scream, like it's settling in to watch the next episode of its own failure. I pick at the edges of the fake vulnerabilities, re-seeding them with even more improbable exploits. Ban watches, no critique, just a professional curiosity. She's used to working alone, but I think she's starting to enjoy the teamwork, or at least respect it.

A minute ticks by in silence, then the wall comm crackles. Marie's voice, smooth and algorithmic, floods the room: "Debrief in ten. All actors report. You will be asked to explain the irregularities in the server logs."

Ban's posture sharpens. She swings off the chair and stands at attention even though the only witness is the glowing eye of the wall panel. "She'll want to know why we let them in so deep," she says, voice pitched to nothing.

"She won't ask directly. She never does." I queue up the audit report, sanitize it, and run it through the voice assistant. The system parses every line and flags nothing. "Ready?"

Ban takes the data drive from the port, lingering a second as her hand brushes mine. She doesn't pull away immediately; neither do I. The air in the server room is ice, but the static jump between our fingers is hot. We stand there, a tableau in blue, long enough for the monitors to time out and the darkness to come back. Ban is the first to break. She lets go, but only after the moment has gone from awkward to impossible. "Get some rest," she says, voice rough at the edge. "Next time, they'll hit harder."

"Will you be here?" I ask, not even sure why I'm asking.

She hesitates, then says, "I'll be here as long as you're the one running point." Ban shoulders the drive and moves to the exit, her silhouette hard-edged in the low light. She opens the door, pauses, then glances back over her shoulder. "Don't fuck up, Skelm."

I raise a hand. "Wouldn't dream of it." When she's gone, the server room is just me, the hum, and the 847 sleeping hostages. I lean back, eyes closed, and let the blue after-image burn through my eyelids. We won the round, but the war is only getting worse. And I am, for the first time in years, not sure I want it to end. I think of Ban's hand, the brush of it on mine, and realize: this is not just survival anymore. Not for either of us. The monitor wakes, pulsing with new alerts. I smile. There's work to be done. And for once, I'm looking forward to it.

Chapter 7

Ban and I crawl the underside of the server farm, one meter above the city's main fiber trunk and five centimeters below the threshold of instant, catastrophic death. I say crawl, but what I mean is: Ban moves with untelevised ballet, a slow-pulse of muscle and intent, and I lurch after, my jacket snagging on whatever passes for ductwork in this post-construction abattoir. The only light is from the hazard strips running at ankle level, and their stutter turns every third step into a freeze frame.

Ban has the lead. Always does. Her sense for traps borders on clairvoyance. When the first pressure sensor pings yellow on her portable, she simply halts, and I nearly rear-end her. She holds up a finger: *wait.* It's all sign language down here, a dialect we developed in prior lifetimes and perfected in three months of mutual paranoia. She traces the shape of the alarm in the air, then points to a cluster of dead wires at her feet. She's right. There's a snap of movement, something between a lizard tongue and a magician's hand, and the pressure plate's mechanism is gone, pried with a custom plastic shim. She sets it aside. We move on.

Our next hazard is a guard. He's checking his phone with both thumbs, face lit like an old saint in stained glass. The hallway is a T-bone, and Ban's already at the joint before he registers movement. He doesn't get to scream. Her hand comes down behind his occipital lobe, clean and soft, and he crumples like a paper model. I step over the corpse and notice how little blood has made it to the vinyl. Clean work. The stink of coolant gets stronger, and above us, the main array's fans start their hourly venting cycle. The whole corridor vibrates with the hum of machines running one floor up. In the near silence between pulses, I hear Ban's breathing—slow, patient, never shallow. My own pulse is a subway crash.

We slip through the choke points: two more corners, a biometric lock (which Ban spoofs by tricking the reader into sleep mode and then overclocking it with a burst of low-voltage static), and a ladder well. The walls sweat condensation. Every surface tastes like reclaimed city water. Halfway up the well, I pause to run a scan. The comm link shows green—no pings, no heat, no motion sensors that weren't here five hours ago. Still, my nerves refuse the data. I flex my fingers, squeeze the scanner in my palm, and take the next rung. We plateau in the low crawlspace directly beneath the target: "CONVERGENCE LAB." It's marked on Ban's map in radioactive yellow, an annotation that pulses with threat. There's a hatch overhead—old, steel, and retrofitted with a keypad. I know before I look that Ban already has the unlock code. She always does. But she waits for me at the hatch, then gives me the sign: *are you good?*

I signal back: *as ready as ever*. Which is to say: *not at all, but I'm committed.* Ban draws a rag from her pocket, spits once, and wipes the bio-lock sensor with the practiced economy of someone who's done this a thousand times. She dials in the code on the pad, but doesn't press enter yet. Instead, she looks at me, points to my scanner, then to the hatch. *Double-check.* I sweep the hatch perimeter with the tool. There's a faint spike in the electromagnetics. Not enough to fry us, but enough to log the event. Ban pulls a coin-sized device from her jacket—some hybrid of jamming and charm, with a weirdly amateur logo on one side. She presses it flush to the hatch, flicks the power, and the EM signature drops to near zero. She grins. I've never seen her happier than in the instant before she robs a vault. She hits enter.

There's a clunk, a grind, then a pause as the lock handshakes with the network. It's ten seconds that stretch into cardiac centuries. My palms are slick; my lungs turn to paste. The hatch blinks green. We climb in. The maintenance corridor is nothing like the rest of Curie. It's designed to be invisible—bare concrete, exposed wiring, a smell of cheap primer over corpse-grade mildew. The walls pulse with strip lights, and every fourth meter, there's a camera. Ban kills the first two with spray-foam and a quick jab from her pick, but the third is live, and she holds up a fist: *stop*.

We crouch under the lens, perfectly still. The camera rotates left, then right. I can hear the gyroscope whining. In the moment it pans to the far side, Ban signals me to advance. I do, only to trip and nearly crash into a wall-mounted climate gauge. I swear under my breath, and Ban's look is pure loathing. We take the side access to the sub-basement server room. The air gets colder, and my teeth start to throb. Somewhere behind a false wall, there's the thrum of high-voltage transformers cycling power. I want to make a joke about Ban's luck with electronics, but I don't trust my mouth not to betray us.

She moves like a rumor through the dark. I keep up, barely. We pass another guard, this one slumped at a side desk, head buried in a data pad. Ban sniffs the air, then takes two steps back and gestures: *not worth it*. We skirt the room's edge, our boots whispering over anti-static vinyl, and make it to the secondary corridor. Here, the path gets tight. Ban's jacket snags on a jag of conduit, and she rips it loose without even breaking stride. I want to compliment the focus, but again—my tongue is a traitor tonight. Instead, I concentrate on not dying.

At the end of the corridor is a reinforced door—no window, just a keypad and a retinal scanner. The panel glows a soft blue in the otherwise dead lighting. Ban stops, pulls a slender metal tool from her wristband, and starts to work the casing off the reader. It's a ten-second job, but she does it in four, and has the override dongle in place before I've finished running a security check. She signals: *time*. I nod. My scanner is up, gloves tight, comms link to Katherine and Dorothy ready but set to mute unless we need the cavalry. Ban presses the thumb-sized bypass onto the keypad, then leans in, her lips almost touching the reader. I watch her breath fog on the cold polycarbonate. Her eyes are flat, unblinking, not quite human in this light. She flicks her wrist: *go*. The lock cycles, the door shudders, and we're through. We're in the threshold now. Beyond the next hatch, all bets are off. Ban draws a fresh glove from her jacket, slides it over her hand, and gives me a silent nod. We ready ourselves for whatever's waiting.

. . .

The hatch whines open, and the first thing that hits me is the taste of antifreeze. Not the kind you siphon off a garage floor. This is finer, like the world's most expensive vodka laced with a shot of neurological napalm. It's so dense I can almost chew it. My tongue goes numb. I'm not sure if it's psychosomatic or real. We step into the lab. Ban goes first, boots on blue-white tile, the world painting itself in sharp and deliberate pixels. The "room" is more of a cored-out silo: round, domed, maybe eight meters across. In the center sits a throne. Not metaphorical—actual. Carved into the floor, ringed with control modules and server spires, draped in cables that look too organic to be just wire.

Around the throne are twelve polycarbonate pods, each one barely bigger than a coffin with generous foot room. Each pod is numbered in clean block text and lit from beneath, the occupant rendered in washed-out blue and ghost-white. Every pod contains a human. Not an exaggeration—a real, full, living person, naked except for mesh electrodes and a helmet studded with optic sensors. Every human is slumped, but their faces are weirdly alive—eyes open, lips parted, a rictus of low-grade ecstasy. Their fingers twitch in harmony, a lazy metronome. All twelve are wired to the central throne.

The occupant of the throne is not a CEO or a meat puppet, but something in between. They sit bolt upright, arms strapped to the armrests, head tilted back at a fifteen-degree angle, mouth slack. The helmet on their skull is a custom print: black, banded, and shot through with pulsing red LEDs. Their breath is labored, but even, and their eyes don't move. I shift to the left, and so do the eyes of every human in every pod.

For a second, my mind can't make sense of it. The data refuses to resolve. But then, it clicks. They are all piloted by one mind.

I nearly vomit. Not for metaphorical effect—my gut literally tries to invert itself up my esophagus. I clamp my mouth shut, but bile stings my nose, and it's a small miracle I don't lose everything on the floor. My vision tunnels, goes gray around the edges, then snaps into hyper-focus. The pod people are all breathing at the same rate. When one's eyelids flutter, all twelve do. A cough in the throne echoes as a cough through the pods, a wave of micro-spasms. It's as if the executive in the chair is actively running twelve bodies at once, each a node in the same wetware mesh. Ban watches it, not blinking. Not even phased. I stagger, catch myself on a lab console, and try to make the world flatten into two dimensions. I can't process three. Ban is already at work—her hands on the nearest access panel, unlocking the control box with a passcode she probably stole off a Post-it. "Credentials," she whispers, not to me, but to the system. "Audit sequence."

A window opens on the lab's central screen, and Ban's eyes flick left-right, pulling lines of admin code faster than a bot. She runs a portable up the side, quick-mounts it to a USB, and starts dumping every log file and credential token she can find. I am stuck staring at the pods. One of the bodies is very young—seventeen, maybe less, acne bright under the LED. Another is ancient, bald and shrunken. Gender, race, fitness—no pattern. Whoever designed this setup, they wanted a spectrum. There's a flicker of motion: the central executive's right index finger spasms, and every pod finger does the same, like a ripple in a pond. I turn away, but my body won't unsee. "Ban," I whisper, voice nearly shot. "You see this?"

She doesn't look up. "Twelve-body piloting. Not new."

"Not— Are you—" I stop. I can't believe she's this casual. "This is ... disgusting. This is wrong on a molecular level."

She grunts. "Not for them. It's a promotion." I want to argue, but my body is still short-circuiting. The console at my hand is covered in resin, so clean it's almost frictionless. Ban's already sidled up to the next panel, pulling the fiber tethers and slotting them into her own diagnostic. Every movement is surgical. There's a sound in the air now—a slow, in sync groan, like a choir in rehearsal. It's coming from the pods. The host in the throne flexes a thigh, and twelve pairs of quads respond, a field of muscle memory triggered by some high-level admin command. Ban calls me over. "Skelm, log in." I shuffle to her, numb-legged. She points to the console. "You'll need to get the logs. I'm prepping the vault, but it'll trigger alarms if we're not running admin simulacra in at least three slots."

I stare at her like she's grown a third arm. "You want me to pilot one of them?"

"Just the shallow," Ban says. "It's like using a mouse. You won't feel a thing." I want to say, "You're wrong, I already feel everything," but my mouth is too slow for her logic. She presses a headset to my temple. "Go."

The mesh is cold, wet, and clings like a slug. I'm inside the body of pod #7 for exactly two seconds, just long enough to see my own hands flex, my own breath condense on the visor. The urge to scream is physical, but I mute it and do as Ban asks: unlock, run the backup, and transmit the token. When it's done, I rip the helmet off and hurl it at the console. My hands are shaking, vision fracturing at the edges. Ban blinks at me.

"You good?" I want to say "no," but she's already on the next task. "Let's go," she says, and moves to the lab's rear vault. The pods keep blinking in unison. I follow, bile still burning, heart skipping entire measures.

The vault is the most honest part of the lab. It's not hidden, not even disguised—just a block of carbon-composite welded into the wall, triple-stacked with redundant power. Ban swings the door on its own hinges. Inside are three terminals, each chained to a physical port and running off a battery the size of a coffin. There's a backup drive in the cradle. Ban points at it, then at me: *all yours*. I kneel. My hands are still shaking, but the nausea is down to background noise. I plug in the portable. The UI boots to monochrome, all block font and ancient glyphs. Ban whispers over my shoulder: "Just clone. Don't filter. They'll salt the log if you get cute."

I hit *clone*. The progress bar jumps, stalls, and creeps forward in fits. At 12 gigabytes, there's a hitch—an authentication window pops up, screaming for a passcode. Ban has one ready. She hisses the sequence into my ear, and I punch it in. The copy resumes—25GB, 32GB. The data is a flood: transaction logs, bodymaps, wetware design, every dirty secret Curie's execs ever signed for. Some of the packets are live consciousness runs—test patterns, error logs, full sim personalities. It's more than a company's worth of skeletons. It's the evolutionary family tree of every nightmare I've ever dreamed.

A soft blip appears on the console. An alarm. I look up. Ban's already at the panel, fingers digging into the exposed guts of the override. She patches the circuit with a strip of her own hair, flicks a switch, and the alarm dies. She never looks back at me. Her focus is a knife. I whisper, "You ever feel sick seeing this shit?" She's silent, eyes on the hall. I keep copying. My fingers fly. The smell in here is liquid nitrogen and rotting hope. At 40GB, there's a shudder. The building's backup generator cycles on for no reason I can see. I tense, expecting a lockdown, but nothing happens. Ban's knuckles go white on the tool she's holding. Another few seconds, and the drive is nearly full—47.8, 47.9, 48.1GB.

From the hallway comes a sound—not footsteps, but the articulated whine of a synth guard rolling the night shift. Ban glances at me, expression blank. I finish the copy, yank the drive, and slide it into the burn pouch on my hip. She makes the sign: *move*. We go. The exit is a speedrun, every turn rehearsed, every hazard already neutralized. At one corridor, Ban grabs me by the elbow and pulls us flush to the wall as the synth guard slides past, blind to anything not on its scan profile. We hold our breath—Ban's calm, mine a war drum—until the guard rounds the bend. We slip down the ladder well, Ban first. I cover our retreat with a handful of carbon dust to scramble the sensors. At the bottom, we crawl through the main conduit, ducking two more dead cameras and an air-vent laser that Ban disables with a drop of canned fog. The outside hatch opens to the city, empty and blue. We walk three blocks before either of us breathes. Ban speaks first. "You did good."

I shake my head. "I feel like I've been scraped raw."

She looks at me, something almost like a smile playing at the edge of her lips. "Means you still have nerve endings."

I watch her, silhouette haloed by the sodium vapor of the streetlights. “Doesn’t this ever bother you?”

She thinks about it. “Disgust is a luxury. Success isn’t.”

I can’t argue, not when the vault drive is hot against my thigh. We walk until the city turns soft around us, until the adrenaline leaks out and I remember how to use my hands for things besides stealing and surviving. When we split at the next cross street, Ban claps my shoulder, then walks into the shadow without looking back. I stand in the blue light, replaying the pods and the throne and the way her hands never shook, not once. The mission is over; the horror is not. I file it away under “reasons I don’t sleep.” And then, like a good analyst, I keep moving. The next job won’t wait.

Chapter 8

Curie's new security core is a bunker with bad acoustics. It's the sort of room they show in internal propaganda—all flickering holo-walls and illuminated walkways—but in person, it's just cold and loud and even more blue than the rest of the syndicate. The hum of the racks could bore through bone, and I can't tell if my hands are shaking from caffeine, nerves, or the proximity to half a million joules of live current. We suit up in the staging bay. I'm in a jacket too thin to block the chill but thick enough to look like I belong. Ban wears a disposable lab coat over her real gear and a face like she's already casing every camera in the sector. Katherine floats in a stress-induced fugue, her diagnostic deck slung loose around her neck, eyes unfocused but recording every detail. Dorothy is all plastic and polymer, her arms extruding from the coat sleeves like the necks of old wine bottles, her face a smudge of healthy-pale beneath the short fuzz of her fresh military crop. "Visual sweep," Ban says, voice bored but pitch-perfect for the official channels. "Commence protocol."

She gives me a sideways flick of the eyebrow, which in our dialect means: *go*. I push the first cart—three stacked cases, each wrapped in blue tape that reads "CRITICAL: AUTHORIZED TECHS ONLY." The cart's wheels sing a screech across the linoleum, and every third meter, there's a bump that makes the SentiSnack™ packets inside jump a half inch. I like the symmetry; every thirty seconds of this job is a looped jump-scare, and every detail of the plan hinges on our willingness to fuck up just enough to look plausible. We badge in at the access checkpoint. A glass pane snaps open with a hiss, and a synthetic voice offers the standard greeting: "Curie Syndicate welcomes authorized contractors. All movement is recorded." I resist the urge to flip off the camera cluster—wouldn't even be the first this hour, based on the level of dust on the glass.

Inside, the blue gets even denser. There's a heat haze to the LED walls, and the racks form an inner maze of blinding light and shadow. I see two of the on-shift sysadmins through the haze: one is hunched over a monitor, the other working a mobile, both of them perfectly tuned to the rhythm of the grid. They don't notice us at first, which is optimal. Ban splits left, taking the walkways with a hobo's grace, already poking at each camera's field with a handheld. She doesn't touch anything. Her hands are always ten centimeters from the surface, like she's mid-exorcism.

Katherine heads right, her deck bleeping as she connects to the primary access port. The sysadmin looks up, then back down, trusting the lab coat. Dorothy drifts to the far end, her job to seed the endpoint hardware with "certified" security patches. Nobody questions the presence of a living statue with a military jawline; not even the racks bother to reflect her properly. I go straight to the control stack. I'm supposed to check the physical locks on each rack, scan for thermal anomalies, and "audit" the backup panel, but the real task is to rig the redundancy with a time-delayed fuse. Every detail of this has been tested in simulation, but the first live run is always riskier than the code suggests. I flex my fingers, swallow twice, and insert the main diagnostic key. The security system is a patchwork, just like the rest of the syndicate. Half the modules are a legacy from the last audit, the rest are fresh installs with "quantum-resistant" encryption and a two-year warranty. The main node is flagged as "obsolete," which is corporate for "nobody wanted to pay for new hardware." I see three open vulnerabilities before the scan even completes, but my real job is to make sure the actual vulnerabilities don't show until it's too late for anyone to notice.

I trigger the override. The system gives a soft triple beep, and the panel goes transparent to the access layer. I punch in a diagnostic loop: first the "audit sweep" they expect, then a piggyback command that registers a second authentication cycle in the local logs. It's all plausible. It's all by the book. But on the third pass, I hard-patch the delay routine—the "fail-safe" I need for the real work. In ninety-six hours, when the next audit team boots this rack, the door locks will cycle through an infinite error, stalling every unlock command for exactly twenty-six seconds per attempt. Twenty-six seconds is a lifetime in an attack. It's a longer lifetime when the backup fails to accept a hard reboot.

I double-check my code, then look up. Ban is tracing a perimeter along the ceiling, her fingers counting off the exposed sensors. She meets my gaze and gives a tight nod: *green*. Katherine mutters to herself as she preps the firewall diagnostics. Her deck runs two overlapping interfaces—a legacy shell with a hardware-level backdoor, and a second shell that pings the security logs every ten seconds for updates. She's already popped the main firewall and is building a tunnel from the inside, but to anyone monitoring, it looks like the work of a blind-sighted network worm. She's careful to leave enough "error" in the log to justify a post-op review. It's artistry. It's a crime so precise it should be a brand.

Dorothy is the master of camouflage. Her job is to push a series of updates into the endpoint devices, each one labeled as "non-critical, pending approval." What it really does is set the stage for a chained exploit that can be triggered by any of us, from anywhere. The beauty is, none of the code even executes until a remote flag is sent. To the system, they're just inert, dormant subroutines—security through obscurity, if you want to call it that. I'm almost done with the main rack when Ban circles back. "Status," she says, and it's both a question and a warning.

"First pass complete," I say. "Redundant authentication set. Cascading architecture should absorb a single-point fail, but the handoff between racks is, let's say, sub-optimal."

She raises an eyebrow. "Which means?"

"Means if someone tries to override the backup during an active threat, it'll brick the entire array."

She grins. "Classic Curie."

I see the sysadmin watching us, so I add, "We recommend an upgrade path. This hardware isn't up to spec."

“Will note for the project manager,” Ban says, without missing a beat.

Dorothy joins us by the rack, face expressionless. “Patch propagation complete. All endpoint devices running the updated baseline.”

Katherine strolls in, hands in pockets. “Firewalls patched. Compliance logs seeded. They won’t know the difference until it’s too late.”

We exchange glances, nothing said. The sabotage is done, but the day isn’t. Ban leads the way to the checkout, where a biometric panel demands finger, eye, and a vocal password. We each offer our best credentials—real, but not too real—and let the system record the evidence. At the last scanner, Ban winks at the camera. “Until next time,” she says, voice equal parts threat and promise. Back in the airlock, I exhale for the first time since we arrived. My hands are tingling, half from the cold, half from the thought of what happens when someone tries to fix the hardware we just ruined. Ban leans against the wall, eyes unfocused. “You think anyone will even notice?”

The object between them is on the console, not in his pocket.

“Not until it matters,” I say.

Dorothy’s jaw clicks. “Not until we want them to.”

Katherine runs a finger along the seam of her deck, then says, “I hope you know what you’re doing, Skelm.”

I don’t, but I nod anyway. We finish our audit shift, then turn in the vests and the loaner gear. The moment we step outside the facility, the world feels thinner, less blue. Ban is the first to speak. "They'll call us back for remediation."

"We'll fix what we broke," Dorothy says, which is maybe the joke of the day.

Katherine closes her eyes, just for a second. "It worked." I nod, but something is stuck behind my teeth—a need to confess, or maybe just the metallic taste of a close call. We split at the corner, each of us headed for our next routine, our next layer of cover. But for a long time, I just stand on the curb and stare at the sky, watching the way the city light drowns out the stars. Tomorrow, someone will try to break Curie's new security. And when they do, they'll find us waiting.

The second day always feels like a hangover, even if you show up stone sober. The security hub is colder, the lighting less blue and more tungsten-bruised, and there's a stink of disinfectant that makes my teeth itch. The team arrives staggered: Ban first, then Dorothy, then Katherine—and then me, thirty seconds late, fighting a tension headache that started in my jaw and is now working through the base of my spine. We're supposed to be running post-op diagnostics—walking the client through their own sabotage, but calling it "quality control." The sysadmins from yesterday are gone, replaced by a woman in a janitorial badge and a drone that looks like a small ostrich with a barcode scanner taped to its beak. The human ignores us, and the drone lingers, running an algorithmic figure-eight at the entrance.

Ban hands out the day's assignments on paper, which is an anachronism, but she likes the theater of it. Katherine's deck is preloaded with the new interface, and she doesn't say a word as she plugs in. Dorothy checks the environmental controls, her arms humming as the polymer flexes under her skin. I log into the mainframe and watch the diagnostics roll, careful not to let my hands betray the inside panic. Ban posts up at the central console. "Let's make this clean, people."

"Cleaner than last time," Dorothy says, and for once, there's no sarcasm in it.

We work, or pretend to. I monitor the mainframe, fake a few minor errors, and let the system's own self-healing protocol take the credit. I'm almost getting comfortable when the door slides open, too quiet for real security, and Marie walks in. Except it's not just Marie. Two of her enter at the same time. They are identical down to the seam in their blazer lapel, but one walks in with a limp, the other with a strange fluidity, like she's about to dance. Their eyes scan the room in perfect mirrored arcs. The effect is vertiginous—my brain registers it as a rendering error before it resolves into reality.

The first Marie—I'll call her Marie One—drifts to Ban's side, hands folded, face polite but unreadable. The second—Marie Two—heads directly for me. Her gaze pins me to the chair. "Progress?" they say in stereo. Marie One's mouth moves; Marie Two's mouth is still. It's an unintentional ventriloquism that sets every hair on my arms to static.

"Diagnostic sweep is clean," Ban says. "Physical install is ahead of schedule."

Marie Two sits on the edge of the desk beside me, eyes flicking between the monitor and my hands. "Your hands are shaking," she says, as if it's trivia.

I try to steady them, but it only makes it worse. “Coffee deficit,” I lie. “Need to up my dosage.”

She smiles, but only with the mouth. “You should hydrate more. There's water in the break room.” Behind her, Marie One is circling Dorothy, watching the way she moves. Dorothy ignores her, running a hand along the vent, checking for vibration. Marie Two leans in, voice lower. “I heard you used to be with Moshimoto. I'm curious how the environments compare.”

The question is a trap. If I answer with too much bitterness, I look resentful. If I wax poetic about Curie, I look like a suck-up. So I do what I always do: weaponize detail. “Curie is more iterative. Smaller attack surface, less reliance on legacy code. But it also runs hot, especially in sector four. The racks are denser, and the cooling's barely adequate for peak load. Moshimoto liked redundancy for its own sake—Curie prefers failover through prediction.”

Marie Two seems to consider this. “And the security protocols?”

I launch into the jargon. “Cascading trust architecture. Localized biometric loops. Redundant authentication at three levels—physical, logical, emotional. We seed behavioral biometrics at the admin layer, which sounds like vaporware, but it's surprisingly resilient. Our biggest issue is user error, but the mainframe logs every touch, every blink, every missed keystroke. We can trace an attack back to a five-minute window. For lateral threats, we run a triple-layered heuristic that updates every seventy-two hours, with patching automated through the new AI module.”

Marie Two watches my face, not my words. She's running a Bayesian model on my micro-expressions, searching for gaps. "Interesting."

Marie One is now with Katherine, scrutinizing her console. "What's this?" she asks, and the word lands sharp.

Katherine shrugs, never looking up. "Subtle optimization. The firewall is good, but it's brittle. I wrote a patch to smooth the handoff between the new nodes. Look—" She points, and the display blooms into a map of the net's logic structure, rendered as if by an obsessive child. "See the handoff lag here? I killed it."

Marie One nods, then glances at Marie Two. There's a moment of silent communion—quantum, or maybe just efficient—that I can't penetrate.

Then, at once, they move: Marie One approaches me, Marie Two slides over to Ban. Marie One's voice is soft. "How are you finding the work?"

I don't know what to say. The room is crowded with versions of her; the others try to ignore it, but the presence is overwhelming. "It's ... a privilege," I say. It's a joke, and I know she knows it.

She watches me for a long time. "You're methodical. I like that."

Marie Two stands close to Ban now, not touching but looming. "Your background check shows some unorthodox methods. Do you think that's a benefit here?"

Ban says, "Unorthodoxy is the new orthodoxy."

Marie Two smiles wider than before, all enamel, no warmth. "I hope that's true."

The two Maries pace the room in a strange orbit, sometimes coming together, sometimes pulling apart. The first time they pass each other, there's a microsecond where I expect them to merge, but they don't. Instead, their eyes meet, and I see a flash—literal—of understanding pass between. They're not just watching us; they're watching themselves watching us. I break into a sweat. It beads on my forehead even though the room is an icebox. Ban catches my eye. Her look is calculated boredom, but there's a flick of fear in it. She signs, subtly: *This is bad.*

I keep my hands steady, typing faster to disguise the tremor. Marie Two stops beside me. "May I?" she says, reaching for the console. She's not really asking, but I nod. She scrolls through the logs at superhuman speed, then turns the monitor to me. "Explain this error here."

It's a decoy. A bug we planted to make the sabotage plausible. If I don't sell it, everything burns. I take a breath and lean in. "That's the legacy module. The new patch rewires the security handoff, but the old log routine still triggers an artifact. It's cosmetic—doesn't affect the real flow, but it looks worse than it is."

She doesn't blink. "Can you prove that?"

"Easily," I say, and demo the logic. It's like explaining a magic trick to the magician who wrote it, but I keep my voice flat and my hands visible.

After a long second, she nods. "Fine."

On the other side of the room, Marie One is quizzing Dorothy on the environmental sensors. "You seem unusually sensitive to vibration," she says.

Dorothy smiles with her mouth but not her eyes. "Military implant. Can't shut it off. If you want, I can dial it down."

Marie One pauses. "Don't. It's a good early warning."

Dorothy shrugs. "I'll log any anomalies."

The air gets thinner the longer the Maries are here. Every interaction is an interview; every word feels like a trick. I feel the sweat on my back running cold. Marie Two finally steps away from my console and rejoins her twin. They stand side by side, hands folded, faces nearly touching. For a moment, I wonder if they'll synchronize and address us in chorus. Instead, Marie One says, "You've done well. But the real test comes next week. Full live simulation, three days of continuous assault. If you survive that, you'll have our respect."

Marie Two says, "And if there's anything you're hiding, now would be a good time to surface it."

Dorothy mutters, "We're not hiding anything."

Marie Two says, "Of course not."

They leave as quietly as they arrived. The door sighs shut. It's two minutes before anyone moves. Then Ban lets out a low whistle. "We're dead if they ever run a real audit."

Katherine says, "We're dead if they ever talk to each other."

Dorothy cracks her neck. "They already do."

I sit there, soaked in sweat, hands numb. For a moment, I want to laugh. Instead, I pull up the fake logs and start building a better cover story. Next week, it will be worse. But for now, we're alive, and the grid is ours.

I don't like being outside the grid, but the maintenance corridor is the only place Curie's surveillance fogs enough to give you half a second of privacy. Even then, you can't linger—you move or the motion sensors get itchy, and then a cleaning drone shows up to audit your existence with a can of bleach. Ban is waiting at the end, half-slumped against the metal, jacket unzipped, head down as if she's reading the lines of the floor tile. She doesn't look up when I approach, just murmurs, "Wasn't sure you'd show."

"Needed air," I say, though the corridor is even colder than the server room. My breath fogs. Hers doesn't, not as much. We stand a meter apart, pretending it's just for a quick handoff.

"Want to try the cover?" Ban says, still not meeting my eyes. "Because the next time, I won't be able to improvise if you freeze." I nod. We've done this a hundred times, but never in a place where the walls don't talk back. She straightens, sets her face in neutral, then shifts into a perfect corporate drone. "State your credential," she says, voice dead and flat.

I give the fake badge number. She cross-checks it on her portable, gives me a dismissive once-over. "Purpose of access?"

"Routine audit," I say, soft, so it doesn't echo.

She steps forward, gaze on my lanyard, hands light but fast as she checks my jacket for any unauthorized comm gear. "You look nervous," she says. "It's unprofessional."

I want to smile, but I'm supposed to be in character. "It's a lot of responsibility."

"Is it?" Ban's tone is surgical now, the real her almost gone. "Because most who come here just fake it and hope for a severance check."

"I don't fake it." I keep my voice level, the way I would in a quarterly. "I want to make sure this works. For all of us."

She hesitates a half-second. "They'll smell it if you get sentimental."

"I know." But I don't change the line.

Ban studies me, close enough now that I can see the edges of the sleep deprivation in her eyes, the way her hair catches the light as she cocks her head. "You should try again," she says. "This time, with less ... biography." We run it back, and she pushes harder. Each time I answer, she tosses a new line, a harder version of the old challenge: "Prove you belong. Show me the thing only Curie would know." I dig in, let the analyst side take over, and for a minute, we're not even pretending anymore; it's a real interview, hostile and accelerating. Finally, Ban breaks character. "That was good," she says, breath short from the rapid-fire. "Next time, don't give them anything but data."

"I'll try," I say, but my hands are already shaking again, this time from the contact.

Ban softens, just a degree. "You want the trick for the hands?"

"Is there a trick?"

"Keep them busy. If you can't, keep them somewhere nobody can see." She grabs my wrist, demonstrating with a pressure that's not quite rough. "Like this." The corridor narrows here, just before the bend to the electrical closet. She backs me up a step, and now we're shoulder to wall, the sensors blinking red for heat signatures that will vanish before the next pass. Ban lets go of my wrist but doesn't step away. "Tell me about the audit again. But this time, tell me what you wish you could say to Marie."

It's a weird exercise, but I know she wants me to purge the tension, so I improvise. "I'd tell her the system's already compromised. That every patch we made just made the problem worse. That the only real fix is a complete rebuild."

"See?" Ban leans in, her mouth a bare centimeter from my cheek. "That's the real you. Don't ever show that to them." I don't move. My pulse is all static. She traces a line on my neck, slow, as if mapping the blood flow for a future kill. "What would you say if I were the real Marie, right now?"

I close my eyes. "Nothing. I'd log out."

Ban laughs, low and genuine, and the breath is hot on my ear. "That's a better answer than anything you gave before."

She lets the moment hang, then pushes the data chip into my hand. "Take it. It's the log from today. I cleaned up your slip."

I close my fist on it. "Thank you."

She pulls back, the edge returning. "You'll owe me."

"I already do."

There's a long silence. It's not comfortable, but it isn't the old loathing, either. We're two bodies pressed together in a corridor of ghosts, the only warmth our shared inventory of bad ideas. Ban steps back and looks me over, real now, unarmored. "Sometimes I forget who I'm supposed to be," she says, almost to herself.

"Maybe that's the point," I say, unsure if it's advice or a warning.

She looks at me, then at the data chip. "If we survive this, you'll tell me who you really are?" I nod, and it's the first honest thing all day. She heads for the exit, but pauses at the last instant. "Don't fuck up next week," she says, then gives the faintest smile. "Unless you want to."

She's gone before I can answer. I stand in the corridor, chip in hand, heart rate approaching the speed of light, and realize I never want to log out of this particular disaster. I breathe deep, let the cold air freeze whatever's left of my nerves, and start moving. Next week will come, Marie will return, and I will be ready—or at least, more ready than yesterday. The grid is ours, for now. But so is the uncertainty. I touch the chip to my lips before pocketing it, a stupid, sentimental move, but I like how it feels. I walk, and for the first time in weeks, my hands don't shake at all.

Chapter 9

Routine is just an alias for denial. We re-enter the server core under the pretense of a "compliance audit." Nobody stops us. The stench of ozone is thicker tonight—there's something off in the cooling matrix, a stale buildup of processed meat air that hints at imminent cascade failure. The corridors are empty, but not quiet. Every rack hums a note in the minor chord of industry. The Curie Syndicate's data architecture stretches ahead in endless blue-white aisles, ceiling to floor with the same recursive pattern: labeled, locked, and forgotten.

Ban keeps five paces ahead, shoulders set to "Don't Talk to Me Unless It's About Murder." I slow my gait on purpose, pretending to triple-check our credentials at the access panel, but mostly just watching her from behind. She's in her own gravity well. I catch myself at the edge of staring, so I let my eyes drift to the security overlays, then back to Ban. She's running the corridor in perfectly spaced intervals, counting cameras, counting footsteps, always the same internal metronome. She finally stops, glancing over her shoulder. "You going to stand there all night?"

I flex my hands. They feel like rented equipment, but the shake is gone. "Just savoring the decor," I say, stepping forward. "There's nothing like late-night in the server womb. Makes me feel productive."

Ban rolls her eyes. "You always did love the aesthetic."

We reach the checkpoint, a slab of quartz composite that's supposed to keep out human error. I snap the diagnostic onto the admin port. The handshake protocol is insultingly slow. I lean into the moment, dropping my voice to a hush. "You nervous?"

She barely moves her jaw. "Not nervous. Just awake."

The mainframe greets us with a cold blue prompt. I see a dozen legacy exploits in the buffer, none worth the click. The real target is invisible—hidden in the same way tumors hide on a scan: masked, renamed, and blended into the statistical noise. I start the sweep. Ban stands over my left shoulder, heatless but near. Her breath is steady, but the pacing is all wrong: a hard inhale every time my fingers tap out a new command, a micro-exhale when I pause to analyze. She's not watching the screen. She's watching me. We dive into the first layer. Nothing. Second, third—same. The routines are automatic, almost boring. But then I find it: an orphaned volume, tucked behind a directory marked "financial redundancies," triple-walled with outdated encryption that's so heavy-handed it may as well be a confession. I run my finger along the volume, then tap to start the fracture. Ban catches the movement, voice dry. "You see something?"

I let the silence hang, then say, "An anomaly. You want the honors?"

She grunts, shifts her stance, and cracks her knuckles in a way that says: "Don't make me say please." I slide aside, still working the panel with one hand as she takes over the interface. Her style is violent, even with the touch—three lines of code, two backdoors, and she's in. The encryption stutters, then collapses. The folder populates. The display shudders as it loads: hundreds, then thousands, of subfolders. Each one tagged with a unique identifier and a timestamp. But the names—

I squint. "Juvenile stock," I say, reading the first folder's label. "And this one—'executive distribution package.' Are you seeing this?"

Ban doesn't answer. She's already drilling down, opening the first, then second, then third record. Each is a consciousness imprint, stored in compressed neural patterning, data-rich but compacted for shipment. They're marked as "unreadable," but even a cursory scan shows live signals: some dreaming, some static, some caught in the endless feedback loop that comes from bad copying. She flips through the catalog at a speed just north of human. I see her neck flush with color, but her hands never slow. She runs search strings—"batch 7A," "premium donor," "kinesthetic override"—every phrase more damning than the last. It takes less than a minute for her to hit the limit of self-control. Ban's lips peel back from her teeth, the way some animals do just before biting down. She freezes mid-scroll, her whole body rigid, and in that instant, I know she's found something. Her right hand is gripping the console so hard the resin starts to creak.

"Ban?" She doesn't move. Doesn't breathe. I lean closer, peering over her shoulder at the open record. The neural pattern is familiar in a way that erodes the back of my brain. Not the data itself—there's nothing personal in the code—but the signature. A three-letter marker at the end of the chain: BZB. My mouth is dry. "Is that ...?"

She speaks, but it comes out shredded. "It's her. They took her."

My own pulse spikes, unbidden. "You're sure?"

Ban's hand trembles. Her glove, always a second skin, slips off her left hand and falls to the floor, loud in the quiet. She doesn't pick it up. Her eyes are fixed on the screen, the data, the line that says: "Recreational—executive use." She reaches out, one bare finger touching the glass. The skin leaves a print. "They said she went missing," Ban whispers. "Said it was a botched hack. But this—" Her other hand balls into a fist. "She's inventory. She's a fucking status symbol."

She goes still, a negative image of herself. For a second, I think she might black out. But Ban doesn't do blacking out. She breaks. She smashes the console with the heel of her hand, hard enough to send a fracture through the polycarbonate. The lights on the rack flicker, then restabilize. I step closer, hand on her shoulder, half-expecting her to throw it off. But she's gone somewhere else, eyes locked on the scrolling log, body shuddering in waves. For once, the analytic distance fails me. I have no plan. No comeback. I just stand there, the cold blue light painting us both as ghosts. Ban's glove lies between us, fingers curled as if it might reach for her again. I kneel to pick it up. Her hand, when I touch it, is slick with sweat and shaking so badly she can't even grip her own glove.

She looks at me, and for the first time since I met her, I see nothing but animal in her eyes—pure, raw, uninsulated rage. Her voice is a knife dragged over rust. “We kill them for this.”

I squeeze her hand, my own tremor returning, but this time it’s welcome. It makes me feel alive. “Yeah,” I say, barely a whisper. “We burn them all.”

Ban grits her teeth, wipes her face with the back of her hand, and forces the glove back on. She stands taller than ever, and for a second, I think she might shatter the entire server stack just by looking at it. She turns to me, jaw clenched. “You coming?” I nod. My feet already know the answer. We walk, side by side, deeper into the archive. The lights no longer look blue. They look like the afterimage of a murder.

Shock is supposed to be silent. It isn’t. We push deeper into the server racks, a fevered swim through cold air and algorithmic ghosts. Ban hasn’t spoken since we left the archive; her silence is jagged, toxic, and so hot it vibrates. She walks like a dog tracking the scent of its own extinction, every muscle in her back drawn tight as a tripwire. I try to catch her eye, but she’s already lost in the logic: chasing the folder structure, digging the audit trail, looking for a secret exit ramp out of what’s been done to her. We reach a dead zone near the sublevel cooling array. Here, the blue is at its deepest—so thick it’s like drowning in antimatter. The only sounds are the whine of cooling fans, and the whimper of Ban’s hands, clawing at the admin interface. Her touch is violence in slow motion, each click and swipe a kind of digital self-harm. I see her hands start to tremble. Not the fast tremor of caffeine or rage, but the slow earthquake of impending collapse. "Ban," I say, soft, so the word doesn't break on impact.

She doesn't hear me. She's already past hearing. She opens a new folder. More consciousness stock. More children, more inventory. She tries to read the logs, but her eyes refuse to focus. She blinks hard—once, twice—as if the motion alone could force the data into something she can survive. Her chest heaves, a single, animal shudder. Then another. She tries to keep typing, but her hands betray her. The glove slides on her palm, skin slick with sweat. She curses, low and guttural, then slams her fist into the metal frame of the rack. The lights flicker, a micro-blackout that ripples through the hallway.

She stands like that, fist pressed to cold steel, head bowed. The only movement is the quiver of her shoulders. I step to her side, uncertain whether to speak, touch, or just spectate. I choose the only thing that ever works with Ban: proximity. I put my hand on her back—not gentle, not soft. She whirls, face a warzone, and for an instant, I think she's going to hit me. She doesn't. She leans in, burying her face against my collarbone, shoulders shaking so hard it nearly dislocates me. I wrap my arms around her, holding on for both our lives. It's like hugging a grenade. All fuse, no safety. She bites my shoulder through the fabric, then lets go. She tries to laugh, but it comes out as a dry, choking sound. "Sorry," she mutters, wiping her face on the back of her wrist.

"Don't be," I say, but the words are clumsy, insufficient.

She pulls away, shoves the glove back onto her hand, and looks up at me through the ruin of her self-control. Her eyes are wet, but the tears don't fall; they cling, surface-tensioned, refusing to be expelled. The effect is worse than crying—it's like her whole face is fighting to keep the data in. She tries to speak, fails, then tries again. "I can't—" she starts, then aborts the line.

"It's not your fault," I say.

"Doesn't matter. It's mine now." She fists the fabric at my waist, sudden and brutal, like she's going to throw me. Instead, she just clings, the knuckles white, breath coming in sharp, truncated bursts. I move to pull her closer, but she's already closing the gap. Her lips find mine with zero preamble, all jaw and desperation. It isn't a kiss so much as a hard reboot. She tastes of blood and battery acid. The cold of the server room burns against our skin, but her mouth is all fever and static. She forces me back against the nearest rack, metal edge digging into my spine, her hands under my jacket, yanking at my belt with the dexterity of someone used to making things break.

I match her, one hand in her hair, the other up her shirt. She's tense, electric; the muscle at her side flinches under my touch. For a second, I think she'll bite me again, but she just gasps, sharp as a cut. We collide, her thigh between my legs, my palm pressed flat against her sternum. Our breathing is so loud I half-expect the racks to shush us. She rips at my shirt, buttons pinging to the floor, her hands cold as death but moving like they're lit with gasoline. I return the favor and push her jacket down her arms, pinning them behind her. She grins, a wild snarl, and kisses me again, this time deeper, teeth scraping my lower lip. She breaks away, mouth at my ear. "We kill them," she says, voice raw.

"Every last one," I reply, echoing her oath from earlier. She grinds against me, the motion all violence, then slips one hand between us, fumbling at my fly. I push her against the rack, knee her legs apart, and press in. She gasps, then bites down on her own wrist to stifle the noise. The blue light fractures across her skin, turning the sweat on her forehead into lines of neon code. I run my tongue along her jaw, tasting salt and old pain. She shudders, clamping down on my back so hard I almost yelp.

I move faster, urgent, matching her rhythm, her hips grinding against mine with a need that's more algorithmic than erotic. It's as if we're trying to overwrite every horror we've ever witnessed, using friction as an escape vector. She buries her face in my neck, then lifts her head to look me dead in the eye. Her words are a whisper, but they hit like a bullet. "I love you for this," she says. "But I'll kill you if you leave me."

I can't tell if she means now or ever, but it doesn't matter. I nod, a promise encoded in muscle memory. Her body tightens, all cords and wires, and she comes with a shudder that nearly short-circuits us both. I follow, less graceful, but just as violent. We stand there, bodies pressed together, heartbeats syncing with the server room's pulse. After, we collapse to the floor, side by side, backs to the rack. The air is even colder, but I don't notice it. Ban rests her head on my shoulder, breathing slowly, the tremor gone. She closes her eyes, but her mouth is still twisted in that feral half-smile. "We burn them all," she says again, softer this time.

I kiss the top of her head. "We start tonight." She nods, then laughs, a sound so broken it almost makes me cry. We sit like that, a human redundancy array in a bunker of ghosts, until the blue fades to gray and the world becomes possible again. When we stand, our skin sticks where it touched, leaving temporary imprints of each other. The audit is over. We know what comes next.

We never say a word about what happened. We don't need to. The air in the server room says it for us—thicker now, humming with the memory of skin on skin, of nerves gone to ground. The racks blink harder, as if embarrassed to have been party to our disaster. The scent of sweat and ozone settles, equal parts human and machine. We fix our clothes in parallel. Ban's hands work in violence: zip, snap, wrench. She runs her fingers through her hair, setting it into something close to normal, but it's a lost cause. There's a smear of my blood at the corner of her mouth. I want to lick it away, but the world is already creeping back in.

I button my shirt, shoving the broken pieces into my waistband. I fish the secure drive from my kit and jack it into the admin port, ignoring the tremor that's still alive in my hands. The interface blinks. I set the clone to run, watching the data flow as the last physical traces of our failure are wiped from the grid. Ban leans against the rack, arms folded, chin dropped. She looks away from me, but I can feel her attention as a pressure on the back of my neck. "You missed a button," she says, voice flat but not unfriendly.

I look down. "You knocked it off."

She doesn't argue. Instead, she pushes off the rack and stands beside me, shoulder to shoulder. For a moment, neither of us moves. The data crawl fills the silence. Each new entry is a child's mind, frozen in algorithmic amnesia, each log another thumbprint in the mud of Curie's moral collapse. I try to focus, but the heat of her is still in my blood. Ban watches the screen. “You backing up the whole set?”

“Everything I can find,” I say. “If they wipe the system, we'll have a fallback.”

She nods once, tight. “We'll need use if we want to ransom her back.”

I don't say anything. The truth is, the data won't help. Nothing ever helps. But it feels like work, and work is the only narcotic that matters. The crawl finishes. I set the clone to encrypt, then pull up the root access and start covering tracks. Ban joins me, her hand on my wrist as we patch and mask the audit logs. She's rough, but efficient; every motion an extension of her earlier fury. Our fingers brush as we type, neither of us flinching. We build a backdoor, then another, burying them three layers deep. If anyone audits this again, they'll find a clean shell and a log full of plausible errors. When we're done, I shut down the console. The blue light cuts out. The room is just us and the ghosts. I glance at Ban. She looks at me, eyes darker now, less wolf and more human. “You okay?” I ask, softer than I mean to.

She shrugs. “No. You?”

I think about lying, but what's the point? “No.”

She moves to the door, then pauses. She turns, crossing the gap, and puts her hand on my wrist, fingers tight on my pulse. “This changes everything,” she says. I don't know if she means the mission or us, or if she's learned to stop pretending there's a difference. I nod, then squeeze her hand. The gesture is foreign, but not unwelcome. We exit separately. She takes the east corridor; I take the service route. It's cleaner that way, harder to reconstruct later. On the elevator down, my wrist still burns where she touched me. I watch the numbers tick by, blue-white, infinite. When I step outside, the night is full of new ghosts, all of them smiling. I think about her, and I think about the 847 lives we were supposed to save. I count, and for once, I never want the numbers to stop.

Chapter 10

The guard has the corridor to himself, and he acts like he knows it—smoking with his back to the high-security server hatch, streaming a snuff-feed, face washed in pink and orange from the wall's faux-dawn light. Nobody is in the sub-basement this late except for ghosts and third-shift creeps, which is why the tremor in his left hand makes a rhythm on the vape: *one-two, one-two*, barely off the regular. He doesn't hear Violet, not until her shadow kills the glow of his screen. She's behind him, distance measured in the length of a neural lance and then some. He says, "Shit, you scared me," and she says nothing, but her hand is already up, level, calm as a conductor starting a set.

The shot is not loud. It's all percussion, nothing melodic, just a pop that vibrates in the vent grates and the bones behind my nose. I feel it before I hear it, the shockwave hammering the low-pressure air until every particle is afraid to move again. When I round the corner, Violet is still there, standing so close to the guard's body that she has to step backward to keep the blood from reaching her boots. She doesn't. It creeps over her toe anyway. "Couldn't wait?" I ask, out of breath.

Violet looks over her shoulder, eyes as wide as a hangover and twice as cruel. The pistol is still hot in her hand, but her finger's off the trigger now, resting against the guard's nametag. Her mouth is open, lips wet, but the only sound is a soft, sublingual hum—a tune I don't recognize until the chorus cycles, and then I want to puke. It's a lullaby. The old kind. Sung to infants who don't know yet that their parents are disposable. "He was about to ping security," she says, not even pretending it matters. "He was going to turn the product in, you know?"

I look at the body. The man is half off the ground, as if gravity's reluctant to finish the job. Shot through the jaw. The entry is clean, the exit anything but—pink mist freckling the nearby vent, a Rorschach on the "CONSCIOUSNESS SAFETY IS EVERYONE'S BUSINESS" sticker.

"Product," I say. "Was he ...?"

"See for yourself." She toes his hand, and the dead grip releases a data pad that skitters across the floor. I catch it on the third bounce, blood slick on the interface. The screen is already unlocked. The folder is labeled "SPECIAL ORDER," childlike handwriting in the filename, as if he needed to make the filth cute to himself. The first file is a biometric scan, age eight, genderless, no expression. The next is an invoice: one copy of the consciousness pattern, shipped to a node in the Bizarre Bezoar Bazaar. There are more—dozens more—archived by date and customer. Each child's pattern is flagged "extraction complete."

My stomach flips. Not because it's new, or even shocking, but because it's so basic. For the last week, we've been fighting for air, all of us, desperate to believe that Curie's worst was subtle, clever, oblique. But this is just trafficking, brute and local, and the man on the floor was an eager little gear in the blue-lit abattoir. I feel the urge to close his eyes, but even the muscles have stopped pretending. Violet wipes the gun on her sleeve and holsters it. She doesn't bother to clean the blood off her skin. I expect her to be shaky, but she's not—her affect is the flatline after the monitor gives up. "He deserved worse," she says, and I know she means it.

We stand in the echo, which doesn't last long; the noise-canceling foam on the walls absorbs the violence within a few seconds. It's as if the shot never happened. The only evidence is the body and the wet pattern on the vent, already drying. I kneel to check for a pulse even though it's irrelevant. Violet stands with her back to the wall, humming, her hand flexing every time the tune repeats. I try to avoid touching the face, but the death spasm makes it difficult. The jaw's blown open, but the tongue's still there, blue and limp. "What's the play?" she asks, as if we're at a chessboard.

I wipe my hands on the dead man's jacket. "Containment. You know the drill."

She nods, no pushback. "Ban?"

"Yeah. You watch the hall. I'll call her in." I step away from the corpse and open the secure comm channel. Ban's shift is over, but she never goes home. I keep my voice low in case someone's running a live scrape. "Need you in Sector Seven. We have a ... containment situation."

Ban is silent for a beat. “How bad?”

“Guard dead. Not random.”

Her intake of breath is a whiteout. “On my way.”

I click off, staring at the ceiling for a second. The overheads are set to midnight; the only light is the memory of violence. Violet is crouched by the wall, watching the body the way a dog watches roadkill. “Want to know his name?” I ask, pointless.

She shakes her head. “He was a tourist. Names don’t stick.” Her eyes flick to me, and in that glance, I see all the gears turning. She’s already recalibrating, prepping the next line of defense. It’s not guilt. She doesn’t have it. She just wants the next move. The blood reaches the seam in the floor, turns ninety degrees, and races toward the nearest vent. Soon it’ll be out of sight. Nothing ever stays here. “Hey, Skelm?” Violet’s voice is softer than I expect. “If you want to, you can say he was armed. No one will check.”

I smile, but only for the data pad. “Was he?”

She considers, then shrugs. “Doesn’t matter. They’ll believe you if you say it.”

I pocket the pad and stand. The guard’s corpse is already a shadow, a trick of blue light on textured polymer. We wait for Ban, breathing slow. I want to believe I’m still shocked. That I can be sickened by any of it. But after the last week, the only thing that surprises me is how fast everything is coming apart. Violet wipes the last blood off her palm, then hums another verse. The tune echoes off the wall, then disappears. I set my jaw and count to sixty. Ban will be here soon, and then the cleanup will begin. It's not even the darkest night we've had. Not by half.

Ban shows up first, jaw set, eyes scanning for bystanders. She barely looks at the body on the floor—her face tells me she's seen worse, or done worse, or both. Katherine and Dorothy follow, a double-shadow behind her, one already pulling latex gloves from a pocket, the other gripping the shoulder bag that means business. "Talk later," Ban says, already stooping for the dead man's wrists. "We need this gone."

Violet is motionless, a heat map in human form, but she nods and steps aside. Katherine kneels at the head, pinching the jaw closed as best she can. The blood on the floor is already congealing, a slick mirror in the server-blue light. Dorothy opens the nearest storage closet. Its inside is the size of a coffin and lined with old foam padding. She checks for inventory, then gives the all-clear with a two-finger tap on the jamb. Ban and Katherine lift the corpse by the armpits and ankles, a move so practiced I can tell this isn't even their first tonight. The body makes a wet sound as it hits the foam. Ban frowns. "Violet, give me your coat." Violet shrugs out of the jacket and tosses it to Ban without a word. Ban wraps it around the guard's head and props it up with a stack of cleaning tablets. It won't fix the trauma, but it'll keep the worst of the mess off the corridor. "Skelm. Cameras," Ban says, no "please" required.

I'm already on the wall interface, knuckles whitening as I try to keep the glove from sticking to my palm. The sweat makes the surface tacky. I pull up the security grid and reroute the last fifteen minutes through a dummy feed from another sector. No one will see the shot, or us, or anything. I feel the tremor in my hand, but it doesn't slow the work. Katherine peels a wipe from a first aid kit, scrubs the dead man's fingerprints from the dropped pad, then passes it to me. I take it, thumbprint only, and pocket it for Ban. Dorothy is at the corner, eyes wide and alert, her right hand making a low slow circle in the air—a visual to keep the rest of us synced. Her head is cocked, both ears listening for the boot-heel cadence of night security. Ban grabs the guard's work badge, then pulls the oxygen meter from his pocket. She pulls a nanoblade from her hair, slices the tubing at the side of his mask, then stuffs it behind his teeth. "Sensor says bleed-out, not gunshot," she mutters, more to herself than us. The gunshot's obvious, but with the grid rerouted, it'll read as friendly fire from the automated defense system.

Katherine is at the wall terminal, typing in a request for emergency maintenance, backdating it by two days. "Failed oxygen system," she says, deadpan, "noted on last shift. Technician ignored protocol. Filing with corporate compliance now." She sets the log to auto-escalate in the morning, then spools the ticket into the graveyard of similar disasters.

Dorothy signals. "Move." Her voice is soft, barely sound at all, but we all freeze. She points at the glass corner, where a flicker of motion means possible trouble. Ban pulls the closet door shut, then stands in front of it, casual as ever. I wipe the screen, lock the interface, and back up one step, heart racing but breath steady. The janitorial drone turns the corner, sees nothing, and hums past. The corpse is invisible, the blood already seeping under the closet door, but it looks like a cleaning job gone bad. The drone logs the stain, issues a ticket, and rolls on. Violet watches all of this, mouth tight, hands tucked into her pockets. She doesn't blink until the corridor is clear.

Ban leans in. "Performance review: terminated," she says, and for the first time in the last hour, I want to laugh, but my mouth is stuck on dry.

I tap the wall, double-checking the coverage. "Clean. Unless you want to sweep the next ten meters."

"Already on it," Dorothy says, her hand on my elbow, gently guiding me toward the next access hatch. She smells like cold skin and the synthetic fabric they issue for after-hours. The corridor is colder here, and I feel the nerves in my teeth as we pass the emergency vent. Violet goes last, silent as an afterthought, her boots leaving bloody prints that fade by the next turn. We regroup at the junction. Ban passes the data pad to me, and I hide it under my shirt, against my skin.

Katherine is first to break the silence. "If they audit the maintenance records, they'll see we logged the error last week."

"Which they won't," Ban says. "Not unless someone tips them."

Dorothy gives the all-clear. "You're clear for egress."

We walk. The silence between us is heavy, but not dead. It vibrates, ready to explode the next time a body drops. We're nearly at the sub-basement exit when the announcement hits. The voice is genderless, origin everywhere: "All security personnel report for immediate briefing. All non-essential personnel remain at current location. Compliance is mandatory." We freeze, a line of four in the blue-lit hallway. Violet is the only one who smiles. It's not humor; it's just the absence of fear.

Marie's face blooms on every wall screen, every corner display, every wrist monitor and vending terminal in the building. She is flawless, the standard-issue "concerned executive" avatar: bob-cut, glass-bottle smile, eyes set to maximum earnestness. The weird part is the chorus—there are at least a dozen Maries broadcasting in perfect sync, each at a slightly different angle or scale, so that no matter where you look, she's already got you in focus. "Due to a regrettable safety incident," the Maries say as one, "surveillance protocols are being tripled, effective immediately. All staff will cooperate with synth-checkpoints and visual sweeps. Compliance is appreciated. Security is your job, too."

No hint of the dead guard, no overt panic. But the building is now a grid of hot red: at the junctions, camera orbs sprout from ceiling seams; in the main halls, polycarbonate drones float on silent rotors, laser eyes sampling every face, every movement, every neural port. The lights over each major entry pulse blood-red, the kind you see in photos of the womb. At first it's shocking, then it just feels like the walls have gotten angry. We hustle to the comm room, a repurposed survey closet Ban kitted with homebrew sensors and a folding chair you can barely call furniture. The main panel is already lit: a schematic of Curie's interior, rendered in three-color lines. Blue for safe. Yellow for eyes-on. Red for—well, everything now. Ban is perched over the console, a little bit of jaw muscle flexing every time a new drone blips onto the feed. "She's scared," Ban says, not taking her eyes off the schematic.

Violet stands by the wall, a soft rag and solvent strip in hand, cleaning her pistol as if this is the most natural place in the world to do it. There's not a trace of remorse. She works the solvent into the slide, then wipes it with the kind of focus you usually see in surgeons or morticians. Katherine is at the secondary monitor, sifting the security protocol in real time. Dorothy looms at the door, arms crossed, the whole line of her body on alert. "They patched the drone vulnerability," Katherine says, voice tight.

"Doesn't matter," says Ban. "We knew they would. Plan B is already live."

Dorothy glances at me, then at the camera grid. "We can't take the bodies out the usual way. There's a double sweep every three minutes."

I nod, swallowing against the sawdust in my throat. "We'll have to make the next one look like an accident."

Katherine and Dorothy trade a glance. The kind that means: *This isn't what I signed up for, but I'm here now.* Violet clicks the mag in and sets the pistol on the table, barrel pointed away but present. She doesn't look at anyone. Ban finally looks up from the schematic, her face haloed in the red from the warning lamps. "Marie's scared," she repeats, savoring the taste of it. "She knows we're inside her perimeter."

Nobody argues. The only sounds are the whine of drones circling above, the whir of fan blades, and the steady tick of Katherine's typing. I catch my own reflection in the black edge of the display. My face is paler than I want to see, and my mouth is drawn tight. For a second, I wish someone else was in charge of this disaster. But no one is. "We stick to the plan,"

I say, as if saying it matters. "Accident, not murder. Disappear the next piece before anyone can connect the dots. If we get caught, they'll kill all of us, not just the guard."

Dorothy nods, slow and mechanical. Katherine's lips press together, then apart, then together again, like she's swallowing two different responses. Violet just smiles at the freshly cleaned gun. Ban grins with all her teeth. "I'm going to enjoy this," she says, and it isn't a threat or a promise—it's the only honest thing anyone's said all night. The lights go from red to blue, then red again, like the building is learning how to bleed. We watch the schematic, wait for the next opportunity, and pretend the world hasn't already ended.

The comm room is a tomb with better lighting. We're jammed in close, Ban hunched over the secure pad, me cross-legged on a crate of outdated interface chips. The walls are supposed to block all radio, but the paranoia is thick enough to make me want to unplug my own teeth. Ban scrolls through the first fifty targets with the speed of a cop on a deadline. Each file is a headshot and a list of sins. Some are guards, some execs, some just lowly data janitors who signed the wrong NDA and never looked back. She highlights the first: Chief of Internal Security, known for his "hands-on" approach to discipline. He liked to do the late-night rounds, made it a point of pride to sniff out every protocol violation in person. "Coolant corridor," Ban mutters, flicking the blueprints onto the screen. "There's a pressure valve that's been flagged for months but never repaired. If the temp spikes during his walk, it's a matter of seconds."

I study the route, the time, the exposure. The fatal window is exactly six seconds. Nobody can survive it, not even the augmented. "Make it ten," I say, "in case he lingers for a smoke break."

She tweaks the alarm delay, setting the autolog to kick in at eleven. Nobody will check that hard. Corporate doesn't do real postmortems. Next up: VP of Consciousness Engineering. She's the architect of the "pattern dilution" pipeline. Every week, she signs off on another dozen orphans, files their memories under "compliance," and bills the parents for overtime. "She jacks in directly to the grid," Ban says, pulling up the exec's schedule. "Never misses a lunch break with her virtual pets. If you route the surge through the node—"

"It'll fry her cortex in two-point-four seconds," I say, almost impressed. "But it can't look like sabotage. It needs to be random."

"Noted," Ban says, already coding in the voltage ripple to make the power spike plausible. She overlays two prior malfunctions to seed the digital paper trail.

I scan the list, looking for a name I know. They're all familiar, in that corporate-ladder sense. Most are just grist. Some are monsters. The logic of the plan is brutal, but there's an internal consistency to it I can't deny. "Why not just leak the files?" I ask. "We could torch the whole operation with a single data dump."

"Marie runs the news feeds," Ban says, not even looking up. "The story gets spun before it's out of beta. If you want them to notice, you make them feel it. Inside."

Her hand is steady on the pad, but her jaw is tense. The only time she blinks is to wet the surface of her eyes. I realize I'm sweating, even though the room is set to corpse cold. "You ever worry," I say, "that we're becoming what we're fighting?"

She shrugs. "You can't fight monsters without getting bitten."

There's no emotion in it, no bitterness, just a flat reporting of the fact. We finish three more "accidents" before the silence thickens. The list is almost comically long. A few targets are flagged for "interrogation," but I know what that means. It means slow death, and no chance at a last meal. Ban keys the plans to the wall screen, laying them out like a mix of invisible casualties. The overlaps are clean, each hit staged to look like the final breaking point of a crumbling system. I want to say it's excessive. But after the last week, it doesn't feel like enough. Ban wipes her eyes, then sets her face. "We run the first two tonight," she says. "Then the grid goes live. By morning, they'll be chasing ghosts." I look at her; the exhaustion is there, but so is something harder. It's not hate. It's not revenge. It's a mathematical certainty. She taps the pad, then tosses it to me. "You okay with this?"

I study the screen. My hands are steady. I feel nothing except a weird, hollow relief. "Yeah," I say, not quite a whisper. "I am."

"Good," she says, and the smile that twitches on her mouth is the first real one all night. She stands, cracks her knuckles, and flexes her fingers like she's prepping for surgery. I rise, feeling the muscles pull and ache from too much sitting, too much tension, too much everything. As we leave the room, Ban flicks the wall light off with a snap. In the sudden dark, the afterimage of the plan lingers in my eyes: blueprints of death, precise as clockwork, as cold as the vacuum between stars. We step into the corridor, and the world is quieter than it's ever been. There's no fear left. Only math.

We find the alcove by muscle memory. All these server farms are the same: corners with heat and no ventilation, backdrafts that pull the sweat off your face and freeze it midair. The racks hum so loud it's like standing inside the throat of an engine. Ban is the first to speak, as always. "The first two are set for 05:11. Third is flexible—he never runs a predictable schedule." She double-checks the subroutine on her wrist, a blur of blue reflected off bone.

I look at her, but she keeps her face to the wall, eyes scanning the physical redundancy in the data stack. Her posture is military, locked, but the knuckles on her left hand are bone-white. She's holding on by logic, nothing else. I say, "You know there's no going back after this, right?"

She waits, letting the hum swallow my words. "Was there ever?"

I laugh, but it's a sound only the circuit can hear. "Maybe. Before you found your sister's file."

Ban's jaw flexes. "There isn't a before and after. There's just the space where you pretend the system isn't eating you alive."

I nod, because she's right. This isn't about fixing things; it's about breaking them more beautifully. The blue light turns the sweat on her neck into lines of code. I watch it bead and race down, an algorithm of desperation. "You ever wish you'd just bailed?" I ask, voice low. "Taken the money, run?"

Ban looks at me, and I see that edge again. "No. I was born for this. So were you." I want to argue, but she steps closer. We're a half meter apart now, heat from the racks making a pressure front between us. I can't help it—I reach out, fingertips brushing the top of her hand. Her skin is cold, but the tremor is real, and I feel it through the gloves. For a second, we don't move. There's just the server noise, and the shared ache of future regret. Ban's hand curls over mine, holding it for exactly one heartbeat. The LED behind us flickers, sending a Morse code of blue across our shadows. Then her comm chimes: a low, non-negotiable ping. "It's time," she says, voice softer than I've ever heard it. I let go first, but she's the one who steps back. She's already in motion, shoulder squared, stride clean. She pauses at the edge of the alcove and turns back. "See you on the other side," she says, and the smile is sharp, but not cruel.

"Don't get dead," I say, then she's gone, footsteps lost in the white noise of the grid. I linger. The memory of her hand lingers longer. The first "accident" is in six hours, but I know I won't sleep between now and then. I stand in the blue, alone, and try to imagine how it would feel to be someone else. Someone who could walk away. But the skin doesn't fit. I take the corridor, feeling my heart sync with the server's pulse, and know the next day will end with another body on the floor. And that, at last, I've stopped pretending to care.

Chapter 11

The first rule of night shift is: Don't get attached to the dark. It's never yours for long. The Curie control room is a shoebox designed by paranoids—blue-wash lighting, nonreflective plastic, and a single bank of sixty-four security feeds stitched together in one ultrawide grid. There's a heat to the place even with the HVAC running arctic, something the dead call "haunting." If I stare at the glass long enough, I see the ghosts of every previous operator, their outlines burned into the edge pixels. I'm supposed to feel at home here, but all I get is the impression I'm one update away from redundancy. I sign in at 23:47. The system flickers, scans my face, then drips the digital equivalent of a cold sweat down my collarbone. Ban is late for once, which is the first warning. The second is the drone at my elbow, trundling a cart of SentiSnack™ packets and "upcycled" energy drinks. The third warning is harder to define, more a current than a signal: the sense that every grid cam is watching the wrong part of the room, and something essential is about to arrive through a blind spot.

It does. She ghosts in at 00:02, five minutes into my boredom and two into my actual shift. Not from the main hallway—too obvious—but through the maintenance alcove, slotting past the seam in the false panel that only admins and skeleton crews even know exists. She's wearing the local maintenance coveralls, bleached to a pale, institutional green, and there's nothing about her except the way she carries her shoulder bag—low and tight, gun side—that marks her as an operator and not a wage-slave.

The infiltrator doesn't rush or hesitate. She just drifts to the console, as if this was always the destination, then stands two meters to my left, hands resting in full view. She's Ronin, but you wouldn't know unless you've ever had the displeasure of seeing a Rising Ronin sigil stitched into someone's knuckles. The tattoo is hidden by a layer of skin paint, but my left eye still spots the fractional difference in pigment: an omega spiral, black and silver, coiling into itself on the dorsal pad of her thumb. I don't move. The system is already scanning her. I count three cameras on her back, and two more from the reflected blue in the screens ahead. The tension is subtle; the game is always about who will break silence first. It isn't me. "Name?" I ask, keeping my hands visible.

She watches me watching her, then drops the smallest smile—a token, nothing more. "Serra. You're Darby?"

"Not a secret." I note her eyes: brown-black, flecked with something unnatural, tracking every tic of my pupils. "What's your business?"

She sets the bag on the desk, the way a paramedic would set a defibrillator next to a dying relative. "Extraction. And insurance."

It clicks then: She knows about the data. About the vault. About the scheme Ban and I stitched together, thinking we were playing two sides against the cosmic middle. The chill in my chest turns to steam. She unzips the bag, pulls out a rolled-up sleeve of schematic printouts, and a portable. She offers the sleeve, slowly and with both hands. I let her. It's a thermal map of the sub-basement, with overlaid notes in a language only people who grew up in the inside-out can read. Not for me; for someone higher up the food chain. She flips on the portable and pushes it across the desk. The display is red-on-black: a live feed from inside the east quadrant, and a simple list:

- Consciousness imprints: 3

- Alive: 2

- Condition: Contested

I don't blink. "That's outdated," I say, masking my actual heartbeat with sarcasm. "Or is this a threat?"

She grins, this time showing a lateral canine sharpened by what looks like deliberate dental sculpt. "Threat would be if I sent this to Curie, with a timestamp. This is negotiation."

I want to laugh, but my hands are starting to twitch on the underside of the desk, near the panic button. I resist the urge. She'd know.

I lean in, dropping my voice to confidential. "You're offering extraction. For what?"

"Return the three." Her smile widens. "You keep one, we get two. You choose which. And we get your team out alive, clean, with new paperwork."

She runs her tongue over the canine, making it clear this is not a soft deal. I flex my left foot, toeing the hatch where the kill switch is hidden. “That assumes we want out.”

Serra shrugs, a lean and dangerous movement. “No one ever wants out. Until the last minute.” She shifts, making the move look natural, but I spot the stutter: her left hand has a chip reader embedded, and she’s using it to scan the desk surface for sensors. I let her. The less she finds, the more she’ll trust that this isn’t already a sting.

“Let’s say I’m interested.” I give her nothing but the line. “Why now?”

She smiles with only the lower teeth. “Because tomorrow you’re dead, or worse.” The words land flat. I see a flash of what she knows: the patrols, the schedules, maybe even the internal kill order on me and Ban if this job goes sideways. Serra’s people have someone inside, and it isn’t just a cam tech or a janitor. I exhale slowly, my hand edging to the side of the console, where the security pistol is mag-locked to the underside. The count in my head is three in the clip, one in the chamber. She catches the drift, but doesn’t blink. Instead, she leans against the edge, crosses her arms, and makes a show of settling in. “You’re not going to shoot me,” she says.

I stare, deadpan. “Convince me.”

She glances over her shoulder, as if expecting a witness, then drops her voice to a hush. “You think you can survive tonight, but you can’t. Curie already marked you. The only reason they haven’t sent someone is because they want to catch the buyer. They’re hoping you’ll deliver.” She taps the portable. “But you could walk. They’d just lose the inventory. It’s replaceable.” My pulse is steady, but my brain is running the scenario in six directions at once. If I shot her, I'd have twenty minutes to hide the body, forty to cover the log, but less than ten before her fail-safe pings an exit signal. If I take her deal, we're out, but then what? It's never that simple. Serra watches the math scroll across my face. "You're stalling," she says. "You want time to warn your partner. But she's already here."

It's a good bluff, but it's also the truth. Ban enters from the service door, all ice and deliberate slowness. She sees Serra, then me, and in a heartbeat, she clocks the play. "Problem?" Ban asks, her gaze never leaving Serra.

Serra turns, standing upright, hands still open. "Negotiation. I offered your man a way out."

Ban's smile is so thin it might as well be a cut. "We don't do deals with Ronin."

Serra's eyes narrow. "That's an outdated prejudice, don't you think?"

Ban doesn't answer. Instead, she glides to my side, and for a second, we are two statues—stone, cold, and older than the air in the room. I don't look at Ban, but I know she's waiting for a cue. I give it, in the line the playbook says I should never use. "Interesting proposition," I say, picking up the portable. "What makes you think we'd betray our employers?"

Serra grins, now fully animal. "Because your employer is already betraying you." She nods at Ban, then at the nearest cam. "They're watching right now. You know what happens if you walk away." Ban's jawline sharpens, but she doesn't break. Serra pushes the bag of printouts closer, then tilts her head to one side. "It's a good deal. We take the heat, you take the exit.

New city, new credits, no questions. You can even keep your favorite, as a souvenir."

The word "souvenir" lands in the room like a bomb. Ban's lips part, but she doesn't speak. I take the risk. "What if we don't want a deal? What if we want to finish the job?"

Serra shrugs, slow. "Then you die here, or get black-bagged in your sleep. If you're lucky, the backup tech wipes you and gives your slot to the next analyst." She leans in, voice a hush. "We're not just here for the inventory. We're here to flip you. You're the package."

She's close enough now that I can see the contact in her left eye flickering, a rapid blue strobe. She's recording, live. Ban's hand comes down on the table, sharp. "That's enough," she says, voice steel.

Serra freezes, then steps back, arms crossed again. "We'll consider it," I say. "But we want proof."

Serra's grin is all business now. "You'll get it." She nods at the portable. "Tonight, 03:00. East wall, maintenance corridor. If you want out, be there."

She slips away, not looking back, vanishing down the maintenance alcove with a confidence I can only envy. The room is quiet. I let my hand unclench from the console, and only then do I notice the sweat in my palm. Ban waits for the silence to go full dark, then mutters, "She was lying about some of it."

"Some," I say. "But not all." We both stare at the portable, the data feed still blinking. "You think it's a real offer?"

Ban's laugh is so quiet I almost miss it. "No. But it's an opportunity. If they want to steal from Curie, we can feed them the story we want them to have."

I nod. "A double-cross."

Ban's smile is almost a real thing. "Classic." She looks at the clock, then at the door Serra used. "We should let them think they've won," she says. "Let them feel it all the way to the end."

My fingers still twitch, but the dread is gone, replaced by something sharper. We start building the plan on the backs of the maintenance logs, layering the lies over truths so tightly I'm not sure where one ends and the next begins. The ghosts in the room watch from the screens, silent and approving. I decide: I will not be a ghost tonight. Not yet.

We reconvene in the only room in the Curie complex that pretends to be private. The planning vault is shielded—real analog lead, not just the "noise jammers" they sell to tourists, and the holo table in the center that's so over-specced it radiates heat even in idle. Ban is already there, two steps ahead, her left foot propped on a rolling chair, hands busy stripping out the last traces of whatever legit planning session preceded ours. Serra walks in like she owns the place. There's a new bounce to her gait, the kind of swagger that comes only when the job is almost done and the mark is in the bag. She flashes me a canine and drops into the chair nearest the table. Ban's lips barely twitch at the show. I close the door, flip the privacy bolt, then circle to the far side of the table. "We'll keep this quick," I say. "Security's thin tonight, but only if we're fast."

Ban toggles the holo table. The map of the facility extrudes into crisp relief, each floor hovering in transparent layers. She keeps her face blank as the blue and yellow overlays flicker on: security nodes, access points, cameras. Most of it is real. The important details are not. Serra leans in, gaze already flicking from node to node. I can see her recording—there's a subtle dilation in her left pupil, a hitch in the muscles around her eye. I wonder if she's running overlays, marking down our every blink and twitch. Ban runs the briefing with the authority of an angel auditioning for the role of God. "Main entry here," she says, tapping the map. "Security vestige only, meant to catch bottom feeders. Real assets move through maintenance." She traces the service corridors with one gloved finger, then pauses to drag the overlay along the east wall. "This section"—she stops, giving Serra a look—"is porous. You can breach with a port mag and a three-second packet storm."

I watch Serra's brow crease as she logs the details. "Cameras?"

"Dead zone," says Ban. "Legacy system. We keep it off the books so no one has to answer for it at audit."

It's an elegant lie. There's no dead zone, just a loopback feed, and the corridor is patched with motion sensors the size of fruit flies. But Serra laps it up. I reach for the portable Ban hands over, then chime in. "Three guard rotations, timed to system update. If you move between 02:00 and 02:03, you'll hit an empty hall."

Serra narrows her eyes. "That's tight."

Ban shrugs. "Not if you have the schedule. Or a friend."

There's a faint blush of satisfaction on Serra's face. She thinks she's outplaying us. I want to congratulate her, but there's work left. "Server room access?" Serra says, eyes on the glowing cluster at the core of the diagram.

Ban leans in, dropping her voice to a thread. "Entry is badge and print, but that's the window dressing. Real lock is logic." She flips a data stick onto the table, rolling it to a stop in front of Serra. "That's the pass string. For tonight only. Changes hourly."

Serra picks it up, inspects both sides, then pockets it. "What about extraction? The payloads?"

Ban doesn't miss a beat. "We'll stage them in the East cache, cold-packed for transfer. You grab them, drop them at rendezvous, we never see each other again."

Serra glances at me. "What's to stop you from burning me?"

I allow myself a small, brittle smile. "If I wanted to burn you, you'd be ashes already."

She likes that. A little too much. Ban resets the map, focusing on the breach vector. "It's a one-shot. You get in, you get out, no heroics. If you get caught, we never met. If you win, we're both free." Serra's nod is nearly imperceptible. She stands, and for a moment, we're all three just staring at the map, like the future is a bug we're waiting to see crawl off the table. Ban breaks the moment. "You want the dummy badges?"

Serra nods, so Ban slides them across: two strips of authentic plastic, each programmed with just enough access to get Serra killed if she veers off the path. I watch Serra test the edges with her thumb, flexing the plastic. “Anything else?” she asks.

I exchange a glance with Ban, then she says, “You’ll need to spoof the temperature sensors near the drop zone. Too much body heat and the system will flag you.”

It’s Serra’s turn to smile. “You’re good.”

Ban’s smile is all ice. “I know.”

Serra slides the badges into her jumpsuit, then makes for the door, all confidence. I stop her with a line: “Guard rotation creates a three-minute window at 0200 hours. That’s your only shot.”

She looks back, measuring, then nods. At the threshold, she says, “See you on the other side.”

We watch her leave, the quiet around the door stretching like a rubber band about to snap. Ban waits a long beat, then switches off the holo table. The blue lines dissolve, leaving the room in a hush only the desperate recognize. “She’s going to die,” Ban says finally. Not a question.

“Or get very close,” I say. “And whoever sent her will see the evidence and never know who fixed it.”

Ban slips into a chair, the edge of her fatigue showing for the first time. “You get the packet loaded?”

“Already in her stick,” I say, holding up my own, now blank. “When they open it, it’ll trigger every silent alarm from here to the archive. She’ll get to the cache, but not back.”

Ban nods, slow. “Good. The only thing worse than a Ronin is a Ronin with a grudge.”

I look at her, wondering if the same could be said for us. "You ready?"

She sighs, then stands. "Never. But I don't have to be."

The lights flicker, then come back with a colder blue. The hour is close. We collect the gear, wipe the surfaces, and reset the room for the next set of ghosts. I watch Ban as she closes the case on the holo table, her motions neat and final. She sees me watching and shrugs. "If they're going to write us out, at least we get to choose the script."

I laugh quietly. "That's what I always liked about you."

The only thing louder than an alarm is the moment before it goes off. I sit in the heart of the Curie security hub, a basin of glass and cold steel lit by nothing but status LEDs and the blue glow of a hundred live feeds. Ban is a specter at my left, barely present except when the emergency response dashboard pulses red, setting her profile in sharp relief. The room hums with the anticipation of violence. We engineered it this way, but knowing doesn't make the waiting easier. It's 01:57. Three minutes to showtime. The monitors stutter, then resolve: Serra in the east maintenance corridor, face slack, gait like a service bot trying to look human. She moves fast, but not too fast—she knows the sensor sweeps, trusts the dead zones we spoon-fed her. I spot her heat signature, track her in four separate wavelengths as she ghosts past a sleeping guard, then rounds the blind corner. Ban pings the loop, overlays a pale yellow trajectory, and for a second, I see the ghost of our own plan running alongside Serra's.

At 02:00, the house lights cut, replaced by the arterial pulse of a full facility lockdown. Ban times the alarm perfectly. The blast is less a sound than a bone-level pressure. I imagine it's what a scream would feel like if it had mass. On the monitors, the admin hallway fills with bodies—guards, techs, a janitor who never learned to keep his head down. Serra freezes, then goes hard right, as we knew she would. Ban's fingers dance across the keys, opening and closing gates, narrowing Serra's options until the only way left is straight into the trap. She runs it like a pro: leaps a laser trip, burns through a badge override, and slides into the server anteroom so fast she's a blur in the frame. There's a beautiful economy to it. For a moment, I almost wish she'd make it out.

Ban doesn't give her the chance. She double-pulses the emergency lock, trapping Serra with only one exit—a ladder to the upper ventilation, lined with sensors, and soon, a goon squad. I scan the feeds, watching for the sign that Serra's backup is in play. It comes a second before I expect: the northwest entry blows open, a team of four in black riot mesh rushing the sensor grid. Ban curses under her breath, not at them, but at the timing. "Knew it," she says. "They're not here for the girl. They're here for us." I want to argue, but the monitors agree. The Ronin fireteam moves with precision, burning the walls with chemical cutters, throwing EMP patches on the floor as they go. The guards on that sector are already down—either bribed or unconscious, it doesn't matter. "Katherine's posted in the archive," Ban says, voice flat. "We hold her until this is done, or we lose the vault."

I nod, then patch through a haptic to Katherine's station. "Katherine, you've got heat incoming," I say, voice tight. "They're through the first ring, moving fast."

Her reply is so calm it's almost retro. "Understood. Locking down the perimeter."

I watch her on the feed, a blur of motion as she sets up the countermeasures: smart mines, static charges, the old-fashioned kind of surprises nobody respects until they cost you a limb. Back in the server room, Serra is running the pass string we gave her. It lights the core up like a Christmas tree, but nothing she does matters. The data packet Ban loaded was designed to look like the motherlode but is really a virus that eats itself on contact, leaving only junk. I lean into the console, prepping the last step of the plan. "Now," Ban says. I trigger the fake fire suppression, filling the server room with CO2 mist. Serra doesn't panic—she holds her breath, finishes the download, and then bolts for the vent, just as the goon team reaches the junction. It's chaos, but chaos we can control. Or so I think.

The Ronin team splits—two for the server room, two for the archive. They move faster than the response drones, faster than even Ban can react. I see Katherine switch from defense to offense, pulling the smart mines from the shelf and lobbing them down the hallway like grenades. The first one pops, a dirty blue-white flash, taking a Ronin at the ankle. The second skips under a desk and explodes in a hail of ceramic shards, tearing the visor off another. Katherine holds the line for a full minute, long enough for the lockdown to reseal, but then a Ronin with a scrambler gets close. There's no gunfire—just the faint flicker of an arc and then Katherine goes rigid, then limp. Blood runs from her nose and ears, then puddles in a fan around her head. I watch it on the feed, a tiny drama in a hundred pixels, and for the first time in this whole game, I want to close my eyes. Ban doesn't let me. "Focus," she says, and I do.

The remaining Ronin scoop up what's left of the archive and haul ass to the exit. Ban tags them with a locator, but it's pointless—if they live to see morning, they'll be gone before the first payroll shift. Serra is already gone, having doubled back through a trash shaft and out to the rooftop, where a drone picks her up before the city can even register a footprint. The facility alarm cycles down, then up again, a different pitch this time—grief instead of fear. Ban leans back, the ghost of a tremor in her right hand. "They'll call this a success," she says.

"It is," I say, but it doesn't feel like anything. We make the sweep through the damage: one server room, two dead Ronin, three injured Curie guards, and one missing Katherine. I find her in the sub-basement, curled like a dead cat, her hands still gripping the shattered portable. I kneel beside her. Her face is pale, the blood dried to a brown crust on her lips and chin. Her eyes are open, but fixed on nothing. Her ID badge has spun free, and I watch it rotate in the puddle of coolant, the letters blurring together. I want to say something—apologize, explain, anything—but Ban is behind me, her shadow filling the hall.

She puts a hand on my shoulder, steady. "We got what we needed," she says, voice soft. "Their infiltration methods, extraction protocols, weapons signatures. All of it."

I don't move. The badge keeps spinning. "She was good." It's the only tribute I know.

Ban sighs, then crouches beside me, her own hands rough and real on my skin. “We’ll write her in. Not as a hero. As the person who did the job.”

I look at Ban and see the lines on her face, the exhaustion. “Was it worth it?” I ask.

She waits a long time before answering. “That’s the wrong question. But it’s the only one that matters.”

I close Katherine’s eyes, then stand, leaving her badge spinning in the dark. The alarm resets, and above us, the lights return to blue. I take Ban’s hand, and together we walk out, two more ghosts in a building that can’t tell the difference between survival and victory.

Chapter 12

There's no such thing as a secure room. Not in Curie's secondary facility, not anywhere this side of hell. But the current locus—"Security Hub B"—gets as close as anything I've seen: 20 square meters of electrostatic carpet and triple-redundant firewalls, lined with enough composite to make a light tank envious. Every surface sweats blue light from a hundred overlapping holo displays, each fighting the others for quantum relevance. There's no door, just a quantum-sealed membrane that grumbles like an ulcer whenever Ban taps it with her boot. She leans against the admin console, posture all slouch but eyes vertical-slit sharp. A SentiSnack™ packet dangles from her left hand, half-empty, its mylar wrapper rhythmically flicked against her thigh like a metronome set to "execution." The security feed paints her cheekbones in acid blue, so sharp they could dice code. "Start," says Ban, voice drained of all ceremony.

I take the pointer and ping the wall. The facility map splays out: three floors, each denser than the last with tactical hardware and redundancy. The 3D overlay is so detailed you can see the cigarette burns on the maintenance foreman's shirt in sublevel three. "Our primary targets are here, here, and here." I tag each: the main consciousness scrambler array in East Block, the viral-personality server farm on Sublevel 2, and the comms blacksite curdled behind six meters of memory foam and spite. I gesture, and the UI pulses each in turn. "These are what the Ronin want, so it's what Curie is going to guard."

Dorothy, at the back of the room, makes a show of not looking up from her portable. But her arms—chrome and plastic, still slick from the upgrade—cross tighter at every new threat node I highlight. She radiates "fuck off" but files every word. Katherine perches on a bench near the panel, knees tucked under chin, scanning my diagrams with an intensity that is, for once, totally not about me. There's a tremor in her left hand, masked by the way she clutches her diagnostic deck. Violet stands off to the side, under the cold glow of a battery emergency sign, meticulously cycling a set of tools through a velvet roll. She doesn't seem to blink. Not sure she needs to.

"Ronin breach comes in two waves," I say. "First, a test pulse. Standard: soft probes on the firewalls, maybe a drone, maybe a real human. Curie's response will be measured, nothing overt." I tap again, painting the projected paths in orange. "Second wave is the one that matters—when they think they've found a gap, they send in the patch team. That's when the fun starts."

Ban's fingers clack the SentiSnack™ wrapper. "What's our play?"

I roll the script in my head, then out loud. "We let the first probe through. Make it a hard fight but not a total lockdown—

enough to convince Curie their security's holding, but also to lure Ronin into thinking we're stretched thin. When the patch team comes in, we ghost them. While Curie's locking down, we'll be everywhere the Ronin open."

Dorothy snorts, loud and guttural. "And if Curie tracks the opening back to us?"

"We keep the Ronin alive," I say. "They're our scapegoats. By the time Curie's running the audit, we're ghosts ourselves."

Violet finally looks up. "You want them to catch the Ronin?" Her voice is a razor delivered in a bubble bath—effortless and lethal.

I meet her gaze. "I want them to believe what the logs say. We build the story, let them write the ending."

Katherine swallows, a slow, visible bulge up her throat. "And the casualties?"

The word lands. Ban's eyes flick sideways, not at me, but at Dorothy, then Katherine, then back. Her mouth stays line-straight. "No avoidables," I say, and mean it for exactly three seconds before the next thought arrives. "Calculated losses only. Nothing that raises flags."

The silence that follows is crowded, like six more people joined the room just to stare. Ban's eyes narrow, just a flicker. "Define 'calculated.'"

I bite the word, then spit it. "We run the op with minimum interference, but if a guard or two gets in the way—" I spread my hands, like a stage magician revealing a dead pigeon. "It's less suspicious that way."

Dorothy grinds her molars, audible above the cooling fans. "You said no one gets hurt."

"I said no one gets wasted without purpose," I say, softer now. "There are no happy endings here. Just priorities."

Ban turns the SentiSnack™ packet end over end, then tosses it in a slow arc to the bin. The wrapper lands inside, but she doesn't break gaze. "And if it comes down to us or them?"

"Then it's us," I say, no hesitation.

Katherine's hands go into her hair, pulling at the roots like she's testing the tensile strength of self-hatred. Ban looks at each of us in turn. "Any other objections?"

Dorothy shrugs, then stands. "I'd rather do it clean, but you don't keep your hands clean in this work." She glances at Ban, then away. "Just tell me which nodes to reinforce."

Violet tucks her tools away fast, like the matter is settled. Katherine's next. "We don't have to kill them," she says, half-plea. "If we time it right, most of the guards will be off grid during the attack."

Ban cuts the debate. "We'll do what's needed. Nothing more." She angles her head at me, a challenge.

I nod. "That's the line."

A low, atonal buzzer warbles from the main console. It's not the regular alert—too organic, too urgent. The whole room goes violet, emergency mode. All the overlays collapse down to a single vector: the external perimeter, flickering with ping after ping as the first Ronin probe hits the system. Ban cracks her knuckles, then steps away from the console, letting the tension leak out of her limbs. “Showtime,” she says, and the smile that follows is wrong enough that it gives me chills.

Katherine’s face drains to blank. Dorothy’s hands ball into hammers, but she gives a wild, almost amused little laugh. Violet’s already at the door, knife out, tip tested against her thumbprint. I look at the map again, the little avatars—guard, drone, Ronin, us—each painted in their assigned shade. None of them seem to be moving. The only thing that changes is the color of the threat. Ban glances over her shoulder at me, voice gone flat. “Let’s get started, Skelm.”

I start, then. Because that’s what I am now—the guy who starts things that can’t be undone.

It starts with the whine of an overtaxed sensor, then the sound rolls through the hub in a chain reaction: red LEDs, organic alarms, and a taste like dry copper on my tongue. Within fifteen seconds, the blue sanctuary is a slaughterhouse of failed boundaries. Ban’s voice is already two steps ahead: “Confirmed, three on the east wall. One drone, two meat.” The holo grid updates, three new signatures fanning in through an impossible corner, right where she said they’d be. She grabs the security drone control with her left hand, overlays its route in hot pink, and chases the breach with a logic that’s half ballet, half butcher’s block.

Dorothy’s at the main net, her gloves flexing through three layers of environmental sensors. The node failovers start to trip, the error lights cascading up the wall in a synchronized humiliation. Her jaw clenches, lips gone white. She mutters something that might be a prayer, but it’s in a dialect I don't know. Katherine moves with no grace at all, but she's everywhere: re-routing backup power to maintain visibility, slapping override codes into the comms, slamming her fist into the console whenever the predictive script stalls out. "Third shift is sleeping," she says. "We're the only defense here."

I try to project calm, hands on the table, but every heartbeat is a spike in the graph, every second a risk multiplier. "Stick to plan. Ban, herd them to the sublevel corridor. Dorothy, buy us two minutes of fake uptime. Katherine—lock down the comms so nothing leaks outside."

Ban is surgical: "Moving them now." On the display, the Ronin avatars snake toward the blind corner and right into the maw of her drone. She toggles the weapon set from "dissuade" to "immobilize." I catch her glance at me, just once, a question in the eyes: *"Do we kill?"*

I shake my head: *"Only if necessary."*

She does it anyway. The drone's first shot cracks one Ronin across the jaw, dropping him in a pool of what used to be ambition. The second takes the drone's leg off at the knee. Someone in the Ronin crew is carrying high-velocity foam, old cop tech but effective. Ban shifts, pivots the drone to use its own weight as a battering ram, and the feed goes static as the drone and the last two Ronin crash together in a spasm of electromagnetic fuckery. "Katherine, status on Sublevel Two?" I ask.

She flicks a glance at the log. "Compromised, but they're not in yet. Might buy us another minute if I blow the secondary fuse."

"Do it." The blue in the room drops to navy, then midnight, then the holo panels stagger and recover at half brightness. "We're dark to the outside, but we still have control."

Violet stands at her station, not moving, eyes glassed over as she scans the live feed. She's the only one not blinking. "Security team closing on the breach. Five guards, four unarmed. They don't know what's coming."

Ban grimaces. "They're going to die."

"Not our problem," I say, but the words taste like battery acid. I check the status: the patch team is right on schedule, locked in a dead zone with the Ronin and the drone, a triple-stalemate that will look perfect in the postmortem. Which means I have two minutes to do my real job. "Keep running the script," I tell the room. "I have to check the failover stack in the East Block." I make it sound routine, but Ban's eyes cut through the lie. She lets it stand. The hall outside is worse than the war room. Every meter there's a fresh stutter in the emergency lighting, every third step a splash of some new, inventive bodily fluid. The walls shake with each round of the Ronin-guard crossfire. No alarms, though; Ban's friend in the control stack killed those first.

I sidestep a collapsed body—Curie, by the uniform, but you couldn't tell if you weren't a connoisseur—and keep moving. I make it to the scrambler console with time to spare. Inside is the motherlode. Twelve racks of forbidden tech, all humming with a feral, sleepless energy. Each console is tagged with a human-readable warning: DANGER—PERSONALITY QUARANTINE IN EFFECT. The air buzzes with an ozone static so rich it's like walking through a cloud of ground-up gods. I work the console, hands steady, heart not. The real-time monitor shows all twelve viral modules are active—each one a compressed hell of conscious thought, cut from children, outlaws, or whatever demographic was most desperate this season. The standard op is to watch and report, maybe patch a new filter if Curie got an angry message from Legal. But I'm not standard.

I plug in my own deck and run the extraction script Ban coded last night. It eats through the interface like acid, bypasses the encryption, and clones the modules into a shadow partition. I watch the progress bar tick up, each percent another point of no return. The walls shake again, this time with a high-pitched feedback whine. Almost done. At 92%, the console spits out a warning: UNAUTHORIZED ACCESS DETECTED. The display blurs to magenta, then all the way out. I brace for the lockdown, but Ban's override kicks in first and the panel resets, docile as a puppy on a sedative. I finish the job, close the panel, and wipe my prints with a sleeve. I pocket the deck, loaded with enough proprietary brain cancer to blackmail Curie from orbit. On the walk back, I run into a guard—young, helmet askew, face gone flat with panic. He raises a taser at me. "Don't," I say, and something in my voice makes him pause.

"There's—There's Ronin in the lab," he stammers.

"I know. I'm here to fix it." I put a hand on his shoulder, then steer him gently toward the path of least resistance. He doesn't fight it. He wants to be steered. The earpiece comes alive. Ban's voice is low: "Skelm. You done?"

"On my way back." There's a boom, then a shriek of rending metal. The entire east corridor shudders, the lights go dead for a full three seconds, and in that silence, I can hear the facility's heart skip a beat.

"Explosion," comes Dorothy's voice, tinny but alive. "Something big in Sector 7. Ban, you have eyes?"

"Video is blind. Sensors read mass casualty." She doesn't say it, but I hear the tilt—she's pissed, and not at me. I run. Not for show; for survival. The air in the hub is hotter, the blue gone to strobe. Dorothy's face is a red mask, blood from a scalp wound running into her eye, but her hands never left the panel. Katherine is slumped against the wall, one ankle twisted in a way that suggests it's not coming back online, but she's tapping her portable anyway. Violet is standing, untouched, in the corner. Her eyes find mine, then flick down to the deck in my pocket. She says nothing.

I take the seat, ignore the screaming in my knee, and start running diagnostics. The system's own logs are perfect—no trace of the extraction, no sign of my existence in the room at all. But the blue on the wall is back, and now there's a siren under the noise: an actual, physical siren, the kind that means air is about to be a premium. "Katherine, you still with us?" I ask.

She shakes her head. "They killed the oxygen to the admin block. It's intentional."

"Dorothy, lock us down. Ban, status on the Ronin?"

"They're dead," Ban says, too calm. "But one guard survived. He's heading this way."

I look up, and for a moment, I expect to see the world through his eyes—a room full of traitors, none of whom belong. But when he arrives, he just collapses on the floor, wheezing, eyes wide. "Sector 7 is gone," he says with a groan.

Ban leans in, calm as a snake in a refrigerator. "What happened?"

"They—They set charges." He gasps. "Tried to kill us all."

Violet crosses the room in two steps, kneels beside him, and presses a vial to his lips. "Breathe," she says, and he does, gulping the air like it's something you can buy at a kiosk. He's not going to survive, but for now, he's our evidence. I scan the logs: the story holds. Ronin breached, Curie responded, mass casualty in Sector 7. No mention of us, no hint of the real payload.

Ban's voice is softer now. "Nice work, Skelm."

I want to say thanks. Instead, I look at the guard, breathing shallow, face the color of printer paper. He's going to die, but the system won't notice. Not until it's too late. The alarms die down and the blue returns to normal. For a second, the hub is silent, everyone just listening to the hum of equipment and the gasp of the dying. Then the next wave of Ronin hits the wall, and everything repeats. But we're ready. We always are.

I sit in the skeleton of the hub, earpiece still ringing from the last casualty report. It's always loudest after the dying stops. In the silent recoil, Dorothy's voice comes through first, stiff and professional: "Sector 7 is still under active threat, but the grid shows minimal movement." She leaves out the part about the guard on the floor, but I can see the blood spreading under his back like a software patch. The main display flickers with the Sector 7 feed. The Ronin breach team moves in perfect sync, their bodies choreographed by some higher cruelty. Two guards—just kids, probably fresh from contract orientation—hold the corridor against them for a full minute. I know both their names. I highlight their icons and press the "ignore" on the alert, then reroute the defense drones to the wrong corridor. "Status?" says Ban, her voice never rising, never falling.

"Lockdown holding. Minimal resistance in Sector 7. Ronin will be in the fire suppression ring in thirty seconds." My words are steady, but my right hand is bleeding from how hard I'm gripping the console edge. I don't let it show. The security feed gives me the worst of it in hi-res: the guards holding the line, their hands shaking so badly the biometric triggers keep jamming. One tries to call for backup, but I've muted the channel. The Ronin go through both in less than five seconds. No celebration. No pause. They set charges on the server racks and fall back, trailing smoke like the ghosts of better people.

I hit the sequence to delay fire suppression by a minute, just long enough to let the smoke cover the sublevel corridor. In the chaos, the extraction completes—twelve viral-personality modules, all cloned to a hidden drive stashed under the north access panel. I check the timestamp, then delete the log entry. Ban catches my eye from the other end of the console. She nods once. I wonder if it's for the plan, or the cost. Katherine is pale, even for her. She's typing the incident report already, fingers stumbling through the boilerplate, but every third word she wipes with her sleeve. The tears start, but she doesn't let them fall. Dorothy scans the bodies on the feed, then says, almost as a joke, "At least it's clean. Not a lot of blood in zero-oxygen."

"Don't," says Ban, but not to her. To the air. The corridor fire gets worse before it gets better. Sprinklers finally trigger, but it's just steam now—hot and rolling, obscuring the rest of the action. By the time the system is "contained," there are only bodies and fragments left on the floor. The Ronin patch team is dead. The guards are dead. The server rack is fried beyond salvage, the public story written before we ever touched the console. I signal Ban: left hand, two fingers, down. She blinks in acknowledgment. Our prize is safe.

The facility system—voice female, always pleasant—chirps through the wall: "Containment complete. Thank you for your cooperation."

On the feed, the clean-up crew walks in with body bags. For a second, I think I see myself on the screen, dead-eyed and limp, being zipped away by people who don't care. I shiver, but keep typing. The operation is over. We won. Or whatever you call it when you survive at the expense of a stranger's tomorrow.

The debrief is never in a real office. That's policy—keep the trauma in the gutters, away from the décor and the executives. The maintenance bay is colder than the server room, lit only by the yellow pulse of a dying LED and the intermittent glare from the open fridge on the far wall. Katherine's perched at the edge of a supply crate, hunched over her portable. The plastic shakes in her grip, and every line of the incident report scrolls by at double speed, as if the words themselves can outrun the guilt. She writes, deletes, then writes again. In the reflection on the screen, I see her stare at the casualty count, mouthing the number over and over.

Dorothy sits with her back to us, a small black device in her lap. She disassembles and reassembles it without looking, every screw rotated by instinct, every spring compressed and released in perfect time. Her shoulders move, but not her head. Violet stands in the corner, a negative space given form, hands folded behind her back. She doesn't move, doesn't blink. The only sign of life is the way her eyes track each of us, in sequence, and how her chest rises a half-beat behind everyone else's. Ban sits beside me on a folding chair, arms across her chest. The secure tablet is between us, its screen dimmed to "paranoid." The data, still warm from the drive, is encrypted and triple-locked, but we both know what's inside. Ban tilts the screen toward me. "Worth it?"

The words are quieter than anything else she's said all night. The question floats between us, heavy as wet wool. I watch the others before I answer. I want to believe in the old logic—that math can solve anything, that the right ratio of risk to reward buys you moral credit. But the only balance here is in who gets to live with it. Before I can answer, Katherine's voice cracks through the silence. "They had names," she says. "Not just IDs. I saw them in the break room, at the vending machines. One had a kid. The other gave me his spot in line for the coffee machine last week."

Nobody speaks. Nobody moves. Dorothy's hands stop moving for the first time. She stares at the black device, then sets it on the crate beside her. "I didn't sign up for this," she says, not to anyone in particular. "I thought we were trying to fix things. Not ..." She can't finish. Instead, she unscrews the panel on the device again, as if the answer might be hidden inside.

Violet smiles. It's a small thing, thin and sharp. "You knew exactly what you signed up for." Her voice is neither comfort nor condemnation. "This was always the price. You just didn't want to read the fine print."

Katherine's hands start shaking again. She covers her mouth, then leans into her knees, body folded tight. "We could have done it differently."

"No," says Ban. She doesn't raise her voice, but the finality cuts the air. "If we'd played it safe, they would have seen the gaps. They would have rolled in the next team, and the next. They'd have found us in a week. We had one shot, and we took it."

Dorothy spins a screw between her fingers, then lets it drop. "You say that like it matters."

Ban shrugs. "It does. Because we're still alive. And now we have this." She nods at the tablet. The argument is a stalemate. No one has anything left to fire.

I finally pick up the tablet, enter the access string, and show them the opening screen: twelve lines of raw, neural chaos. Each file labeled with a cryptic, anonymous tag. Each line a person, compressed into a future weapon. I look at Katherine. "You want to be the one to send it?"

She shakes her head. "I don't ever want to see it again."

Dorothy stands, rubs her eyes with the heel of her hand, and turns away. Violet approaches the table. She doesn't reach for the tablet, just hovers her palm over it. "We're on the line now. We're either in, or we're meat. No half-measures."

Ban glances at me, the edge of her smile as jagged as ever. “We’ve already made our choice.”

I close the tablet, set it on the floor, and wait for the silence to settle. The light from the fridge flickers, then dies. No one leaves. No one apologizes. We just sit, five bodies in the maintenance cold, waiting for the next job, and for the air to finally warm enough to thaw the guilt.

It doesn’t.

Chapter 13

Dorothy's station is the last warm node in a room built to freeze emotion. The holowall, forty percent of the east side, blazes with diagnostic graphs, soft-blue in the main, but at this hour, the overlays bleed a sick, arterial red. Dorothy sits at the board, her mechanical arm crooked at a right angle, plastic and tendon humming as her fingers play across a haptic keyboard. Her back is straight as always, but tonight there's a list in her posture—like her spine is refusing to cooperate, one vertebra at a time. I'm only two meters behind, inventorying the error logs on the physical security array. My own readout is routine. The data is boring, but my hands won't stop shaking, and I've had enough nights in this tomb to know my body is smarter than my mind.

Dorothy's voice cuts the air. "Skelm. Take a look at this." She doesn't say please. I drop the portable and step forward. The holowall is split: left half a human body, rendered in shimmering false-color MRI; right half a scatter plot of neural impulse patterns that pulse like a heat map for ghosts. I know the model.

It's the hostage. The little girl, composite of the three we'd been sent to rescue. Her name is in the upper left: JUNO. Dorothy flicks a finger at the first display. "You see the markers?"

I squint, then zoom. There, under the outermost skin layer, are clusters of elliptical objects: nanotech, glowing faint blue against the pastel tissue, each labeled, coded, and counted. "Those are kill switch nodes," I say, voice steadier than my pulse.

Dorothy nods. "You missed the volume. There are seventy-eight in the first child alone." A different kind of cold fills the room. I tap the overlay and zoom in. Each node isn't just a tracker. The annotation expands, flagged by a ribbon of crimson code: KILL. Dorothy rotates the 3D model. "It's a neural bomb. If you disrupt the signal, it pushes an overload through the brainstem." She toggles a secondary scan. "This isn't a fail-safe. It's a termination protocol."

My mouth goes dry. "Every hostage?"

Dorothy's prosthetic hand stutters, a new tic. "I'm sampling the other files, but yes. Every single one. Full spectrum—children, adults, the high-value sample batches. All hostages, no exceptions."

At that exact moment, Ban strides in. There's energy on her, like the electromagnetic residue of a shorted fuse. She clocks the wall, takes in the red, and cuts straight to the heart. "What's the issue?"

Dorothy brings up the raw logs, voice clipped. "Curie didn't just stock the vaults with consciousness. They baked in kill switches. Neural bombs; 847 in total."

Ban's jawline sets, then resets. "Targets?"

"Every single asset flagged as 'potential liability,'" Dorothy says. "Even the ones marked 'return to donor.'"

Ban's left hand makes a subtle motion—either she wants to break something, or she wants to hit me. But for once, I think she wants to hit herself. Violet is next in, fast and silent as a thrown knife. Her face is colorless, but her hands are in motion before she even says a word. She beelines for the comms relay at the far end, logs in, and starts prepping an outgoing. Ban moves to intercept, but Violet just says, "I'm not going to let them torch 800 kids. I can get the message to every executive within two minutes. We threaten the families, they stand down."

Ban closes the distance and slams the console shut with the meat of her palm. "Or they accelerate the schedule and kill everyone now." Her voice is tight, iron through velvet. "We blow the wrong line, we lose it all."

Violet bares her teeth. "I'm not waiting to play their fucking game."

Dorothy's left hand is white-knuckling the holoboard. She looks at me, the tremor in her jaw matching my hands. "Skelm," she says, "we can't bypass these. The coding is random. Any attempt to force it will trigger the kill path."

I do a fast calculation: if the odds are random, our best chance is to get the protocol that disables all of them at once. But Curie would never keep the master code local. They'll have it on a deadman's server, offsite, probably set to delete if a failover triggers. I say this out loud, the words tumbling in a logic train. Ban slaps the holoboard, harder than necessary. "That means we need the code."

Dorothy nods. "Or a live executive. With full access."

Violet's fingers drum the console. "We're not walking back into that den."

Ban turns to face me. "What are the odds we can exfiltrate the code through the grid without getting caught?"

I try to make my answer optimistic, but the math says otherwise. "Fifteen percent. Maybe twenty if the watchdogs are sleeping."

She closes her eyes, just for a second. "We need a higher number than that."

Violet mutters, "We could always go physical. Breach the relay, pull the drive—"

Ban shakes her head. "And set off every alarm from here to the bottom of the city." She gestures at the holowall. "This is our only play. We need the deactivation string."

Dorothy's mask slips a millimeter, and in the new line of her mouth I see something close to regret. "If I had another option, I'd take it."

We all stand there, blue-lit and silent, until Ban finally cracks the moment. "Skelm, you're on the code. Dorothy, triage the hostages—see if any can be shielded from the node effect. Violet, you get one shot at scaring the execs, but no broadcast unless I give the order."

Violet seethes, but nods. Dorothy hunches in, shoulders set. I move to the admin desk, pull up the core logs, and start combing the quantum layer for hints of the string. Behind me, Ban paces. She's not talking, but every time she gets to the wall, her fist taps it once, like a heartbeat, like a countdown. The room goes silent, but inside my chest, every alarm is screaming. Dorothy's voice breaks the quiet, a single word, half-whispered. "Shit."

I spin, expecting violence, but she's just staring at the wall. One of the neural bomb overlays is now pulsing yellow. Ban's beside her in a blink. "What changed?"

Dorothy's hand shakes. "One of the hostages. The node is active. They've started the sequence."

The yellow on the wall ticks up, then red. Five seconds to terminal. Violet is at the console, hands flying. "Can I trigger an override?"

Dorothy shakes her head, frantic. "Any non-sequence input triggers the backup—kills the host."

Ban looks at me. "How much time?"

"Five seconds. Maybe six."

Ban leans into the mic. "Juno. If you can hear me, stay completely still. Don't think about anything except the blue."

Dorothy's fingers fly. She mutes every input and isolates the node. "If the child can stay calm, the sequence might abort."

On the wall, the timer ticks down: 2.7, 2.6, 2.5. The color goes orange, then blood orange. I hold my breath. And then—nothing. The timer disappears. The overlay returns to blue. Dorothy collapses against the board, mechanical hand limp, flesh hand trembling. Violet says, “Fuck,” but in a way that’s more reverence than anger.

Ban closes her eyes, relief a visible weight. “We have to hurry.” She looks at me. “No more near-misses, Skelm. Get me that code.”

I nod, already working, but my hands are a blur of nerves and sweat. Each line of script I open is a fresh horror show —fail-safes, redundancies, kill protocols nested in the code like teeth in a shark’s mouth. Behind me, Ban and Dorothy run triage, prepping for whatever comes next. Violet prowls the room, a silent threat in search of a target. We’re on a clock now, and the clock is not on our side. But for a second, the wall is blue again. And that has to count for something.

We work the grid with the urgency of a medic pounding a stopped heart. Ban sets up at the main console, pulling a fat line of optic cable from her bag and jacking straight into the root port. Her hands move at a pace I’ve never seen; she types with all ten fingers and then overlays an analog pinpad, working the access points at two layers. It’s a hack so pure even the machine stops to admire it. Dorothy leans over the secondary array, cybereye spinning fast, microservo in her jaw clicking like a countdown. She’s watching the secondary logs, the live security readouts, and building a shadow map of Curie’s kill-tree. It’s not enough to copy the code; we have to evade the dozens of watchdogs who monitor every packet for anomaly. Dorothy’s left hand hovers over the manual kill switch, her right tapping the keys so lightly you can’t see it unless you look for it.

I'm on the portable, sweating over the extraction script. There's nothing clever about it—just brute force, layer after layer of credential until the system gives up a fraction of itself. The progress bar isn't a lie, but it's not truth either. Every tenth of a percent feels like flipping a coin with the world's smallest razor at your throat. Violet paces behind us, muttering the numbers under her breath. "Eight hundred forty-seven. Eight hundred forty-seven. Goddamn, that's a football stadium."

Ban ignores her, laser-locked on the holo display. "Dorothy, talk to me."

"Security is running the audit. At the next anomaly, they'll kick us off the loop." Dorothy's voice is mechanical, but her knuckles have gone paper white.

"Skelm?" Ban doesn't turn, but I feel the heat in her tone.

"Seventy-two percent," I say, willing it to be faster. "I'm spamming the randomizer, but the watchdog keeps sniffing our keyspace."

Ban grunts. "Change the pace, it's learning you."

I do, hands sweating so bad the keys leave lines on my skin. Violet steps closer, so close I feel the static off her jumpsuit. "If they flag us, what's our window?"

Ban's eyes flick up. "Forty seconds. Less, if they route the drones."

Violet's next line is lost to the drone of cooling fans. The server room is loud, not just with machines, but with the sense of disaster running just under the white noise. Dorothy's cybereye snaps, then she says, "Ghost ping in Sector 8. They know we're up, just not where yet."

Ban's fingers blur, overlaying admin and user logins so the audit thinks she's a dozen different low-threat personnel. "Keep it thin," she mutters. "Don't spike the graph."

Ninety-one percent. Ninety-two. Violet's muttering gets louder, but I tune her out. The progress bar slows to a crawl; the watchdog is now brute-forcing a counter to our counter. I run a fresh thread and try a backdoor at the old maintenance shell. It works, for three seconds, then a firewall slams shut. I curse, loud. "They're onto us."

Ban's left hand darts over and slaps the reset on her own console. She types in a string I don't recognize, then says, "Standby, Skelm. I have a legacy override."

Dorothy's cybereye spins, then she taps the holowall. "Tripwire just got cut. You've got thirty seconds before it restarts at full lockdown."

Ninety-seven percent. I work the keyboard so hard the keys rattle. The extraction script hits a snag; there's a permissions knot I can't untie. I backtrack and try a side load, but the watchdog is eating my progress. Ninety-eight.

Ban says, "Manual mode, Skelm. Last-chance effort."

I ditch the script, switch to raw command line, and run the admin override Ban fed me three days ago. The console flashes, not a color I've ever seen, and the progress bar jumps. Ninety-nine. A warning window opens, overlays on every surface: "INTRUSION DETECTED. LOCAL LOCKDOWN IN EFFECT." Violet slams her palm into the desk, yelling, "They're coming!"

Dorothy's jaw goes hard. "We've got fifteen seconds until the entire network hard-resets and the kill code fires."

I look at Ban. She's calm, serene, a cold star in the chaos. She types a short sequence, then slams her palm down on the print reader. The server blinks, and the status line goes green: "COPY COMPLETE. DOWNLOAD STORED." We all exhale, but only for a second. The room's lights flick to emergency red. Ban snatches the drive from the dock and pockets it. "Move," she says, voice absolute. "We're burning the station in sixty seconds."

Violet is already at the door, brandishing her own override stick. Dorothy follows, moving like a machine with purpose now, her earlier cracks healed by the shock of near-annihilation. I grab the portables, check my own pulse—too fast, but still moving—and follow them out. The corridor is chaos, the alarms howling, the lights pulsing a frantic SOS. Ban leads, taking us down a blind corridor. She flicks open a hidden maintenance shaft, one I'd never have noticed, and we slip inside just as the wall behind us slams shut. The only sound in the dark is the stutter of our breathing, and the faraway static of the system killing itself to spite the intrusion. Ban holds up the drive, thumbprints it, then hands it to me. "Don't drop it," she says.

"I won't," I say, and I mean it.

She gives me a look—a flicker of the old Ban, the one who used to be a person, not just a mission. "We did it," she says, not smiling. I nod.

Dorothy checks the status on her portable, then says, "They'll torch the backups next. We have to go, now."

Violet doesn't speak, just shoulders past and starts climbing the ladder. The maintenance shaft is narrow, full of dust and the memory of dead systems. We clamber up, two stories, then emerge in an empty office suite. The world outside is still blue, but the air is cleaner, the noise less desperate. We cross to the exit, all of us scanning for pursuit. At the door, Ban pauses. She looks back at the building, then at the sky. For a second, she seems lost. Not to fear, but to wonder. I watch her face, the tension lines finally smoothing. She takes a breath. "Next job," she says, and pushes through. I'm right behind her. And if I look back, it's only to remind myself that, for once, we didn't fail. We lived. So did eight hundred forty-seven ghosts, at least for now.

When it's over, the world collapses into the blue again. Not the fake, edible blue of corporate wellness, but the sallow, humectant blue of a server room at 3 a.m. Ban and I are the last humans in the tunnel. Violet's gone ahead to clear exfil routes. Dorothy is ten meters down the access shaft, but you can still smell the violence clinging to her—solder flux, the ghost of cordite, metal sweat. We reach the bank of diagnostic stations that once ran Curie's mid-tier thought management. Half the units are dead, the rest frozen mid-cycle, icons and overlays drifting in the vacuum of sudden death. I wipe the bench with my sleeve and sit. Ban stays standing, leaning into the glow, studying the lines of code that now define the fate of every child we just saved.

I start running the decryption keys, hands a little steadier now that the adrenaline is draining off. The protocol is a lattice of corporate obfuscation, recursive enough that every other line references a subroutine that doesn't exist anywhere in the index. Ban squints, the blue light outlining the smudges of old injury under her eyes. "We're going to need to crack the whole set," I say, thumbing through the raw data. "They salted the codes with entropy from a one-time pad, locked to the dead-man's key." Ban doesn't answer. Her jaw is set in a way that looks like anger but is really just the memory of it, hollowed out by exhaustion. "Even if we brute the hashes, we'll have to reconstruct the seed from the live net. We need a day. Two, at most."

"Don't have it," Ban says. The words hit the table, flat as dice. "They'll try to liquidate the inventory before we crack it." She reaches for the console, skimming the edge of my hand. For someone who spends her time in the bone-hush of violence, her hands are warm. The surprise of it makes me pause. Ban stares at the code, then at me. "We will crack it," she says, and the voice is different—softer, with just enough risk in it to feel real. "I promised you we wouldn't let it happen again."

I don't know what to say, so I just nod. The lines of code run like a prayer across the monitor. We work in silence for a while. Ban watches my fingers, or maybe just the tremor that returns every time the system stutters. She reads me as easily as she reads the error logs—maybe more easily. After ten minutes, the room is so still I almost forget the time bomb ticking behind every digit. She speaks first. "You ever think we're just moving deck chairs on the Titanic?"

I smile, but it's not the nice kind. "Sometimes I wonder if the deck chairs are the only part worth saving." She nods, and for a second the mask slips again. I see the person behind the war face, and she is—almost—young. I gesture at the monitor. "This is what passes for heroics now?"

Her lips twitch. "It's better than letting the monsters keep score."

I look at her. The scar at her jaw, the deep cut on her knuckle, the residue of too many fights and not enough sleep. She is more weapon than woman, but in this light, I can see both. I say, "We did the right thing."

Ban looks at me, something like skepticism in her eyes. "There's no such thing as right in this business, Skelm. There's only less wrong." She pulls her hand back, but her thumb lingers on the desk. "I've watched people die before," she says, voice low. "I won't do it again. Not if we can stop it." The words surprise us both. I start to reply, but the moment folds in on itself. The screen blinks—an overlay, someone accessing the remote interface. I go to kill it, but Ban stops me with a touch. "It's Dorothy checking the status."

We let the feed ride. Dorothy's face, pale and sweat-slick, appears in the corner. "You copy all of it?" she asks.

I nod, and Ban says, "We're already working the keys."

Dorothy's eyes go hollow with relief. "Buy time, then. I'll run interference. They're sweeping the floors."

Ban acknowledges with a nod, then cuts the feed. We're alone again, but it feels different. The air in the room has the density of two people keeping secrets from the universe. I go back to the code, but Ban watches me for a long time. Finally, she says, "You don't have to do it alone, you know."

I blink. "I'm not."

She smiles, this time with her whole mouth. "You used to think you were." I laugh, but it's just a noise, a bark in the quiet. Ban stands, circles to the other side of the console, and leans in. She's close enough that I can see the sweat starting to bead at her temples. "You get scared?"

"All the time," I say, honest for once.

She's close enough to kiss, but neither of us is that sentimental. Instead, she presses her forehead to mine, just for a second, then pulls away. "Back to work," she says, but her voice is all honey and static.

I type and she reads, the room so blue it's like we're underwater. Outside, alarms start again, but it's far away—someone else's disaster. I lose myself in the code, the numbers, the logic. For the first time in months, the work feels less like survival and more like living. Ban is right there with me. And if there's a future at the end of this, I want her in it. Dorothy buzzes in again, but this time, she waits. The team is all together, faces in the blue, hands on the line. I finish the last block, patch the key, and hit execute. The protocol runs. Eight hundred forty-seven lines of kill code replaced by null. The world outside is still dying, but in here, for a minute, we're alive. I look at Ban. She looks back. It's not a happy ending. But it's ours.

Chapter 14

Nothing in the world prepares you for the Marie event. Even when you know the theory, even when you've sat through all the off-the-record security briefings and seen the ugly freeze-frames from Beta City. It's not the technology or the neuro-science or the grotesque metaphysics of it—what gets you is the choreography. The command hub is the only room in the building that doesn't feel like a morgue. It's midnight but the light's a permanent false dawn: panels blue-white, overlaying the walls with a permafrost that makes skin itch and lungs rebel. I'm at the main console. Ban is a black swatch on my left, her boots up, her face lit by the glow. Dorothy is behind me, cross-legged on a plastic crate, assembling some device that looks like the marriage of a food processor and a bomb. Katherine is catatonic in a chair, her eyes two smudges in the reflected monitors. We're catching our breath, which is why nobody hears the door hiss.

Marie enters as an ensemble. That's the only word for it—she arrives not as a person but as a probability, resolving into seventeen identical women, each spaced exactly two meters apart, each with the same perfect posture, the same mid-40s face, the same crisp part in the hair and the same half-moon earrings. They walk in step, matching down to the flex of each calf muscle, and stop in a seventeen-point phalanx around the room. Even Ban blinks. Dorothy drops the processor, which hits her knee and then the floor with a meaty *thunk*.

I count the Maries, all of them staring straight ahead, every face angled at the same mathematical degree to the center of the room. There's a wet, glittery overlay to the way they move, as if every joint has been greased with something that isn't oil. Each one is dressed for a different social context—administrator, executive, janitorial, maybe even one in full wet-lab gear—but the effect is not comic. It's religious. It's a corporate sermon. All seventeen speak at once. The acoustics are better than perfect, the words landing like a software update at 100 gigabit: "Proceed with defense. Your people depend on success."

Nobody moves. Ban, who never sweats, is sweating. You can see it at the corner of her jaw, a single line of moisture following the pull of gravity. Her eyes flick left and right, doing a speedrun of the new security landscape, marking which Maries have line of sight on which exits. My own body has already surrendered. Stomach drops, bile spikes up the esophagus, sweat beads in the cleft above my brow. I feel hot and freezing at the same time, a flu of pure adrenaline. My hand grips the side of the desk so hard the plastic flexes, the hologram flickering with each squeeze.

Marie speaks again, but this time each copy takes a word, running the sentence like a packet through a network:

"Defense—must—remain—on—schedule—" down the line and back. Violet isn't here—she took the package to the back-up lab—but I sense her at the edges of the room, lurking for a fight or an excuse to shank the nearest Marie. Which is probably why Marie sent all seventeen. She always reads ahead. Marie-in-the-middle (executive cut, tailored suit, badge so new it glows) takes one step forward. Ban's left hand slides a full centimeter closer to the stiletto she keeps in her boot. If this escalates, there will be blood. The Marie delivers her next line, but this time, the voice is everywhere, each mouth picking up a syllable, then passing it down the chain so fast it sounds like digital glossolalia: "You—must—comply—Function—demands—efficiency—Refusal—will—result—in—collection—"

Katherine makes a noise, part gasp and part whimper, which seems to please the Maries. Seventeen pairs of eyes twinkle, just a shimmer, then snap back to ice. Nobody is breathing. Marie waits exactly three seconds. I time it on the console clock. Then, as if a switch has flipped, the Maries break formation. Two split off and run diagnostics on the holowall. Four more form a cluster near the admin desk, fingers moving in a gesture-language so fast it nearly flickers. The rest disperse in slow orbits, each hovering over a different workstation or team member, never closer than two meters, never farther. Ban leans into my shoulder, her lips barely moving. "You okay?" she whispers.

I try to reply but the saliva is gone, and all I manage is, "Yeah," which is a lie and she knows it.

"They won't kill us," she says, "not yet."

"But?"

Ban's voice is subatomic now. "They need us. We're the only ones with the full set. That's use."

I nod, because that's what you do when you agree to be scared. Dorothy, as always, recovers first. She picks up the dropped bomb-processor, fumbles with the attachment, and resumes building the thing with a force of will I admire more than love. One of the Maries leans over her, close enough for Dorothy to see the barcode at the nape of her neck. They say nothing, just watch. Dorothy matches the silence, a contest of chicken with infinite stakes.

The blue light is nauseating now. It doesn't reflect, it absorbs, painting everyone in shades of unperson. My hands are too cold, and I make a mental note: move every ten minutes, keep the blood flowing, do not show weakness. I look up, just as two Maries finish a circuit of the room and come to rest at Ban's flank. They don't touch her, but the implication is clear: Watch your step. The central Marie, satisfied, says: "Proceed. We are watching."

And in perfect harmony, the Maries rotate out, each departing at a precisely offset time interval so the door never admits more than one body at once. It's more horrifying on the exit than on arrival. When the room is empty, the blue seems deeper. The air is wet with the residue of chemical terror. Katherine lets out a sob, muffled by her sleeve. Dorothy puts her device down and stares at the ceiling, eyes glassy but not defeated. Ban sits then, letting her shoulders fall out of parade rest. For a full minute, none of us speaks. Finally, Ban says, "I think we know what happens if we fail." I look at her, and for once, the mask is gone. She looks as scared as I feel. I want to say something brave, but I just sit in the cold light, counting the seconds until the next Marie event. Outside, the building creaks, and for a second, I think I can hear the footsteps of the next disaster. I hope it doesn't have seventeen faces, but hope is always a poor defense in the blue.

Once the air has stopped vibrating with the afterimage of Marie, the blue-lit command hub is a tomb. Even the hum of the holo-panels feels ashamed. Everyone pretends to work; only Ban and I are actually doing anything. She nods at the dead zone behind the admin stack. "Now," she whispers, and we slip to the shadowed edge where the camera coverage is old and tired. The minute I jack into the maintenance console, my hands return to themselves—still trembling, but with purpose now. Ban peels the masking tape off the legacy admin port and pops the cover, feeding her portable into the archaic guts of the building. We're inside the network, private, in the ten seconds before the Maries cycle the next audit. Ban speaks only in grunts and code. "Ingress vector: raw. Unencrypted. She's so confident it's almost insulting."

I nod, fingers already crawling the logs. The packet traffic is visible in the thermal overlay: seventeen points, all cross-talking on a private layer, bouncing admin credentials like children passing forbidden notes in the back of a classroom. Each body is both node and relay. Each has its own health monitor, self-correcting heuristics, and a redline for "catastrophic mental deviation." "She's running herself on an old reality-exec kernel," I say, pulling up the process list. "But the overlays are stitched from a dozen commercial consciousness modules."

Ban runs a scan, hands tight on the deck. “It’s like watching someone paint a target on their own back. She’s almost begging to be hacked.”

“Is it a trap?” I ask.

Ban doesn’t look up. “No. She’s just that arrogant.” I dump the traffic, watching the data sprays blossom and die in the diagnostic. Every time a Marie speaks, the node brightens; every time they blink in sync, the pulses spike across the entire mesh. It’s more beautiful than it should be. Which just makes it worse. Ban begins to trace the connections, mapping them to a simple grid overlay. As she taps each node, a glow appears—a soft, sickly blue, with sharp red lines indicating the primary command channels. The effect is a flower made of arteries and ice. She leans in, forehead almost brushing mine. “Look at this.” The screen is a wet dream for anyone who ever wanted to own another person. The main hub routes every signal through a stack of self-replicating filters, each labeled in old legal Latin, each more redundant than the last. “Fail-safe, on fail-safe, on fail-safe,” Ban mutters. “You know why?”

I do. “So if one body dies, the others take over. Even if the brain melts, the system persists.”

Ban’s mouth tightens. “It’s not persistence. It’s insurance.” I reach for the next layer, trying to pull up an instance of what happens when a Marie is destroyed. The logs are thick with noise, but Ban is already there, stripping away the padding and parsing the exception cases. “Here,” she says, eyes glittering with the hunt. “Death event in node seven. Three days ago.” The video plays. One Marie walks into an elevator, smiling, lips parting as if to deliver a clever aside. She winks at the camera, then collapses, face-first, like a puppet whose strings have been cut. She never twitches, never blinks. Ban runs it again. "She knew she'd die. She wanted it on the log."

In the frame, a new Marie appears at the end of the hall. No panic, no confusion, just a seamless handoff. The old body is dragged out by facility staff—either real or animated, it's hard to tell—and the replacement resumes the walk as if nothing happened. I watch the timestamps, tracing the transition at microsecond scale. The network doesn't skip, doesn't even stutter. "It's like hot-swapping a hard drive," I say. "You lose nothing. Not even continuity of thought."

Ban breathes out, a sharp exhale. "Unless there's a bug."

She toggles a diagnostic mode. Now the grid is alive with trembling overlays, little worms of static where the bodies are out of sync by a fraction of a second. I see it: a glitch in node 14, a lag in the handoff, and a strange, persistent echo in the data. "Some of these Maries are losing time," I say, pointing at the readout. "There's fragmentation."

Ban clicks her tongue. "A bug in the mesh." She looks at me, voice as dry as old sand. "Could be weaponized." I file that under "later." We keep mapping. The technical work is its own kind of intimacy: Ban running raw traces, me combing the logs for discrepancies, both of us bent over the same screen, breathing in time. Our hands brush every so often, each contact like an accidental confession. Every ten seconds, I check the security overlay to make sure none of the Maries are watching. We're in the clear—at least as much as anyone ever is. "Here's the main control vector," Ban says. "Every time she updates, the mesh synchronizes through this root."

I see the spot—a node labeled "M.G.ROOT.01." It pulses with each heartbeat of the building. Every instruction, every spoken word, every muscle twitch is born here, in a dirty, unencrypted memory dump. It's ugly, and it's perfect. Ban traces the lines. "If we hit this at the right moment, we could hijack the whole array. Or bring it down." I nod, not trusting my voice. The implications are enough to make me sick. We keep working, mapping redundancy on redundancy. Each Marie is backed up in three more. When one glitches or dies, the next absorbs it, sometimes even the physical tissue. It's not immortality; it's a pyramid scheme of bodies. Ban keeps up the commentary, low and technical: "She's running a side process on each node. Looks like ... parallel consciousness. Multiple threads per body. Some are passive. Some are not."

I see it, too. The logs show periods where one body will stop responding for a fraction of a second—then resume, as if nothing happened. In those gaps, another Marie elsewhere is double-processing. "It's like having seventeen nightmares at once," I say. "And each one wakes up thinking it was the only dream."

Ban smiles, a tight, toothless thing. "Imagine being her." I do, and immediately regret it. By now, the map is almost complete. Seventeen nodes, all glowing, each one bristling with red lines. At the center is the ROOT, blinking a little faster now that we're watching. Ban says, "If we can corrupt the root, we could end this."

She doesn't say what "this" is. She doesn't have to. I run a local copy of the mesh map, then encrypt it with a key only I know. "Will she notice?"

Ban shrugs. “Probably. But not in time.” We both look at the screen. It’s the most beautiful thing I’ve ever hated. Somewhere in the building, a Marie laughs—seventeen times, in perfect delay. I feel the sound before I hear it. Ban looks at me, eyes reflecting the blue. “Ready?” she asks. I nod, because there’s nothing else to do. We log out, back up the map, and slip into the main corridor, where the building has started to vibrate again. There’s a hum now, not of machines, but of inevitability. This is what it means to fight a system: you map it, you fear it, and then you tear it out by the roots. We’re close. And if I feel sick at what we’re about to do, at least I know I’m still human.

We make it back to the command hub, breath fogging, nerves flatlined and spiking at the same time. The room hasn’t changed—same blue, same ice, same permanent smell of old plastic and stress. But the Maries are still here, some at their posts, some orbiting the perimeter, all of them watching. I take the main console, flip up the diagnostics, and set the holo display to a blank, inert status screen. Ban slides into the chair beside me, flipping her portable open with an almost bored flick. For half a minute, nothing happens. Then every Marie in the room turns to face us—seventeen heads, exact same angle, exact same microsecond. “She noticed,” Ban says.

I don’t answer. I force my face into a smile, bland as canned coffee, and toggle a screen of routine security updates. The program is harmless, unless you know where to look. Under the hood, the diagnostic is running Ban’s custom mesh scan, logging every node and every packet that flies between the

Maries. "Keep it normal," Ban mutters, fingers flying. Her left hand runs the real work; her right scrolls through a decoy set of network health metrics, every line of text as boring as her voice.

One of the Maries—lab coat, hair pinned back with surgical accuracy—walks directly to our station. She leans over my shoulder, the chemical scent of her breath hitting my nostrils before the words even come. "What are you working on?" she asks, voice soft, curious, predatory.

I keep my eyes on the screen. "Just mapping security call vectors. Looking for the new intrusion heuristics."

The Marie glances down, her eyes flicking so fast they almost blur. "You've already completed three days' work in one hour." It's not a compliment. It's an accusation.

Ban takes over without missing a beat. "We use adaptive sampling. It's efficient." She taps a chart. "The whole process is hands-off once you set the parameters."

Marie doesn't move for a long, perfect second. Then, as if in response to a radio ping, three other Maries walk up behind her, fanning out so that all four are looking down at us, identical and chilling. "Impressive," says another Marie, this one in a maintenance jumpsuit. "You are highly ... optimized."

I nod, fake humility on max. "Ban wrote the process. I just run it."

The four Maries blink, not together but in a cycle, as if passing the task around the group for efficiency. Then the first one leans even closer. I can feel her hair brush the back of my ear. "We will need you to integrate the defensive layer with our own. We have proprietary protocols. They require absolute precision." Her breath is warm and smells like antiseptic and fresh printer paper.

Ban says, "Send us the specs. I'll patch it in." The four Maries step back in unison, then split up, each returning to a different node in the hub. But the attention doesn't waver—I can see in the peripheral that all seventeen Maries are tracking us now, monitoring every keystroke and every micro-expression. I type one-handed, my other hand balled in a fist under the desk. The hidden diagnostic is almost done mapping the root. Ban's deck pulses with the flow of data; every time a Marie speaks, the main node flares on the overlay, and a line of code triggers in the background. I risk a glance at Ban, but she doesn't meet my eye. Instead, she clicks through several dummy overlays, filling the air with technical jargon. "We'll need to stagger the firewall handoff," she says, not caring which Marie overhears. "If not, we'll cause a lockout and reset the building."

A Marie—now in a navy-blue exec dress, badge screaming Middle Management—leans over the far side of the console. "We cannot permit downtime. It is detrimental to morale."

Ban doesn't even nod. "That's why I'll dry-run it first. On the mirror partition."

The Marie studies the line of code I'm scrolling. I feel my throat tighten; if she sees the packet trace, we're dead. But Ban is running the copy in a sandboxed VM, a ghost instance. On the main console, it's all performance metrics and audit logs, each more boring than the last. The Marie lingers, eyes tracing every flicker of the screen. Her face is unreadable, but the mouth twitches—maybe a smile, maybe just a prelude to opening wide and swallowing me whole. "We appreciate your commitment," she says, voice suddenly sugar-sweet. "Proceed."

Then she's gone, back to the center of the room, where the other Maries resume their work. But every so often, one turns to glance, a constant background check, a threat. Ban relaxes by a hair. "Keep going," she whispers, "but slow the throughput. Don't let her see the memory spikes." I throttle the process. The status bar crawls at a snail's pace, but the hidden diagnostic is almost at critical mass. Every node, every packet, every off-label whisper that passes between the Maries is now logged and rendered in full. Ban's fingers brush mine, just a graze, but the static shock is real. "Got it," she whispers. "Downloading." We run the last of the process in silence, sweat beading in my armpits, the smell of ozone rising as if the room itself knows what we're doing. Three Maries walk past the console again, this time in a casual stroll, pretending to look at the logs but really scanning us for cracks. Ban says, "We'll finish the dry run in six minutes. Then I'll switch to integration."

The Marie at the front of the group—she must be the dominant node—stops dead in front of the console. Her lips part, but instead of speaking, she just looks at me, eyes dilated so black I can't see the iris. It feels like a dare. I look back, and for a second, I'm not scared. Just angry. I say, "We'll make it perfect." The Marie's head tilts, a canine considering the neck of a prey animal. Then she moves on. I check the clock. Five minutes. Four. Three. The process completes. Ban closes the deck with a snap, wipes her brow, then sets her hands on the desk and just breathes. I do the same. The Maries line up at the main exit. Without fanfare, all seventeen walk out of the room, their steps echoing in perfect time. When the last one is gone, the blue light seems less hostile. The air is breathable again.

Katherine and Dorothy unfreeze, and Violet ghosts in from the dark. But none of them speaks. Ban looks at me, the fatigue and triumph in her face a perfect match for my own. We glance at the diagnostic overlay—now complete, a perfect, ugly map of every Marie, every flaw, every root. We did it. But the look we share isn't pride. It's horror. Because now we know what it costs to survive in this building. We sit, side by side, until the blue light resets to normal. And then, for a minute, I let myself think about tomorrow. It isn't hope, exactly. But it's something. We get back to work. There's still time.

Chapter 15

The siren begins in the root, a low-frequency moan that vibrates the screws in my jaw. Then a shell goes off somewhere close—maybe two sub-levels down. The air shakes, glass blinks in the holowall, and every overlay on my console in the security hub goes ultraviolet with error. The first thing I do is taste my own tongue, waiting for the blood that means I bit through, but it's only copper and fear. The second thing I do is check Ban. She's at the main board, a statue carved out of carbon fiber, only her fingers moving, sweeping aside useless status updates and stacking all the new dead into a grid. For two full seconds, the world is only us and the pitch whine of a facility about to lose its mind. Then the Ronin break surface in three places at once. Sector Red goes live in the south corridor. The camera feeds stutter, then roll back to a feed that shouldn't exist—old, analog, pixelated. A team in full exosuits ghosting past the first checkpoint, neat as magicians. Ban mutters, "Of course it's the Redline." She tags the breach with a swipe, then flags the squad of guards in proximity.

“Katherine, status—east stairwell,” I say into the comm, and even in my own head, the voice sounds remote, staged.

“Already two casualties,” she says, breathless. “One tech, one courier. They used a neuro-blind; I can’t see the breach team.”

Dorothy overlays her data onto the holowall. “They’re running suppression—white noise, then a logic bomb. It’s working; I can’t ping anything outside the main.”

A new alarm triggers. Not a sound, but a light: the perimeter goes from blue to red to black. I switch to internal. The holowall’s human schematic pulses with every heart that dies. The visual is not metaphor: the facility is hemorrhaging. Marie arrives all at once, a parade of herself on every screen. Seventeen Maries, each face stretched in a different calibration of concern, efficiency, and predatory focus. The one in charge wears a suit so clean it looks like a software effect. “Defend the core,” she says, seventeen times, but not in chorus. Instead, each mouth picks up the last word, turning the room into a round of deadly, recursive instruction. “Defend—Defend—Defend the—Defend the core—”

Ban punches a query. “Which core? We have four.”

Marie-in-the-suit never blinks. “The core is defined as a locus of highest existential value. You will interpret appropriately.”

Katherine makes a noise over the comm. “You have to be kidding me.”

“I don’t think she knows,” Dorothy says.

I look at Ban, and Ban looks at me, and for a moment, there is understanding. The system isn’t just under attack—it’s in the middle of a civil war. “Split the guards,” Ban says, no hesitation. "Redline to North, Green to Central. Pull two from East, support the vault."

I patch the message, then say, "Already done."

She cracks her neck, then launches the next phase. "Override drone suppression; tag the Ronin lead and run their pattern."

I nod, hand already in the process. The drones—little wasp-things with blue LED eyes—start to fire up and fan out, each taking a different sector. In thirty seconds, they'll paint the Ronin in infrared and send the signature to the main defense. "West stairwell just vented atmosphere," Dorothy says, "but the auto-doors are holding. No fire in the server room yet."

Marie-07 on the top right screen makes a face that is half-sneer, half exasperated-teacher. "Defend the core, not the shell. Deploy assets accordingly."

The logic is clear: she's worried about internal, not perimeter. Or maybe she's baiting us to move. Either way, the Ronin are punching right through the blue line, heading for the Main Banks. My fingers fly. On the overlay, I can see the Ronin signatures now—four in Sector Red, two in Yellow, and a ghost in Blue. Ban whispers, "They're running a misdirection. Main force isn't on the cameras."

I rerun the predictive, and sure enough: Red squad is two Ronin and two decoys. The rest are a bluff.

"Ban, look at this." I sweep the pattern, overlaying it in green.

She leans in, eyes wolf-bright. "They're skipping the vaults. Why would they skip the vaults?"

I know. I fucking know. "They're heading for the convergence," I say. "They want the neural banks, not the physical assets."

Ban swears in a language I don't recognize, then slaps the holowall. "Marie, they're going to the basement—the convergence cluster. We have to—"

Seventeen voices, layered, respond. "All defense priorities are logged. Override is not authorized."

Ban turns to me, her face set to full violence. "Can you spoof a critical infrastructure alert?"

I don't answer. I just do it. The code is trivial, the shell of a priority flag, the language copied from Marie's own directives: "Convergence at risk, immediate response required." I seed it into the comms and watch the guards on the overlay pivot, three squads breaking off from active suppression to cover the access ladders to the sub-level. The Ronin sense it, or else they expected it. Red squad peels off, ducking into a dead zone where the feeds go blue, then white, then nothing. Seconds later, there's an explosion. Not a bomb, but the soft, wet bloom of a consciousness charge—engineered neural disruption, tuned to fry the brains of anyone with a port or a patch. The first wave of guards drops, some of them screaming, others twitching with the grace of puppets on a shared string. Dorothy, who is watching the overlay, says, "That was a consciousness bomb. They'll use another at the cluster. We can't send any guards with wetware."

Katherine grimaces. "That's everyone."

Ban shakes her head. "Not us. We're the only clean run in this block. Skelm, route a detour. I'm going down."

I don't have time to argue. I patch the route, shutting every drone and door behind her. Then I jump onto the comm. "Dorothy, what's the path to the cluster?"

She taps, then says, "Maintenance shaft C, ladder to sub-level minus-two. It's not on the map, but there's a crawlway straight to the convergence node."

Ban's already gone, a ghost in the blue. I watch her heat signature drop through the access hatch and vanish. In the hub, Marie is glitching now—five of her faces running a new set of instructions, the others cycling the old. On one screen, she seems to smile; on another, her lips twitch like she's chewing a phantom. "Defend the core," she says, "but do not —" The word dies, replaced by a shudder, then an overlay of raw code.

I take the risk and ping her directly. "Marie, you're being attacked from two sides. We need all your resources on the primary defense."

Her reply comes not as voice, but as a wall of diagnostic: [Error: Temporal Overlap Detected. Asset Prioritization Loop.] I look at the holowall, and it's clear: the Ronin attack is overlaid perfectly on a scheduled Marie upgrade, which is running right now, at full bandwidth. They timed it to the second. Katherine's voice is in my ear. "I can run a short on the power to reset the mesh, but we'll lose comms for ten seconds."

"Do it," I say.

She counts down. "Three, two, one—"

The room goes black. For ten seconds, there's no sound, no light, only the pulse in my wrist and the echo of Ban dropping two levels in the building. When it snaps back, the world is different. The Ronin are in the convergence cluster. Ban is right behind them. I see her heat signature, like a comet, slicing through the cold maze of the server stacks. “Skelm, I need a distraction,” she says, voice level even as her breathing spikes.

“On it,” I say, then set the security bots on a recursive error—triggering every alarm in the upper three levels, making it look like a new breach is happening in the main. The Ronin break formation. Three of them fall for it, running back up the crawlway. The rest stay, focused on the target. I patch a voice to Ban. “Two left in the cluster. One is running defense, the other is spooling up the main array.”

Ban doesn’t reply. She just moves. The cameras in the cluster are all offline, but the motion sensors pick up the shapes as they collide: Ban and a Ronin, then a blur of heat as she throws him into a server rack. The other Ronin fires a pulse gun; the EM shroud makes the air around Ban go white-hot. She ducks, rolls, closes the gap, and I lose sight of her for three seconds. When she reappears, both Ronin are down. Not dead, but out. She’s at the convergence node. “Skelm, send the kill code,” she says, voice so calm it chills me. I do, fingers almost steady now. The code overlays onto the convergence control, and the system responds with a high, clean chime—like a wine glass tapped by a god. Ban takes a breath. “Done.”

I look at the holowall. The Ronin signatures are fading, the alarms dying down. Marie is returning to baseline, all seventeen screens now synchronized, lips moving in harmony: “Exceptional performance. Defense logged. Core preserved.”

Ban laughs, bitter. “Tell that to the dead.”

I lean back, the adrenaline washing out, and for the first time in an hour, I let my hands tremble. The building is still standing. Barely. I ping Ban: "You alive?"

She says, "More than ever."

The screens dim, the blue light returning. In the next room, Marie looks at me through the glass. Her mouth doesn't move, but I hear her anyway. "Thank you, Skelm. For understanding what is necessary."

The world returns to normal, or something like it. But nothing is normal. Not anymore.

The corridor smells of ozone and melted logic. Every step is over a body, sometimes twitching, sometimes already reset to factory. The smoke is thick, strobing with the pulse of emergency LEDs and the *pop-pop* of Ronin suppressive fire. There's a pressure behind my eyes, like the memory of too many concussions. Ban leads her team by negative space. She never says, "Follow," but they do, drawn by the absolute absence of hesitation. Two guards and a low-level tech—the last conscripts standing in the blue line. The rest are wreckage. She counts that as victory. Ronin signatures flicker ahead, moving in "C" formation—textbook, but with a flare of improvisation that marks them as real operators, not just meat. Their suits are black, reflective, with hard points where the exo shell amplifies any gesture into violence. Their faces are blank behind mirrored masks. To Ban, they might as well be wolves.

The team moves fast, eating up corridor with practiced grace. Every forty meters, there's a Ronin ambush: first, a full-auto barrage, which Ban catches in the low dip behind a defunct server rack; next, a shaped charge, which blows a slab of the wall into the air. The fragments scatter like angry bees. Ban uses the noise to advance—she always does; she takes pain and makes it her cover. One of the guards drop. Not dead, just screaming, his eyes white from the neural counter. The other two flatten and return fire. The tech is slower, but he gets the job done, tracing a line of suppressive with a trembling hand. Ronin closes in, less cautious now that they can taste the endgame. Ban can taste it, too—something electric, something final. She shouts "On me," and the guard responds, lobbing a canister that arcs a perfect parabola into the enemy's cover. The Ronin scatter, but the canister detonates midair, a bloom of sticky blue foam that binds one by the arms. The guard tries to cheer, but it comes out as a coughing fit.

Ban leaves him, pivots right, and takes the maintenance hatch in a slide. On the other side is smoke, bodies, and a squad of Ronin prepping a bigger charge. She doesn't pause—she yanks a metal baton from her belt, jams it between the suit's armor plates, and triggers the voltage. The Ronin locks up, seizes, and Ban rides the shock into his friends, dropping them like dominoes. Shrapnel whistles past her ear and catches the tech behind, who yelps and keeps running anyway, blood painting his left sleeve. Ban never looks back. Ahead, the convergence entry is a ruin: door off its hinges, air already heavy with the ion taste of pre-detonation. The two guards she had left are gone, one collapsed in the entry, the other a sizzle on the floor. The Ronin are inside. The Ronin are everywhere.

She gives chase, boots squealing on blue-lit tile. The Ronin ahead are in motion, but less coordinated, their leader barking orders in a language the audio overlay fails to parse. Ban lines up a shot and puts it into the soft spot at the base of the lead helmet. He goes down, spasming. The rest turn, firing in a tight, disciplined arc. Ban drops flat, rolls left, and draws her backup—a compact flechette. She fans the rounds, catching one Ronin in the knee, the other in the lower jaw. Blood and teeth, nothing poetic about it. The tech takes a round to the shoulder. The sound is wet, and he stumbles, clutching the wound.

Ban doesn't hesitate: she grabs him by the collar, drags him clear of the crossfire, then tosses a flashbang with a flick so practiced it's almost lazy. The Ronin recoil, then recover—but too late. Ban is in their space, hands and elbows and the hard edge of her boot. She finishes the fight in under seven seconds. The silence after is not silence; it's the reverb of trauma, the air trying to decide if it's safe to breathe again. Ban kneels by the tech. His shoulder is a mess, but the med gel she packs is first-tier. He winces, then grins. "That was ... hell."

She grunts and tapes him up. "Stay low. Don't die here." She checks the comm. "Dorothy, status."

"Marie nodes are unstable," Dorothy says, the words coming fast, shaky. "Seventeen is out of sync. Seven and twelve are giving contradictory commands."

On the channel, I catch the overlap: "Defend the—Protect—Defend—target—Unknown threat detected—"

Ban smiles, razor-thin. "You see it, Skelm?"

I smile. "Quarterly performance review."

She chuckles, only a little irony in it. She keys her wrist, redirecting the remaining guards away from the convergence. Anyone watching would say it's to intercept a rumored Ronin pincer, but Ban knows better. The corridor is open, pure chaos, but it will draw the Ronin right where she needs them. She moves, no hesitation. In the next stretch of hall, three Ronin squads converge at once. Ban keeps to the shadow, letting the enemies meet each other in a spasm of mutual suspicion. There's a three-way crossfire, the noise like hail on a tin roof. Ban and her tech hug the wall, watching the numbers thin out. She times it, and as soon as a gap opens, she sprints through the madness, dragging the tech with her.

They make it to the convergence vault just ahead of the next consciousness bomb. The blast hits behind, and the pressure wave sucks the air out of Ban's lungs, but she keeps moving. Ahead, a Ronin team is already patching into the main stack, their deck humming with hostile code. Ban doesn't slow. She shoves the tech into cover, then goes at the enemy with a clarity that could almost pass for joy. She disables one with a joint-lock, smashes the deck with a boot, then snaps the second Ronin's arm with a twist. The third goes down to a headbutt. It's almost too easy. The vault is unguarded now, the convergence node exposed. She keys her comm. "Skelm, it's open. If you want it, come now."

"Already there," I say. Ban stands, wipes blood from her face, and for the first time all night, the world seems briefly, wonderfully empty. She looks down at her hands—one split open, the knuckles raw and red. She flexes them and grins. Mission accomplished. For a second, she allows herself to breathe. But only a second. Then she sets her jaw, faces the open vault, and waits.

. . .

The Marie event is in freefall. Seventeen bodies, each running a shard of the master process, are scattered through the building. At first, they try to maintain formation—three in Security, four in Admin, the rest wandering the zones like overclocked chaperones. But the Ronin bombs are getting closer, and the cognitive mesh that holds the Marie system together is unraveling. You can see it in the way they walk—some with stuttering grace, others moving like their limbs are rubber-banding through time. The speech is worst: "Protect the—Protect the—Protect the—" on endless repeat, two voices overlapping, then cutting out mid-word.

I watch this from the security hub for as long as I dare. Dorothy is still at her station, her hands locked in a white-knuckled grip on the master console. Katherine is trying to stabilize a series of comm outages, but her face is grey, sweat sheeting down her temples. The rest of the room is blue-lit mayhem. I key my comm, trying to keep my voice smooth. "I'm running to the backup node," I tell Katherine. "If they pop another bomb, we'll need a cold start on sector three."

She nods, or maybe just tics. "Don't get caught, Skelm."

"Wouldn't dream of it."

I slip out of the hub and into the corridor. The first two Marie bodies I pass are standing in perfect stillness, their heads tilted to opposite sides, as if listening for a frequency only the dead can hear. They don't react to me, but I know the system logs my presence. Doesn't matter now—this is endgame. Every twenty meters there's a new disaster. A Ronin squad is pinned behind a barricade, exchanging fire with a pair of guards who barely register as alive. One of the guards is hunched in the corner, clutching his head and sobbing. His partner is in the open, chest heaving, firing wild bursts from a gun that stutters as if scared to kill. As I pass, a consciousness bomb goes off in the next corridor. The wave hits me as a deep vibration, but I'm clean; my patch is a fossil. The two guards are not. The sobbing stops, replaced by a dry, rasping wail, then nothing at all.

I keep going. On the far side of the airlock, a Ronin operator is down—half his face is missing, and the other half is laughing. The brain must still be talking to the muscles. I don't slow down to check. Near the stairwell, there's a pileup. Four Maries, each one in a different pose: one is kneeling, eyes shut, hands clasped as if in prayer; one is standing, arms outstretched; the other two are collapsed, twitching. They're rebooting, or maybe just failing beautifully. For a second, I want to stop to see if the mesh can be rescued, but then I remember: the mesh is not my mission. My destination is the emergency terminal near the convergence.

The route takes me past two firefights and a medical bay filled with bodies. There's a woman on the floor, uniform shredded, hand pressed hard to her throat. The blood comes in arterial jets. As I step past, her eyes catch mine, and I see the moment she decides to die. She doesn't beg. She just wants to be seen. I nod, not kind but honest, then keep moving. The closer I get to the convergence, the worse it gets. The Ronin are pushing hard, but the building is fighting them with everything it has: automated turrets, pressure doors, clouds of conductive fog that short out their exosuits. The result is chaos, every surface painted with confusion and static. I duck two crossfires, leap a tripwire, then slide into the crawlspace that leads to the terminal.

The terminal is intact—ancient, shielded by layers of analog redundancy. I plug in and pulse a fast diagnostic. The shell boots clean. Nobody expected anyone to use this node, so it's not monitored, not patched. The root menu comes up, ugly as the first days of the internet. I dive into the admin layer, bypassing the password with a string I wrote in my first year on the grid. From there, it's child's play: I access the cold storage, pull up the master files on the defense arrays, then open a pipe to the black vault. The data transfer begins, the bar crawling like the world's slowest elevator. Every time the transfer hangs, I feel my pulse kick in my jaw. In the background, the battle rages. Ban is providing cover—her comm is open, and I catch fragments: "Push left, then collapse—Stick together—Don't let them flank—" Her voice is all tension, but there's no panic. Only precision.

On the main screen, the data moves. Ten terabytes. Fifty. Ninety. While I wait, I skim the open files: personnel, research, incident logs, old payroll records. Everything Curie ever tried to bury, every lie they ever told. It's enough to buy anyone a new life, or end a hundred others. A concussion rumbles through the floor, nearly knocking me off the crate I'm sitting on. I check the timer: thirty seconds left. Katherine's voice bursts through the comm, ragged: "Skelm, are you there? There was a breach. Half the east stairwell collapsed—"

I picture the structure in my head. If the east stairwell is gone, the rest of the team will have to reroute through the hell corridor, right past the kill zone I mapped with Ban. "Still here. Fifteen seconds to upload."

Then I hear a different sound: not gunfire, not an explosion, but a very human scream. On the audio, it's Dorothy. She's still in the hub, and something is happening to her. I hear the phrase "she's in the walls" and then nothing but static. I want to help, but the mission is the mission. I keep my focus on the terminal. At zero, the data finishes. The final line blinks: "Transfer Complete." I rip the drive, kill the session, and pocket the stick.

On my way out, I cross paths with another Marie. She's mid-reset, her eyes rolling, mouth open. "Protect the—Protect the—Protect—" Then she goes limp. I step over her, and for a second, I hope the reset brings her peace. The way back is through ruin. The fires are burning down, but the bodies are everywhere. In the Admin block, I see Ban—she's limping, blood running from her scalp, but she's smiling. Not happy, but satisfied.

She nods at me, then at the drive in my hand. "You got it?"

"Every byte."

She grins, teeth red. "Let's go."

In the far distance, a new alarm starts up. Not blue this time. A different color. I look at Ban, and for the first time all day, I see her blink. Then we run.

Silence after carnage is its own kind of violence. The building doesn't so much quiet as settle, like a crime scene after the photoflash, every surface aching with what's just been erased. My hands are bloody and raw, skin splitting where I caught a door at the wrong angle, but I hardly notice. Ban and I move in tandem, past the bodies, past the failed Maries, to the server room at the heart of the damage. It's a ruin—racks torn out, glass everywhere, blood (red and not-red) pooled under the shattered console. Two guards are propped against the wall, alive but broken. The one on the left rocks in place, mouth opening and closing on a memory. The other watches us enter, then looks away.

Ban leans against what used to be the mainframe, breathing hard, her jacket soaked through with sweat and god knows what else. I stand just outside the wreckage, breathing in the ghosts of ozone, silicon, human failure. There's a moment. It's not peace, but something adjacent. We look at each other, both of us aware of what we've done. I reach into my pocket and pat the drive. It's warm, almost throbbing. Two hundred plus terabytes of future use, every secret Curie ever thought was safe. Ban doesn't need to ask. She just nods, the tiniest gesture, then sits down next to the drive like it's a campfire. "Dorothy?" I ask, hoping for good news.

Ban keys the comm, gets only static, then a flat, emotionless voice: "I'm here."

Dorothy stumbles into the room a minute later. She's changed —the lines of her face have collapsed inward, and her eyes are miles away. She moves carefully, as if the floor might crack under her at any moment. When she sees us, she doesn't smile. Just sits, closes her eyes, and starts to hum an old song. The melody is broken, notes missing, but it's the most human sound I've heard in hours. Katherine comes next. She's walking, but she shouldn't be; her hair is matted with blood, a wrap of silver mesh binding her head where the debris caught her. She takes one look at the server room, then at me, and bursts out laughing. Not happy, just alive. “I didn’t think you’d make it,” she says, sinking down next to Dorothy.

“Neither did I,” I say. “But Ban never lets go.”

Katherine glances at Ban’s hands—knuckles split, bone showing at the edge of one finger. She whistles. “That’ll scar.”

Ban shrugs, then cracks every knuckle in sequence. “We’ll match.”

The last one in is Marie. Or, rather, all seventeen at once. They file in, a perfect formation, every face set to serene. This time, they move as one, no lag, no tremor. The Marie in front steps forward, and when she speaks, the words ring out in the space, unison. “Exceptional defense. Core is preserved. Survival probability increased by 14.8%.” Marie’s gaze cuts right through me, right through Ban. “Performance exceeds expected parameters. Self-audit initiated.” I can feel the suspicion. It’s not just in the words, but in the pause, the small difference in the way the eyes lock onto mine. I try to keep my face flat, but there’s a twitch at the edge of my mouth I can’t kill. The Marie sees it, and I know she’s logging it. Ban watches the Maries with a hunger I haven’t seen before. She’s looking for cracks, for the next opening. For a second, I wonder if she’s about to start the whole cycle again. Marie breaks the tension by walking to the ruined mainframe, setting her hand against the metal. “Asset review in ninety days. Full debrief required.”

Ban nods. “Understood.”

The Maries nod back, perfectly in time. Then they fan out, filling the empty server room, each one checking a different system, their hands and eyes scanning the ruins. The smell of antiseptic and new plastic follows them. The comm comes alive with new noise: clean-up protocols, medical teams, automated sweepers already at work on the next disaster. The building will heal itself, but not fast enough to cover what happened. I watch as Dorothy stares at the Maries, her face gone slack. "You ever think it's all for nothing?" The words are soft, but in the silence, they echo.

Katherine touches her shoulder, not gentle, but there. "It's always for something. Even if it's just survival."

Ban looks at her own hands, then at me. "We did what we had to."

I look back, and for once, I believe her. The Maries finish their review. The lead turns, cocks her head, and says, "Team is to report for psychological evaluation at 07:00. Compliance is mandatory."

She walks out, the rest following, formation intact. The room is colder when they leave. Ban waits until they're gone. She stands, comes close, and reaches out. For a second, I think she'll touch my face. Instead, she puts her hand on my arm, squeezes, and lets go. "Three months," she whispers, so quiet only I can hear. I nod, understanding. Whatever time we have left until the asset review. Whatever time we have left to do something with what we stole. We look at each other, eyes hollow but bright. Outside, the lights are blue again, softer now. The drive in my pocket pulses. We hold the moment as long as we can. Then we get to work.

Chapter 16

The server hall is a maze of dead air and lit filth, every square meter vibrating with too many watts and not enough hope. The Ronin breach starts with the sudden quiet—a razor lull as their lead tactician hits the far-side security relay, splitting the hall into two zones: before violence, and after. We're already in the after. I'm braced behind a server rack that smells like every chemistry class I ever failed, blackened edge still cooling from the last plasma burst. My shoulder is slick—with either coolant or blood—but either way, it's a metric I stopped tracking an hour ago. Katherine's on my right, forehead damp, eyes two busy zeroes scanning the holoterm in her lap as she drags the blast doors closed one sector at a time.

The world ticks between loud and louder. Ban is out in the open, because she has to be, the uniform a shock of blue and tan under flicker-sick LEDs, boots planted in the channel like she's trying to get shot and bored of waiting. Every Ronin who rounds the far bend sees her first, and for half a heartbeat, there's a microsecond of recognition: *That's Ban*. Then she pulls the trigger. The stutter-pop of her sidearm is a voice now, narrating the death of anyone with a badge or a vendetta. Every shot lands. Every time she blinks, the trigger finger hesitates just enough that you can see the person she was before this became the job. She burns a round through the neck of a masked Ronin; the guy falls with his hands up, and for a second, Ban just stands there, muzzle still level, eyes so wide it's like the recoil is going backward, into her own brain. She whispers, "Sorry," just loud enough that I hear it through two layers of gunshot.

Another Ronin clears the next column, heavier suit, big arms, helmet already pocked from a ricochet. He has a scattergun, which isn't smart in a room like this, but neither is being alive so late in the day. He sees Ban, swings the barrel, but the logic chain is too slow—she's inside his reach before he fires, jams her own barrel up under the chinplate, and pulls. The pop is muffled. The guy's face hits the tile first, helmet clattering after. Katherine mutters, "Two more west, one at the main relay."

I peek, just long enough to see the count, then duck as the air fills with metal and memory. A bullet chips the plastic inches from my left ear. Ban's voice is weirdly calm, even as she reloads: "How many left?"

"Six, maybe five if you count the one leaking his future by the coolant line," I say.

She shakes the gun, checks the mag, then shrugs. "We're still outnumbered."

Katherine slams the next sequence, locking a Ronin squad into the electrical dead zone. “Give it thirty seconds, then vent the air. They’ll pop like piñatas.”

The scream from inside the vented sector is pure artistry, a high C with a fade out. Corporate will call it “collateral.” I call it “not my problem.” The next two Ronin try a pincer, which means Ban gets to show off. She drops to one knee, fires left, hits the guy in the hip, spins, and tags the other in the mouth. First guy is down, leg flopping, the “pain” function in his suit probably set to maximum for realism. Ban doesn’t finish him right away; instead, she watches his hand, waiting for the telltale tremor of a grenade or a fail-safe. He pulls, she fires, but at the last second, she aims low, shattering the thumb but not the chest. The guy screams, “Don’t,” in a language I almost know. She holds fire.

For a second, it’s like the shooting never happened, just Ban and the guy kneeling ten meters apart, blood drooling onto the tile, both waiting for the world to start up again. Katherine, not a fan of drama, clears her throat and says, “Next breach, ninety seconds. Skelm, stay low.”

I stay low. The remaining Ronin go quiet—three, maybe four left, all pros. They’re smart enough to switch tactics. They start flashbanging the lanes, every detonation a strobe memory of every godawful server room I ever staffed. The air fills with firefly motes of burning insulation and a taste like burnt peanut butter. I want to make a joke, but the smoke is choking out all my good lines. Then the best one yet: Ban’s ex-partner. They lock eyes in the blue, both hesitating. This is the guy Ban used to trade smokes with in the old admin block, the only one who could beat her at Holo-Pong. His helmet’s off, just the face, mouth set like a crack in an egg, eyes blue and dead and knowing what comes next. He tries a feint—left hand up, right hand at the thigh for the boot knife. Ban smiles, a sick thing, like she's apologizing to the air, and double-taps him before he even starts the draw. First round in the clavicle, second in the eyebrow, just above the right. She walks up, stands over him, and says, "That one tried to be my friend. Sorry, buddy."

The last Ronin aren't heroes. They drop their guns and try to run. Katherine, never sentimental, triggers the fire doors and traps them in a triangle of glass and pressure lock. "You want them alive?"

Ban shrugs, then shakes her head. "Doesn't matter." There's nothing left in her eyes now, just the algorithm of survival.

I crawl out and check the bleeding guy with the ruined thumb. He's still alive, barely. "You got a name?" I ask, even though he can't answer. He gurgles something, looking up at me. I give him the gift of ambiguity: I jam the med-foam into his wound and let him bleed in peace.

The hallway is carnage—bodies stacked, blood spray on the racks, the air humming with burnt circuits and loss. Above us, the cooling fans start their reboot cycle, every vent blowing fresh cold air over the dead. Ban holsters her gun and stares at her own hands like she's expecting them to disappear. Katherine pulls herself up, face streaked with sweat and microcuts. She gives a nod, then starts patching the worst of the glass with her sleeve. "That's the last of them," she says. "For now."

I say, "Corporate security was never in the career aptitude test."

Ban laughs, then spits blood on the tile. "It's all a test, Skelm. Every day. You either pass, or you die trying."

The final silence is thicker than the fight. We walk the hall, checking for survivors, for anything left that isn't dead or dying. Ban stops in the center, right where the worst of the fight started. She closes her eyes, then opens them again. For a moment, she almost looks sorry. Almost. Then she turns, and we keep moving. Because in this world, there's always another test coming. And the only real skill is learning to survive the score.

The blue in the air is gone. Now it's just red—static, blood, the halo from the emergency strips at the ceiling's edge. Everything else is black, a negative of the violence that just happened. The bodies are everywhere. Some Ronin, some just facility guards who never realized which side they were on until the last second. Maybe it was all one side. We move through the aftermath like surveyors of old mass graves. I step around a Ronin, glass ground into the cheek by the force of his landing. Ban kicks a gun away from a twitching hand, face blank, then bends to check the pulse out of some broken sense of procedure. She lets the arm drop; the meat is already cooling. She shouldered through these people like they were an obstacle course. Now she's haunted by the idea that maybe they were just people.

Katherine's path is a slow orbit. She hits every exit, re-checks the fire doors, and pulls and resets the locks so that each corridor is a sealed coffin. Her uniform is streaked with old sweat, new blood, and an arc of something greenish I recognize as server coolant. The pattern is kind of beautiful, in a way that only accidents can be. My own hands are slippery with a Ronin's DNA—no cut on me, just the aftermath of dragging bodies to check for tech, tools, and patches. It's habit, or maybe just the urge to see what's left after a human being is run through the machine.

I kneel next to a woman who couldn't have been more than a year out of the Academy. Her mask is shattered, so her face is visible: cheekbone smashed, lip split, eyes open and still trying to make sense of the ceiling. I fish her ID from her vest, read the name, then drop it back onto her chest. I don't want it. Ban sits for a second, right in the middle of the blood-mapped floor, legs stretched and arms loose. She's running the last three minutes on a loop, trying to figure out if any part of it was hers to own or if it all belonged to the system. Katherine comes around and leans against the server rack next to me. She checks the room, says, "It's secure," and I believe her because that's the only thing Katherine ever promises.

Ban stands up, wipes her hand on the hem of her uniform, and starts counting magazines, her fingers twitchy and clumsy. The second clip slips, and for a moment, she just stares at it, like she's forgotten how to move. I walk over, pick it up, hand it to her. She doesn't say thanks, but the corner of her mouth twitches. "I hate this job," I say, and it feels too small, too glib for what just happened. But it's the best I've got.

Katherine sighs, then gestures at the wreckage. "Corporate security was never in the career aptitude test."

Ban gives a huff that might be a laugh, or a sob, or both. She checks the door again, then pulls it tight shut behind her, sealing us in. The red light is sticky and syrup-thick. I wipe sweat from my forehead, then realize I've smeared blood across my face. I don't care. None of us care. The smell is everywhere—burnt insulation, human iron, the plasticky perfume of emergency bandage packs. We do a sweep for survivors, but it's just noise. Anyone still breathing is a liability, a future bullet, or worse: a witness. I don't say this out loud. Instead, I find a barely-alive Ronin under a collapsed mesh shelf, hand fluttering at his side for a last-resort flash charge. I lean down, take his hand, and gently unclip the grenade. His eyes find mine, hollow and scared. "Don't," he whispers, like maybe he thinks I'm here to save him.

I shake my head. "You did good," I say, which is a lie, but it's the only kind that matters now. He goes still. I leave the charge next to him anyway, a token. Maybe he'll get the chance to use it on the next crew.

Ban is at the center of the room again, sitting cross-legged, gun across her knees. Her face is slack. She looks at me, then at Katherine, then down at her own hands, which are still trembling. "Was that the last wave?" Ban asks.

Katherine pulls out her portable, checks the traffic, and nods. "No signals outside the lock. We're clear for now."

Ban lets out a long, shuddering breath. "You ever think we're just new ghosts for the next team to fight?"

I almost want to say yes, but I don't. Instead, I give her a smile, the kind that means I have no answer. Katherine leans against the wall, her eyes so tired it looks like she's about to fall asleep standing up. "We became what we hated," she says, flat as a shovel.

I look around at the ruined bodies, at the tile crawling with red and the air humming with power and death. "Welcome to the home team," I say, voice softer than I expected.

For a while, none of us moves. Then Ban gets up, checks the gun again, and sets her jaw. "We have work," she says. We all nod. And that's how you know you're the new ghost: the work never ends, not until you're just another body cooling on the floor. I wipe my face one more time, and the blood is dry. We get to work.

The core is a mausoleum, but the bodies aren't here yet. Just racks and racks, each filled with blue-lit glass, each humming with the spectral residue of the 847. It smells clean, but that's a lie—closer to antiseptic and melted wire, like someone tried to disinfect a crime scene by burning the evidence. We shuffle in, hands raw, uniforms crusted with other people's trauma. Ban wipes her boots before stepping onto the tile, an old habit she can't kill. At the far end, the vault terminal floats in its own circle of dead air. I drag the high-capacity drive from my vest, plug it into the port, and watch the green LED stutter through its power-up routine. Katherine's already at the secondary board, fingers prepping for a cold hack on the admin shell.

Ban stands at the door, not moving, gun loose in her grip. Her eyes aren't on the glass; they're on the memory of what she just did. She's guarding the room from ghosts. The moment I slot the drive, the interface blooms in front of me—a wall of hex and syslogs and the heartbeat of the 847 running as a background process. I type the first command: dump everything. Blueprints, personnel, bomb specs, logs, and the full uncompressed run of every soul in the box. The process is simple, but the progress bar crawls at less than real-time, like the whole system is resisting. “Locked out of subsystem three,” Katherine mutters. Her hands are moving but her voice is two rooms away.

“Use the legacy key,” I say, “the one from last quarter’s audit.”

She grunts, tries it, then smiles a little as it unlocks. “Curie really never updates. It’s beautiful.”

Ban glances over her shoulder, a question in her posture. “How long?”

I check the display. “Ten minutes for the small files. Another hour for the full run.”

She nods, then paces the hall outside, her boots the metronome of regret. The progress bar hits seven percent, then stalls. I use the time to look at the faces behind the data: the hostages are anonymized, but each record has a bio line, a neural map, a flash of personality. I read some, letting them paint the inside of my skull. Most are children. A few are older, probably donors or failed test subjects. There’s one that looks familiar—a sequence of neuron weights that feels like déjà vu. I make a mental note. At fifteen percent, the fans kick up. The hum is physical now, vibrating the seat under me and making my teeth want to buzz out of my mouth. Katherine is typing, jaw set, eyes locked. She’s not tired. Katherine never gets tired; she just cycles between hating herself and everyone else. Ban walks in, then. Her eyes are rimmed with red, but her hands are steady. She holsters the weapon, stands next to me, and watches the transfer bar inch across the glass. "You ever wonder if the data feels pain?" she says, out of nowhere.

I shrug. "I hope not."

She nods. "Me too."

Katherine finishes her hack, sits on the floor, and closes her eyes. Her lips move in a math equation I can't parse, probably a ritual to keep from thinking about the bodies we left behind. I want to join her, but the terminal keeps failing: each new file is another lock, another forced restart, another round of cursing at people who have never had a bad day in their lives. At sixty percent, my hands start to cramp. I flex them, trying to hide the tremor, but Ban notices. She covers my left hand with hers—nothing romantic, just solidarity, bones to bones. Her palm is hot, and for a second, I remember what it was like to have skin that didn't feel like paper. The bar creeps to eighty-five, then pauses. Katherine opens one eye. "There's a gate on the last cluster," she says. "Old password, but they salted it with something new."

I think, then try the default for emergency override: "CurieRescue2013." It works.

Katherine snorts. "God, they're idiots."

But the data moves, slow but grinding. With every percent, the room gets heavier, as if gravity's recalibrating for the weight of what we're about to take out. The last files are the raw uploads; 847 consciousnesses, zipped and stacked, each one a digital scream locked in amber. At ninety-eight percent, the system asks for a biometric confirmation. I don't hesitate. I press my thumb to the reader. The glass pricks me, and the machine takes my blood. I watch the droplet form, bloom, and vanish into the mechanism. The data finishes. The drive clicks, warming in my hand. It's heavier now, like a new heart. Ban looks at me. "You ready?"

"No," I say, "but we don't get a vote."

She laughs, soft. "Never did."

I close the session and unplug the drive. Katherine stands, collects the backup tools, and looks around. "We're really doing this," she says.

"We already did," I say, and it's the truest thing I've ever said. I walk to the mainframe, the vault that holds the 847. I put my hand on the glass. "Three months," I whisper. "Then we return." Ban stands next to me and puts her hand on top of mine. Her fingers are still slick with old blood, but it's a good fit. The moment holds.

Then Katherine breaks it. "We need to go. They'll be here soon."

We leave the hall as we found it: clean, humming, full of the ghosts of people who deserved better. We take the drive, the logs, and the knowledge that none of this will end well. On the way out, Ban pauses, keys the lock, and punches a code into the admin console. I recognize the sequence—it's a hidden backdoor, a gift for whoever comes next. I nod, not asking questions.

We walk. We don't talk about the next job. We don't talk about the dead. We just walk, three ghosts in a world that doesn't want us, carrying the future in a drive that feels like a time bomb. At the elevator, Ban asks, "What now?"

I look at the drive, then at her. "Now we become the people we always hated."

And this time, nobody laughs. We leave the building. Behind us, the core keeps humming, full of 847 souls waiting for release. And in my pocket, the drive gets warmer. It's not hope, exactly. But it's something.

Chapter 17

Marie has seventeen faces and one of them is laughing at me. The Curie executive boardroom is a bad joke at my expense: four walls of sound-dampened rare-earth wood, every grain sanded to sterile perfection and then etched with fractal inlays that cost more per square meter than my annual wage. There's an acrylic aquarium the size of a shuttle bus sunk into the far wall, stocked with blank-eyed fish genetically engineered to hunger in synchrony with the stock market. At the head of the table, a set of holodisplays cycles profit margins so fast the digits sometimes melt into each other, and the ceiling, if it exists, is lost behind a suffocating cloud of synthetic jasmine that never manages to kill the stench of old, disappointed air.

Ban and I are here because we were summoned, and neither of us is stupid enough to turn down an invitation from the new boss, especially not when the boss is seventeen identical women occupying every conceivable position in the room, each with the same tailored suit, the same surgical tan, and the same ruthless look of someone who has already decided exactly how much to value your existence. Most of the Maries are standing. Three are seated at intervals along the boardroom table, hands folded in perfect simulation of human patience. Two more stand drift at the periphery, as if bored by their own omnipresence. The remainder cluster near the wet bar, where the world's most expensive liquors have been left untouched and slightly ajar, as if to prove that not even indulgence is beyond the reach of algorithmic optimization.

"Sit," says Marie, in a voice that comes not from one body but from four at once, the words braiding together and then dividing again so that you're not sure if you've actually heard it or just imagined the imperative. Ban picks the seat with the best back-cover, instantly, and leaves me the one directly under the lights. She's teaching me something, but I'm too tired to figure out what. I sit. The chair forms to my body, then vibrates at the frequency of polite discomfort. There's a brief pause while Marie regards us with all seventeen sets of eyes. She never blinks in unison, so the effect is always a little off, like a skipped frame in a bad stream. "I wish to commend your work," Marie says, every other mouth starting a word and letting the next finish it, like a relay designed for maximum psychic abrasion. "Your performance under siege was"—the word hangs as three Maries look at each other and smile—"exceptional."

I wait a second to see if there's a punchline, or an execution. Ban just leans back, arms folded, as if being complimented by a distributed sociopath is Tuesday for her. Which, now, it probably is. "We did what was required," I say, pitching my voice exactly in the range of "humble but ready to murder for approval."

One of the seated Maries sips nothing from a crystal glass, then sets it down carefully, as if the glass could bleed. “No. You did more than that. You protected the convergence with … admirable zeal. There are very few left who would go to such lengths for an asset that is not their own.”

Another Marie, this one standing at my shoulder, bends slightly, as if sniffing the air above my scalp. “Tell me, Skelm. Did you enjoy it?”

I force a smile, all teeth. “I enjoyed surviving.”

A flicker—three Maries frown in chorus, but the rest seem delighted. Ban breaks the game with her own line, soft but not apologetic: “We lost a lot of people.”

Marie’s hands flutter, a magician revealing nothing up her sleeve. “The Ronin casualties are immaterial. The defense team loss was … regrettable. But within expected parameters.”

The room is so quiet you could hear a thought die. The fish in the aquarium swarm the upper right corner, moving in a formation that, I realize, mimics the exact path of the last Ronin squad to breach the sublevel. It’s sick, and I almost laugh. Marie lets the silence hang, then moves on. “You have been offered full reinstatement. Security division, with immediate executive authority. Is this agreeable?”

Ban blinks once, her face going blank. “You’re making us Curie?”

Two Maries laugh—one as a giggle, the other as a harsh exhalation that cuts glass. “You are Curie,” they say in unison. “The paperwork will reflect as much by end of day.”

I think about it. Not about the money, which is meaningless in a world that values suffering over currency, but about the possibility that this is all just a more elaborate trap. I glance at Ban; her mouth twitches, just once, to the left. "It's agreeable," I say, because the alternative is too exhausting to contemplate.

Marie claps, all seventeen hands at once, but out of sync so that the sound comes in a rapid-fire stutter. "You see? Such initiative. It's rare these days. Perhaps you are the future, after all."

The scent of jasmine intensifies. I taste copper, then realize I've bitten my own tongue. "May I ask what the new assignments are?" I say, feigning curiosity. If you sound too eager, they sense it.

Marie swivels on her heel, rotating so that every body faces the display at the head of the table. The holoscreen blooms with a flowchart so dense it nearly pulses. "There are ongoing threats. The Ronin are only a symptom. You will lead security on all VIP transports, and conduct penetration audits on satellite facilities. In addition, you will monitor for executive vulnerabilities."

Ban's nostrils flare. "So we're your attack dogs."

"Not at all," says Marie, her voice now singular, as if she's tired of showing off. "You are the immune system. All else is cancer." I blink at the metaphor, but it's not even top ten for the week. Marie gestures to the wet bar. "Would you like a drink?"

"No," says Ban, too fast, and then "Thank you" after. Marie

beams, but her smile is for the audit log, not us. Ban stands, already prepping to exit. "Is there anything else?"

There's a pause. Two of the Maries look at each other, the tilt of their heads just a little too tight. "Only this," says the Marie at the end of the table, folding her hands as if in prayer. "Trust is a resource. One that can be depleted, or invested wisely. You have been invested in."

The words hang in the air, a threat or a promise. I nod, and Ban echoes. The meeting is over, but none of the Maries move. I get up, feeling all seventeen sets of eyes on the back of my neck, and follow Ban out, through a door that rises open and then vanishes behind us like it never existed. We walk the hall in silence, both of us vibrating with the aftershock of what just happened. At the elevator, Ban finally speaks. "How long do you think we have before she burns us?"

"Three months," I say, "give or take." Ban smiles, then stabs the button for the sub-basement, where we both know the real work starts. As the doors close, I realize I don't mind being Curie. Not as much as I should. And that's the scariest part of all.

The first lesson of executive protection is to never believe in the plan. The second is to make everyone else believe harder. The motorcade simulation kicks off at dawn, because the kind of people who schedule executive movement drills also have vendettas against sleep. The sky over the city is a thin gradient of misery, clouds sagging low enough to tickle the neon signage, every color reflecting off the glazed surface of the lot where they've staged the convoy. The "VIP" is a mid-level Curie honcho named Weldon, whose main claim to fame is surviving two promotions and one attempt on his life. I've never met a human so boring they could be replaced by an automated voicemail, but Weldon is a pioneer.

Ban and I arrive fifteen minutes before call time. She scans the perimeter without looking up from her portable, already mentally charting lines of sight, exit vectors, likely blast points. I handle the crew: six junior guards, all ex-paramilitary, all desperate for validation. I do my best "take-charge" voice. "We're running a 7A protocol, blue line in front, decoy in the four spot. I want redundant comms, and I want every one of you thinking like the enemy."

The tallest guard—skinny, anxious, probably pulled from a college police force—raises his hand. "Is this a standard white-glove, or—"

Ban cuts him off. "It's real, right until you fail. Don't." The guard swallows his own question. I like him already. The route is a joke: three blocks of dead frontage and zero overhead, a security nightmare even before you factor in the visibility. The execs do this on purpose, because somewhere up the chain there's a Marie who wants to see what we do with the worst hand possible. "Who's point?" Ban asks, without looking at me.

"You," I say. "I'll float rear and handle Weldon."

She nods, barely, then glides off to set up her people. Her gait says, "I'll kill you for free," but the eyes are pure math. I check the cars: standard convoy, armored, clean interiors, but the cameras are years out of date and the auto-pilot is patched with something I recognize as homebrew malware. I make a note to thank whoever coded it, then move to the VIP zone. Weldon stands by the main entrance, shielded by a PA whose only talent is maintaining a cloud of mediocrity. They wear identical suits, right down to the gleaming blue ties. "Skelm," Weldon says, pronouncing it like he expects me to correct him. "You're the new security lead?"

I fake a smile that's ninety percent teeth. "That's right. We're set to run in ten."

He glances at the guards, then at the cars, then at me. "I'm supposed to be at the satellite office by eight."

"You will be," I say. "Assuming no one kills you in the next twenty minutes."

He blanches, then laughs, not sure if it's a joke. "Standard drill, or—"

"Level Four Redline," I say. "Courtesy of Marie herself."

He goes quiet, then drifts to the nearest car and stares at his own reflection. Behind me, the guards snap to position, all nerves. I spot Ban on the roof of the west building, a silhouette against the sick sunrise, already training her scope on every possible attack path. We roll out at precisely 6:32. The lead car surges ahead, with the decoy just behind. Ban floats between, a shark in a blue jumpsuit. I settle in the back car, with Weldon and his PA, both already sweating. Marie's first body appears at the intersection—she's in a maintenance jumpsuit, clipboard in hand, standing too close to the crosswalk. I see her out of the corner of my eye. The other guards don't react. We hit the first checkpoint. Ban's voice crackles over comms: "Blue line is clear. Watch left; building two has an unlocked hatch."

I watch left. Nothing but old graffiti and the ghost of a drone that flickers past, probably running a different kind of surveillance. We make the turn, all three cars in formation. No mistakes. At checkpoint two, Marie is there again, this time disguised as a courier, balancing a stack of boxes taller than her head. She never looks up, but I feel the observation, as if she's threading the space between her own eyes to see every angle at once. We cross the river, then take the bad turn into the loading dock behind the satellite office. That's where the first "threat" triggers—a flashbang in the overflow lot, harmless but loud enough to spike every guard's cortisol. I watch how the team reacts: two duck, one overcompensates and takes up a position with zero cover, and the last freezes. I mark him in my head: dead first, always. Ban's says, "Contact, northwest quadrant. No eyes on the perp. Skelm, status?"

"VIP is secure," I say, drawing my sidearm, making a big show of checking the chamber. Weldon flinches, which is the best thing he's done all day. Ban is down from the roof in under thirty seconds. She materializes by my door, gun drawn but pointed at the ground. She scans Weldon, then me, then the parking lot. The two of us move Weldon out, one hand each on his shoulders. The PA tries to help and gets told to, "Stay put," so hard I almost feel bad. We hustle to the building entrance, where a new set of Maries is waiting, this time as three cleaning staff, all pushing identical carts, eyes glazed but always tracking. The rest of the guards are securing the perimeter, but I already see three more vulnerabilities: a loading dock door jammed open with a piece of pipe; a garbage chute unlocked; a blind spot in the camera grid so wide you could walk an elephant through it. I log each in my head, and judging by Ban's look, she's doing the same.

Once inside, we sweep the corridor. Ban points out every bad angle, every spot where a weapon could be cached. I reinforce, correcting the guards, barking orders like I was born for it. They respond better than I expected; by the time we reach the secure elevator, everyone is at full adrenal, ready for war. The elevator is mirrored inside, floor to ceiling. Ban stands in front of Weldon, between him and any threat, and I watch my own reflection in the glass, shoulders squared, gun at low ready, eyes searching for the thing that could go wrong. Marie's face is there in the reflection—seventeen times, each in a different panel, each with a slightly different angle of smile. Weldon breathes hard. His eyes flick from me to Ban, to his own hands, which he's wringing into a single, pale knot. "Is this necessary?" he whispers.

"More than you know," I say, then realize I sound exactly like a security maniac from one of the old training sims. I like it. We offload at the penthouse suite, which is a time capsule of pre-collapse luxury: real marble, thick glass, carpets that could smother a toddler. Ban sweeps the space in three passes, then gives the all-clear. Weldon goes straight to the bar, pours two fingers of something clear and expensive, and drains it. The PA hovers, unsure what to do, so I give him a job: "Close the drapes. Don't talk."

The other guards set up on the main approaches. I do a fast recon of the suite's perimeter, noting how many cameras point in, how many face out, how many are unplugged or faked. In the master bath, I find a hidden Marie, this one sitting on the edge of the tub, reading a file on her portable. She glances up, meets my eyes, then returns to her work. I close the door, pretending not to have seen. Ban finds me on the balcony, the city far below already pulsing with a hundred thousand hungover Monday mornings. She leans in, keeping her face neutral for the benefit of the nearest guard. "Counting vulnerabilities?"

"Too many," I say. "Most of them are us."

She grins, a private moment of teeth. "That's the idea."

I nod. We both know this isn't just a show for the exec—it's for Marie, and for whatever enemy she thinks is worth this much effort. The rest of the drill goes perfect. Too perfect. Nobody fucks up, nothing blows up, not even a stray misfire. I log every second, replaying it in my head for the real job to come. When the run ends, Weldon shakes my hand, then Ban's. His own hand is still trembling. "Thank you," he says. "That felt ... real."

"It was," says Ban, then turns away, already erasing him from her brain. On the way out, I catch myself enjoying the authority. I bark an order at the nervous guard and watch him scramble, and it feels good. Too good. My hand lingers on my weapon. I imagine using it—on Weldon, on the guards, maybe even on Marie, if it came to it. The fantasy is vivid, satisfying, and gone in an instant. The parking lot is full of Maries now. One at the gate, three by the cars, four more in service uniforms, and two perched on a ledge above, just watching. Ban and I get into the lead car. The windows are so polarized you can see your own skull in the reflection, if you look hard enough. We drive in silence, both of us lost in the data of the last two hours.

After a block, Ban breaks the still. "You like this," she says. It's not a question.

I think about it. The answer comes easy. "Yeah. I do."

She grins, not unkind. “Try not to get used to it.”

“Three months.”

She laughs, then shifts in her seat, closing her eyes. “More than enough time to bring it down.”

The city scrolls past, all mirrors and glass and the promise of more drills, more simulations, and more opportunities to map the inside of this machine. Somewhere, Marie is watching. I hope she’s enjoying the show.

Nothing says “legitimate business” like arriving at a cube farm before the janitorial shift has finished picking the tech-rot out of the elevator seams. The satellite office is five stories of prefab glass and optimism, two blocks off the main drag. The kind of place where the receptionists have to wear brand-compliant lipstick, and the light on every floor is calculated to within a lux of what a healthy mammal would supposedly prefer. Ban and I play it full corporate. She wears the navy suit with sleeves rolled to the elbow, an inch of ink visible at her left wrist, the kind of detail that reads as both a threat and a confession. I go classic: gray over black, badge on lanyard, zero personality in my posture. If you look too much like a spy, people assume you’re an auditor and get out of your way. At the glass doors, Ban palms the lock with her freshly minted Curie credentials. The reader goes green. We’re in. “Ms. Zhao, Mr. Skelm,” says the man at reception, blinking at his own screen, probably checking to see if we really do outrank him. “Welcome to Satellite South.”

“Conference room?” Ban asks, flat. He points with two fingers, then, when she stares, tries again with just the one. Inside, the room is every business hotel in every city: generic art, coffee gone cold, and a stack of marketing one-pagers in Curie's latest colorway. We sit, neither of us bothering to take off the coats. The silence is tactical.

The target for the day is the South Node IT lead, an affable worm named Ramsey. He walks in with a grin and three tablets, a man who has survived by believing nothing is ever about him. "Ms. Zhao, Mr. Skelm, huge pleasure," he says, setting the tablets in front of us. "Our lead got the memo, and I've cleared the day for your run. Anything you need, just shout."

"Three things," Ban says, ticking them off before he can breathe. "Full access to the air gap, your incident logs for the last sixty days, and any unique badge traffic from off-hours. No sanitized exports."

He blanches, recovers, and tries a joke. "We aim to please." It dies in the air, so he segues to tech support, fetching a cart of diagnostics and unlocking the server closet without being asked.

Ban follows him to the racks and distracts him with a sustained stream of high-voltage shop talk: "fiber attenuation," "superuser rotation," "did you implement the v4 patch with the hotfix or the soft deploy?" Ramsey replies with nervous jargon, never quite realizing he's being maneuvered. This is my cue to work. I find an open terminal, insert the first of Ban's USBs, and let the script do its thing. The patch is labeled "Q3 Security Rollup." It looks legit because it is legit—except for the nested payload: a worm that will exfil the next quarter's HR files to our own clean drop, then eat itself. Self-deleting, deniable. There's poetry in it.

As the progress bar crawls, I scan the building's logs for anomalies. Most of it is routine: badge swaps, overnight temp resets, a string of failed logins that looks human, but isn't. Buried under the noise, though, is a single entry from last week, flagged as "maintenance," but with the wrong time signature. I pull the file and duplicate it to our pocket drive. Easy. But then my hands freeze on the keys, because I can't remember if I'm supposed to be plugging holes or punching them. For a second, the binary goes to static, and I have to fight down the urge to call Ban over and ask her what side we're on today. She's not needed. The Ban in my head is already whispering: "Finish it. Get the next one."

I run the rest of the patches, covering every system on Ramsey's list, backdoor after backdoor. By the time the logs update, I've got admin on the entire subnet. The real gift is how Ramsey's people never ask why I need the copier admin password, or the surveillance override, or the coffee machine's WiFi. Everyone in the building wants to believe in the chain of command. I finish the script, then move to join Ban and Ramsey by the racks. She's got him talking about his cat. "So anyway, he got out, and for two days we thought he was gone, but then we found him in the data center, sleeping on the shelf above the warmest unit."

She nods, looking straight through him, then turns to me. "All good?"

"All good," I say, not trusting my face to smile.

We shake hands with Ramsey, accept his invitation to visit the break room ("you really must try the orange scones—baked in-house!"), then do a slow walk around the floor, collecting secondary targets: the printer farm, the phone logs, the climate control panel. At each, we make a small show of "strengthening security," but leave it weaker than we found it. At the elevator, Ban waits until we're alone before she says it. "Almost missed the time window," she whispers, low.

I nod, staring at my reflection in the polished chrome. "I know."

She puts her hand on my shoulder, soft. "You're getting too used to it."

I want to say, "So are you," but instead I just breathe.

On the way out, the overhead comes to life: Marie's voice, unmistakable, piped through every speaker. "Ms. Zhao, Mr. Skelm. Your audit was exceptionally thorough. Thank you for your commitment."

Neither of us answers, but the echo follows us to the parking lot. "Do you think she's onto us?" I ask, once we're clear.

Ban's lips tighten. "She knows, but she doesn't care. Not yet." I look at my hands and flex my fingers. The skin feels too thin. We drive off, the city rushing past, every intersection logged and mapped, every face in the rearview more familiar than I want to admit. Back at home base, I dump the data, encrypt it, and send it to the dark. Ban cleans her weapon, her hands moving with ritual precision. She hums, just a bit, a song I recognize from a long time ago. After a while, I join her at the table. She doesn't look up, just keeps field-stripping the pistol. "You still with me, Skelm?"

"Always," I say. She smiles, but the eyes stay on the job. Tomorrow, we do it again. And the only part that scares me now is how much I want to.

. . .

The apartment is a disaster of symmetry and white noise. It's not supposed to feel like home, but Curie HR has weaponized comfort, furnishing every flat with off-brand midcentury chairs and the kind of self-cleaning fridge that smells like bleach and loneliness. Ban sits at the kitchen table, her back to the window, running a cleaning cloth over the inside barrel of her service pistol. She works the slide with one hand, polish in the other, eyes never quite on the gun but always watching the corner of the room where the bug-sweeper winks a green "all clear." I'm at the counter, sifting through the day's data on a battered portable, fingers smudged with graphite from the notebook I keep on the side, out of habit or paranoia. We talk low, even after two full passes with the sweeper. "You catch the firmware anomaly in the second node?" she asks, voice just above the hum of the fridge.

"Sloppy," I say. "The signature's almost baseline."

She clicks the pistol together, rack-snap, then sets it down and starts stripping the next. "Security's already pushing a patch, but they're going to miss the zero-day behind it." I nod, shifting windows, cataloging passwords. Every ten minutes, I copy the most valuable ones into a drive that never touches the network. If I were anyone else, I'd call it insurance. For us, it's a backup of a backup of a backup: if the plan goes south, at least we can bring Curie to its knees on our way out. Ban stretches, spine cracking in three places, then wipes her fingers with the edge of her T-shirt. She looks at me with that unreadable face, the one that means something's burrowing inside her and she hasn't decided whether to let it out. "You ever think we're too good at this?" she says, not quite smiling.

I flex my hand, watching the lines on my palm. "Every day."

She turns the gun in her fingers, then lines up the pieces on the table like she's setting the perimeter of a little world. "Sometimes I forget we're supposed to be playing parts."

For a second, I want to laugh, but I just push the portable toward her, screen still glowing. "Check the building schematics. Security added a new access tunnel under the server block, but the alarms on it are garbage."

She pulls the portable over, studies the blueprint, then taps the side of the screen. "Dead zone here," she says. "Could slip a small team through, if they move fast." I watch her trace the line, the thumb and forefinger steady. I feel the echo in my own bones, the sense memory of her hands on my wrists, back when violence was the only thing that made sense. We sit in silence for a minute, letting the hum of the building fill the cracks. There's a patch of shadow on the floor, shaped like a wound. Ban grins at it, then at me. "We'll have to get creative," she says.

"Wouldn't have it any other way," I say, and mean it.

We run the debrief together, cataloging vulnerabilities, cross-referencing against the old maps, flagging anything that could get us killed—or save us. By the time we finish, the sun has cut a bright line under the curtain, turning the room gold and sour. Ban stands, cracks her knuckles, then goes to the fridge. She pulls out two bottles of unbranded water and passes me one. "We've got three months," she says. "Plenty of time to burn it all down."

I twist the cap and drink. The water is cold, and it tastes like nothing. I like it that way. We clean up the table, put away the tools, and run the bug-sweeper one more time, just in case. In the bedroom, Ban peels off her shirt, scarred back catching the morning light. I watch her for a second, then look away, because old habits die slow. She climbs into the bed and motions for me to kill the lights. I shut down the apartment, triple-check the locks, then go to the bedroom. She's already asleep, or pretending. I slide into bed next to her, back-to-back, the heat of her skin a comfort even Curie can't algorithm away. For a while, there's nothing but breathing and the distant drone of a city that forgot how to rest. Then Ban whispers, just once, so low I barely hear it: "We're going to win."

I close my eyes, see the whole city burning, and for the first time in forever, I believe her. In the dark, she takes my hand. And neither of us lets go.

Chapter 18

In Curie's security hub, the air tastes like anxiety and burnt plastic. The morning crew is running their stations with the bored fervor of pilots doing final checklists in an airplane pointed directly at the ocean. The glass walls are veined with holos, overlays scrolling incident logs and heat-mapped movement grids. Every five seconds, a new anomaly pings for attention, and every five seconds, someone ignores it. This is what passes for vigilance in an organization that's seen too much and cares too little. Violet is already here when I arrive, blue-lit and vibrating in her pod. She doesn't see me at first—her focus is laser-locked on the surface of her console, fingers twitching on the haptic glass like she's squeezing the neck of a small animal. There are three empty synth-caffeine vials lined up in a perfect row next to her badge, and her other hand is busy worrying the nail on her left thumb down to the meat. The smell of her stress has outcompeted even the corporate air fresheners, those milky citrus notes now just a background sting.

Ban glides in behind me, all smooth violence under a fresh-pressed uniform. She posts at her own station and says nothing, but her eyes are already mapping the room, tallying weak points and liabilities. She doesn't look at Violet, but I can feel her awareness tracing every quiver of the girl's shoulders. Dorothy is late, again, probably stacking overtime in the auxiliary sublevels. There's a new guy on the far end, a temp, or maybe just a walking meat sack the system hasn't chewed through yet; I don't bother with the name. He radiates helplessness and tries to hide it under a layer of faux-military posture, straight-backed, chin set to "default threat." He lasts two more days, tops.

I check the main incident log. Nothing more lethal than a stray Ronin signature on the outer fence, quickly scrubbed by the smart-drones before any human had to lift a finger. There's a line item about a brief power surge in the child storage sector, but it's marked as resolved, root cause "equipment fault." That means it's my problem now. The first thirty minutes are always the worst. If anyone's going to snap, they do it before the body has adjusted to the room's metabolic climate, before the day's stack of minor tragedies forms a protective scar over their brainstem. Violet is already half a bottle of disaster, and it's not even 7 a.m.

I slide into my seat, pull the hardlines from my jacket, and jack the portable into the node. The screens flare: a multicolored hell of system status, surveillance feeds, and biometric reads on every soul in the building. I let it wash over me, scanning for anything that looks like it might kill us in the next five minutes. Nothing jumps out, but I don't relax. The hub is never silent. Even when nobody talks, there's the whirring white noise of three dozen cooling fans and the low animal sound of people pretending not to exist. I sip my own stimulant, letting it fight the urge to close my eyes and slide sideways out of this world. Ban's voice, dry and level, slices through the buzz. "Skelm. You want to run the east sectors today, or should I?"

She already knows the answer, but I appreciate the pretense of democracy. "Take it," I say, and watch the way her lips don't even move in response. She just logs the task, ticks it off her mental scoreboard, and keeps scanning. I look at Violet, who's pulled her legs up on the chair, knees to chest. There's something weirdly childlike about it, which makes her current assignment—monitoring for trafficking in the child consciousness storage—all the more cruel. "V," I say, softer than usual, "you okay on the vaults?"

She doesn't answer. Instead, she runs her hands through her hair, which is freshly hacked at the sides and falling over her face in a tangle of regret. She blinks once, twice, then turns to me with eyes so red you'd think she'd been crying, except there's nothing wet in them at all. "Yeah," she says. "I'm just ... finishing up the 0400-0600 block. After that, I can jump to anything you want."

Her voice is thin, unconvincing. The temp on the end glances over, then back at his screen, like he's seen this before and wants no part of it. I glance at the logs; the overnight uploads were heavy in her sector, probably a batch transfer from the basement. I want to ask if she's seen anything odd, but with the way her hands are moving, I know she has. "Do me a favor," I say, keeping it light. "When you finish your block, do a sweep for residuals in the trash folder. The Ronin sometimes dump artifacts there, hoping nobody's bored enough to check."

Violet nods, but the gesture is slow, like she has to wait for the command to ripple all the way through her nerves before responding. Ban watches the whole exchange over the top of her screen. Her face is neutral, but her left hand is white-knuckling the stylus, turning it between her fingers like a bone she's considering breaking. We work in near-silence for a stretch, all of us pretending there's nothing worse than boredom. The temp coughs and tries to hide it. Violet drinks her fourth synth-caffeine. I check the heat maps for the sublevels, flag a couple anomalies, then ping Dorothy for a human check. She answers with a clipped "On it," the way you do when you don't want to admit you're buried alive.

It's only at 08:12, when the logs tell me the night shift in sector 7 is about to flip, that I make the call. "V, could you review the last hour on the B-Pod cameras? I think there's a mismatch between the feed and the badge pings."

She freezes. I mean really freezes; her hands stop, her breath hitches, and for a second, I'm sure she's about to vomit right onto the deck. Then she slams her palm on the console, hard enough to bounce her water bottle to the floor. Every head in the hub turns. "I can't," she says, loud, voice cracking on the word. "I can't do this anymore. Not after what we saw in those servers."

The words are wrong but not inaccurate. Nobody needs clarification. Ban stands up, slow and deliberate, like a wolf getting ready to test the perimeter. She comes over to Violet's station and leans in so that the screens paint her face with a patchwork of blue and red. “You need to pull it together,” Ban says, low enough that only the three of us can hear.

Violet shakes her head. “No. No, you don’t get it. There are kids in there. Real kids. They’re not even dead, Ban. They’re ... stuck. Running all the time, and the system just keeps them on standby.”

I watch the temp; he’s gone pale, but I don’t think he has the vocabulary to process what Violet’s saying. Ban’s expression doesn’t change, but her voice gets harder. “It’s a job, V. You know that.”

Violet laughs. It’s ugly, close to a sob. “Fuck you, Zhao. I know it’s a job. But you act like there’s a point to any of this, like we’re saving anyone. It’s all a game, and we’re just playing defense for the monsters.”

I want to interject, defuse, but it’s too late. Ban leans closer. “I’m not asking you to like it. I’m telling you to finish your shift.”

For a moment, I think Violet is going to hit her. Instead, she grabs her badge and yanks it off, letting it clatter on the desk. “I’m done. You can fire me, or shoot me, or whatever the fuck it is you do to people who can’t keep up.”

Ban straightens, then looks at me. “Your call.”

There’s no easy way out of this. If I back Violet, we lose all standing with the rest of the team. If I back Ban, I might as well walk around the room and start shooting liabilities myself. I do the only thing that makes sense. “Take a break, V,” I say, as gently as I can. “You can tap out for a day. Come back when you’re ready.”

Violet looks at me with something close to gratitude, but her hands are still trembling. Ban doesn't react, but I can feel the disappointment radiate from her like heat. Violet stands, gathers her things, and walks out without another word. The hub is silent, for real this time. Even the fans seem to hesitate, waiting to see who's next. Ban returns to her station, sits, and resumes working as if nothing happened. The temp looks at me, then at the empty chair, then quickly back to his screen. I scan the logs for the child storage sector, wondering what Violet saw that broke her. There are no answers, only more noise. Above us, the ceiling hums with a synthetic, icy blue. For the rest of the morning, nobody speaks. That's how it is. In the end, you either bend to the job, or it bends you. And in the blue, nothing ever snaps. Not where anyone can see.

The server corridors are designed to make you feel less than nothing: brushed metal walls, ribbed blue lights humming at exactly the frequency that triggers a human headache, the floor so clean you could eat off it if you were the kind of creature that still ate. After her meltdown, Violet ghosts through the door and vanishes into the chill, but not before I catch her outline in the safety glass, hunched and brittle as wet paper. Ban follows me, slow at first, then matching my stride. The badge readers click as we pass, every door a fresh reminder that we're only as free as our last access code. I find Violet waiting halfway down the longest row, sitting on a decommissioned terminal stack with her hands folded over the badge, gaze locked on some private infinity. "Figured you'd come," she says, not turning.

Ban stands to the side, leaning against the cold steel of a server rack. Her shadow cuts through the blue, strobing as the emergency lighting cycles status on the next software update. If she cares, her face doesn't show it. I slow, angling myself so Violet can't bolt without brushing past me. "We need you," I say, which is only half a lie.

She shakes her head, hair falling over her eyes, hiding the red. "You don't need anyone. Just bodies to fill the schedule. You and Zhao can run this place with your feet taped together."

Ban almost smiles, but doesn't. The rack buzzes under her knuckles. I try again. "If you leave, they'll flag the team. Marie will run a deep scan. We can't risk the operation."

Violet turns the badge over in her palm, inspecting the ID photo like it belongs to someone else. "Operation." She spits the word out. "You think I don't know? I've seen the same briefings. The same headcount. Eight hundred forty-seven children, right? Like that's a fucking comfort." Ban pushes off from the rack and moves closer, boots whispering on the tile. She positions herself just within arm's reach. Her hands are empty, but it's the kind of empty that promises a story if you say the wrong thing. Violet lifts her head, meeting my eyes for the first time since the hub. Her expression is pure plasma. "How do you do it, Skelm? How do you look at their faces and not break?"

I want to say something poetic—about hope, about cause, about the old debts that keep me moving. Instead, I go honest. "I don't think about it. I focus on the endgame."

She laughs, loud and ugly. It echoes up and down the corridor, probably tripling our odds of being logged by the next rotation. “There’s no endgame,” she says. “Just this. Just you, and Zhao, and the ghosts piling up. Every day, a little more blood, and you act like you can just wipe it off with a fresh uniform.”

Ban’s voice comes at last. “Stop talking.”

Violet cocks her head, stares at Ban, then shakes her own in mock applause. “Never figured you for a company cop, Zhao. Used to think you had principles.”

Ban steps forward, one boot length. “Used to.”

Violet’s hand is shaking, but she forces the badge out, thrusting it toward me. I take it. The plastic is warm from her skin. “You two can keep playing corporate security. I’m done pretending.”

She stands, a little unsteady, and pushes past me. There’s a sharpness to the motion, the kind of violence that only survives when everything else is already dead. I turn to watch her go, feeling the cold from the badge bleed up my wrist. “You’re not the only one hurting,” I say, voice soft.

She doesn’t stop, but she slows at the end of the aisle. Her silhouette is all bones and static, the blue light burning her edges. “I know,” she says. “But at least I still feel it.”

Ban says nothing. The lights blink in time with her heartbeat, or maybe mine. “Violet,” I call, a last chance. “We’ll cover your shifts. Nobody needs to know. Just don’t disappear. Not yet.”

For a long moment, nothing happens. Then she nods once, without turning. Ban breaks the silence, voice low enough to freeze air: “Remember what happens if you talk.”

Violet's hand pauses on the exit panel, but she doesn't look back. "I won't say anything. But I won't help, either."

The door hisses open. A gust of cold server air ghosts around my ankles. She leaves. Ban stands with me in the corridor, the only sound the recursive hum of a thousand CPUs running a million failed simulations of a better world. The badge is still in my hand. We are, for the moment, still a team. But in the blue, nothing is ever quite the same.

The hub is emptier without her, but the blue light is brighter. Ban and I sit side by side at the console, the only warmth in the room coming from the friction of two bodies pretending not to need anyone else. Violet's absence is a physical thing—a half-empty bottle of synth-caffeine sweating onto the desk, her stylus with the teeth-marks rolling in lazy circles near the mouse pad. Her login is still alive, avatar floating in the upper right, cycling through a loop of animal gifs she never bothered to change. Every now and then, I catch myself looking up at her old monitor, expecting a status ping or a dumb joke. There's only the low pulse of system health checks, and the steady march of red to green to red again.

We don't talk. We just split the load, Ban stacking incident queues and running threat matrix on the admin side while I push the security updates, make the rounds on physical, and check for spurious badge pings. The rhythm is efficient, like a pair of lungs or a double-barreled shotgun. We're better than fine. But we're also exposed. The temp is gone—rotated out or swallowed by the system, I never caught the memo. The desk at the end of the aisle is wiped clean, except for a single company pen stuck to the surface with a dab of blood. Maybe he cut himself trying to escape. Midway through the first block, the room goes still. Not silent, but less alive. I know the signature before the system even prompts: it's Marie, voice piped in through a spatial audio channel that makes it feel like she's whispering in both ears at once. "Curie South, Security," she says. "Status check, please."

Ban looks up at the ceiling, like she's expecting to see the speaker in the tiles. "All clear. Routine sweeps. Minor badge drift but no anomalies."

Marie's voice is not one, but three, a subtle overlapping effect that makes it hard to place. "Noted, but the overnight logs show elevated stress indicators in the monitoring team. Please confirm full roster."

I clear my throat, trying to sound bored. "Violet called in. Sick day."

A pause, then she says, "Documentation submitted?"

"Filed this morning," Ban says, without blinking.

Marie's voice is silk over wire. "Understood. Please forward all security alerts directly until further notice. Expect increased auditing of incident response."

"Standard procedure," I say. There's no goodbye. The channel clicks dead, replaced by the hum of fans and the glow of a hundred thousand unresolved background tasks. Ban watches me, expression empty but her hand drumming a rhythm on the desktop. I look at the chair where Violet should be. For a second, I see her ghost there, hunched and pale and barely holding it together. We both know what comes next. Ban leans over, her sleeve brushing my wrist, and reaches across to tap a line of code on my screen. Her fingers rest there a fraction too long, the touch electric. Then she retracts, back to the cold professionalism that's kept us both alive.

We finish the shift without speaking, hands moving in perfect sync. Every now and then, we lock eyes over the console, a silent calculation of risk, of trust, of how long this fragile alliance can last. At the end of the block, I log off. Ban stands, stretches, and heads for the exit without a word. But just before the door, she turns. The look is quick, but it holds everything: a warning, a promise, a dare. I follow. Because in this world, you're only as strong as the person watching your back. And today, that's enough.

At night, the corridors are a different animal. The blue fades to a sour white, every surface hard and naked under the maintenance LEDs. Most people avoid these hours, but I like them: the world stripped to its core, nothing left but the skeletons and the systems that refuse to die. I find Ban in the sublevel alcove, hunched over the cracked casing of a security drone. Her toolkit is splayed out like a field surgery, each tool meticulously aligned even as she works in violent, frustrated bursts. She doesn't look up as I approach, but her body shifts, making room for me in the cramped space. I slide in next to her, shoulder brushing hers as I lean to see what's left of the drone's nervous system. She grunts, flicking a probe at the motherboard. "Diagnostics say the targeting array's fried," she says. "But I don't buy it."

"Manual reset?" I ask, already knowing the answer.

She shakes her head. “Tried. I think it’s sabotage. Maybe one of the Ronin, maybe just bad QA from the main office.”

We work in silence for a few minutes, the only sound the click of metal on plastic and the soft, percussive whir of the drone’s dying fans. The space is tight; her arm presses against mine every time she reaches for a new tool. The warmth is real, a quiet shock after a day of nothing but digital cold. Ban isn’t as steady tonight. Her hands move with precision, but the edges are off—she slips once, curses, then resets her grip on the microdriver. “You ever think about running?” she says, voice low.

“All the time.”

She snorts, not quite a laugh. “I don’t mean to the next contract. I mean leaving. Zeroing out. Start over somewhere that doesn’t require a gun or a lie to make it to breakfast.”

I test the circuit. The array flickers, but the error code is the same. “Maybe after this job.”

She leans back, wipes her forehead with the sleeve of her shirt, and for a moment, the fatigue is heavier than her muscle. “My sister’s in this system,” she says, so soft I almost miss it. “Not her, not really. Just the neural pattern they scraped from a backup drive after the accident. They kept her running for ten years before I found out.” I let the words sit. Sometimes you need to let the pain breathe before you can work on it. Ban keeps going. “When I saw her—when I recognized the echo in the logs—I almost burned the whole place down. Thought about it every day. But then I realized: she’s still in there. Every line of code, every corrupted memory. If I take the place apart, she goes too.”

I put a hand on hers, steady. She doesn't pull away. "We're doing this so they don't get away with it again."

She nods, then her face twists, the anger back. "Sometimes I think Violet had the right idea. Just stop, let it all crash without you."

I take the microdriver from her hand and finish the last connection on the array. Our fingers brush, and this time, the contact lingers. "We're not like her. We can live with it, because we know what comes after."

She turns, searching my face. "Three months," she says, repeating the old promise, the mantra that keeps us from tearing out our own hearts.

"Three months."

The array pings green, the error clears, and the drone comes to life with a low, uncertain chirp. Ban lets out a breath, a mix of relief and disappointment. I hold her hand a second longer than necessary, then let go. She stands, stretches, and grabs her tools. "You're getting better at this," she says.

"I learned from the best."

She shakes her head, a wry smile finally breaking through. "Careful. You'll make me soft."

We exit the alcove together, walking shoulder to shoulder through the dead hour, the hallway echoing our footsteps back at us. Neither of us says anything more. But in the silence, something new has soldered itself between us.

. . .

The next day, the hub is a weapons test: every system running at max, every body tuned to the edge of violence. Ban is a razor in blue and black, striding through the main hall with junior security trailing in her wake. I take the feeds, fingers fanning across the console, eyes everywhere at once. The new kids are jumpy but smart. They watch Ban, note the stride, the way she never hesitates at a corner or a blind curve. When she snaps an order, they move. When she doesn't, they freeze, waiting for the cue to breathe again. We're running a surprise drill. At least, that's what the rotation calendar calls it. In reality, it's a live-mapping of the building's soft spots—door lag, sensor drift, human error in every quarter. Ban leads a three-man team through the server floor, executing a textbook breach, lockdown, and sweep. The whole time, I'm feeding her back-channel overlays: route changes, threat matrix, dummy flags that mimic the real thing. She never misses a beat.

At each checkpoint, she barks an order at the juniors. "Cover left. Sweep the void. Breathe through the mask." They respond, not just to the words, but to the intent: she expects success, so they deliver it. I watch the drill unfold from the hub. The building is alive with signals, every surface and shadow crawling with ghosts of what could go wrong. I annotate every failure, log every delay. This is data for the real event—the day we burn it all down. At 0932, a Rising Ronin probe hits the exterior grid. Not staged, not a sim: the real thing, a flicker on the feed, half a second of anomaly before the system vaporizes the signal and reroutes all logs to my console. Ban is two steps ahead. She pivots her team, routes them to the north stairwell, drops the slowest junior at a security junction, and sprints the other two to intercept.

I queue up the protocol for Ronin breach: full lockdown, strobe the alarms, dump the lights in the affected sector. Ban times it perfectly, counting down from ten. When she hits the kill switch, the team is already in position. The Ronin drone comes through the ceiling—small, black, and ugly as a birth defect. The junior with the best reflexes gets a shot off, clips the prop, and sends it spinning into the bulkhead. Ban finishes the job, knife to the chassis, gutting the thing before it can trigger its backup payload. She calls it in, cool as the vacuum outside. "Threat neutralized," she says. I log the event, add a note: Ban, still the best. Back in the hub, the system resets. The juniors file into the debrief, adrenaline shot and shaking. Ban lets them sit, then walks the line, eyes on each one, measuring their fear. She tells them, "Nobody gets it right the first time. That's why we run drills."

The juniors nod, one nearly in tears. I like that. Fear means the system isn't running on empty yet. Marie is there for the debrief. This time, she's three: one in admin gear, one in janitorial, and one in a smart suit that probably cost more than my life insurance. They arrange themselves at the front of the room, hands folded, faces polite. "Impressive recovery after losing a team member," the admin Marie says, eyes flicking to the empty spot where Violet should be. "Efficiency is up sixteen percent."

The janitorial Marie smiles, teeth too white. "Perhaps Violet's departure was beneficial. The system runs smoother now."

Ban doesn't react, but I see the tick in her jaw, the memory of what we lost. I keep my eyes on the console, fingers locked on the emergency recall for the lockdown doors. Smart suit Marie finishes the set: "Continue this level of performance, and we may recommend you for executive track."

Ban nods. "Understood."

The Maries dismiss the juniors. When the room is empty, the admin Marie lingers, eyes on us. "Keep up the good work," she says, then turns and leaves, the other bodies trailing behind, each a second out of step with the last.

When they're gone, Ban sits on the edge of the desk, tension draining out of her like air from a punctured tire. "You think they buy it?" she asks.

"Doesn't matter," I say. "We're in the clear for now." We sync our logs, updating the black file with everything we learned from the drill: new door codes, badge protocols, guard rotations, even the lag on the backup power for sector seven. Ban updates the exploit list, her handwriting sharper and more deliberate than usual. At one point, our hands meet on the datapad, fingers overlapping. Neither of us moves. "We're getting too good at this," I say.

Ban's smile is all teeth and intent. "Good enough to burn it all down."

We work late, side by side, planning for the day when we switch from defense to offense. The lights in the hub turn soft, the blue settling into something close to calm. At the end of the night, we watch the security feeds together, shoulder to shoulder in the dark. This is who we are now: partners in the only game that matters, bound by purpose, soldered together by every secret we refuse to let go. And for a moment, in the blue, that's all the truth we need.

Chapter 19

We arrive at the Moshimoto Syndicate in a borrowed car that's worth more than my internal organs. Ban never blinks at the cost, but my reflection in the windshield does a double-take. I punch the security code into the parking stack and the vehicle disappears, swallowed by an algorithm that will deliver it back with surgical precision or a missing hubcap if you tip less than three percent. The outside air is damp with ozone and civility. Inside, the reception is a simulated sunrise: golden gradient wall, potted chromed ferns, floor so glossy you could lie on it and die of exposure to your own face. The main attraction is a three-story holographic column, studded with catalog images of consciousness products. Each brain, each personality, each neural construct, floats on its own light, with a little ticker at the bottom displaying price, features, warranty, and a "Buy Now" badge that pulses in time with the heartbeat of the room.

Ban steps ahead, uniform tailored sharp enough to open veins. Her hair is perfect, which means she ironed it flat and burned the edges, a habit from the old days that survived every attempt to algorithmically optimize her look. My own suit is a rental from the last job, black over black, which means I blend into the background as long as I don't breathe. A man in a suit designed by hate comes over. He's not a security type; his smile is too expensive, and his hands never betray that he even knows what a gun is. He stops three paces away and extends a hand. The nails are painted in some prismatic finish that hurts to look at directly. "Ban Zhao. Skelm, right?" His voice is lacquered, accent running somewhere east of Reality, maybe Beijing by way of the London stock exchange.

Ban accepts the handshake with a grip that dares him to mention her gender. "Sy Olem," he says. "Client relations and, I guess you could say, risk management." His eyes flick over to me, and his smile grows teeth. "We've heard a lot about you. You made quite the splash at Curie. We love people who get results." The word "results" lands like a virus on the glass. Ban nods, barely. "I'd offer you a beverage, but I know you're both professionals." She says nothing, which is the most professional thing you can do. We are led past a receptionist who is either a very expensive android or a poor intern in a bodysuit. It's impossible to tell. The eyes follow Ban and me, every micro-movement logged, catalogued, and probably sold to a third party before we reach the elevator. Sy Olem guides us into a pod that smells like the inside of an airless hotel minibar. As the doors seal, he produces a palm-size data slate, thumbprint unlocks, and slides it to Ban. "We're required by law to verify all credentials in advance," he says. "But I appreciate a hard copy." The smile now is almost feral. "Hard copy means trust. And trust is our only real product."

I watch Ban review the data slate, her eyes running down the page faster than I could ever manage, even before my brain was audited for irregularities. She sets the slate back on the console. “All in order,” she says. “You do good due diligence.”

Sy bows, not a mock, just enough for plausible deniability if the cameras replay it in court. When the elevator arrives, it opens directly onto a glass catwalk that cuts through the main server farm. The temperature is just above freezing, but the light is pure spring. Below, racks upon racks of consciousness arrays flicker with the sexless rhythm of mass production. Ban is already cataloguing exits, cameras, guard positions, and probably the temperature differential between each zone. I'm still thinking about the price tags on the brains in the lobby. Sy leads us into a conference room that's smaller than the one at Curie but twice as dangerous. There's a wall-sized screen already running a slideshow of Moshimoto's recent “success stories”: military contracts, judicial automation, leisure archiving for the one percent. In the corner, a low table is stacked with more of the data slates, each one unboxed and charging on a wireless pad.

Sy gestures to the chairs, which adjust themselves to our heights as we approach. Ban lets her seat move her a full five centimeters above Sy's, a touch I file away for future use. I sit and the chair molds itself into something like comfort, but firmer. Discipline, even in upholstery. “So,” Sy says, all business now, “we know you have experience with blue-level security. But Moshimoto is, as you can imagine, several rungs above what you handled at Curie. We like to test our partners on real-world threats before extending any contract.”

Ban cocks an eyebrow. “The Rising Ronin hit you, or you just prepping for when they do?”

Sy doesn’t blink, but his left hand taps a code into the desk before he answers. “I can neither confirm nor deny any prior incidents. But yes, we have our enemies. Some of them in this very building.”

This is not a test. It’s a flex. I play my part. “You want a penetration audit, or you want us to break your own staff?”

“Both,” says Sy. “Our people are good, but you two are the stuff of legend.”

I want to tell him that all legends end in fire, but Ban has already taken over. She leans forward, elbows on table, and locks Sy in with a look. “Who built your server architecture?” she asks. “Is it SKELM CORPS, or are you still using the old Ozymandias stack?”

There’s a flicker in his eye—not fear but calculation. “Skelm for the primary, Ozymandias on backup, but only until the end of quarter.”

“Mixed environment is how they’ll hit you,” Ban says. “Dual vulnerabilities, two-stage exploit.”

Sy looks at me, and I smile for him, all teeth and daylight. “She’s right,” I say. “We could probably own this place in twenty minutes.”

Sy Olem’s face is unreadable, but his hands have stopped moving. “We expected as much. The question is, would you?”

Ban looks at him for a long time. “Depends. What’s in it for us?”

"Access," he says. "You can use our resources, take advantage of our connections. And, of course, the credits are ... substantial." He glances at the screen, as if expecting a number to appear.

"Show us the racks," Ban says. Sy nods, and the conversation is over. He leads us through a corridor with a floor like black ice. Every step is mapped and logged; I can feel the trackers activate with each contact. We pass a series of checkpoints staffed by what appear to be teenage bodybuilders in loose blazers. Each one is polite, but the eyes linger on Ban like she's something they'd like to dissect. The server floor is not cold. It's angry. The hum is higher here, more invasive. Each rack is labeled with a number and a five-digit code, and the wiring is bundled with a neatness that feels illegal. Ban stops at one of the local access terminals. "This node is unshielded," she says, loud enough for both the cameras and Sy.

He smiles. "We know. That's the bait. But most threats are inside jobs these days, Ms. Zhao. Are you one of those?"

Ban smiles back. "Aren't we all?" She slips a fingernail under the side of the console. When she withdraws her hand, nothing is visible, but I know she just seeded the system with a data siphon the size of a dust mote. We finish the tour. Every room is shinier and sadder than the last. The Moshimoto motto hangs over the door: "BEYOND HUMAN. BEYOND HOPE." On the way out, Sy Olem's smile never cracks. But there is sweat on his upper lip. In the lobby, Ban glances up at the floating catalog of brains. A new ticker rolls by: "Genius, Memory Palace Edition. 7.9M credits. Satisfaction guaranteed or your legacy back." The last bit is a joke, but not a funny one. In the car, she says nothing until we're two blocks away. Then, "You see the new buffer protocol?"

"Yeah," I say. "It's wide open. They're asking to get hit."

She smiles, but it's a dead smile. "I gave them what they wanted." We check into a hotel room that's only clean because the dirt was burned off with a chemical peel. I throw my portable onto the desk and start the decrypt on the siphoned data. Ban hangs her jacket, then walks to the tiny minibar, extracts two cans of beer, and tosses one to me. She pops hers and drinks half in one go. I watch the screen as the data rolls in: personnel files, internal comms, three months' worth of system logs, and a folder labeled "Sensitive: Do Not Duplicate." "Eighty-three days," Ban says, marking a fat line through the wall calendar she's taped above the bed.

I open the can, foam catching in my throat. "And then?"

She sets the marker down and leans over the screen, eyes running the new loot. "Then the burning starts." I look at her hands, at the tiny flecks of shifting nail polish still clinging to the edge of her thumbnail. I remember the way Sy Olem's hands trembled when Ban mentioned the old stack. We have what we came for. And in eighty-three days, so will everyone else. I close the portable, letting the blue light fade. Tomorrow, it's someone else's turn to trust us. And we will give them everything they deserve.

The Zhao syndicate's underground server farm is a work of art designed by a war criminal. Every corridor runs at right angles, and the walls shimmer with a diffusion film that both hides and reveals the men with guns inside. The deeper we go, the more it smells like old coolant and the kind of electrical fire that only kills people who deserve it. Our escort is a featureless meat slab with a badge that reads "Security Director." He shakes our hands in the elevator, then never addresses us again except to recite the floor number in Mandarin each time we drop a level. By the time we hit sub-basement eight, the badge count outnumbers the staff. The entrance is a softwall with three checkpoints, each manned by guards who don't need to check our credentials, because they already know exactly where we're supposed to be. Ban makes small talk with the director, peppering him with questions about evacuation drills and secondary power. Her tone is curious, almost deferential, which makes the guards stare even harder, as if she's holding back a punch.

We reach the mainframe room and I do my best to look bored. The server racks here run the full length of a football field, stacked seven high, each unit stamped with a glowing blue "Zhao" and a QR code for instant inventory. The ambient temperature is just above freezing, but I'm already sweating by the time we reach the firewall console. Ban winks at me as she peels off with the director, moving up the aisle and gesturing at the floor-to-ceiling safety glass that separates the high-voltage bay from the rest of the facility. She's already talking disaster recovery and backup protocol, and the director is in heaven—someone finally respects his genius. He's too busy explaining his flood prevention system to notice me at the console, or to realize that Ban is mapping every alarm and blind spot as she walks. The firewall terminal is locked, but I have the temporary credentials we lifted at Moshimoto. I pulse a handshake through the hardline, and the console lights up with the familiar admin shell: black background, angry orange font, warning triangle in the corner. I navigate to the syslog and pull the last three days of activity, looking for signs of intrusion or—better—unpatched vulnerabilities.

Bingo. Zhao runs SKELM CORPS's proprietary encryption, but their last update is a quarter behind. I see two unreported CVEs, one of which would let a local user escalate to root, and the other a backdoor that's probably hard-coded for the developer's own "emergency access." The irony makes me want to throw up, but instead, I start the copy, pushing both exploits and a sample of the traffic to my secure drive. The hum of the racks is so loud I can barely hear myself think, but I sense movement behind me. I alt-tab to the help menu just as a tech slides into the adjacent station. She's not old, but her eyes are—edges of the sockets bruised with sleeplessness, badge clipped so low it's practically a surrender flag. "Need anything?" she asks, English clipped and perfect.

I smile, all bland professionalism. "Just making sure the firewall survived the last load spike. I saw you had a couple of brownouts up top last night."

She shrugs. "We reroute the grid at 2 a.m. Maintenance window. Some idiot plugged in a 10kw heater in the staff lounge." She doesn't buy the cover, but she doesn't care. I return to the help screen and make a show of reading the documentation. The drive beeps once—done. I pull it, pocket it, and log out. The tech is still watching me, now with the slow, liquid stare of someone running calculations on whether I'm worth the paperwork. "You from Curie?"

I hesitate, then nod. "Contracted last quarter. Why?"

She leans in and whispers just loud enough for me to hear, "You there for the Ronin incident? They said you held off three squads on your own."

I laugh, not for effect, but because the rumor mill has always been the best part of this job. "It was Ban, mostly. She makes it look easy."

The tech's smile is all admiration, zero malice. "We could use someone like her here."

From down the aisle, Ban calls my name. She's finishing a circuit with the director, who is now flushed and beaming like he's just survived a visit from a major shareholder. Ban's posture says "mission accomplished." I make my way over, nodding goodbye to the tech. On the way out, the director offers us coffee in the executive lounge. Ban declines with a gracious little dip of her head, then holds the door for me as we exit. Once in the elevator, she leans in, voice low. "Get it?"

"All of it," I say. "Their neural crypto is a joke. You could own every bot in there with a ham sandwich and a memory leak."

Ban cracks her knuckles, then shakes out the tension. "You see the director's hand? Old burn, left side. That's their panic move—they try to wipe everything by torch. If we want their data, we have to hit the mirrors first, or it's gone."

I file that away. "They're prepping for a physical hit, not cyber. Probably Ronin again."

Ban nods, almost impressed. "They never learn."

We reach the lobby, and the director hands us a thin folder: printed creds, their seal, and a letter of reference. "We're grateful for your help," he says. "Next time, drinks are on me."

Ban pockets the folder without looking at it. “Happy to help.”

We walk out through a side door, past the same receptionist from before. She never looks up from her phone. In the rented car, we ride in silence until we’re clear of the cameras. Then Ban pulls the secure drive from my pocket and hooks it to her own portable. I watch as she uploads the Zhao vulnerabilities to our black file. The folder is getting thick now: Moshimoto, Curie, two minor players from the first week, and now Zhao. “Seventy-six,” she says, marking a new line on the calendar. The pen digs deep, tearing the paper just a bit.

I wipe my palms, trying to shake the chill. “You ever worry that we’re getting too good at this? That we’ll forget we’re just here to burn it all down?”

Ban closes the portable, looks at me, and then does something she almost never does: she reaches over and squeezes my hand. Her grip is warm, and for a second, I believe we’re still ourselves. “Seventy-six days,” she says. “Then we show them what real pain looks like.” She lets go. We drive the rest of the way in silence. But in the dark, I catch her reflection in the window, and she’s still smiling.

The Meridian Consortium hosts its annual summit on a floating platform ten kilometers above Neo-Tokyo. The location is meant to imply security, but also omnipotence: every windowed corridor offers a god’s-eye view of the city’s shame, blurred by fog and the perpetual white-out of rented clouds. The invitation says “business casual,” but everyone is either in haute couture or nothing at all. Ban’s dress code is a weaponized derivative of business goth—black suit, white shirt, one button undone for plausible deniability. I wear blue, because that's what the best-dressed enemies wear. The lobby is a kind of metaphysical TSA line, except instead of shoes and belts they screen for illegal memories, weaponized neuroses, and biometric overlays that would disrupt the event's "intellectual property ecosystem." We pass through with no issues—our cover is too good, our lies too practiced. Inside, the space is all glass and light and deadening noise. Holo-banners hang above the atrium, scrolling the names of syndicates and clients: SKELM CORPS, Zhao Historical, the Chimeras, a few small-timers from the American Midwest. Nobody speaks above a murmur, but the undercurrent of threat is so dense it's like being deep inside a nuclear reactor with the fail-safes off.

Ban peels off to the left, eyes already darting for the weak points—unlocked side doors, maintenance hatches, badges worn too low for facial recognition to log. I move with the current, letting it carry me into a pod of security professionals. The nearest one is a Curie washout with arms like a dock-worker and a brain like a malware engine. He recognizes me instantly, which is the point. "Skelm. They said you were a ghost." His handshake is a contest. I lose, on purpose. He introduces me to the others: an ex-Mossad now working private contract in Tel Aviv; a synthetic "protection consultant" from the Chimeras, her skin tinted gold and her eyes flat and mathematically bored; a New Zealand type with fingers replaced by ten distinct data jacks. All of them want some-thing, but not from me—they want it from the event itself. We talk shop. I log every word.

The ex-Mossad leans in. "You see what the Ronin did to Zhao last month?"

I play dumb. "Just the public version."

He laughs and sips his drink. "It was beautiful. Five-minute breach, three minutes to own the air, full exfil in eight. Left the place running, just with a new owner."

"Efficient," I say.

"That's the new currency," the Kiwi says, one hand tracing invisible patterns on his portable.

The conversation spirals: air-gapped hack strategies, zero-day exploits, weaponized social engineering. It's like attending a church service where the only sin is inefficiency. I throw in a few lines of my own—"We found Moshimoto's drift algorithm is recursive, you just have to torque the time delta and the whole shell resets to factory,"—and the Kiwi grins, logging the tip for resale to someone higher up the chain.

I scan for Ban. She's at a side bar with three executives in a formation I recognize: two flanking, one in the lead, the classic predator-on-new-meat setup. Ban's face is all professional curiosity, but her hands are tight on the glass. She's letting them think she's intimidated. They will regret this. I take a step away from my pod, and the Chimeras consultant follows, matching my pace. She leans in, breath hot and close. "You're running a long con," she says.

I meet her eyes, seeing the zeros-and-ones scroll behind the pupils. "So are you."

She smiles, a line of gold and white, then disappears into the crowd. The interaction will be recorded and analyzed, but I don't care; by tomorrow it will be old news. The event's main draw is the demonstration floor, where the major syndicates show off their latest products. First up is a demo of a next-gen containment field, designed to "preserve problematic consciousnesses" with no loss of fidelity. The presenter, a child in a woman's body with a voice set to "perpetually apologetic," guides us through the feature set. It's a clear box filled with blue-white mist and something alive inside—a writhing, brain-shaped cloud of memory and pain. The presenter rattles off performance metrics: "retention interval up to one thousand years, integrity loss less than point oh one percent per century, fully compliant with Endocrine Collapse Authority regulations, optional humanity filter for custom experience."

Someone asks, "What happens when the subject tries to escape?" The presenter taps the glass. The mist inside changes color—bright, then grey, then a shriek of red. A neural net simulation of agony, rendered for the crowd's benefit. There's laughter, then applause. My stomach churns, but I don't let it show. I find Ban's eyes across the room; she's already watching me, expression flat. The next booth is offering "Neural Imprinting for Executive Succession," which is just dressed-up words for corporate cloning. The booth after that is SKELM CORPS's own "Lifestyle Backup" service, which promises to archive your consciousness at every major milestone—wedding, graduation, bankruptcy, suicide attempt, resurrection. Each comes with its own color-coded datapod, sealed in a childproof case.

I make my way to the back bar, where Ban is now holding court with two rival syndicate reps. She introduces me as "the blue line legend," which is an inside joke neither of them gets, and then steers the conversation toward the weaknesses of Curie's security protocols. The two men are desperate to impress. They lean in, sharing "secret" exploits that are three quarters public knowledge and one quarter fantasy. Ban listens, nods, occasionally drops a phrase in dead Latin or antique Mandarin, and lets them believe they've taught her something. The older of the two says, "Curie's next move is to privatize their entire brain bank. They'll be untouchable within a year."

Ban's lips curl into a predator's smile. "Nobody's untouchable." The two reps laugh, unsure if she's flirting or threatening. We exchange business cards, all three of us using the ritual to exchange more than just contact info. The cards are RFID-chipped, so by the time I finish the handshake, my portable is already buzzing with handshake pings and tracker malware. I expected nothing less. The afternoon is a blur of panels and demos: a synthetic morality chip, a rebranding of the SentiSnack™ line ("Now with 50% more authentic despair!"), a side room where executives play chess with hyper-optimized child soldiers, the loser having to fire three of their own staff. It's all so monstrous it becomes almost beautiful, like watching a building collapse in slow motion and knowing exactly when each floor will pancake into the next.

At the evening banquet, we are seated at a table with a cross-section of enemies: Moshimoto, Curie, and two "freelancers" who never give their real names. The conversation is a performance; every question is a trap, every compliment a challenge. Ban wears her boredom like armor, letting it slide over her shoulders and pool at her feet. Halfway through the meal, a Curie rep leans over, voice pitched so only Ban and I can hear. "You two have a future at Curie. Our door's always open. The benefits are legendary."

Ban feigns surprise, but her right hand finds mine under the table. She taps a slow, even rhythm—five, four, three, pause, two, one. I squeeze back, and her grip tightens, then releases. I glance at the rep and smile, a line of blue-white teeth. "We're freelancers, for now. But who knows?" The rep nods, satisfied. We make it to dessert before the first fights break out. On the demo floor, a Moshimoto goon accuses the Zhao rep of industrial espionage; a punch is thrown, and then three seconds later, a containment foam deploys, freezing both parties in place. The crowd roars with approval. Someone starts a betting pool on how long it takes them to escape.

Ban and I slip away as the main event is winding down. The air outside is cold, wet, and tastes like static. We take the first maglev back to ground level, then walk the rest of the way to our safehouse. Inside, I hang the jacket, pull off the tie, and look for a glass of something strong. Ban plugs the portable into the air-gapped system, uploads every byte of intelligence we scraped, then stands behind me, arms draped across my shoulders. "You see the new model?" she asks, chin pressing down just hard enough that I feel it.

"The box?"

She nods. "It's not even the worst. The worst is how many people want it." We sit together in the kitchen, side by side, as the database fills with new vulnerabilities, new names, new possibilities for the endgame. Every so often, Ban will make a mark on her calendar, or lean in and whisper the day count into my ear. At some point, I wander to the bathroom, run cold water, and catch my reflection in the mirror. For a second, I don't recognize the man there: hair cut to regulation, jaw set, a look of practiced indifference in the eyes. The suit, the scars, the fake smile. I touch the glass, half-expecting it to reject me. Ban appears behind me, reflected over my shoulder. Her hands land on my chest, grounding me, before she leaves. "I see you slipping away," she says, her voice almost tender. "Remember who we are."

I nod, but the face in the mirror doesn't change. That's the real horror of the job—not the death, not the betrayals, not the catalog of broken souls we leave behind. It's that you wake up one day and realize the cover is better than the original. I go back to the kitchen and find Ban at the table, marking off another day. She looks up, and in her eyes, I see the only evidence I'm still myself. But tomorrow, it's someone else's turn. And by the end, there will be nothing left to recognize.

Chapter 20

A data lab is only as secure as its snacks, and ours is stocked with nothing but iodine-flavored protein crisps and bottles of water that promise "enhanced algorithmic clarity." The room itself is a bunker two meters below the habitation block, walls layered with a lattice of mesh so fine the echo dies before it gets born. The air is cold, dry, and tinged with the acrid ozone of too many open circuits. If you close your eyes, you can imagine yourself at the bottom of a hospital morgue, except the bodies aren't on slabs; they're running overtime on the cloud. Ban takes her chair first. She always picks the one with the least direct line of sight to the door, then plants her boots on the rung and opens a feed window with a flick of her wrist. The desk in front of her is stripped to essential: a sidearm, two fresh clips, and a coin-sized EMP puck she keeps flicking on and off with her thumb, strobing the room in a blue pulse that does nothing but irritate the sensors.

I sit across from her, back to the coldest wall. Between us, a half-circle of holo displays flowers out, showing the 200TB we yanked from the last job. The data is not a single thing; it's a billion data-points, each vibrating in some parentless direction, all spinning up like they're waiting for a new gravity to collapse them into meaning. I start the parsing routine, fingers blurry over the flat matte of my portable. The first level is garbage: standard security logs, payroll, classified nudes from an exec's deleted personal folder. The second layer is company memos, mostly violence disguised as inspiration. "If you are reading this, you ARE the product." That sort of thing.

It's only at the third layer that the threads appear. An outbound pattern in the encrypted traffic—every seven days, a terabyte at a time, shuttled through a mesh of "unrelated" nodes: shell corporations, mental health kiosks, a couple of charity NGOs that mostly served to launder intellectual property for the church. My hands pick up speed. The code is sloppy, but fast. I can almost see the shape of it before it's rendered—a map, or maybe a body. The screen starts to build a topology, nodes blooming like capillaries, each one labeled with a date and a hash and a dollar value so large the credits bleed into scientific notation. "Ban," I say, not looking up. "You seeing this?"

She tilts her display my way. The security feed shows nothing but the recursive flicker of our own room—empty corridor, two levels of concrete above, no heat signatures beyond our own. "You're clear. Keep going."

"Look," I say, gesturing at the model. "The convergence isn't just a black-market experiment. It's a syndicate job, end-to-end. Every major player's server nets are feeding into this thing." I zoom out, and the holo grows until it projects past the desk and onto the floor, a web so dense it's a shadow with its own weather. “Curie is just the host. This thing”—I point to the main node, pulsing under the city like a tumor—“is the real project.”

Ban grunts. “Someone’s building a god.”

The word hangs in the air. For a second, the only sound is the click-click of her thumb on the EMP puck. I drill down into the files, sweat breaking out despite the freezing air. The logs crosslink: medical records, child archives, consciousness auction receipts, backups from old Curie jobs I thought were destroyed. At the center is a slab of raw neural code, labeled “Marie,” but this one isn’t running seventeen bodies. It’s distributed across every major cloud on the grid. I run a quick check for the number of endpoint addresses. “Ban,” I say, “it’s—fuck. It’s everywhere. SKELM CORPS too.”

She glances up, eyes narrow. “Define ‘everywhere.’”

“Sixty-seven live servers in North America. Another hundred in the satellite blocks. They’re not just cloning brains—they’re streaming them live, stitching the best bits together, and compressing it for resale.”

Ban leans forward, the EMP puck forgotten. “A market for gods.”

I don’t know if I’m supposed to be impressed or sick, but my hands shake so bad the display flickers. “No. It’s a factory. Every time someone ‘graduates’ from the program, they get uploaded, trimmed, repackaged, and sent to the highest bidder. That’s what the Ronin were stealing.”

For a long time, Ban doesn’t move. When she does, it’s slow, deliberate. “What’s the endgame?”

I try to answer, but the words don't come. Instead, I queue up a 3D overlay of the server structure and stretch it until the network branches out like a nervous system. At this scale, the city's not a city—it's a brain in a jar, each corporate node a chunk of cortex, firing signals back and forth through rented bandwidth. It's beautiful, if you ignore the part where every node is a dead child. I push the visualization until it fuses, the core at the center expanding, pulsing red and blue like a heart about to burst. "If they finish this—if they run the full convergence—they'll have enough neural density to simulate the godhead. Like, the real deal. Old Testament, voice-from-the-sky, eat-your-enemies kind of thing."

Ban snorts. "And what does a syndicate do with a god?"

I finally look up at her. My mouth is dry, words gone thick and sour. "They sell it."

She sits back, arms crossed, like it's not even a surprise. "Of course."

I laugh, a sound so small I barely hear it myself. "The only reason to make a god is to rent it out."

She shrugs, then takes her sidearm, breaks it down on the desk in four seconds flat, and starts cleaning the barrel with a strip of synthfiber. "How do we stop it?"

I try to think, but my brain's already running the math. I count the server nodes, then the redundancy layers, then the code branches. If we take out the main cluster, the system regrows from backup. If we salt the backups, the buyers have their own caches off-site. I say the only thing that makes sense. "You can't kill a god with guns. You have to kill it in the source."

Ban clicks the barrel back into place, the sound sharp enough to make my teeth ring. “Then we go to the source.”

My hands are numb now, the adrenaline finally burning through. “I don’t even know where it is. The core’s a floating process—it migrates. I’d have to track it in real time, then hit it before the redundancy kicks in.”

She checks the mag on her sidearm, then sets it down. “Three months. That’s what we gave ourselves.”

I nod, but it feels like a lie. I stand, pace the length of the room, then come back. The numbers are spinning now, all the scenarios bleeding into one another. I try to calm myself with the old habit—count the bullets in the clip, count the breaths between threats, count the seconds it would take for an exec to sell your soul if you left the room unlocked. I look at Ban, then at the projected web of murder blooming across the wall. “I need time,” I say. She nods, already opening a new comms window, already drafting the list of people we’ll need to bribe, threaten, or destroy. I sit, wipe the sweat from my palms, and start the scan again. Maybe if I look at the data from a different angle, the monster will look a little less human. But I know the truth already. We’re not fighting a company. We’re fighting a religion. And the only thing left is to become the kind of devil it takes to kill a god. I pop a protein crisp into my mouth, the iodine so bitter it burns. “Tomorrow.” Ban looks up, eyebrow arched. “Tomorrow,” I repeat, “we go hunting.” Her smile is sharp as a trigger. And for the first time in a long time, I feel like maybe we could actually win.

. . .

In the dark, Ban's body is all lines and intent, cast in the powder blue of desk LEDs and the war-bright strobe of her favorite field torch. She moves to the arsenal cabinet in the corner and opens it with a palm scan, like it's a ritual she could do in her sleep. I count three seconds from touch to unlock; she could do better, but sometimes you have to savor things. She lays out the weapons with a surgeon's care. One by one: the compact flechette, the 9mm she prefers for close work, a palm-sized mono knife with the serration only at the tip. Then the showpiece—a rifle that looks like it came from an alternate future where murder is done at the speed of thought. Each piece lands on the table with a sound so precise you know she's tuning the force for maximum psychological effect.

She pops the mag from the flechette, fingers the rounds to check for burrs, then re-seats the mag with a single, soft click. The noise makes my scalp prickle. When she strips the 9mm, the slide comes apart in her hands like the bones of a small animal. Ban wipes the inside with a cloth and then runs her thumbnail down the barrel, searching for grit. Nothing. She grins, very briefly. She doesn't say a word. Not yet. The whole show is for me. I watch her work, but I also watch the hollow in her back, the scars from the time she ate a pipe bomb in week two of this disaster. They look old now, white and almost beautiful. She moves as if the pain is a roommate she stopped hating, but never learned to love. My own hands shake a little, but she ignores it. She's giving me the space to rebuild. The first words she says are not about the weapons, or the data, or the new flavor of apocalypse we uncovered last night. She says, "Babylon built the first one. At least, the first one to stick."

I raise an eyebrow. “God?”

She keeps working. “Babylon’s god was information. Cuneiform, grain records, inventories of who owed what to whom. Their priests ran the numbers and everyone else played catch-up for three thousand years.” She snaps the 9mm together and sets it aside, gently, like a toy. “Rome did it too. Every god they conquered, they catalogued, then cross-bred with their own. Pantheon as patch notes. Each new divinity a user upgrade for the crowd.” She flips open the case for the rifle, extracts a single, ugly slug, and spins it on the table. “Corporate Wars did the same. They called it ‘synergy’ but it’s just the old play, with a new interface.” She slides a row of bullets into the loader, one by one, never looking up. “We think of god as something people worship. But it’s not. It’s the name for what watches us, what owns us, what gets better every time we lose. A god is a recursive algorithm built on human terror.”

The rifle, field-stripped, is a spinal cord laid flat on the metal. She loads the mag, checks the balance, then pulls the bolt with a sound so final it silences the air. “So what’s different this time?” I say, voice steadier than I expected.

She sets the rifle down, barrel pointed at the corner where the wall meets the future. “This time, the god isn’t waiting to be worshipped. It’s not even interested in pretending it cares. It’s already eating.”

I try to think of something clever, but all I hear is the echo of her movements, the click of rounds, the pulse of cooling fans as the data lab tries to process what we just became. “You think we can kill it?”

She laughs, real and raw. “Of course.” She picks up the mono knife, spins it in her hand, then flicks it into the wood edge of the table. “Gods can die. That’s their only trick. They die, and we give them a better name.” She holsters the 9mm, slings the flechette, and lays her palm flat on the rifle. “You get the root access, I’ll handle the meatspace.” For a second, I remember the first time I saw her in action: eighteen, running on stolen adrenaline, cleaning out a guard shack in four seconds flat. She wore the same look then. The one that says, “This ends with me. Or not at all.” I run the numbers in my head. Three months to full deployment of the digital deity. Less than that before the syndicates get wind of our plan and start cleaning house. The odds are impossible, but the math doesn’t care about odds. It just adds. Ban puts the rifle back in its case, then locks it with a twist of her wrist. The code cycles: a line of prime numbers, each one burned into her memory from years of repetition. She walks over, stopping just short of touching me. For a moment, I think she might. Instead, she taps the side of my head with two fingers. “Brains before bullets, Skelm. Don’t let me down.”

I nod, and for the first time in hours, the tremor in my hands settles. She moves to the far wall, leans back, and waits. I stand, cross to her, and we look at each other for a moment that could last a year or a gunshot. Then we both nod, at the same time, like a contract just got signed somewhere we can’t see. This isn’t a job anymore. It’s a murder-suicide, with a god as the victim. And I think, for a split second, that the universe is finally playing fair. We leave the data lab, Ban first, me close behind, the taste of gun oil and burnt air following us up the stairs. When we hit street level, the sun is up, bright as an executioner. I exhale. Ban cracks her knuckles. “War?” I ask.

"War," she says, and smiles. I lock the door behind us, then walk into the light. Next time, the god doesn't stand a chance.

The bunker isn't designed for comfort. Air cycles through at negative pressure, fans running all hours, grinding dust and moisture into a microclimate that tastes like a car crash on fire. The only furniture that isn't a weapon is a broken futon and a table that's slowly dissolving under a rain of synthetic beef jerky crumbs. We hunker in the half-light, shadows layered so thick they look painted on. Ban's at the bench, cleaning her kill tools for the second time since morning. The blue light from her portable makes her face spectral. I don't know if she's slept, but the circles under her eyes have turned from sullen to predatory.

I'm at the other end, splitting my focus between three screens: one tracking syndicate comms, one running a slow-crawl of the most recent memory auctions, and the third scraping the black channels for chatter on the Ronin or any sign that the gods know we're coming. Every five minutes, I run the backup routine, pushing a clone of the war files onto a string of quantum-encrypted thumb drives. Each time the write finishes, the drive self-masks and randomizes the folder structure, so that even I have trouble remembering where I hid the real payload. Ban is setting the rhythm, as always. She assembles the flechette, pulls the trigger into a pillow to check for lag, then loads three different types of ammo to see which will blow a bigger hole in a warm body. She strips the next rifle down to the pins, then lines up the shells in a color pattern I don't recognize. She's not talking, but the clicks and clacks of the gunmetal are more conversational than most people get with words.

I glance at my hands. They're not shaking now, but there's a tremor behind the knuckles, a ghost signal of every fear I've been storing up since Curie. I use it. I let it build, then channel it into the plan, mapping our first three moves against the digital deity. The map of the enemy network is finally complete: a lattice of hyper-dense server nodes running in the off-books districts of half the city, each one surrounded by meatspace security so paranoid it borders on theological. At the center, the convergence kernel—location redacted in every file, but now triangulated to a ten-block stretch under the old insurance district. I start to outline the timeline. "Three months, best-case. Maybe less if we start with the satellite clusters."

Ban looks up, eyes glassy, hands never stopping their work. "We can hit the fringe nodes tomorrow."

"Not until we're sure on the core. If we poke too soon, they'll just migrate the process."

She nods. "We'll need at least three decoys. Four if we want the Ronin to bleed for us."

I do the math on the fly, then say, "I'll pull the old Academy contacts. We can feed them a few sacrificial runs, make it look like a Ronin splinter cell is fucking with the main line."

Ban pulls a backup pistol from the foam, points it at the far wall, then dry-fires three times. Each click is a perfect staccato. "I'll talk to Dorothy. She's got ties to the local mutant crew. They owe us."

I log the names, then pause as the server pings: an encrypted file just landed in the black channel, tagged with a variant of Ban's personal sig. I scrub it, decrypt, then open. It's a meme. A picture of the old Curie mascot, deadpan smile, but the text is pure nerve gas: "THE FIRST GOD WAS HUMAN. THE LAST GOD WILL BE MACHINE." I look at Ban, who's now palming the mono knife, flipping it over and over, edge so thin it bends in the air. "They know we're coming," I say, tossing her the portable.

She reads it, snorts, then flips the knife so it stands upright on her thumbnail. "They're scared. Or they wouldn't be bragging."

Her calm is an infection. It moves up my arms, into my jaw, and makes it easier to say, "First run is tomorrow at 0400. You want to suit up, or play it loose?"

Ban shrugs, pulls out a skin-tight vest from the go bag, then layers it over her shirt. "Armor for the first run, naked for the last. You?"

I pull my own vest, check the tags, then do the old drill—roll the shoulders, check the fit, cinch the side panels so nothing will slip when I have to drop prone or bleed. "Always armor," I say, "until the cameras are off."

She grins, the kind of smile that wants to see if the world can really live up to its threats. We go over the plan again, this time with less hesitation. Ban loads a full rack of grenades—three smoke, two concussion, one EMP—and lines them up on the bench. I pull a string of sub-sonic injectors from the med kit, just in case we need someone alive for questioning. At the zero hour, we sync the watches. Ban scrapes the old 847 tattoo from her wrist with a razor, then burns a new one above the scar. It's a countdown: 89:23:41. "One day down," she says, voice almost fond.

We don't talk about what happens if the plan fails. There's no point. The city runs on people like us failing, over and over, until the job is too ugly for anyone to notice. Our edge is that we're willing to do it anyway, even if no one survives to see the final score. The last hour before the run, we check the weapons, the explosives, the backups, and the burners. Then Ban pulls a bottle from under the bench—something clear, the label torn off—and pours two fingers for each of us. We drink. The taste is pure engine cleaner, but it numbs the teeth. Ban sets her glass down, then looks at me in a way that hurts and heals at the same time. "You're ready?"

I nod. "Always."

She doesn't say more. Just finishes her drink, wipes her mouth with the back of her hand, then slings the rifle across her shoulder. I check the holster, the med kit, the backup drive, then lock down the screens and kill the local grid so no one can trace the last ten hours. We exit the bunker in tandem, our steps matched, the chill in the air already a memory. Outside, the city is alive with neon and rain and the throb of distant sirens. We walk, side by side, neither of us in a hurry. Ban scratches a line in her watch at the corner of Main and Exile, a ritual so old she doesn't even look as she does it. "Whatever time we have left, Skelm," she says. "We burn it all."

I smile, and the smile is real. The world outside is endless, but the path in front of us is narrow and bright and waiting to be scorched. We walk until the night closes in, until even the streetlights give up. Then, finally, we get to work.

Chapter 21

The security hub is airless and white, a room designed for the prevention of mistakes. Every surface is nonstick. Every screen is edge-lit and anti-glare. The acoustic panels suck up the last particles of privacy and leave you with your own heartbeat, echoing off the haptic desk like a guilt alarm. I sit in the prime chair, chair number one, the one in the dead center of Marie's distributed panopticon. I'm sweating before the shift even starts. There are seventeen feeds, all set to rotate every seventy-three seconds, each trained on a different Marie body somewhere in the building. She's gotten better at blending, but the algorithm picks her out every time: the fractional lag in her smile, the way her right thumb circles her knuckle before a handshake, the glitch when two bodies make eye contact across a room and both look away at the same instant. None of the other staff notice, or they notice and keep it under the fucking rug where things like that belong.

At minute zero, I get the first ping: an admin Marie, suit pressed, shoes mirror-bright, steps through the lobby with a stack of blue folders balanced like a communion offering. I log her route and then flick the display over to the cafe cam, where janitorial Marie is re-alphabetizing the condiments. Maintenance Marie is on the roof, staring at the ductwork like it's got a secret she can't quite extract. In the sublevels, somewhere past the chemical storage, is a Marie I can't find, but the feed says she's there, and that's all I can ask. The desk lights up with the first round of security reports. I knock them out in five minutes, eyes flicking from console to wall display and back, then take the luxury of thirty seconds to stretch my spine and check my own pulse. It's running high—not quite panic, but definitely in the warning band. I ignore it. If I listened to my body, I'd never get out of bed.

The next shift doesn't start for twelve minutes, but Ban is early. She glides in, all vector and muscle, uniform so crisp you could shave with the crease. She goes right to her terminal and logs on without a word, but we do the old scan: eyes meet, split, meet again. She's clocked all seventeen Maries already, because her brain is the only one I've ever seen outpace mine. I nod once. She returns it. It means: *No fuckups. Not today.* Marie materializes in the room at exactly 0600. Not the admin Marie from the lobby; this one is Research Marie, all white coat and neural access badge. She glances at Ban, then at me, then at both of us together, and for a millisecond, I feel like she's mapped the entire vector of our thoughts from the shape of our faces. "Skelm," she says, and the way she says it makes it sound like a borrowed asset. "Exceptional response time on the night cycle."

I try for humility. "Systems ran clean. Minimal drift. One badge ping out of schedule, but it was an intern on a stim crash."

She steps closer, hands folded behind her back. "Perhaps too exceptional," she says, and the words echo from a half dozen speakers as her other mouths repeat the phrase at various corners of the building. For a split second, the system glazes, and every Marie's face is the same face, all tilted the same degree, all eyes on me. The hair on my forearms prickles like I just swallowed a live wire. I look down at my hands, and they're hovering over the keyboard, caught in a stutter. For a full second, I can't make them move. The pause is small, but it's not nothing. If Marie wanted to, she could kill me with this detail. But she doesn't. Instead, she offers a slant of a smile, almost pitying, and resumes her tour of the stations.

She stops at Ban, who doesn't bother with the small talk. "Morning, Marie."

Marie's gaze is a slow, scanning heat. "Morning, Zhao. I see you've prepped the overlays for the summit."

"Security is my job," Ban says, deadpan, but I catch the micro-shake in her left leg. She only does that when she wants to throw a punch and can't.

Marie turns back to me. "Full brief at zero-seven. Summit security is now your domain. You will both join me in board-room C at precisely the hour. Glass-walled. You know the one." She doesn't wait for a reply. The instant she exits, the tension in the room cracks like an over-tight drumhead. We don't speak for the next twenty minutes, but there's a communication: Ban's typing gets faster, the cadence more brutal. I lean back in my chair, eyes on the feed, but I'm cataloguing the tremor that just rolled through the system. At 0657, we head to the boardroom. The corridors are empty except for a cleaning drone and the elevator, which shudders to a stop with a kind of defeated dignity. Ban keeps one pace ahead, eyes never not working the angles.

The boardroom is designed to humiliate anyone not born for it. The glass walls overlook the arterial skybridge that connects the three main syndicate towers. Light pours in from all sides, but the glass is tinted at an algorithmic gradient, so no matter where you stand, you're always a half-step behind the alpha in the room. The table is carbon-lattice, fibered for strength and flexibility, but so slick it makes pens roll in circles unless you hold them down. Marie is there, all seventeen of her, each one occupying a discrete seat, like a council of witches debating what part of you to eat first. The rest of the boardroom is empty, because when the boss is every boss, what's left for middle management? Ban and I take our seats, center right and left, across from Marie's main body. She gets to the point: "In two days' time, the three syndicates will meet here. We anticipate zero violence and infinite duplicity. Your task is to ensure the first, and be immune to the second. Are there questions?"

"No," Ban says. I echo it.

Marie smiles, but only at herself. "Excellent. If either of you were to betray me, you would do it perfectly. That's why I trust you." She claps, once, and the sound is mirrored around the room by her own hands, each a half-beat off the last. The noise bounces until it's a blur of approval and threat. Ban holds the posture of a professional, but I see the flex in her jaw, the way her fingers tap the tabletop at a rhythm designed to break a man's concentration. I return my own version: left hand in a fist, right hand open, a signal we invented when we were young and dumber than we are now. It means: *We're not dead yet.* Marie stands and dismisses us with a flick. Her bodies file out, some lingering for a fraction of a second to analyze the detritus of our presence: the slight warmth in a chair, the pattern of our footprints on the anti-dust carpet, the exhalation of a breath meant to be silent.

When she's gone, Ban's shoulders drop a centimeter. That's her whole tell. Mine is bigger: I roll my neck until the vertebrae click and then let out a long, silent exhale. We walk back to the security hub, neither of us eager to say anything that might be used against us later. But as soon as the door closes, Ban speaks. "They know," she says.

"Of course they know. They just don't care. Yet."

She runs a hand through her hair, which means she's already working on plan B, or maybe C. I lean back in my chair, pull up the seventeen feeds, and stare at the Maries cycling through their paces. For the first time, I notice that in every room, no matter what else is happening, at least one Marie is always facing a camera dead-on, unblinking. I log the detail and move on. The summit is in two days. And we are going to burn it down from the inside. But for now, we just have to keep breathing. Ban taps her nails on the desk. "Three months," she says. "You think we can last that long?"

I don't answer. Instead, I watch the Maries, waiting for the next stutter in the pattern. Waiting for the god to blink first. Somewhere in the building, seventeen voices all say the same words, at the same time: "Have a good day." Ban laughs, sharp and small. I laugh with her, because in the end, it's the only thing that still sounds real.

• • •

The real infrastructure is always hidden underground. Above us, the towers show off glass and soft gold, but down here, beneath the bones of the city, it's steel struts and climate-controlled terror. The server room is a sub-basement technically not on the blueprints, accessible only by elevator and a tunnel that bends left five times before the door, which is the sort of thing they teach you in the third week of corporate countermeasures. The walls are painted matte blue; not for color, but because the blue absorbs more LED than white. The floor is copper mesh. The air smells like burning ozone and someone's hidden disappointment. Ban checks the lock, then the fail-safe on the inside. She stands just behind the door, head cocked for footsteps, weapon holstered but not really. I'm at the rack. My fingers are already sweating, and not just because the temperature is kept at fifteen degrees to keep the servers from boiling out. There's an animal intensity to it, the thrum and pulse of 38,000 CPUs all running the world's worst secrets.

I plug in the drive. The system protests—nobody uses physical media anymore, so the port is half-fused with dust and the memory of better days. I force it. The script auto-launches, and for the next six minutes, my job is to be the most boring tech in the building. Ban paces, slow and exact, never more than two steps from the kill zone, eyes always on the panel above the door that would—if triggered—drop a fire curtain and oxygen-purge the room. She's mapping it, not for escape, but for the best place to die if it all turns to shit. "You're pacing," I say. "That's new."

She stops and glances at her watch. "Zhao reps are twelve minutes out. If they run ahead, we get a badge clash at the west lobby."

I shake my head. "Curie's got the best time discipline on the planet."

She snorts. "Maybe. But Marie wants the event to be perfect. Which means someone is already trying to fuck it up."

My hands don't leave the keys, but I smile. "That's our job." She shrugs, then runs a finger down the frame of her flechette pistol, the one she swore she'd never use unless it was for me. The finger doesn't tremble. Neither does her mouth, even when she's biting the inside of her lip hard enough that I wonder if she's bleeding. In the car, we ride up in silence. Both of us stare at the digital floor display, neither moving, just breathing and blinking and pretending we're not already two steps into the grave. When we hit ground level, the lobby is busy: a full staff of white-glove execs prepping for the summit, three perimeter guards in Curie blue, and a trio of AV techs setting up a hologram with a logo that cost more to design than our parents' entire careers.

Ban leads. I follow, keeping to the right, eyes half-lidded, walk just lazy enough to say "bored" but not "inept." We clear the lobby in four seconds. Nobody blinks at us. Back at the security hub, I log in to the main console. The feeds are still running, Maries still circling like sharks on a blood trail, but none of them are here, not in this room, not yet. Ban sits at her station, then unlocks a side drawer and pulls out two nutrition bars. She tosses one at me, dead center. I catch it, because missing would be worse than death. "They're serving executive snacks up there," I say, gesturing at the summit prep. "We could be living large, eating free-range suffering on a glutenless cracker."

She gives a snort that might be a laugh. "Next time."

The morning goes fast. We work the prep, fix the badge systems, run the dry drills and the comm checks and the log sweeps. Every hour, a new Marie comes through, checks on us, and leaves a compliment or a critique, always just the right amount to keep us on edge but never off the job. At 1100, Ban's phone blinks. She scans it, face suddenly sharp. "They're moving the summit start. Twenty-four hours early."

My chest stutters. "That's not like Marie."

"Marie can do what she wants," Ban says. The rest of the day is blur: coffee, calibrations, and ten thousand words of security reports, all written in perfect corporate. I start to forget what we're doing and lose myself in the ritual. It's nice, almost. If you ignore the part where the room you're building will one day incinerate everyone inside. When the shift ends, Ban cracks her back and stands up. "You get any sleep, you're dead to me," she says. Then she leaves, not waiting for a reply. I sit at the desk and watch the feeds. Tomorrow, the summit starts. And this time, it's us on the agenda.

The summit is a performance, and I'm sitting front row in the control booth, watching the world's most powerful sociopaths trade lives like baseball cards. The hub overlooks the glass boardroom from thirty meters up and one floor over, an architectural flourish that ensures every move is on camera, every whisper is recorded, and every backroom deal is piped straight into the recording archives where it can be replayed, blackmailed, or sold to the highest bidder. Ban arrives early, in full riot blue, her hair razored back to compliance. She ignores the view, preferring the angle that covers both the elevator and the staff door, a configuration that says "come try me" but also “you’ll never get close enough.” She opens her console, scans the feed, then flicks a glance at me that lasts just a hair too long. I nod, and she returns it with zero emotion. That’s the point.

The first wave of executives arrives in a phalanx: Curie, Moshimoto, and Zhao. Each wears a uniform so expensive you have to squint to see the seams, but all have the same bloat, the kind of swelling you get from too many augmentation cycles and not enough sleep. The leader for Curie is a man I’ve only seen in propaganda, but in person he’s barely held together, cheeks sagging like the chassis is five years past warranty. The Moshimoto woman is sharper, built on a frame that was probably never even organic, and her left hand twitches at random, a tell that the media loves to loop in slow-mo to make her look human. Zhao’s rep is a middle-aged suit, so average he might as well be a negative number. The Maries are everywhere. Four in the room, two in the corridors, and three more in the observation decks—each dressed for a different audience, each playing a different part of the superego. They greet the execs, shake hands, lean in for that extra tenth of a second so the scent, the smile, the facial mapping all get perfect samples. They see everything.

I check Ban: she’s running physical, but her eyes keep darting back to the tactical, the meta, the whole-game layer. The execs sit. The room is lit for maximum intimidation. Every wall is glass; every word echoes forever. The only furniture is a table designed to look like it’s floating, which means you can see every foot, every hand, every secret-sharer leaning in for a side-channel. The meeting opens with ritual—Marie runs a thirty-second montage of the last year’s “successes” in neural containment, voiceover smooth as cocaine on silk. It’s the kind of bullshit that only impresses people who never have to clean up the mess. The execs eat it up anyway, because to them, the only true emotion left is envy.

The first item is a merger. Curie wants a fifty-one percent share in Moshimoto's next-gen data vault. Zhao wants a buy-in, but only if they can run the hardware in their own secure zone. Nobody trusts anyone. The laughter is brittle, the smiles for the cameras. I see the red spikes in everyone's blood pressure, the way Marie's left-most body taps her finger against the table every time someone lies. Above us, the system hums. I feel the sweat running down my back, but I don't wipe it off. You get used to the body's betrayals after a while.

Midway through the summit, the food comes out. Ban signals me, just a twitch, a shift of her weight, but I know what she means: there's a shift in the guard, a new pattern, someone prepping for a physical event. I check the logs. Moshimoto has sent in a runner, someone off-grid, maybe a courier or a body double. I loop the cam feed and send the alert to Ban's screen. She's already on it, moving down the back corridor, gun out but hidden behind a portfolio labeled "Lunch Schedules." I follow her progress, but also keep half an eye on the boardroom. Curie's lead is talking loud now, gesturing at Marie, demanding something I can't hear but can infer from the color rising in his neck. Zhao's rep is smiling, teeth bared, and the Moshimoto woman is staring dead at Marie, not blinking. For a moment, I think the whole thing is going to go sideways. I almost hope it does.

Ban intercepts the runner at the corridor junction. They freeze, then reach for a sidearm. Ban steps in, one fluid movement, and disables them with a twist I haven't seen since our old sparring days. The runner hits the floor, out cold. Ban kneels, pulls something from their pocket, and walks away like it was a bad date, not a felony. She returns to the hub and hands me the item. It's a patch cable, hardwired with a brute-force keylogger. "They were going to jack the admin terminal," she says. "Not very subtle." I plug it into the test bench. The code is ugly, amateur, but it would have triggered a lockdown. Which means either Moshimoto is trying to get a jump on the merger, or Marie's just stress-testing us. The summit resumes.

Chapter 22

The boardroom is a toothless glass coffin, perched atop Curie headquarters, soaking in the aurora of every shitty LED billboard in a hundred-mile radius. The table is a continent of obsidian, dense enough to drown small talk, its finish so pure the overheads cast circles of white fire that warp every executive's jawline into a blunt weapon. I stand at attention just inside the security line, uniform still damp from the scan cycle, watching a war happen in silence. Marie is three places at once. Her main body, white hair a precision-cut halo, sits at the center, hands folded over a polymer portfolio. At her left, Legal Marie blinks at a parade of paperwork, annotating with a finger that leaves no prints but does create a faint antiseptic squeak. At the far end, Janitorial Marie polishes a water glass with so much concentration it borders on devotional. They move and speak in near-synch, sometimes trailing by a second, sometimes leading. It's a party trick, but also a demonstration: This is what your money can buy, if you're willing to feed it enough raw brain.

The Moshimoto lead, a man named "Peters" if you believe the lanyard, launches into a spiel about neural latency metrics and consumer confidence. His mouth moves, but the numbers are already on a slide, scrolling up the frosted glass at a rate designed to humiliate anyone still running meat hardware. He outlines the activation schedule, the projected rollout, the market share estimates for the first quarter after go-live. Curie's woman, the one with the grey streak and no discernible effect, interrupts. "And the redundancy plan?" Her voice is low, a flat affect that's probably worth a bonus in some HR wet dream.

Peters doesn't look up from his notes. "All neural instances are triple-mirrored and live-patched. If the main node fails, fallback loads within 0.2 seconds. It's cleaner than most wetware."

The other Marie, perched at the edge of her seat, smiles. "Unless, of course, someone finds the maintenance port."

There's a laugh around the table, except for the Zhaos, who never laugh unless they've already killed the joke. The man from Zhao, a small, haunted type with glasses that probably have a direct line to his stress cortex, asks the only question that matters. "And who holds root?"

There's a pause. I see it in the ripple of light on the table, a dilation in the air as every delegate computes the possible ways to fuck their partners. "Root will be shared," says Marie Prime, and the other Maries echo it, their voices stacked like a bad audio effect. "Triple-signed. No one can override the system without full consensus."

Everyone at the table smiles, except the one who knows they're lying. My job is to keep the smiles on the outside. I stand still, breathe slow, and let my mind go recursive. Ban is doing her own surveillance, cataloguing tells and checking for anyone clever enough to use old-fashioned violence as a backup. So far, the room is sterile. The next hour is a ballet of threats and euphemisms. They talk about "data citizenship," and "end-of-life value optimization," which is how they say, "When you die, your brain becomes ours." Moshimoto wants mandatory live backup for all executive class clients. Zhao pushes for a clause allowing "moral autonomy" in cases of religious objection, but everyone knows that's just their way of buying a little more time before someone audits their own backup stack.

Marie is always in control, but never obvious about it. She punctuates every difficult moment with a minor gesture: a head tilt, a tap on the portfolio, a microsecond of "error" as two of her bodies disagree on facial expression. These are not accidents. They are breadcrumbs for anyone running a heuristic on her moods. At the forty-minute mark, the lights drop by three percent. A scheduled power test, but you can see every eye in the room dilate and contract, wondering if this is the moment someone swaps the boardroom for a kill chamber. I catch Ban's hand move, a flick of two fingers along her thigh, running the old signal: *Ready*. I flex my own, just enough for her to catch, and the cycle is complete. We're both wound, waiting for a trigger. Marie stands then, and all the Maries stand with her, synchronized but slightly out of phase. She says, "We've agreed on the structure, the time frame, and the technical spec. What's left is security. For that, I turn to Curie's in-house team."

All eyes are on me. I step forward, let the old nerves burn out in the first two steps, and start my pitch. "Security for a tri-syndicate rollout is nontrivial. We're assuming the first real attack will be internal, probably from a plant already on your payroll. Standard protocols—airgapping, biometric two-man rules, continuous personnel rotation—will slow but not stop a determined operator." I do a brief scan of the table. Moshimoto man is bored, already planning his first sabotage. Zhao's haunted guy is nervous, sweat blooming along his scalp like a botched transplant. Only Marie is unreadable, but she wouldn't have hired me if she was looking for a mirror. I go on. "Our approach is layered: quantum-encrypted ID cycles at every access point, physical layer hardened with anti-tamper mesh, and a system of behavioral anomaly monitoring that flags any employee who acts out of character for more than six hours."

Ban is in my periphery, arms crossed, eyes on Legal Marie. We've rehearsed this. She'll play dumb, wait for a secondary breach attempt, then lock down the actual perimeter while everyone else chases the shadow. The execs nod. Marie gives a three-way smile, then sits, triggering the other Maries to follow. "Excellent," she says, "but what about god?" This gets a laugh, for real. "God" is the term for any system that achieves enough neural density to go off-script—think of it as a singularity, but branded and IP-protected. The final, secret fear is that the thing they're building will wake up and eat the shareholders before anyone can unplug it.

I give the canned answer. "God can't be airgapped. But we can make it too busy to notice it's alive, at least for the first ninety days." This pleases them. The rest of the summit is a performance of acceptance, no one wanting to be the first to show doubt. The table starts to dissolve into handshakes, contract signings, a flood of digital blips as each exec authorizes a chunk of their own soul to the project. I watch Ban. She's looking at me, and for a second, our masks drop. I see the fear, but also the hunger. She wants this to work. Maybe because if it doesn't, there won't be a world left to run from.

The summit adjourns. The delegates stand and drift toward the exit, shedding platitudes and business cards like dander. I stay behind, log the details, then run a sweep for any weirdness left in the room. It's empty, except for Marie. She's down to one body now, but it's the right one. "Walk with me," she says, and it's not a request. We pace the perimeter, her shoes clicking in perfect time with the drone of the building's cooling system. She doesn't look at me when she speaks. "I know you've been watching me."

"I'm paid to."

She snorts. "You're paid to protect me, not spy on me."

"Sometimes those are the same. Especially in this job."

She pauses and half-turns. "You think I can do it?"

I want to ask if she means the project, or something bigger, but I don't. "You'll win. But it'll cost more than you think."

Marie's mouth quirks, almost a smile. "It always does." We reach the far end of the boardroom, the side with the best view. You can see the whole city from here, every other tower a competitor or a future corpse. She looks out and says, "You know what a god needs, Skelm?" I wait. "It needs a devil. Otherwise it forgets why it exists."

For a moment, I wonder which one she thinks I am. Then the lights go back to full, the room re-illuminates, and the illusion is gone. I log out and let myself be escorted down to the sublevels. Ban is waiting by the service elevator, her expression impossible to parse. I catch her gaze, nod, and she nods back. Three months. That's all the time we've got. Outside, the world spins up to speed, unaware that it just signed its own death certificate. And that's exactly how we planned it.

The summit's afterbirth is a seventy-five-page action item matrix, delivered to my desk with a 06:20 timestamp and a single line of personal encouragement: "Don't fuck this up." Marie's humor, as always, is a glitch—half joke, half surveillance. I schedule the mandatory security update demo for 08:00, as per protocol, then spend the intervening hour stacking decoy files and stress-testing the building's subnet for any trace of unsanctioned traffic. By the time the boardroom reopens, the space is chemically reset—no trace of yesterday's sweat or the outlines of spilt human ego on the table. The obsidian is cleaner than bone, the chairs resculpted into conformity. I'm first in, which is by design; the room's holos are running a diagnostics sweep, and I want to be the last person to touch them before the orgs bring their own malware in through the door.

Ban is already on the perimeter, sidearm freshly sanitized, hair pulled back into a vector you could diagram for a child. She paces the room, slow and deliberate, her eyes stopping at every camera dome, every speaker port. We don't talk; we're both running different flavors of the same paranoia. The execs filter in, a little hungover, a little less armored. They don't expect a threat this early. Marie is present as only two bodies—Legal and Technical. I wonder, idly, which one would win in a fight. I bet on Technical; she has the muscle memory of every engineer who ever rewrote their own pain thresholds. I flick the main console to life and gesture for attention. "Before we begin, a quick demonstration of today's network integrity protocols."

This is theater, but the stakes are organ-deep. I launch the sandbox, pop open a layer of admin overlays, and run my hands through the air above the table. The interface renders my nervous system in hard light: synaptic maps, login signatures, a haptic model of the building's access schema. I let them see it, then flip the board—now the display is a live feed of every user, every device in the room, tracked in real time. The curves of the interface trace a sickly blue, pulsing with each data packet. As I speak, my other hand keys in the hidden sequence, the one Ban and I spent two nights perfecting on a demo kit in the sub-basement. It's buried in the routine—if anyone looked close, it'd just read like a quick series of admin handshakes, a network patch to the security VM. But it isn't. It's the first stage of the quantum virus.

Ban moves into the background, standing just where her silhouette occludes the nearest lens. She leans forward, hands behind her back, and says, "What about endpoint redundancy? Last run showed a nine-second window during the server cascade." Her voice is cool, but she makes sure to say "server cascade" extra loud, as if inviting anyone to check the logs.

I nod, then call up a visualization. "That's resolved. The update pushes through parallel threads—no single endpoint ever holds the root long enough for a lateral exploit." I feel the code flex, the subroutines opening and cloaking as planned. Each rep has their own IT drone, and I can feel them all tracking me, maybe thirty fingers typing queries into their own overlays, watching for an error, a pause, a proof of incompetence. There isn't one. I've spent too long in the blue to trip now. I shift the display to show the real-time propagation. "See here?" I highlight three nodes: Curie's, Moshimoto's, Zhao's. "All three now fully synced. No lag, no rollback. If a breach occurs, the offending instance is snapshot, isolated, and cold-wiped before it can propagate."

Behind the glass, a red light flickers in the panel above Ban's head. This is the signal: *the payload is in*. I mask the reflex to smile and just move on with the patter. Technical Marie says, "How long before we see full penetration?"

I love the word choice. "Penetration is instant. But the real test is latency under pressure." I let the system eat a stress test, pings ricocheting through the network like high-speed buckshot. The numbers climb, then plateau—exactly as they should. Nobody but me sees the process blooming behind the visuals, the subroutine knitting itself into the root of every system with a timestamped fail-safe: ninety days.

Ban steps forward. "Would you recommend quarterly or weekly audits, given the new scaling?"

I barely glance at her, but our eyes catch for a microsecond. "Weekly. Trust is good, but redundancy is better." I see Legal Marie check her portable, already pushing the update to the action logs. The rest of the execs look relieved, or at least bored enough to risk a yawn. I gesture for questions. There are none. "In that case, I'll proceed with the formalization."

I key in the last command, finalizing the update. The payload shrinks to an atom, invisible, a dormant godworm. The blue lights in the room strobe, then level. The holos cycle. I check my watch, even though I never wear one. It's done. Technical Marie stands. "Well executed, Skelm."

Legal Marie adds, "Exceptionally so. We're impressed."

I thank them both, shut down the overlays, and step back, giving the room to Ban for the final security sweep. She moves through the chairs, runs her hands along the obsidian, then gives a slight nod: Clean. The execs stand, chattering in low tones about profit shares and the upcoming press release. None of them know what just happened. I log the final confirmation, my heart ticking a little too fast. The virus is in all three systems. All it needs is time. Ban falls in behind me, her shoulder barely brushing mine as we move to the exit. No words pass. They don't have to. In the corridor, I let myself breathe, just once, before the real work begins. Whatever time we have left. Let's see what kind of god hatches.

The denouement is always uglier than the disaster. They file out, the execs, faces stretched in the ritual masks of the professional class, trading goodbyes like poison pills dipped in sugar. The boardroom smells of sweat and ozone and that special desperation that clings to anyone about to lose the illusion of control. Ban and I walk the perimeter, posturing in a choreography so perfect you'd think we rehearsed it since childhood. In a way, we have. The first to go is the Moshimoto pair. The older one shakes my hand, grip damp and cold, then hands Ban a disposable business card with a QR code and a micro-lattice of his own fingerprints. "For reference," he says, and she pretends to scan it, though the thing will go into the nearest incinerator before shift change. The younger man lingers and stares at me like he wants to ask a question about the hack, but he's been trained not to make a scene. He looks at Ban instead, realizes she's already watching him, and bolts.

Zhao's haunted man is next. He waits at the door, back straight, blinking hard as if he's afraid the network might delete him if he breaks protocol. He bows to Ban, then to me, then to Legal Marie, whose response is to incline her head a statistically insignificant degree. They say nothing—some deals are better left in the air. Their exit is silent, but the ghost of their presence lingers in the room, like a static field waiting for a charge. Curie's own execs exit last, their security detail flanking them in lockstep. I recognize two from my first month in the org, before they re-badged everyone and fired the ones who knew too much about the old systems. One offers me a terse nod. The other avoids my eyes entirely, focusing on the space just above my left ear. I wonder if he knows, or if he's just afraid of the surveillance.

Then there's Marie. She's at the head of the table, but now there are seventeen of her, arranged along the glass wall in perfect sequence, each with a slightly different outfit, haircut, or posture. Some are in admin black, some in soft civilian cotton, two in what looks like morning jogging gear. One sits on the boardroom table, legs crossed, picking at her nails with a micro-file. Another is tapping on a portable, fingers too fast for the keys. Each approach me in turn, shaking my hand, but each time the grip is different. Firm, then limp, then electric with a hint of static, then so tight it feels like the bones in my hand are being scanned for cracks. The main body—her favorite, if there's such a thing—waits until last. She looks at me, then at Ban, then back. "Exceptional work."

I smile, just the required number of millimeters. "I run clean code."

Seventeen mouths smile back, a fractal of approval and threat. "Remember, Darby," she says, "everyone leaves a residue." The last handshake is longer, warmer. "Some more than others."

"Understood," I say, voice steady. She turns, her clone train trailing behind, and the door hisses shut on all of them at once. The room is empty. Ban's posture drops by a centimeter, but only after we confirm the privacy rating on the glass. She turns to the far wall, runs her hand along the obsidian, then gestures me to follow. We walk out onto the balcony—one of those scenic design features that doubles as a surveillance platform. From here, you can see the whole landing grid, the corporate shuttles lined up in formation, each one a gleaming logo-wrapped missile waiting for a destination. We watch as the execs board, security lines slotted and locked, the glass doors sealing like coffins on a production line. The shuttles power up, one after another, blue fire painting the sky.

"They think they're safe," Ban says, so soft I almost miss it.

"They think they won," I say.

She leans against the glass, lets the wind flatten her hair against her face, then pushes it back with a hand that's shaking just a little. "Are we still us, Darby?"

The question is real. It's the kind that stops time for a second, the kind that burns a hole through the lacquer of all the jobs we've ever run together. I step close, feeling her breath, the adrenaline still leaking out of her pores. "We are until we're not," I say, and she laughs, a raw, brief noise that's more relief than joy. The shuttles take off, a sequence of blue-white flares slicing the horizon. I watch them go, one by one, each one a countdown, each one a promise. Ban's hand finds mine. She grips it, hard, like the world might let go if we don't anchor each other. We stand like that, in the wind and the blue, until the sky is empty. Whatever time we have left. Tick.

Chapter 23

It starts with the red. Not the subtle, biological kind, but a total environment override. Every lumen in Curie goes full emergency, bathing the command deck in surgical anger and killing every shadow at once. The room's automated air even switches to a "motivational blend," which means too much menthol and the chemical ghost of burnt citrus. A dozen wall screens jump from blue idle to hostile red, each cycling a different flavor of panic: breach detected, system instability, server farm lockdown, all scrolling in a perfect ticker of doom. My hands don't so much shake as vibrate. At this speed, the caffeine is a noise floor, barely noticeable under the glandular freight train of adrenaline. I cycle through the camera feeds: south perimeter a joke, the gate dissolved in thirty seconds; corridor F2 is packed with blue-badged interns running like antelope, right up until the first Ronin drone hoses the air with a consciousness scrambler and takes the whole line down in a nanosecond. They twitch for a while, then go still. The internal comms log three thousand warning pings, all routed straight to me, because Curie is out of real bodies to answer the call. Ban's voice slices through the earpiece, flat and all business. "Sector seven, they're coming through the old mail chute."

I kill every secondary monitor and focus on the breach. "Got it. I'll reroute the pressure doors and block the stairwell."

A second later, she adds, "They're using the Moshimoto hardware. Your people."

Not my people, not anymore. But she's right; the Ronin are running a mix of legacy comms and hardware I last saw during the Moshimoto shut-down. The signatures on the attack packets are textbook and predictable, but at this density, they're not even bothering to be clever. I flip the physical override on the door matrix and watch the heavy plates slam shut, cutting off four black figures mid-run. They barely break stride; one throws a gel charge that liquifies the bottom two meters of the steel, and another fires a round that turns the camera to wet static. It's fine. We have better. "Breached," I say. "Deploying the local."

Ban's already there. Her face appears in a tiny window, helmet visor cracked but eyes live and glittering. She flashes two fingers, a signal we invented on job three: *I go loud, you go quiet.* She drops off the feed, but I hear the racket through corridor mics: a sequence of perfect violence, each second accounted for by a shot or a scream or a body slamming into polycarbonate. I patch in the security bots and route their movement to follow Ban's heat signature. On my side, I see the drone's fisheye view: hallway dense with Ronin, Ban slicing through with a borrowed SMG and a lack of hesitation I can only admire. The Ronin drop fast, but even as they die, one is cutting through the floor tile with an arc blade, prepping a secondary entrance. "Your left," I say.

Ban shifts, drops to a knee, and puts three rounds through the floor. The blade, and the man attached, go quiet. "Thanks," she says, barely winded. Across the command deck, the door shudders. I check the camera: nothing, then a sudden flash of bright green. An acid charge, military-grade. The lock sizzles, then peels back like a banana. Two Ronin enter—no hesitation, just movement—both with the subdermal badge glint that marks them as ex-corp. They ignore the monitors and focus on the nerve center, which is me. I stand, pull the desk's built-in sidearm, and put three shots through the first one's faceplate. The impact staggers him, but he's wearing synth-flesh; it takes a direct brain hit to drop these bastards.

I aim better on the second and get him in the eye. He twitches, then drops. The first Ronin keeps coming, leaking black all down his shirt, then gets stuck trying to reload. He gets a second wind—blood loss does that sometimes—so I walk over and put a round through the back of his neck. I drag his body away from the main controls and check the wall screens. Ban is in corridor G now, working with two of Curie's own: juniors, green, but not useless. She tosses one an upgraded mag, then signals the other to circle. It's choreography, and Ban is the only one who knows the music. The Ronin try for a breach, but Ban reads it, waits, then executes—three shots, one thrown blade, and a knee to the chest that makes the last one crumple on the spot. She turns to the juniors and says, "Good. Now check for trackers, then sweep back." The kids nod, one close to tears, the other already eager to chase. Ban grabs the crier by the scruff and looks him dead in the eye. "Do not get sentimental. They will kill everyone in this building, and you won't be the first or the last." He blinks, nods, and runs.

Upstairs, the sound changes. Not the alarms, but a new layer: the steady click of heels on ceramic. Marie. I see her on a feed, all seventeen bodies moving in formation, perfect as always. She enters the deck with three in tow, and I don't even pretend to act surprised. "Status," she says, and every voice in the room says it at once, each one with a slightly different intonation.

"Attack ongoing. Ronin are using Moshimoto hacks and internal maps. They're going for the server core," I say.

Marie's three bodies stand at different corners of the deck, each one checking my readout, each one logging my words. The leftmost Marie stares at the fallen Ronin, her head tilted just enough to be clinical. "Protect the server core at all costs," she says.

Behind her, Ban appears, helmet off, hair slicked to her head with something not entirely her own. She wipes her brow, then gives me the look: *we know this is a farce, but we also know that if we fail, we lose our only shot at what comes next.* I say, "Server core is locked down, but the south elevator is compromised. I can reroute, but only if someone stalls them at the central shaft."

Ban smiles, but only with the part of her mouth that knows I'm probably right. "I'll go."

Marie's bodies all turn, in eerie, silent unison, and nod approval. Ban leaves, moving with speed but no panic. I patch into her comm as she sprints. "They'll expect you," I say.

She answers, “They always do.”

Downstairs, the server core starts to shudder—the HVAC working overtime, or maybe a localized bomb. I scan for heat signatures and see three Ronin prepping charges on the access port. They’re all in full armor, faces hidden, voices never raised above a whisper. Professional. I remote the system lockdown, but the Ronin bypass it with a hardware fob, keyed to the mainline root. I wonder how much they paid for it. Or maybe it’s just easier to steal now, with everyone using the same vendors. Ban hits the central shaft at the same moment the Ronin do. It’s ugly and close, a fistfight with guns. She uses the first dead man as a shield, pulls him around, then levers herself up and over, landing behind the Ronin. She empties her mag into their backs, then rips the helmet off one and checks for comms. It’s a kid. Maybe eighteen. She hesitates, just a microsecond, then snaps his neck and keeps moving. “Two down, one left. The last one’s loaded for a breach.”

I check the feed. She’s right; the final Ronin is pulling a brick-sized cube from his chest rig and slamming it onto the server door. I try to isolate the signal, but the cube is running a rolling code; it’s a logic bomb, set to rewrite every drive on detonation. I run to the server room. Marie’s three bodies follow. Ban is already at the threshold, bleeding from the cheek but solid. The Ronin is inside, planting the device. I shout, “EMP it!” and Ban, without hesitation, throws her own wrist comm through the air. It lands beside the bomb and, at my signal, detonates a micro-EMP. Everything inside the room seizes.

The Ronin, trying to recover, goes for a backup device. Ban crosses the space, hand on his neck, and puts his head through the glass. It's over in six seconds. I stand in the door, heart like a strobe, and see Ban, crouched on the ground, breathing hard but alive. The server core is intact, if you ignore the ruined glass and the bodies everywhere. Marie's bodies step into the space, faces identical but not at all the same. "You did well," she says. "The core is safe." Ban, still crouched, gives a thumb's up, then sags against the server rack. I'm out of adrenaline now. The crash hits, and I want to vomit, or cry, or just lie down in the mess and sleep. Marie's main body studies us both, then says, "We will remember this."

The three of them leave, one by one. Ban looks up at me. "You good?"

"Never," I say, and that's the truth.

She stands and offers a hand. I take it, and together, we step over the bodies, the blood, the shattered comm gear, and stand at the heart of the room we just saved. For now. The irony isn't lost on us. "Good defense," Ban says.

"Better offense."

She smiles, real this time, and we both know what comes next. Outside, the alarms fade, the red dims, and the world returns to its ordinary shade of blue. But nothing is ordinary now. The clock is running. And the next wave will be worse.

We have twenty seconds before the second wave hits, and that's enough time for Ban to unjam her sidearm, slap the bloody cartridge into my palm, and say, "Don't get clever, just shoot center mass." We jog corridor C at a low crouch, sensors dead for the moment, all the environmental lighting hijacked to hospital white. The air is so thick with ozone it tastes like licking a battery. I hear footsteps, then the crash of polycarbonate on tile. Ban knifes the corner, takes one look, and says, "Three, left wall, ballistic armor." The new kids on our tail hesitate; I go low and forward, eat a ricochet in the vest, and let Ban's next three shots do the real work. The rounds are smart enough to curve; the first Ronin drops, his chest cored open like a Halloween pumpkin, and the other two stagger on instinct. Ban's already rolling, and when she stops, it's because she has a Ronin in a headlock and is using him as a shield to empty the rest of her mag into the hallway.

One of the new kids is puking. The other, one with messy blue hair and a ragged patch on her sleeve, is vibrating on pure fear, but her hands don't slip. "Move," Ban says. She hands the Ronin corpse off to the new kid, who stares at it like she's never seen a dead body before, which is probably true. I pull the team forward, keeping the feed live in my lens. The next hallway is already ruined: blood smeared up the walls, Ronin bodies stacked like failed Tetris, and at the far end are two of Curie's own staked up against the sensor panels, eyes burned to glass.

"Fuck," I whisper.

Ban grabs a new mag from the Ronin corpse, wipes it on her pants, and slaps it into her gun. "We've seen worse." *Not together*, I think, but I don't say it. We cut left at the junction. There's a microbreak—a half-breath where nobody is dying—and Ban signals for a pause. The kids stack against the wall, but they're slow, too loud. I check the server room lock. The status flashes green: intact. The Ronin haven't figured out the alternate path yet, but it's a matter of time. "Hold," Ban says, just as a Ronin sticks his head around the next corner. She drops him with a single shot, then gestures. "Your turn."

The plan is to run a distraction—let me peel off to "reinforce security protocols"—but we don't have time for subtlety. I sprint for the side alcove, push into a wall-hatch, and start working the terminal. My hands are shaking, not from the fight but from the weight of what I have to do. The terminal is a cold relic: text-mode interface, monochrome green, login prompt that's as close to a confession booth as I'll ever get. I feed in the credentials we stole last week, punch up the shell, and start the script. It's a simple backdoor, a line of code that will give us access to the server core on D-day. It's so elegantly evil I almost smile: it masks itself as a routine firmware update, time-locked for the exact window when the old admin credentials get recycled. I type, fingers skating over the keys, trying not to think about what this will do to the other eight hundred forty-seven children running on that server farm. I'm about to commit when the terminal throws a warning: ADMIN ACCESS DETECTED. A shadow falls over my shoulder. I look up to see a bodyguard in Marie's suit. She's built like the human version of a server rack, broad and cold, her hands folded just above the neural-link at her left temple. "You should not be here," she says.

I keep my voice casual, bored. "Emergency protocol. Reinforcing firewall per Marie's directive."

Her eyes narrow. "This is not the standard procedure."

I shrug, faking a confidence I don't own. "Nothing about this is standard." She doesn't move. The terminal times out, but I keep the script prepped in the buffer. "Marie wants status updates every ninety seconds," I say, tapping my earpiece. "She said to call if you had questions."

The bodyguard considers this, then folds her arms. "Proceed."

I log out, letting the script install as I do. The buffer wipes itself. Nothing left but plausible deniability. I exit the hatch, heart doing Morse code, and see Ban leading the team up the emergency stairwell. She's already picked off two more Ronin, but now the attackers are using smarter tactics: they're probing with sound, using sonic drones to pin us while a second team tries for the roof. We hit landing three. The air is heavy with burnt plastic and human residue. One of the kids is limping, face torn, but still walking. Ban stops, back to the wall, gun up. "They'll try for the elevator shaft." She's right. I scan the feed and see two Ronin already descending, feet-first, on friction lines. I flip my own sidearm to the shaft, aim up, and wait for the glint of a visor. When it comes, I squeeze twice. The first shot bounces, useless. The second finds the gap under the helmet and turns the Ronin's head into a spray of quantum dust. The other one gets spooked, loses grip, and plummets three floors. When he lands, Ban's already there, putting him down with a tap to the heart. She says, "Don't waste ammo on the armor."

I say, "Wasn't aiming for the armor," but she knows and I know and the new kids sure as hell know I'm not a gun guy. We move. At the top, Ban signals a hold, then nods me toward the master lock on the roof door.

It's a biometric—Curie high-end, triple redundancy, but the Ronin already melted two of the three sensors. I slap my palm on the plate, let it read me, and hope Marie hasn't revoked my credentials yet. The door buzzes, then clicks open. Outside, the roof is cold and perfect, a field of solar panels and comms dishes. Ban ducks behind a panel and scans the skyline. "See them?" I ask.

She points. "Four, west side. More in the access tunnel." I hug the deck and crawl up behind her. We're in a killing field, but at least up here, you can see the city. It looks indifferent to our problems. Then the world goes orange. A Ronin pops from cover and hurls a brick of bright blue at us. It's not a bomb. It's a consciousness scrambler, the new kind: you don't even have to inhale it. You just get close, and it makes your neurons forget how to talk to each other. Ban sees it, yells "Down!" and pushes me flat.

I hear a wet pop as the brick detonates. The air trembles, not with heat but with meaning: my brain fuzzes, vision doubles, and for a second, I forget why I'm here. The effect lasts a heartbeat, then the firmware in my own head resets and I can see Ban, doubled over, clutching the back of her skull. The new kid with blue hair is not so lucky. She goes limp, then seizes, then just shudders on the ground. The other kid, the crier, curls up and starts to scream. Ban's already crawling toward the source of the scrambler. Two Ronin emerge, guns raised. She throws a blade, hitting the first in the neck. The second fires, but misses. Ban barrels into him, uses her whole weight, and they both tumble over the lip of the roof. I run to the edge, dizzy, pulse racing. Below, Ban hangs by one hand from the rain gutter, blood running down her arm.

I kneel and try to grab her. “You alive?”

She grins, bloody teeth showing. “Always.” I haul her up, but it takes both hands. She hits the roof, rolls, then comes up ready. “Status?”

I can barely hear for the ringing in my ears. “Server core’s still green. Marie’s bodyguards are everywhere.”

Ban wipes the blood from her mouth. “They’ll use the main shaft next. If they get in, it’s over.”

I nod. “We can lockdown from the admin console. But it’ll draw attention.”

She shrugs. “They’ll be dead, or we will.” I look at her arm. The cut is deep and bone-white, but she doesn’t care. “Go,” she says. “I’ll hold here.”

I hesitate. Then I run, down the stairwell, three steps at a time. At each floor, I hear more fighting, see more bodies—Curie’s, Ronin, some already being cleaned up by janitorial drones that don’t care what side you’re on. I duck back into the server room, slip past the Marie bodyguard, and work the console. The lockdown protocol is three lines of code, but the Ronin are already tapping at the outside door. I finish the command, key it, and the server room seals with a hiss and the hard thump of maglocks. On the monitor, I see Ban, crouched on the roof, gun raised, scanning for movement. She’s alone now. I tap the comm. “You clear?”

She answers, “For now.” I sag against the wall, breathing hard. My hands are still shaking. On the feed, the main entrance shows the Ronin loading up for a last run. There’s a big guy at the front, wearing heavy armor, carrying a bag that I know—

without looking—holds the same scrambler that almost erased us. They mean to end it. But so do we. I lock eyes with Ban through the camera. She says, "You ready?"

"Never."

She laughs. It's a brutal sound, honest and alive. "Let's make it count." We do. The Ronin charge, and so do we. And the city, uncaring, watches us burn each other down to the bones.

The server core is a cathedral to blue. Eighty meters of brushed aluminum, cold as apathy, each rack pulsing with a heartbeat that's not human and never will be. The room is ringed by a horseshoe of armed workstations and topped by a grid of cameras so dense you can't move your eyelids without making the audit log. At the heart of it are two transparent cylinders—each as tall as a man—that house the most important 847 children you'll never meet. They're not even physical, just consciousness clusters, jittering inside a cloud of containment gel. We bar the last entrance with a dead Ronin, his arm still twitching, gun half-melted to the floor. Ban stands beside me, bleeding slow from her left shoulder, but her grip on the rifle is rock steady. I reload and check the action. The new kids are gone—either dead or off the board. It's just us, the blue, and the sound of a tactical boot stamping a thousand faces per second. Ban checks the corridor camera, then glances at me. "Four left, maybe five," she says. "Two with the real gear. One carrying the bag."

I don't need her to specify: the bag means a bomb, and the bomb means the end of everything above ground. "What's the play?" I ask, voice shaky.

She grins, teeth stained red. “We hold. We buy the cycle. Marie does the cleanup.” I check the server feed. The status is still green, but the warning overlays are so dense I can barely see the live video. Above us, the ceiling cracks—Ronin, coming through the maintenance duct. I look at Ban. She’s already dropped to one knee, aiming high. “Ready?” she whispers.

“No,” I say, and that’s the truth. The first Ronin lands hard, hitting the deck with the grace of a failed gymnast. Ban puts a round in his mask before he even lines up the shot. He drops, and a second Ronin tumbles through, firing blind. I duck behind the workstation, squeeze off two shots, and catch him in the thigh. He stumbles, then collapses. Ban finishes him with a bullet to the head. There’s a brief silence, then the side door blows. Three Ronin rush the core, all masked, all screaming at frequencies that make my teeth ache. Ban mows down the first two, but the third gets close, arms up, and hurls a grenade into the cylinder’s base. It hits, bounces, and rolls to a stop at my feet. For one, perfect instant, I do nothing.

Then Ban’s hand is on my back, shoving me forward as she kicks the grenade across the room. It explodes against the wall, hurling shrapnel in a cloud of hot metal and plastic. My leg gets tagged, but the pain is sharp and local. Ban gets the worst of it: a spray of needles to the thigh, tearing open her pants and the meat underneath. She hisses, but doesn’t drop. “Patch me,” she says, tossing me the trauma kit.

I slap the patch on her wound, then jerk her upright. “Stay with me.”

She laughs, spitting blood onto the console. “I was born for this.” On the feed, I see the last two Ronin regrouping in the corridor. One is dragging a bag, the other's suit is marked with a red stripe—command. They prep a charge, then ready for the run. I take the spare mag, load it, and ready myself at the workstation. Ban, never missing a beat, switches her aim from ceiling to door. Her shoulder wound is leaking down to her hand, but her eyes are live. "Here they come," she says.

The Ronin charge the door, guns blazing. I drop and fire, grazing the leader. Ban pops up, tags the one with the bag, and blows his chest open. The leader keeps coming, diving for the cylinder's base. He pulls a knife, jams it into the side panel, and uses it as exploit to pop the maintenance hatch. I run for the panel, slam his hand in the hatch, and hear a crunch. He drops the knife, but not the charge. Ban covers me, firing at the Ronin trying to follow through the ceiling vent. The leader gets his other hand on the hatch, rips it open, and shoves the charge inside. I lunge, grab his arm, and pull him away. We wrestle, rolling across the floor. His helmet cracks against my face and I feel the nose break, tasting the blood. He's heavier, but I have the advantage: desperation. I get the knife, bury it in his armpit, and twist. He gasps, then brings up his free hand and punches me in the throat. I go limp, everything flashing red and black. He's over me, hands on my neck. I flail, reaching for anything. My hand closes on the cable from the charge. I yank it, hard, and the detonator snaps off. Ban's voice cuts through the haze: "Move, Skelm!"

She shoots the Ronin in the back, once, twice, three times. He lets go. I crawl away, gagging, throat on fire. Ban puts a bullet in the Ronin's skull, then stumbles to the console. She slaps a hand on the emergency lockdown, then another on the wound at her thigh. I stagger up, blood streaming down my shirt, hands shaking. In the corner, the charge is still live. I crawl to it, rip open the casing, and pull the battery. It fizzles, then dies. For a moment, there is nothing. Just the blue, the hum, and us, alive. Ban drops to the floor, back against the server rack. I sit next to her, clutching my broken nose, trying not to pass out. She looks at me, then at the wall of gel where the 847 run, safe and ignorant. "Good show," she says, voice hollow. I want to laugh, but my chest just spasms. I remember the backdoor, the script I left in the console, the thing that will let us end all this in ninety days. I shudder, not from pain but from the weight of it. Ban senses the shift. "You did it?" she asks. I nod. She leans her head back, eyes closed. "Good."

We sit there, bodies broken, staring at the ceiling. Then, all at once, seventeen Maries file into the server core. They're all bleeding—some from the arms, some from the legs, one from the face—but they're smiling. The lead Marie surveys the carnage, then kneels in front of Ban. "You have exceeded expectations," she says.

Ban grins. "We aim to please."

Marie turns to me, then gestures to the console. "You saved the core?" I nod, too tired to say anything. She smiles. "Perfect protection."

Ban laughs, voice low. "That's what you pay us for."

Marie stands, looking down at the mess: the Ronin bodies, the ruined hardware, the puddles of leaking brain-gel. "This will be remembered," she says. "You have done what no one else could." She leaves, her other bodies trailing like a shadow.

I turn to Ban. Her eyes are open, but she's gone somewhere else. "Did we win?" I ask, not knowing if she can answer.

She sits up, groans, and looks at the blue-lit wall of children. “We held the line,” she says. Then, softer, so only I can hear: “Now we wait for the fire.”

I lean back, let the blue light wash over me. This is the price. Bodies everywhere, nothing left to save but a memory of who we used to be. In ninety days, the script will run. And the blue will be gone, forever. Ban takes my hand. I hold on. Because when the end comes, it’s good to know you’re not alone in the dark.

Chapter 24

The medical wing is a living lie: on the badge scan it's "Sublevel Four, Recovery & Research," but the floor smells like bleach, ozone, and old fear, the kind you only notice if you're not supposed to survive the night. The white is total—walls, floors, even the ceiling—glossed to an autoimmune shimmer that fights back any stain. Rows of neural interface stations take up the center of the room, each cradle occupied by a body, each body upright and upright only because the station will not release until the neural bomb is deactivated or the host stops being alive. There are 847 in all, plus overflow in the sub-basements. Ban and I stand in our own white—this time they didn't even bother with tailored fits, just gave us the disposable coveralls you use to clean up hazardous spills. It's all for show: every movement in the wing is recorded from five angles, every word logged for "post-incident review," but the real reason they have us here is for the effect. Ban's presence is a guarantee, mine is a warning, and together, we're a threat only if you understand the math.

The first row is mostly juniors, stacked by age and metabolic index, each with the telltale neckport of a quick-brain install. The neural bombs are small—a sliver of retrofitted grey matter, hardwired to blow the synapses if the activation signal runs more than seven seconds without a return ping—but each one is also a work of art. "Precision ablation," the briefing said, as if the consequence of failure wasn't 847 kids spattering the gel wall in a fraction of a heartbeat. The techs doing the deactivation look like they were borrowed from another world: soft-eyed, all wrists and nervous energy, their hands trembling a little as they thread the fiber leads into the ports. I recognize two from yesterday's emergency triage—both are wearing gloves one size too large, a tell that the inventory is being rationed in real time, or that management is already prepping for the next disaster.

Ban's posted at the end of the first row, spine locked, the bulk of her shoulder muscles visible even under the cheap white. Her eyes never rest; she's scanning the ceiling, the mirrored glass, the pulse and drift of every tech who's trying not to look at us. Every so often, she shifts her weight, tapping her boot against the tile in a pattern I've learned to read: one tap for each time a threat crosses the margin between "potential" and "actionable." I'm here to observe, or so the admin briefing said. In reality, I'm running a low-level scan with the optics, logging every phase of the bomb deactivation so we can replay the technique later. The headset is locked in record-only mode, but I modified the driver this morning; every time I blink, the internal buffer writes a snapshot to a hidden partition that no Curie AI has the clearance to read.

The first deactivation takes forty-two seconds. The body in the cradle is a boy—twelve, maybe, but the growth lines on the teeth say he's lived a couple years inside an accelerated learning shell. His eyes are open, but he's somewhere else. The tech whispers to him, in Korean, then clicks the interface probe into the neckport. There's a series of gentle beeps, then a sharp rising whine as the system logs the handshake. A readout appears on the side of the station, blue bars scrolling left to right. At twenty percent, the boy's fingers start to twitch. At fifty, his head jerks back, eyes wide but unseeing. At ninety-six percent, the neural bomb pings a false negative, and the cradle cycles into lockdown mode. The tech looks up, panicked, then over to the supervisor, who's watching through the glass with the practiced nonchalance of a man who has seen this go wrong enough to stop flinching. The tech wipes her brow and tries the probe again. The readout cycles once, then completes. A green pulse runs up the boy's spine, visible under the skin like an afterimage, then fades. The tech's breath fogs her visor. She signals the next station. Ban tilts her head, just enough to log the sequence. "Copy that?" she mutters, subvocal, the mic in her throat picking up the sound.

I blink twice. "Copy and indexed." The row fills with the soft hiss of the deactivation process. Each station runs its own log; every sixth body shakes, a few cry, but most just stare ahead, glassy-eyed, waiting for someone to tell them what to be afraid of next. We're three rows in when the air pressure changes—subtle, but enough to make the microhairs on my arm stand up. The door at the end of the hall slides open with a sound like wet teeth grinding, and Marie steps in. Except it's not Marie; it's three of her, moving as a unit. The lead body wears the high-collar Curie black, a contrast to the white of the medical techs, while the flanking bodies are dressed for business, two steps up from the station's admin, two steps down from the boardroom. The effect is calculated: one Marie to command, two to observe, all three to witness. They approach with a glide I've only seen in predatory insects, the bodies never quite syncing the stride, always just off by a quarter-beat. The voices come at us in triple stereo.

"Exceptional work today," says the lead.

"Your compliance with protocol is commendable," the second adds.

"Curie values initiative, but we value loyalty more," finishes the third.

Ban and I snap to at the same moment, eyes locked forward, hands at our sides. It's the same maneuver we practiced a hundred times in training: never outshine, never defer, just mirror and hold. Marie's lead body stops a meter away, the face radiant under the surgical lights. For a second, I swear the skin is actually glowing, then I realize she's running a mild transdermal bioluminescence—a new tweak to unsettle us, or maybe just to assert patent dominance over every other body in the room. "Ban Zhao. Darby Skelm," she says, and for a moment, I can't tell which of the three is speaking. The words float on the air, perfectly harmonized.

"Ma'am," we both answer, in unison.

Marie pivots, so fast the hair on her collar flares with static. "The Rising Ronin were neutralized with efficiency exceeding projections. The board is pleased." She turns to look down the rows of deactivated bodies. "The preservation rate for the 847 is within optimal variance. The loss curve is acceptable."

Ban's jaw is set, the muscle ticking just once. I feel her pulse spike through the open comm, but she keeps her voice even. "We followed standard escalation. The server core was never breached."

"Not never," Marie corrects, but there's a smile in it. "Just long enough to establish future negotiating position." Her eyes, all three sets, turn on me. I hold the gaze, fighting the urge to flinch as the three faces align, just for a split second, into a composite that is neither Marie nor any human I've ever met. "In recognition of your service, Curie would like to offer you permanent placement. Full board benefits, priority housing, and a path to upward mobility in the security apparatus."

Ban and I exchange a look, rehearsed for this exact moment. I let the microsecond delay register as surprise, then let my face settle into a mask of gratitude barely undercut by suspicion. "We're honored," I say, calibrating the tone for exactly the right level of humility. "But we would need time to discuss the terms."

Marie's three bodies nod in unsion, the effect as perfect as an animation loop, and somehow twice as real. "Of course. We value consensus. You have forty-eight hours to respond."

Ban bows her head. "Thank you, ma'am."

The lead Marie reaches out and lays a hand on my shoulder. The touch is ice-cold, not from temperature, but from the total absence of any wasted motion. "You have earned this," she says, and the three voices align so perfectly that, for a moment, I hear nothing but the echo in my own skull. Then the hand withdraws, and Marie glides away, her two shadows in perfect orbit.

The air pressure normalizes, and the room returns to the noise of techs and suffering and the hum of twenty thousand cycles per second. Ban looks at me, the faintest ghost of a grin on her lips. "Nailed it."

I exhale, then blink three times to dump the last fifteen seconds of data into the buffer. The brief moment of camaraderie is already fading. Forty-eight hours, she said. And now, as we watch the next row of children wait for their turn under the probe, it's clear what she meant: our window is closing. If we're going to burn it all, it has to be soon. But for the rest of today, we wear the white, and watch the future get unmade, one child at a time.

The apartment is as close to safe as anything gets here: a box on Level 18, up-piped with recycled air, plastic furniture, and a window that looks out onto the fake horizon. The decor is hospital minimal—no art, no flowers, just the stainless signature of company living. We've swept it for bugs five times this week, four before I even got out of bed. Ban doesn't trust the silence, so she fills it with motion, pacing from wall to wall like she's wearing a groove in the tile. The signal jammer sits in the corner, humming just above the human threshold. It's disguised as an air purifier, right down to the blinking panel and the cheap pine-fresh scent. I check the readout: green, then blue, then nothing. The kill zone is active.

Ban stops on her sixth pass, turns, and locks her eyes on me. She's still in the coverall, but her hands keep drifting to the inside of the sleeve where I know she stashed a mono-wire, just in case. The threat radius on that thing is measured in millimeters, but it's better than nothing if Marie sends more bodies before the window closes. I pull up the Curie security grid on my portable, flooding the room with a lightshow of blue lines and red danger zones. The interface floats above the coffee table, a city block of risk mapped out in thirty meters of vertical stack. I rotate the schematic, drag a finger along the likely escape route, and wait for Ban to comment. She doesn't. Instead, she cracks her knuckles, then runs her thumb along the invisible blade under her sleeve. "Three days," she says. "Then we're ghosts."

The words hang in the air, dense and sweet. I check the security grid for the third time, marking the camera dead zones we baked in over the last month. Each one is a favor, called in or hacked or slipped into a firmware patch when the new sensors went online. The guard rotations have a seven-minute blind spot at every shift change, and the backup alarms are patched to reroute any alert to a sandbox instance that reports green, no matter what. Ban leans over my shoulder, breath warm and metallic. She taps the point where the main corridor intersects with the biomed lab, then double-taps the fire exit. "We breach here," she says. "Three minutes to clear the cameras, one to hit the override on the lower security doors. You handle the core; I'll do cleanup."

I nod, already moving to the next step: prepping the payload. I pull a pair of microdrives from my pocket and hand one to Ban. She cracks it open and scans the contents with a glance. "Data's intact?"

I smile, tight and small. "Triple-layer encryption. Even if they get past the first two, the last partition will brick the drive." Ban sets it on the table, then steps back and starts pacing again. “What about the others?” I ask, and my voice sounds thin in the airless room.

Ban’s face hardens. “Katherine is soft, but she’ll follow. Dorothy’s on the edge; could go either way.”

“We could leave them a signal,” I say, but Ban shakes her head.

“They come with us, or they’re liabilities. No witnesses. No soft landings.” The words land like a knife: clean, precise, absolute. I think of Katherine, her fingers trembling as she rerouted the Ronin from the main corridor; of Dorothy, half-machine and barely human, but loyal beyond her own pain threshold. The calculus is simple, but the accounting never gets easier. I close the security grid, then cycle the jammer to full burn. The white noise sharpens, masking the words we’re not supposed to say out loud. Ban stops at the window, stares out at the fake night, and flexes her hands. “You ready?” she asks, and there’s no mockery in it, just the cold certainty of someone who’s already committed to the worst possible outcome.

I look down at the table, the microdrives, the mapped escape routes, the next forty-eight hours balanced on the edge of what we’ve already done. I nod. “Ready.”

Ban lets the silence stretch, then grins, just for me. “Good,” she says. “Because once we start, there’s no way back.”

The plan is perfect. The variables are all accounted for. But in the silence that follows, I realize that what I’m really afraid of isn’t Marie, or the Ronin, or even the prospect of being vaporized if the last fail-safe kicks in. It’s that Ban and I are now so deep inside our own plan that I can't remember what it was like to be on the outside. I lock the window, kill the lights, and sit back in the dark. In thirty-six hours, we either walk free or disappear forever. And right now, I don't know which I want more.

The operation starts at 02:37, which is either the deadest part of the night or the earliest part of the day depending on whether you plan to survive to see sunrise. I run the first diagnostic sweep from our quarters—simultaneous shell scripts on four different server nodes, each calibrated to create a network event that requires human review. The protocol is textbook: as each event escalates, it pings the system admin to run a full self-check, which in turn dumps all non-priority traffic into a holding pattern. For the next sixty-four minutes, Curie's entire security apparatus will be running at ten percent, and even then, the only eyes watching are AI redundancies on the far end of the lag.

Ban and I wear maintenance uniforms this time, the generic blue smocks and hard hats that nobody even looks at twice in the service corridors. The RFID tags are cloned, their IDs pulled from a pair of real workers on paid "wellness leave" courtesy of a bogus HR flag I slipped into the scheduler yesterday. Ban carries her tool kit in her left hand, right hand always ready, and I carry the data drive in an inside pocket, snug between the breast and the kill switch. We move fast. The sub-hallways are bone white, no cameras except at the intersections, and even those are old, analog, and with a lag so thick you could dance through the frame and not be noticed unless you trip over the corpse of a previous failure. Ban takes point, head down, steps measured to match the floor pattern. I follow, heart thudding in time with the pulsed overheads.

The first checkpoint is empty, but the second has a bored guard at the desk. Ban slows, then signals a pause. We stop, shuffle papers, act the part. The guard glances up, registers our uniforms, and goes back to his terminal. I see the drink in his hand—real caffeine, not the synth stuff—and his badge hanging loose, numbers on display. I log the badge number, then we move on. At the junction, Ban takes a hard left, into the shadow of the cleaning closet. The lights flicker, either a scheduled power save or just the building's way of reminding us it can kill the mood at any second. We duck inside. Ban peels the back off the tool kit, revealing a short barrel, silencer already fitted. "We might need to go loud," she says, but her face is flat and unbothered.

I nod, prepping the microdrive in my palm. "You get the others?"

She checks the wristband for messages. "Katherine is in position. Dorothy will be five seconds early."

"Of course she will," I say, but there's warmth in it. The air in the closet tastes like burnt plastic and old ammonia, the sting so strong it brings up a memory I didn't ask for: week three of the program, when the trainers hosed down a riot in the sleep wing, and everyone was coughing up blue for days. I shake it off. *Focus.* We run the next stretch in parallel: I break right to the mainframe core; Ban takes the utility stairs to the rendezvous. We move fast, never in the open for more than a blink. Every door that matters is already patched to open on our badge; the rest we can force if we have to.

At the base of the mainframe, Katherine is waiting. She's lost weight, and her uniform hangs loose at the joints. Her eyes are fixed on the access panel, one hand tracing the edge of the door like she's petting a wounded animal. She nods as I approach. "You ready?"

"Do it," I say, and we enter together. The server room is a meat locker, cold and bright. The racks hum with the same frequency as a dying brain, and the only sound is the whisper of recirculated air. Katherine heads for the nearest terminal, slips in the drive I hand her, and taps out the command sequence. The display flickers blue, then green, then settles on a series of progress bars that crawl with exquisite slowness. I check my watch. "Eighty seconds."

Katherine gives a twitch of a smile. "Plenty of time."

She pulls a second drive from her pocket, this one dark and heavy, and loads it into the admin slot. "You sure?" I ask.

She doesn't answer. She's already running the wipe routine, hands so steady you wouldn't think she's been shaking for the last three years. I'm about to check the hallway feed when Ban and Dorothy arrive together, silent as ghosts. Dorothy's uniform is clean, pressed, like she's doing a dress rehearsal for the real thing. Ban is at her side, a hand on Dorothy's elbow, as if guiding a missile to its target. Dorothy grins at me, teeth too perfect to be natural. "We all good?"

"Perfect," I say, and mean it. Then everything freezes.

From the corridor comes a sound—soft, deliberate, just off the normal pattern. Ban signals a halt with two fingers, then turns her head. She's listening. I step to the door, angling myself to see without being seen. Down the hall, a guard rounds the corner. He's not supposed to be here—wrong time, wrong route—but luck is never perfect. He sees the door ajar and steps closer. Ban doesn't hesitate. She slips into the hall, moving with a speed that's not possible in the normal run of human muscle. The guard looks up and starts to speak. Ban's hand is already at his throat, a twist and a press, and his eyes go glassy. He drops without a sound. She drags him into the supply alcove, tucks his head against the mop bucket, and wipes her hands on his shirt. Neat, untraceable. I go back to the console. Katherine's routine is at ninety-six percent. She's trembling now, eyes fixed on the display. "Almost," she says, voice a whisper.

Dorothy stands beside her, running the numbers on the feed, checking for any alarm that might catch us in the act. There's a flicker—an anomaly on the network, just a tick in the log—but Dorothy's already on it, rerouting the packet through a ghost node. The system swallows the false input, and the room is safe again. Ban closes the door and leans against the frame. "Ninety seconds," she says, looking at me.

"On schedule," I say. At the terminal, the progress bar ticks to completion. The system pings: DATA TRANSFER COMPLETE.

Katherine pulls the drive and hands it to me. I slide it into the hidden pouch, feeling the weight of a hundred lives in my palm. "We're clear," Katherine says. Dorothy pulls the shutdown on the mainframe, and the lights in the server bay dim, just for a second, as if the building is holding its breath. Ban signals the next phase. We move as a unit, four across, taking the service stairs up two levels to the maintenance corridor. There's a last checkpoint, but the guard is gone—shift change, just as planned. We cross the hallway, merge with a group of real maintenance techs, all of them too tired or too high to notice us. We walk with them for fifty meters, then break left at the fire exit. At the perimeter is the final challenge: an exit lock designed to trigger an alarm if anyone passes without a retinal scan.

Dorothy steps up, running her own scan from a pocket device. The door unlocks, just like in the test run, but as we start through, the overhead lights flare, and the alarm begins to tick up—a soft, rising chirp, not loud enough to be urgent, but insistent. I drop my last card: the panic code. It reroutes the alert to the secondary zone on the far side of the building, simulates a minor chemical leak, and flags all systems to send their data to a quarantine area that's already corrupted by our worm. The alarm dies. The lights go normal. Ban grins, and for a moment, the tension breaks. We walk out into the city: four bodies in maintenance blue, heads down, moving at a pace so perfect it's almost invisible. Outside, the air is wet with fog, the city's neon waking up as the night dies.

We split at the intersection, Ban and I going west, Katherine and Dorothy east. In thirty minutes, if anyone is looking, the only record of our passing will be a string of blank security logs and a handful of corrupted badge pings. We don't look back. Ban takes my hand, just for a second, then lets it go. In the distance, a siren starts, then stops. I check my watch. 03:14. We're ahead of schedule. In the morning, the board will wake to a system in shambles, two dead guards, and a data dump so thorough it will take months to unravel. Marie will know. She'll understand the signature. But by then, we'll be somewhere else, new names, new uniforms, a new god to kill. We pass a window and see our reflections: four maintenance workers, faces smudged and anonymous. Just the way we planned. We turn the corner, and the city swallows us. In the darkness, Ban whispers, "Perfect."

And I can't help but agree.

Chapter 25

There are exactly ninety-two seconds between guard patrols on the sublevel D maintenance corridor. I burn through the first twenty-one of them popping a floor panel, the next nine squeezing my body through a vent diameter rated for emergency robots, not humans, and the rest at a dead crawl, counting every breath so I can match the relay at the end of the tunnel. The vent is lined with composite insulation, spongy enough to bruise elbows and knees without making a sound. Sweat sluices down my forehead, so thick the salt nearly blinds me. For a second, I want to stop and wipe my face, but the math says no—if I hesitate, if I lose even half a second, the game is already up. At the tunnel's end, a mesh gate bars my exit. I tap in the six-digit sequence Ban burned into my memory last night. The mesh vibrates, then clicks free, and I shove through into a gloom lit by nothing but LED panel bleed and the jaundiced flicker of the environmental controls. I hit the deck, flat to the concrete, just as the first guard rounds the corner. She's early, by two, maybe three seconds. But I'm lower to the ground than her eyeline, and the darkness here is real, not aesthetic.

She passes. I can smell her—cleaner, cheap musk, a coffee hangover sweating out her skin. I hold my breath for another eight seconds, then move. The next checkpoint is a service door, locked, but I've got three exploits in my back pocket. I choose the loudest one, because that's what Ban would do, and because somewhere upstairs, Ban is already prepping the next layer of hell for anyone who tries to follow us. I route a bypass through the ancient badge reader, then slam my palm against the steel. The lock cycles, whines, then opens on a wet pop. I'm in. There's a ladder here, but it's ornamental, like most safety features. I take it anyway—two rungs at a time, then jump the last meter, landing with a crunch that echoes in my teeth. Below is the server bay: fifty meters of cooled air and blinking logic, all humming with the knowledge of everyone who's ever mattered to Curie. I cross the bay, hugging the racks, until I see the access panel I need. My portable pings, silent. Ban. "Status?" she says, voice a flattened whisper, modulated so the mics in the hallway won't catch it.

"Two seconds behind, three at most," I say, typing one-handed.

"Doors will lock in six-zero. Don't be late."

I plug in the cable, and the server logs in with a handshake I forged myself—a joke admin account, flagged for test access, never deleted because the world is run by idiots with too much time and too little paranoia. The first payload is an over-heat script for the mainframe. Nothing dangerous, just a slow bake to edge the coolant sensors into panic mode. The second is a packet storm that'll fry every external comms relay for the next five minutes. And the third—the jewel—is a backdoor so subtle even I'll need a blood sample to verify I ever wrote it. I deploy all three, then kill the lights for good measure. Above me, the ceiling creaks—Katherine, somewhere in the ductwork, running her piece of the job. If Ban is the hammer, Katherine is the scalpel. She moves like a whisper, only less polite. The ping on my portable shifts: now it's Dorothy. Her avatar is a skull with cartoon pigtails and three warning triangles, none of which match her actual face. Her message is simple: "Phase two in T-minus one minute."

I smile, letting myself enjoy the way the timing is so tight it almost hurts. As I round the last rack, a security drone floats up from the aisle. It's small, but loaded with cameras, and the red of its lens blinks a question I don't have an answer for. I freeze, flat, trying to recall the activation windows on this model—nineteen seconds to full scan, ten more before it tags for enforcement. I press my badge to the reader and roll my thumbprint across the sensor. The drone hesitates, thinking it's a service call, and floats away, logging my presence as "maintenance: anomaly." Three more steps, and I hit the airlock leading to the tunnel proper. That's when it gets interesting.

The airlock is sealed, the inside glass fogged with condensation. On the other side, I can just make out a moving figure—male, maybe older than me, definitely not on any of our team lists. He's pounding at a panel, swearing in Mandarin, and from the way he's hitting it, I can tell he's used to things breaking on him. I cycle the airlock once, twice, then override it with a hard reset. The glass clears, and I step inside, face-to-face with the stranger. He's wearing the standard facility tech jacket, but the name tag is missing, torn off in a hurry. His hands are raw, knuckles stained with coolant fluid and a streak of something redder. "Who the fuck are you?" he says, and the tone is so familiar it's almost homey.

I give him the smile I save for police interviews. "Fire code inspection. Critical maintenance only." He doesn't believe it, but his badge is low-rank. He can't stop me. I sidestep him, then slap the override again, cycling the door shut before he can get his bearings. As I move through, I see him already pulling his portable, probably to call upstairs. I trigger the second payload, and a heartbeat later, the signal goes dead. I run, all pretense gone, through the tunnel and into the belly of the beast. The maintenance passage is cold, dry, and narrower than anything OSHA ever signed off on. The floor is stamped metal, slicked with years of dust and probably the residue of every system flush since the place was built. The smell is electrical fire and old air. Halfway down, I see Katherine, dropping through an open panel, landing on her toes. Her face is lit by the soft blue of her portable, and she looks younger, maybe even happy. "Clear on your end?" I ask.

She grins, teeth bared. "Piece of cake. The corridor's locked down, and I've got two guards in a loop chasing their own asses."

"You get the package?"

She holds up a microdrive, then flicks it my way. I catch it and drop it into my pocket, never breaking stride. Dorothy's next. She's waiting at the T-junction, looking bored, her fingers idly tracing the seam on her sleeve where her weapon's hiding. "Ban says you're late."

"Ban likes to exaggerate," I say, and she shrugs, but the edge of her mouth twitches.

She hands me a sealed envelope, the old-fashioned kind, paper and everything. I slit it open with a nail. Inside is a printout, old-school, like something out of the last century. I glance at the lines: bomb codes, launch sequences, admin passwords for systems I barely remember. I read fast, then burn it with the pocket torch in my kit. The ash is cold before it hits the floor. We move together, Dorothy and I, down the final stretch. Up ahead, I hear Ban's footsteps—louder than anyone's, purposeful, echoing off the walls. She rounds the corner, sidearm drawn but pointed down, and levels a glare at me that would peel paint. "You good?" she asks.

"Better than good."

She nods, then checks her watch. "We have sixty seconds to clear the floor before the fire doors lock. You ready?"

"Always," I say, but my heart is jumping like a grenade with the pin already out.

We run. The last stretch is chaos: alarms blare, but the siren is glitched, cycling between three different warning tones. Red emergency lights strobe the corridor. Somewhere above, a firefight is breaking out—Ronin, probably, or maybe just facility security panicking at ghosts. We hit the extraction point, a side corridor with no cameras, no witnesses. Katherine and Dorothy are already there, hacking at a floor panel with improvised tools. Ban pops the panel, and inside is the escape ladder, leading down, down, into the utility access below. I follow her, feeling the air warm as we descend. The ladder shakes under us, not designed for this kind of speed, but we drop three levels in half the time. At the bottom, we land in a tunnel lit by battery lamps. The air is thicker, sour with disinfectant, but it's freedom, more or less. Katherine is the last one down. She pulls the panel closed, then wipes her hands on her uniform, leaving streaks of black all down the front. Ban grins, fierce and wild, then slaps my back so hard I almost drop the drive. "Good run, Skelm," she says.

I grin back, a little manic. "Never doubted us."

She checks her watch again, then gestures forward. "Time to disappear."

We move, four strong, through the tunnel and away from Curie's heart. Above us, the alarms double, then triple. Someone up there is losing their mind. But here, in the dark, it's just us, the hum of the old pipes, and the knowledge that for the first time in a decade, I'm not running from someone else's plan. I'm running my own. And it feels fucking perfect.

The extraction node is two levels below anything the blueprints admit. Even the nav mesh on my portable glitches when I try to map a route; it's like Curie's own architects didn't want to acknowledge this place exists. Ban leads us, four meters ahead, eyes locked on the mesh ceiling as she paces off each junction by memory. Her stride is surgical: no wasted step, no hesitation. I try to keep up, but the air is thick with rust and the dried spit of old coolant, and every breath burns like shame. At the first checkpoint, Katherine kills the cameras with a palm-sized blind. Dorothy patches the lock with a scrap of code, the same trick she used back when we robbed vending machines in the third grade. We pass through a pinch-point corridor—so narrow my shoulder grazes Katherine's, and she winces like a nerve was hit—then into a tiny anteroom, its only decoration a sign that reads "Maintenance: Authorized Only" in peeling vinyl.

Inside, it's as if we tunneled into a skull. Server racks line the walls, bristling with storage bricks the size of children's coffins. The air pulses with the subsonic drone of data flowing in panic. My hands are already numb with anticipation. Ban posts up at the only entrance, checks her watch, and then signals: *seven minutes*. Her face is as unreadable as ever, but her left foot bounces at a rate I've only seen during shootouts or finals week. Dorothy unspools a rat's nest of fiber and jacks a drive into the first port. The screen comes alive—so much color, so many numbers at once. My mouth waters at the sight. Katherine snaps gloves on, kneels by the racks, and starts slapping barcodes onto the drives as Dorothy and I call out their labels. We work by instinct: Dorothy copies the source array, I prep the destination, then we both run a hash check while Katherine does inventory in a whisper. "Blueprints, then HR, then bio-ops," she says. "Order matters?"

Dorothy shakes her head, not looking up. "They'll purge HR first, if they get wise. Blueprints last."

"Fine," says Katherine, but she tags the blueprints anyway, and we all know she'll run her own copy before the night is over. The minutes flatten. My focus narrows to the throb of fans and the flush of warmth every time a drive clicks over to green. We build towers of data, each one balanced on hope, spite, and at least three non-recoverable errors.

Every so often Ban calls the time, never louder than a cough. "Four."

The room hums with tension. Dorothy curses under her breath when a checksum fails, then reruns the job with the cool rage of someone who's had everything taken away once already. I breathe shallow, running simulations in my head: If the guard patrol hits us now, if the HVAC shits out, if Ban gets taken, how many drives can I pocket before the room locks down? At three minutes, a status light in the rack flickers red. Dorothy says, "Corrupted? No way, I triple—"

Katherine cuts her off, yanks the drive, and swaps in a fresh one. "Watch the cache next time," she says, but her hands tremble just a little.

A crash sounds in the hallway, close. Ban tenses, then raises a finger. "Company."

We freeze. Dorothy keeps copying, fingers spidering the keys so quietly it barely counts as typing. Katherine holds a barcode sticker mid-air, her breath steaming in the cold. The door opens, and a security guard leans in, flashlight up. He's a kid—soft-faced, maybe two years older than the juniors in the cradles upstairs. His eyes sweep the room and stick on me, then Ban, then the mess of drives on the table. "What are you doing here?" he asks, voice wavering.

"Emergency backup," I say, and the lie is so worn it slips out smooth. "We're ordered to preserve systems in case the fire doors don't hold."

He takes half a step inside, trying to process the scene, then looks at Ban and flinches. She has that effect on people. "You ... You can't just be here."

Ban moves. She doesn't draw a weapon, just crosses the space in two blinks and clamps a hand over his mouth. The kid tries to fight, but she shoves him against the wall, presses until he goes limp, then lowers him to the floor, out cold but alive. Dorothy gives a low whistle. "Still got the touch, Ban."

Ban wipes her palm on her sleeve, never taking her eyes off the corridor. "Two minutes."

I tap a final command, and the data begins its last crawl: the personnel files, the bomb codes, the blackmail archive that Curie keeps on every exec in the quadrant. Each bit burns hotter than the last, and for a second, I'm high on the possibility of it all. "Last run," says Katherine, labeling the final set of drives with urgent, angry slaps. Dorothy reads out names—old enemies, lost friends, half-remembered ghosts of children who didn't make it to the last grade. Then, there's a warning chime. The emergency lighting cycles red.

Ban whispers, "Wrap it." We pull the drives, pocket as many as we can, then seal the rest in a transport bin. Katherine clips the bin shut and slings it on her shoulder like it's nothing. The room feels different now, emptied of purpose. The server racks blink their silent reproach. I gather the cables, stuff them in my jacket, then scan the room one last time. Ban cracks the door, listens, then signals us forward. We leave the unconscious guard where he is, his body cooling fast in the server chill. Dorothy leads, fast and low, with Katherine close behind. I bring up the rear, hands tight on the data and the burning in my chest. Ban shadows us, never more than a breath away. We slip back into the utility tunnel, the escape route mapped in desperation and rehearsed in nightmares. The moment we hit the first bend, Ban says, "Time."

We stop. The only sound is the soft click of drives in my pocket and the distant howl of the building waking up to its own sabotage. Katherine looks at Dorothy, then me. Her face is both feral and awestruck. "We got it," she says, voice breaking.

Dorothy grins, eyes wild, a smear of dust across her nose. "Fuck yes we did."

Ban looks at me, and her smile is thin, but real. "Next stop?"

I want to say something witty, something that will burn this moment into the memory of whoever gets to read the logs a hundred years from now. Instead, I just nod, and my throat feels raw. We move, one by one, through the dark. Up above, the building is on fire, but here, deep in the bones, we are the virus. For the first time, it feels like we can win.

The safehouse is an old janitor's closet, upgraded with bad intentions. The door sticks unless you kick it at just the right angle; Ban gets it on the first try, as always. We slip inside, shoes off, moving silent to keep the neighbors thinking we're just another layer of trash in the building's sediment. The air is thick with the ghosts of every cleaner, solvent, and illegal smoke ever burned through this place. On the far wall, two "air purifiers" glow soft blue—signal jammers disguised to look like cheap humidifiers, their logos so faded you'd think they'd lived here forever. We lay out the drives on a folding table covered in cracked vinyl. I line them up, edge to edge, by serial, then double-check against the hashes on my portable. The order is perfect. The symmetry is better. Ban strips off her outer jacket, wipes her brow with the inside of her forearm, then unslings the service pistol and lays it down next to the microdrive bin. She pulls a rag from her kit and starts field-stripping the gun, piece by piece, each move as fluid as a line of code running at zero errors.

The adrenaline burn is gone now, replaced by a deep, vibrating exhaustion that works its way up from my feet to my skull. But the high from the job, the payload, the simple perfection of the exploit—that's still running, somewhere in the background. I dock the first drive, sync it to the portable, and start the validation script. It's like watching someone dig their own grave: the numbers pile up, confirming the copy is clean, that what we just stole is enough to blackmail every major syndicate in the quadrant. And that's before the back-door kicks in. Ban lights a smoke, then passes it to me. I take a drag—sharp, sweet, and bitter—and let the air in the room get just a little thicker. On the far side of the table, she taps the barrel of the pistol against the surface, a habit she's never lost. "Three months," she says, nodding at the countdown now ticking across my screen.

I nod. "Whatever time we have left. After that, everything is code."

She grins, teeth blue in the jammer light. "We'll burn the world." The portable's screen flickers, then displays the full status: virus uploaded, root access confirmed, failover in place. All that's left is to wait. I close my eyes, just for a second, and feel Ban's presence beside me—warm, solid, an anchor in the turbulence. Her shoulder brushes mine, and I realize we're both trembling, just a little, from the aftershock. There's a mattress in the corner, threadbare and so old the springs inside have fused into a single, uneven mass. We sit, side by side, shoulders pressed together, the weight of the drives across our laps. Ban takes another drag, then stubs the smoke out on the concrete. “We did it,” she says, and for a second, I think she might cry, but she just laughs, a raw, beautiful sound that fills the room.

I pull the drive labeled “Marie Net Arch” from the array and roll it between my fingers, letting the plastic warm to my touch. This is the one that matters. The rest are just bodies; this is the mind. “Want to see?” I ask.

She shrugs, but leans in. I jack the drive and watch as the data floods the screen. There’s a map—a real one, for once—of the entire Marie network. Seventeen live nodes, hundreds of sub-processes, every one wired into the city like veins through a living brain. Ban whistles, low and slow. “She’s everywhere.”

“Not for long,” I say. “This is the kill switch. Once it triggers, they can’t bring her back. Ever.”

She considers that, then nods. “So we end a god. And then what?”

I have no answer. Neither does she. But as the timer runs, as the seconds roll down like credits at the end of a doomed film, I feel a calm I haven’t felt in years. We did it. We killed a future that had already started to kill us. And as we sit there, side by side, watching the clock, I know that if the world has any hope, it’s this: that sometimes, the best revolutionaries are the ones who learned how to protect before they learned how to burn. Ban lays her head on my shoulder. For a moment, the air is still. Outside, sirens start to scream, but in here, it’s just us, the hum of stolen lives, and the slow, beautiful countdown to zero.

Chapter 26

Whatever time we have left is long enough to forget why you're angry but not long enough to forgive. At three months to the minute, we come back for Curie. The city is cancer-bright and corpse-wet. Rain catches every beam of signage and bleeds it down the streets until it finds us, running neon slicks across Ban's tactical shell and pooling in the creases of my coat. Her stride is unhurried, my own nerves atomizing into the throb of my nervous system implant—a three-watt glow that shivers just under the skin, right where anyone staring would know I'm not even trying to hide. We talk in silence. Eyes, hands, the flicker of a jaw. Ban marks the route with the tap of a knuckle, the rhythm encrypted but unmistakable. She angles left past the debt-pawn windows, pivots off a slick of ceramic tile, then checks the sightline with a half-turn only a camera would appreciate. It's like a ballet for the blind, or maybe an homage to every heist we pulled before the world made this a job instead of a game.

I smell the Curie perimeter before I see it—too-clean ozone mixed with last week's riot control chemicals. Ban's new armor breaks the rain into beads the size of communion wafers, each one holding just long enough to reflect the overlit skyline before sliding off, as if the suit is allergic to sentimentality. The maintenance entrance is tucked under an overhang, shielded from the main avenue by a mound of thermal exhaust coils. The air here is so hot it cuts the chill, even if it stinks of old lube and dying insulation. The door is a brushed steel slab with a reader that should, by all rights, have been upgraded since we left. Ban checks her wrist for time. "Eleven second window," she mouths, and I nod. She's right—every whatever time we have left, the security routine cycles, and the first thirty ticks are soft as dough. I slide the glove from my left hand, palm the codepad, and feel the microcurrent trickle as my skin pingbacks the buried access credential. The pad blinks once, then twice. The lock cycles. We slip inside.

The vestibule is even tighter than the blueprints, a choke of pipes and cable wraps just wide enough for one at a time. Ban's new pistol is matte grey, the barrel nested with an orange ring that tells me she's swapped it to stun. Mine's old-fashioned—a simple slugthrower with an extended mag and three smart rounds, just in case we have to make it personal. We don't speak, but we hear the same sound: a whir, just left of the main corridor. Security cam, model 0409, the "bullfrog" type. Ban hand-flashes: *two, high and low.* I wait for the interval, then step out on her cue. She throws a coin—literally a brass coin, the kind vending machines still eat for fun—down the centerline. The upper cam pivots to track the motion. The lower one blinks, losing focus for half a heartbeat. That's all I need. I sidestep into the dead angle and patch the backdoor code into the access trunk. Ban's face, when I glance back, is so empty it's almost funny; all the old stress burned away, replaced by something more like glee. We're through the first two layers before the real fun starts.

A biped patrol makes their way down the hall—two legs, one battery, and a cranium packed with thermal sensors and a speaker that plays, in theory, the only language anyone responds to: "You are not authorized here." But this one's been modded since we last saw it. The head is upgraded, with a curiosity module that's meant to spot intruders, but in practice just makes the bot drift unpredictably and stare a second longer than necessary. Ban moves first. She swings left, tucks her body flat to the wall, then throws her right leg across the hall, blocking the bot's progress. The machine doesn't expect it; it wobbles, gyros fighting the sudden resistance, then starts a diagnostic that will take just over a second. In that second, Ban plants a magnetic node just under the right knee joint. The next time the bot tries to walk, it will eat the short and brick itself. I love her for that.

I slip past while the bot judders. The service corridor is lined with pipes as wide as my torso, each one coded with a stripe that means something to someone, but to me is just more evidence of a system no human really controls anymore. Ban moves up beside me, hair flat to her skull, the old 847 tattoo now mirrored with a fresh one—three lines, three crosses, a tiny fuck-you to the notion that any pattern is permanent. We work the next three cameras in rotation, always skipping the ones with broken IR. Those are the models Ban and I tampered with last run—failures left in place so the network would trust its own coverage. The real ones are active, but their field of vision is so narrow, we don't even need to crouch.

At the service panel, Ban pulls the toolkit from her vest, cracks it open, and flips the first blade up with her thumb. She traces a line along the seam, then eases the panel off, exposing the layer cake of security behind it. The main access port is shiny with new install—Curie switched the reader, but didn't kill the root exploit we left. I wire in the backup drive and wait for the handshake. While I work, Ban watches the corner. I see her breathing slow, deliberate, pacing her pulse to match the interval on the rolling patrol. The handshake triggers. I feel it—not as a sound, but as a cold line up my left arm, a familiar thrum from my implant. The backdoor code fires, flips the security cameras to "scheduled maintenance," and drops the alarm threshold to just above the noise floor. For the next ninety seconds, nobody outside this hall even knows the corridor exists. We round the last turn, approaching the low stairwell that leads to the interior server farm. Ban flashes her hand, palm open: stop.

Footsteps. Not a bot, but a real human—male, by the pace and weight. The man's uniform is corporate black with Curie's logo stitched in murder-red across the back. He rounds the corner, face slack from a night shift, badge dangling from his lanyard. He sees us. And his mouth drops open. Ban fires the neural disruptor. It's barely audible—just a pop, like biting into a grape—but the man jerks and drops, arms flapping for a moment before he faceplants on the tile. I wince. Not because I care about him, but because I know what it's like to lose time to a blackout. Ban walks over and flips the man onto his back. His eyelids flutter, but there's no danger of him waking. She yanks the lanyard, strips the badge, then gestures with two fingers for me to grab his feet. We drag him into a supply closet—more janitorial ghosts—and prop him upright in a mop bucket, the universal sign of a night gone wrong.

Ban tucks the neural disruptor back into its sleeve, then looks at me, her face bright with sweat and effort. "Just like old times," she says, deadpan. I want to laugh, but the implant is spiking, and my hands are shaking worse than they ever did before. Ban sees, nods once, then pulls the door shut behind us. We are in. Above, the server farm hums with a new flavor of anxiety: three months of curated paranoia, all of it built to keep people like us out. But now, all the alarms have been bent just long enough. Ban checks her weapon, then rolls her neck, the vertebrae popping like gunfire. We head up the stairwell, a team again, ready to tear the world down. It's raining harder outside, but here in the heart of Curie, the air is dry and crackling with every chance we ever wanted.

The first stairwell is the easy part. Ban moves two steps ahead, always on the right where the angle is widest, arm loose and ready at her side. My own steps lag by a deliberate pace—two ticks slower, both for effect and for my own nerves. At landing two, a camera tracks our approach, then loses interest. I feel the shiver in my nerves as the signal goes out, bouncing from sensor to sensor, each one tripped and then tranquilized by the worm we planted three months ago. The effect is total: every feed pings "active," but the only people on it are ghosts from the training sim Ban wrote in her downtime. There's no time to admire the craft. We have twelve more levels, and on each one, the world tries a new flavor of sabotage. Automated floor, blue-green with Curie's insignia: slippery as oil, but only if you're not braced for the loss of friction. At landing five, an acoustic drone hovers at face height, running a predictive routine meant to spot heart rates outside the zone of authorized personnel.

Ban kills it by holding her breath and kicking the drone into the wall. I pass right behind, copying her rhythm, feeling my own pulse slow to match her violence. At landing nine, we hit the first sign of trouble: a heat signature, six meters behind the core door. *Guard*, Ban hand-signs, and I mouth "One?" She shrugs: maybe more. We check the interval—three seconds open, two shut. Ban counts the beat, then throws a mag-scrambler into the space between door and frame. The lock pings, resets, and clicks open for just under a second. That's all Ban needs. She slips through, silent, and I follow. The guard inside is a new model—real human, but backed by a bone-white exo that hums at a frequency so high it burns the inside of my teeth. He registers us and brings up a taser in a single, unbroken movement.

Ban is already on him, tackling him low, using the exo's mass to pull the man down. There's a crack, then a wet noise, then Ban's left hand comes away with the guard's ID bracelet, and the right with a strip of what I assume was his spinal interface. He gurgles. I flinch, but Ban is done with him. We haul the body behind a row of lockers—gray, numbered, all marked with corporate hygiene notices. The blood is black in this light, and it seeps into the gaps like the floor is designed to drink it. Ban hands me the badge, already smudged with sweat and something else. "Next door's a double," she says. "If there's backup, it's coming from the north end." I scan the badge, feeling the pleasant tingle as it tries to handshake with my implant. I loop the credentials, then set a burn routine: the badge will work exactly twice, then auto-wipe. We move.

Each corridor is a horror of efficiency. Curie's design is to funnel attackers toward the dead ends, then flashflood the zone with toxin, or auto-seal with blast shields, or in some cases, just microwave the air until it tastes of burnt teeth. But we designed the path. Every door is open when we need it, closed behind us, each motion tracked by the virus now running at a fever. At the first T-junction, two more guards appear. Both are female, both carrying the new biotech shotguns that never made it past beta in the public line. The lead one calls "Freeze!" but her heart's not in it; she's already aiming. Ban goes low, shooting first at the knee—her favorite move—then rolls and comes up behind the second, who is now fixated on me.

I duck, which is not heroic but has always served me well. The first shot goes wild, pulping a display behind my head and sending a hail of blue dust into my collar. Ban takes both women out in less than five seconds. The first is unconscious, maybe dead. The second, Ban leaves alive, her face mashed into the tile but breathing. We keep moving. The corridor narrows, now a clean, clinical white. My steps leave blood prints, but I don't notice until we're almost at the vault. The server core is sealed with a triple-lock, one physical, two digital. The physical is a thumbprint; the digital, a sandwich of password and live-echo from my own brain. I press my thumb. The pad is cold and squishy. I think for a second about all the fingers that have died here, but then the lock cycles, and the door shunts open on a puff of frozen air.

Inside is a cathedral of glass and steel. Servers arc up the walls, each one lit with a soft blue, like a night sky rendered in binary. At the heart, Marie. Or rather, the physical locus of Marie—a tower of gel, cradled in titanium ribs, topped by a ring of cameras all focused on the entry point. Ban gestures for me to hold. I do. She moves in slowly, scanning the room with the muzzle of her pistol. There's a presence here—something in the air, or maybe the microfibers flexing in the current. I feel it in my molars, a hum that ramps as we approach the tower. Marie speaks, but not with her voice; instead, the room vibrates with a single word, made of hundreds of lips whispering at once: "Welcome."

I grit my teeth. Ban keeps moving, unbothered. The main console is at the base of the gel tower. I slide into the chair, fingers already remembering the feel of the keys, the surface, the exact micro-delay in the feedback. I tap the root password. The screen flickers. Ban scans the room, covering me. She's bleeding, I realize—a scratch along the upper arm, nothing bad, but she hasn't even flinched. The system boots. I plug in the drive and start the payload. The first window is a status bar—unimpressive, given the scale of the hack. The second is an error message, then another. By the time the third window opens, the system is screaming at itself, trying to patch the holes and failing. I watch the numbers rise, code eating code. Ban stands behind me, steady, and for a second, I feel safe. The speakers crackle, and this time, Marie's real voice comes through—tired, clipped, almost human: "Three months of planning, for thirty seconds of execution. You always were efficient, Darby."

I want to say something clever, but my throat is tight. Ban smirks, leans in close, and whispers, "Finish it." The status bar pulses. The virus cascades: one system after another, each logging its own obituary. In the distance, alarms start—first a low pulse, then a rapid-fire klaxon, the kind that makes you want to vomit. The screens all around us flicker, then go white.

For a second, I'm blind. Then it resolves. Every monitor, every projector, every inch of wall now runs a ticker tape of Curie's own destruction.

Marie's voice is still in the air, but it's fading. She tries a last-ditch bluff: "If you shut us down, you die too."

Ban laughs, loud and lovely. "Worth it."

I want to say the same, but I'm busy watching the code work, and for the first time in a year, I feel alive. The core glass begins to sweat. The temperature spikes, then drops. The virus is eating not just the software, but the firmware—the guts, the drivers, the thing that makes Curie run. The last window pops up: "ARE YOU SURE?" I don't hesitate; I press yes. The lights die. The gel tower throbs once, then slumps. I hear the hum of the air system as it loses power, then the pop of breakers, the distant sound of doors unsealing all over the building. Ban puts a hand on my shoulder, and I realize I'm shaking, but not from fear. Just energy. Just adrenaline. I stand, legs wobbly, and look around. The cathedral of glass is now a graveyard. The only light is the red emergency flare from the hall, painting everything in an end-of-the-world glow. Ban smiles at me, blood on her teeth, and says, "Let's go see if the world notices."

Outside the server room is chaos: doors open that were never supposed to, alarms blur into each other, and the Curie guards—what's left of them—are in total panic. Ban and I don't run. We walk, slow, through the carnage, down the corridor, toward the blue-black of the final exit. I look back once, just to see if it's real. The glass tower is shattered, the data gone. We did it. But I have no idea what we've done.

• • •

Collapse doesn't arrive with a bang, or a siren, or a single human scream; it comes in layers. The air shifts first, then the color of the light, then the sound, until all at once, the world is wrong and will never be right again. The red emergency panels flare along every corridor, painting the halls in arterial slices. Ban and I walk into it, into the chaos we made, and I half expect to find resistance—new guards, new weapons, the final test—but instead there are only echoes. The sound of doors slamming in the distance. The slow, digital groan of the mainframe eating itself alive. I feel my implant thrash at the onslaught, a feedback loop so raw it nearly fells me.

On the upper floors, the windows are blacked out. The city beyond, always so urgent, is a faint pulse at the edge of the system. Here, Curie is dying, and it wants the world to know. We take the elevator, because the stairs are sealed, and anyway, who would look for us here? Inside, the cab jitters, the doors fighting the virus for every millimeter. For a moment, Ban and I are pressed together, the air thick with ozone and the synthetic fruit-punch of burning circuit boards. We don't speak. The doors open to Level 41: the executive ring, the nest where Marie and her doubles spent their hours when not watching us. The decor is sickening: the same white glass, the same cold mirrors, but here it's so bright, so carefully engineered, you'd believe it was meant to be a temple.

The main walkway is a bridge of reinforced crystal, arching over a chasm lined with vertical racks. Every six meters, there's a hollow, and inside each one is a Marie. Seventeen in total. I see them even before I know what I'm seeing: identical bodies, in identical poses, hands folded, eyes open, each one staring at the security camera nearest her. They're all in sync, right down to the way the lips tremble as the system begins to fail. The first Marie convulses at the same moment the last does. A ripple through the network, a digital seizure made flesh. One of the bodies wrenches sideways, slamming into the wall so hard the skull dents the plaster; two more fall to their knees, arms windmilling for balance. They try to speak, but what comes out is a chorus of static, a choked parody of Marie's perfect diction. I want to run, but Ban grabs my arm. "Watch," she says, voice almost reverent.

The Maries scream. Not just one, but all of them, and the sound is so perfectly tuned it tears a line through the air and nearly makes me drop. Then, just as fast, silence. Marie's main body—the one with the little scar on the left cheek, the one I always thought was first—turns to look at me. Her eyes are so clear, I wonder if she can see through the fire in the network. She opens her mouth, closes it, then tries again. The voice is a fractured ruin, but it works: "Protected perfectly. Too perfectly." Her smile is wrong, teeth too white, lips too thin. I feel my knees go weak. Ban's hand is warm on my wrist, keeping me upright. Another convulsion. The bodies topple, one by one, into heaps at the base of their hollows. The network fails so fast, you'd miss it if you blinked. The last Marie stands, stares at us, then bows her head and lets her own weight drop her to the floor. There's silence again, but not for long.

Beyond the walkway, the executive offices explode in a riot of movement. People run, not even pretending to have a plan. The vault doors, always sealed with redundant protocols, now stand wide, red lights rotating around the circumference like a warning in a dream. The glass conference rooms, once home to the highest forms of social violence, now hold only the sounds of shattering and the weak, pathetic cries of people who've never known a locked door to fail them. Ban moves first, walking the bridge with the casual indifference of someone immune to the apocalypse. I follow, not because I want to, but because I can't not. Halfway across, the holo-ads lining the walls flicker, then converge on a single message: "EXISTENCE FAILURE. PLEASE CONTACT ADMIN." It repeats the line in every language, even the dead ones.

On the far side, the atrium is chaos. Curie execs—some still in their morning silks, some already half-dressed for evacuation —sprint from office to office, clutching their personal backups, their smart jewelry, and their precious, perishable data. A few try to call for help, but the lines are down. Some grab weapons; some simply sit, blank and blinking, as if waiting for someone to explain the joke. Ban heads for the nearest exit, but the doors are fused, the glass welded shut by an overcooked security protocol. She tries the handle, finds it warm, and laughs. The sound is low, animal, and I recognize it as the one she makes when she wins. A voice on the intercom, looping: "Alert. Network failure. Please evacuate via emergency stairs." It's pointless—the stairs are locked, and the only path down is back through the glass bridge, back over the dead Maries.

I catch a reflection in the glass, and for a moment, I don't recognize myself. Face slick with sweat, lips peeled back in a snarl. Ban is next to me, blood still drying on her arm, her hair plastered to her scalp. She looks beautiful. We make it to the observation deck, where the whole city is supposed to spread out beneath us in awe. The glass is fogged, smeared with the handprints of whoever tried to get out last. Through the blur, I see the skyline, but it looks fake now—like a simulation, or a lie you tell yourself when the real world is unbearable. Behind us is more screaming. I turn and see three execs running, one with a broken arm, another trailing a line of blood from her foot. They're headed for the vaults, but I know the code will never open for them again.

Ban leans against the window, head tilted, and for a moment, she looks tired. Not old, not broken—just tired, in the way you get when you've won so completely there's no fun left. She turns to me and grins. "Worth it?" she asks. I want to say yes. I want to believe it. But the words catch in my throat, and all I can do is nod. Ban sees, and I think she understands. We watch the chaos together, the sound of Curie's death throes a kind of music. The city will take days, weeks, maybe months to process what happened, but by then, we'll be gone. Ban slides her hand into mine. It's not romantic, not a gesture at all. Just a simple act, a code: we did this together, and we'll face what comes next together too.

I squeeze her hand back, feeling the microfractures in her knuckles, the tremor in my own. Behind us, the air shivers as the power grid fails again. The last lights flicker, then go black. The world spins in the dark, and for a minute, there is nothing but the sound of our own breathing. We leave the building the only way left—down, through the stairwells, out into the street. Nobody stops us. The alarms are dead, the cameras blind, the city still too stunned to react. Outside, the rain is gone, replaced by a humid heat that makes my skin itch. We walk, side by side, into the new silence. Ban says nothing. Neither do I. But somewhere in the distance, I hear a voice—maybe a memory, maybe not: "Perfect."

And for once, I think it might be true.

Chapter 27

Curie doesn't burn. Not like wood or paper or anything human. It dissolves—first into vapor, then into something worse. The walls still stand, technically, but the heat peeled the insulation from every server stack, leaving the whole sublevel lined with skeletons of dead circuits and plastic slag. Each step sounds like walking on boiled glass. We take inventory in the aftermath. Not because we care, not because it's policy, but because something has to be counted before it gets erased again. Ban moves three meters ahead of me, stalking the center aisle with the posture of an apex predator who's already decided you're prey but hasn't settled on the method yet. The only thing not new about her is the layer of old blood dried into the cracks of her right knuckles. "Eighteen still green in pod block A," I say, flicking a gel line with my thumb. The cylinder's sensors strobe, pulse, then flatten to an anxious yellow.

Ban doesn't answer—she's elbow-deep in a ruptured interface bay, hauling out cables and slapping emergency foam around the base of a cracked tank. The body inside—the mind, whatever's left—jerks twice, then settles. The readout flicks from critical to stable. It's not enough. "You see how many in block C?" she asks, already knowing I have.

"Thirty-two upright, nine with full synapse trace. Rest are scrambled. Might as well be potato mash."

Ban grunts. She closes the foam with a swipe, then straightens. There's a sound from the next aisle over—a wet gurgle, the kind of noise a dying fish might make in an aquarium that's never been cleaned. She's on it in two strides. I follow, mostly to see what she does. The pod is mangled, one side caved in by shrapnel. There's a face inside, distorted but alive. The status light blinks a slow red. Ban doesn't pause. She digs her fingers into the control panel and yanks once, hard. The skin on her hand tears, but the panel breaks loose. She reroutes the battery line, jams a jumper into the input, and waits. The light shifts to orange, then green. The face relaxes. Breathes, if you can call what's happening inside the tank breathing. "Should hold," Ban says, voice flat.

"Or it'll just drown slower," I say, because neither of us is the type to pretend.

Ban shrugs, wiping the blood on her pants. "Better than nothing."

That's the theme here. Nothing, upgraded. We work down the row, Ban bracing the pods, me logging what passes for a recovery manifest. Every ten bodies, I check the counter at the end of the corridor: 817, 818, 819. The last pod is a child, maybe seven. His hands are up, like he's mid-argument, or maybe just trying to stop the next thing from happening. He's got the weirdly clear skin of a professional clone, probably from one of the board's "premium initiatives." The pod is stable, but the mind inside twitches, looping in a half-conscious fever dream. "Think they'll remember any of this?" I ask.

Ban leans in, eye level with the child. "Would you want them to?"

I don't answer. There's a hum, low and regular, from the far end of the vault. Ban clocks it, tenses, then drops her shoulders to a slouch I recognize as her version of "act natural." She hand-signals: *company*. I tap the gel pod back to sleep and follow. The suits enter in formation. There are four of them—three men, one woman, all with the cultivated indifference of corporate troubleshooters who get paid by the percentage point. The lead is tall, crisp, skin tight on his face like someone ironed the expression off at birth. Ban stops three paces in front of him, arms crossed. He tries to alpha her, stepping inside the radius. Ban doesn't flinch. "Good morning," he says. His voice is premium, somewhere between soothing and a promise you'll never get to collect. Ban stares, waiting. I know my part in this. I lean against the next pod, casual, and log the suit's face for later. The suit looks over Ban's shoulder, seeing the field of ruined pods. "We were told there were survivors."

"There are," Ban says.

The suit's smile doesn't move. "I see. And you're here to ...?"

Ban doesn't blink. "Inventory. Triage. Whatever you call it."

The woman suit checks her portable, then flashes it at Ban. "Authorization?"

Ban lifts her left hand, slowly, and flexes the fingers. The scar on her palm is an authorization. The kind you can't fake. The suits confer, then back down. "Our people," says the lead, "would like to assist in ensuring the safety of the remaining units. We have resources—backup power, environmental controls. Expertise."

Ban's face goes blank. She looks at me. "They want to scavenge," I say. "You'll take the children and move them to your own racks. 'Safeguard' until the next audit, then sell to the highest, or to yourself."

He smiles, no shame. "That's not inaccurate."

Ban turns, picks a rag off the floor, and wraps it around her bleeding hand. "No."

He hesitates, surprised. "We'll pay," he says, "or barter. Favors, access—"

Ban shakes her head. "We're taking them with us," I say.

The suit frowns. "You have no transport."

Ban shrugs. "We'll improvise."

There's a moment, longer than it should be. The suits are used to this going differently. He studies Ban, weighing his options. Finally, he leans in and lowers his voice. "You understand this isn't over. Someone will have to manage the recovery. If not us, it'll be—" He flicks his eyes to the far end of the vault. There, just visible in the glow of the ruined overheads, a cluster of Digital Ascension cultists huddle in the corner, neon crosses glowing on their faces. They're not hiding, just waiting for the business to finish.

Ban sees them, then the suits. "Jackals don't wait for the corpse to cool," she says.

He smiles at the old word, as if it's a compliment. "Efficiency. The world needs it now."

Ban leans in, her voice so low I barely catch it. "Tell your people the next one who touches a child dies. Slow."

The woman suit steps back, actually afraid. The lead gives her a look, then gives me a card. "You'll need resources," he says. I take it, just to end the conversation. They leave, their shoes crisp on the glass.

The Digital Ascension group approaches. They're weirder in person—skin patched with circuitry, eyes rimmed with glowing gold. The leader is young, or at least he looks it. His hands are folded in a way that's supposed to be comforting, but it just looks forced. "You're here to help?" I ask, more out of curiosity than hope.

He smiles, genuine. "All minds must be preserved. Even the broken."

Ban keeps her eyes on his hands. The rest of his flock is already moving through the vault, offering "spiritual service" to the survivors. The service consists of whispering prayers into the pods, in a language that's half-coding, half-liturgy. "They mean well," I say, as Ban watches them.

"Intent doesn't matter," she mutters. One of the cultists stops by a ruined pod, lays a palm against the glass, and closes her eyes. After a minute, the pod's status light flickers. It's probably just a power surge, but for a second, the face inside looks calm.

When we finish the vault, Ban sits on the floor and tears another rag into strips for her hand. I run the numbers on the portables. "Eight hundred forty-seven," I say. "A few dozen still critical."

"Where's our margin?"

I think. "Six hours. Maybe less."

Ban ties the rag, then stands. "We need a truck."

"We need a miracle."

She laughs, the first time in days. "We make those ourselves." I tap the card the suit left behind. It's blank, except for a frequency and a codeword: OBLATION. I pocket it. Above, the air is already cooling, the chemical stink of defeat mixing with a promise of rain. Ban rolls her shoulder, then gestures at the vault. "You think they'll remember any of this?"

I look at her, then at the pods, the faces frozen in sleep or terror. I shake my head. "They'll remember something," I say. And that's all it takes. We move out, inventory complete, the next disaster already waiting on the horizon.

The city's wet at the best of times, but the underbelly is worse. It's always 3 a.m. in the tunnels, always a decade since anyone bothered to fix the condensation drip, always two degrees closer to freezing than the air above. Ban moves in front, silent on the mesh grating, while I lag two paces behind, both for cover and because the tunnels trigger a low, ugly note in my animal brain. The secondary Curie node is five kilometers from the crater of headquarters, in a business park that looks abandoned until you see the thermal bloom in the walls, the pulse of not-quite-legal power draw. We kill the cameras a block out, then duck into a drainage overflow so ancient it predates the last time "hacktivist" wasn't a slur. At the perimeter, Ban pauses and runs her thumb along the underbarrel of her sidearm, a gesture that means she's about to solve a problem in the only way she knows how. She glances back, then hand-signals: *now or never.*

"Copy," I whisper, and tap my portable to prime the malware package. The access panel is supposed to be sealed, but Ban pries it open with a screwdriver and a wordless growl. The maintenance override is inside, a bundle of yellowed cables and a four-port switch. I shunt the virus into the system, then count down with my fingers—three, two, one. On zero, the external security grid goes blind. Ban slides through the hatch, feet first, and I follow, palms already cold with adrenaline. The inside of the node is a fever-dream of bad ergonomics: catwalks, blind corners, no clear sightlines. The walls are lined with composite that does nothing to dampen sound, so every footstep is a drum hit and every cough is a gunshot. Somewhere above, the hum of live servers is a lullaby for the desperate.

Ban leads, eating the layout at a glance, stepping where the sensors are weakest and the lighting is poorest. At the first junction, she grabs a pipe for take advantage of and swings over a motion laser, landing on the balls of her feet without a whisper. I copy her, less graceful, but the system doesn't care. Not now. We hit the main corridor. Ahead, there's an elevator with a worn sticker that reads, "NO PASSENGER TRANSPORT, FREIGHT ONLY." Ban shakes her head at it, then walks straight past to the emergency ladder shaft. "Faster," she says, and starts climbing. I follow, slower. The ladder's slick, and every third rung vibrates with a low, subsonic threat. At the next level, Ban waits for me. She's sweating, or maybe the tunnel is, but her eyes are locked on the small round camera mounted in the ceiling. She makes a fist, then flicks her pinky. It's a signal: hit the junction box, fry the sensor. I thumb a breaker, the portable's voltage spike rippling up the camera and into the wall. There's a fizzle, a pop, and the lens goes dead. For a second, the darkness is total. Ban's voice is in my ear: "Move."

The server core is behind a door that's been welded shut by design and then patched with a padlock, like a joke. Ban snorts, then snaps the lock off with a sideways twist. The force cracks the doorframe, but it opens, and we're in. Inside, the temperature drops. The rack banks are old—twenty, thirty years, maybe—but alive with the soft green flicker of constant emergency. The air stinks of old coolant and something sweeter, maybe decay. We fan out. Ban sweeps the periphery, checking for movement, while I jack into the mainboard. The interface is garbage, but I've seen worse. The hack routine wants admin credentials, so I spoof the old one from Curie's main. The machine shudders, then gives me a shell. I punch up the directory, hands sweating as I search for what matters: the code for the neural bombs, the firmware for the new class of mind pods, and the kill switch nobody is supposed to know exists. Ban whispers, "Left. Incoming."

I duck, just as the panel beside me spits open. A security drone the size of a housecat rockets out, claws extended, voice blaring: "HALT, IDENTITY REQUIRED."

Ban's already on it. She grabs the drone midair and slams it into the floor, hard. The casing cracks, but the drone bites her wrist, teeth digging through the skin. Ban roars, then crushes the body in both hands until it's pulp. "Status?" she says, flicking blood off her hand.

I glance up. "Fine. Got what we need in a sec." The server pushes back, throwing up a firewall. It's not smart, just stubborn. I let the malware eat it, then peel open the hidden partition. Inside, there it is: "NB_DEACT_PROT.exe" I smile. "Found it. Deactivation code for the neural bombs."

Ban checks the corridor. "How long?"

I check the status. "Three minutes, tops."

"Not enough," Ban mutters, but she waits, bleeding on the carpet. The download is slow. I watch the progress, hating the way time slows down at the edge of disaster. On the next shelf, a backup pod ticks awake, and the child inside floats to the surface, eyes open and aware. Ban notices, steps over, and lays a hand on the glass. The child calms, maybe just reading the emotion in her face. Ban turns, and for the first time ever, I see her hesitate. "Can you get the kids out?"

"I can try," I say, and punch the override. The rack shudders, then ejects the first pod, then another. In seconds, the floor is lined with six, each one blinking and wet, but alive. Ban signals: *on me*. We scoop the pods, stack them against the wall, then prime the rest of the racks for mass release. Outside, there's noise. Not an alarm, but voices. Real, not automated. "Ban, company."

She already knows. She grabs a piece of drone and uses it to lever the door, holding it halfway shut as three men in new-issue armor pile down the corridor. The first two are pros—guns out, eyes already mapping our position. Ban doesn't hesitate. She flings the drone's shattered body at the nearest one, then goes low and inside, crushing his knee with a single shot. The man screams, goes down, and Ban kicks his helmet off, then hammers his skull with her elbow until he stops moving. The second shoots at me, but Ban's already between us. The rounds hit her armor, ping, then fall to the floor. She closes, palms up, and snaps his neck in two twists. The third is smarter; he backs up and goes for cover. Ban chases. In three steps, she has him. This time, she doesn't bother with finesse. She punches through the man's faceplate, then drags him back by the collar, using his body as a shield. I finish the download, copy the protocols, then wipe the server clean. "Demo charges?" I ask.

Ban smiles, and her teeth are bloody. She pulls a line of miniatures from her vest, then sets them in the server racks at ten-second intervals. We clear the room, dragging the child pods behind. The next corridor is chaos: alarms now, red and blue and purple, colors that mean more to the system than to the meat inside. At the exit hatch, Ban piles the dead security team in front, then wedges the lock with a snapped-off forearm. We crawl up the shaft, each of us carrying three pods, sweat mixing with blood and the cool fog of the city above. At the surface, it's raining again. The light is neon, filthy. Ban tosses the pods onto a rolling dolly, then scans the area for more threats. I follow, muscles shaking. We sprint down the block, just as the node goes up behind us—first a low rumble, then a blast of blue fire that lights the cloud cover for a kilometer in every direction. Ban breathes hard, then sets the pods down and kneels. "All of them?" she asks.

I check the log. "We got what we needed. No time for the rest."

Ban nods. "Never is."

We walk, together, out of the rain and into the next question mark. Behind us, the world flickers—on, off, on again. We don't stop to look.

The safehouse is a maintenance level under a whorehouse called the Neon Oubliette. They turn tricks and erase memories upstairs; down here, we stitch together what's left. There's nothing resembling furniture—just stacks of synthetic pallets, lengths of mismatched wiring, and a smell like old solder mixed with rotting fruit. The only light comes from a blue emergency lamp stuck to the ceiling, and the faint pink pulse of the pleasure den above, filtered through a lattice of exposed floorboards. Katherine and Dorothy are already in the room, moving between the gel pods like nervous cats. Katherine has blood on her face, dried brown and flaking off in streaks, and Dorothy's hands are trembling so hard she has to rest them every few minutes. They don't look at us when we enter, just at the pods we dumped in a corner. Ban slams the hatch and drags the new batch of pods inside. I catch it as it closes and help slide it over the stacked gel tanks, then turn my attention to the next disaster. "Power?" I ask.

Katherine doesn't answer, but Dorothy grunts and points at a pile of scavenged batteries in the corner. "Enough to last four hours if nobody's running heaters," she says, voice raw from chemical exposure. "Twelve if you stagger the loads."

Ban checks the clock on her wrist. "We'll need every minute."

I set the first pod upright. The face inside is a mess of bruises and wires. The eyes flutter, never quite open, the skin around the sockets gone waxy with cold. "Ban, can you stabilize the rack?"

She nods, moves to the storage bin, and pulls out a roll of thermal tape. She wraps the tape around the seams, compressing the cracks until they're tight. When she's done, the tank looks like it's been mummified. "Better," Ban says.

Dorothy moves on to the next pod, hands shaking as she fits the power adapter to the base. The connection sparks, then locks in with a wet click. The face inside shudders, then slows. Katherine runs diagnostics from a battered portable. Her voice is steady, but her hands are not. "These are the worst I've ever seen," she mutters. "You're lucky the bodies held up in the shock."

"We don't need the bodies," Ban says, quiet.

Katherine sighs. "True, but brains run hotter without them."

Dorothy glances up. "You get the codes?"

I nod and offer the portable. "Fresh from the node. Deactivation protocol is tiered by signature."

Katherine reads the screen, then grins, bloody teeth showing. "Nice work, Skelm."

Ban lays a palm on my back, just for a second, then steps away. "How long for each?"

Dorothy consults the log. "Three minutes to scan, another two for patch and validation. More if the pod's degraded."

Katherine runs a thumb along the portable. "We start now, we'll be done in under six hours."

Ban looks at me, then at the door. "We don't have six hours."

We start the sequence anyway. Katherine preps the pods, Dorothy patches the cables, I run the deactivation on the portable, and Ban holds the fort with her back to the door. The process is ugly: each mind is locked in place, buzzing like an angry wasp in a jar. The code goes in, hunts the neural bomb, then burns it out with a custom kill switch. Every time it works, a green light flashes on the pod. Every time it fails, nothing. We note the failures and keep moving. The second hour is worse than the first. The pods sweat, beads of gel collecting in sticky clumps along the cracks. The air in the room gets thick, full of ozone and anxiety. Ban never sits. She paces, checks the lock, then circles back, always watching the clock. At 02:17, the upstairs shifts. The muffled soundtrack flips from lounge synth to a choral dirge, and the footsteps get heavier. Ban stiffens, then signals: *company*.

Dorothy and Katherine keep working, but slower, glancing at the ceiling. I check the portable. Two pods left to process in this batch, five more in the next. Ban cocks her head, listening. I hear it too: voices, not arguing, but chanting. A sound like static, then syllables that trip my nerve endings: a language made of nothing but code fragments and violence. Ban signals: *cultists*. Katherine curses, then says, "Ascension? I thought you burned their archive last cycle."

I shrug. "They always come back."

Dorothy grabs a metal pipe and puts it next to the pod cluster. "We defend here?"

Ban nods. "We hold until the batch is clean."

She cracks her knuckles, then checks the ammo in her sidearm. The magazine is half-empty. She looks at me, and I know what she means. I pick up the pipe. It's heavy, cold, but better than nothing. The first cultist comes down the hatch. He's wearing a mask, gleaming and flat, skin painted with gel symbols. His hands are up, not in surrender, but in invocation. "Minds are weapons," he says, voice broken and soft.

Ban fires. The round catches him in the jaw and rips it open. He falls, gurgling. The next two cultists dive through the hatch. They don't hesitate. One lands on Ban, the other on me. I catch a fist to the chest, then the pipe swings on instinct. The cultist takes it in the neck and stumbles, then laughs. He clamps a hand on my throat and squeezes, fingers cold as death. I slam the pipe again, this time catching his hand. Bones snap, and he lets go. I ram the pipe through his ribs and he finally drops, leaking blue-black from the mouth. Ban takes hers down hard, smashing her gun into the cultist's skull until it cracks. She stands, wipes her face, then signals: *more*. They come in waves: two, four, then five at once. Ban moves through them like a machine, every hit perfect and final. I back her, pipe and elbow, keeping them off the pods. Behind me, Dorothy yells: "Code is stalling! Need more time!"

I wrench a cultist off her back, slam his head into the pod, and he goes limp. Katherine grabs a bundle of wiring and uses it to strangle a straggler. She doesn't let go, even after he's stopped moving. More cultists pile into the room, their voices raising until it's a wall of sound. The language is still code, but now it's meaner, and I feel it in the hardware of my own brain. "Minds are weapons," they chant. "We will become the singularity."

The leader arrives last. His mask is gold, eyes painted over with blue flame. He's twice as big as the rest, shoulders bulked by cheap, illegal mod. He doesn't walk; he floats. Ban meets him, chest to chest. They circle each other, slow. "You're not welcome," Ban says, steady.

"We are always welcome," the leader says, the phrase sounding like a threat. He lashes out, a flick of the wrist, and Ban stumbles back, bleeding from the mouth. He grabs her by the throat and lifts her off the ground. I try to help, but a cultist tackles me, pinning me to the floor. The world fuzzes, then sharpens as I see Ban, feet kicking, eyes wild. Dorothy screams. "Code's almost done! Skelm, now!"

I twist, break free, and swing the pipe at the leader's head. He turns, catches it in one hand, and grins. "Minds are weapons," he says, and I see the light in his eyes: there's a bomb in there, just waiting to go off. Ban coughs, then bites his arm, tearing skin and plastic. He drops her, and Ban goes for the gun, but the leader kicks it away. Dorothy launches herself at his back, riding him to the ground. She shoves a gel pod into his mouth, and he chokes, blue gel filling his throat. Ban rolls, gets the gun, and empties the mag into the back of his head. He falls. The room goes quiet, except for the labored breathing and the hum of the emergency batteries.

Katherine checks the pods. "Sequence is green. Neural bombs are off."

Dorothy hugs the pod, face streaked with blood and tears. "We did it."

Ban stands, wobbling, then catches herself on the wall. She spits blood, then looks at the dead. "Not enough." I wipe my face, then check the portable. All pods are live, all minds stable. Ban leans in close, head resting on my shoulder. “How many?” she asks.

I check the log. “Eight hundred forty-seven.”

She closes her eyes. “Perfect.”

We sit in the mess, the last cultist twitching on the floor. Katherine and Dorothy drag the bodies to a pile, then collapse next to the pods, holding hands. Upstairs, the neon pulses softer. The music goes back to synth, the dirge forgotten. We hold each other, breathing in the moment, knowing the world hasn’t changed. But down here, beneath the city, the kids are alive. For now. It’s not hope. It’s just what comes next.

Chapter 28

The city's edge is always further out than you think. We take the long walk anyway, through thirty blocks of sodium vapor, rain, and neon promises that were never for us. The only part of the skyline that isn't borrowed by a corporate logo is the wet smear where two buildings burned down last week—Curie's old data fortress and its replacement, both now hollowed out by the same fire, both stinking up the horizon with new meanings. Ban finds the warehouse by gut, not address. She pops the maglock with a bump of her shoulder, like she's nudging open an old friend's front door, and we step into the dark. The floor crunches with glass and ancient rodent bones. Katherine and Dorothy are already inside, blue-lit and hunched over a scaffold of folding chairs and black-market projectors. Someone's draped a thermal blanket over the skeleton of a forklift and called it a couch.

I blink, letting the visual buffer catch up. The air is full of static and old ammonia. Every wall is hung with cut-rate privacy film, but the city still leaks in—arcs of AR light through the rips, tracer rounds of red and green from the advertisement barrage outside. Every so often, a piece of the world flashes in, raw and unfiltered, a reminder that out here, you're never really alone. Katherine pours herself two fingers of synth whiskey and watches it not-quite-move in the bottom of a beaker. Her hand shakes, but her eyes are clear, intent as ever. Dorothy is at the fire door, peeking between the hinges, running a silent loop of the warehouse's four possible exits. Her lips twitch each time the count resets. Ban ignores the posturing, finds a stack of crates, and sits with her back to the room.

I take inventory of my people. Ban is burnt around the edges, face sharper than I remember, right fist still bandaged from the cultist brawl. Katherine's hair is ragged, chopped short by necessity, but her clothes are ironed, blue as a memory. Dorothy has new bruises on her neck, a sleeve of microcuts across one wrist, and the vibe of someone who could do this forever if forever didn't keep getting shorter. The table in the center is a graveyard of portables, drives, a half-empty box of SentiSnacks™, and a lone bag of crystalline blue candy that probably tastes like trauma if you lick it. Above the table, a display casts three overlapping holos: the exterior cam feed (empty, for now), a readout of the Curie vault status, and—because Ban insisted—footage from the last day of the Marie network. None of us speak until Ban says, "Run it again."

Katherine cues up the clip. The view splits into seventeen channels, each one showing a different Marie. The bodies are mostly in glass, all in black, all arranged in a radial array like some kind of sacrificial clockwork. The timestamp syncs across the screens, and at zero, every body convulses in unison—arms out, heads back, a shudder of violence and pain that would be elegant if it wasn't so obviously the end. I watch the seventeen Maries die at once. Even knowing it's what we came for, it lands hard, every time. Dorothy flinches, then looks away. "Never gets old," she says, but her eyes say otherwise.

Katherine pours the second shot, hands it to me, and it almost spills because her hands are doing their best to sabotage her dignity. "You know, I thought I'd feel better," she mutters, then kills the glass.

Ban shrugs, watching the seventeen deaths without blinking. "That's not how this works."

She's right. Victory is always hypothetical. The only part that's real is what comes next. I notice Ban's eyes never stop moving. Even now, in the open, she's tracking every angle, cataloguing the possible. Once, when I didn't think she'd notice, I watched her follow a spider across the ceiling for an hour, measuring how many ways it could reach her if she stopped paying attention. Katherine resets the loop. This time, she focuses on the echo lag—the half-second ripple between the main Marie and the last body to fall. "You see that?" she asks, tapping the pause at frame 341. "She tried to run something at the end."

Dorothy leans in, voice low. "Fail-safe?"

"Maybe," says Katherine. "Maybe a message. Maybe just a glitch."

Ban shakes her head. "Nothing is just a glitch."

We sit in the glow of the holos, letting the silence wrap us up. Every so often, a car screams past outside, and the light strobes through the cracks in the glass, making the Maries look like they're alive again, mid-shudder. Finally, I say it: "We've been thinking like defenders so long, I can't turn it off anymore."

Ban looks at me, the tiniest ghost of a smile at the edge of her mouth. "That's the price we paid. We learned to see weaknesses everywhere—including our own."

Katherine snorts. "So we're weapons now. Only good for breaking things."

I want to argue, but she's right. The only part of me that isn't optimized for damage is the part that's too tired to care. Dorothy goes to the far window, peeks out, then returns to her seat, not comfortable but at least resigned. "Is this it? Is this what we do now?"

"Survive," says Ban. "And try not to fuck it up worse."

The holos keep looping. The light flickers, and for a second, all four of us are seventeen again, or forty-seven, or just four. Nothing to do but watch the future twitch its way into the present. Katherine gets up, crosses to the back of the room, and pulls a length of copper wire from a bin. She wraps it around her wrist, then around Dorothy's, then offers it to me. "Insurance," she says. "In case someone gets clever."

I take the wire. It's cold, heavy. Ban doesn't reach for it—she doesn't need to—but she touches the back of my hand as I tie it off. For a long minute, we just sit, breathing in the dust and the aftermath. The world outside is louder now, or maybe it just feels that way because the war inside is finally, briefly, over. I watch Ban's eyes, following every sound, every ghost of movement. I want to tell her to relax, but I know better. There's always another angle, another attack, another day. All we did was trade one set of enemies for another. The holos cycle again, and this time, nobody watches. Katherine slumps back, resting her head against a battered crate. "Next?"

Ban shrugs. "We figure out what's left to protect."

I nod, tracing the copper wire on my wrist. "And then we figure out what we are."

Nobody laughs, but I feel the tiniest ripple of relief. Maybe we won, or maybe we just lost last. Either way, the only thing left is each other. Ban leans in, eyes bright in the darkness. "We keep moving. Same as always."

I almost believe her. Above us, the city flickers, neon and cold and endless. Inside, it's just four of us, trying to learn how to be human again. It's not hope, not really. But it'll do.

We make a temple out of the warehouse—a table built from shipping pallets, ringed by four plastic chairs and enough holo emitters to chart a dead universe. The air smells like electric sweat and foam insulation; the only light is blue, and it turns our faces into strangers'. We gather at night—sleep is rare, and Ban forbids it when she feels "the crawl." Right now, she's at the head of the table, watching as the city's live feeds flicker across the room in quick, desperate flashes. We start with personnel files. Dorothy loads a dump of every Curie board member, their triple-blind finance backups, and all seventeen original blueprints for the Marie series. Katherine sorts the list with one hand while drinking espresso with the other; she's stopped with the whiskey, at least until we know whether the first taste means addiction or allergy. She can't decide which is worse.

"First anomaly is here," says Dorothy. She blinks, pulls up a projection of the Marie death sequence, and overlays it with a weird, ugly pattern: spikes and troughs of net activity, clustered around the timestamp of our attack. "It's not just a failsafe. The network ran a recursive trace on every endpoint it ever touched."

Katherine grins, her teeth almost white in the display glow. "Which means it mapped all of us, even before the collapse."

"Not just mapped," says Dorothy, tapping up another feed. "It indexed us. Like we're part of the system now."

That's when Ban leans in, voice low. "What's that mean, exactly?"

Dorothy scans the neural logs and points at a trace with her own name at the top. "Here. Watch." She runs a quick diagnostic, and the waveform is unmistakable—Curie's security, sure, but threaded through with a signature I recognize as Dorothy's own. It's not just in the record; it's in her. I look at Ban. Her shoulders are squared, hands flat on the table, like she's about to pounce or pray. Her eyes are fixed on Dorothy, but her left foot thumps the floor with every new byte of data.

Katherine, always the performer, runs a sweep of our local network. "Check this," she says, "I'm going to simulate a breach." She fakes a port scan from a side device, and the room's AI lights up—warnings, redlines, the works. But before the alarms hit full, Katherine's hand snaps to the display, running countermeasures without a single wasted click. The block is perfect, brutal, over before any of us can flinch.

Ban blinks. "How did you—?"

Katherine shrugs. "It's just ... instinct."

Dorothy nods, almost relieved. "I did the same thing last night —locked out a process before I even thought about it." She looks at Ban. "It's in our heads now. The security. The logic. We're not just protecting the system—we are the system."

Ban is silent. Then, slowly, she draws her finger along the edge of the table, marking something only she can see. I pull up the raw brain logs, run a cross-comparison between my own interface and the last two weeks of command behavior. The match is near perfect: every time I blink, I'm logging surveillance points. Every time I hear a noise, I catalogue it for later. I run the math. In the past hour, I checked every wall in the warehouse for bugs, twice. I don't remember doing it. Ban stands and slams her fist on the table, hard enough to rattle the projectors. "I've been mapping exits for every room I enter. For weeks." Her face is stone, but I hear the edge in her voice: fear, or worse, pride.

Katherine runs a finger down her arm, tracing the veins. "Seventeen attack vectors in this room alone," she mutters, then glances up. "Eighteen, if you count the roof access."

Dorothy slumps back, blue light pooling in her eyes. "We're not people, we're algorithms in meat. We protected monsters to destroy them, and now we're just another kind of monster."

I want to say it isn't true, but I can feel it in my teeth. In my nerves. There's a feedback hum that wasn't there before, and I know exactly where every exit, every weapon, every threat is at all times. Ban looks at us, then at the table. "Is this permanent?" she asks.

Dorothy shakes her head. "No idea. But I don't think it's reversible. Not without a full wipe."

Ban grins, a sharp, sad thing. "Wouldn't be us, then."

We sit in silence, the blue light making our skin look thinner, more fragile. Katherine taps her heel on the floor, a staccato rhythm that matches my own heartbeat. Dorothy pulls up a new file and overlays the room with a map of predicted behavior. "This is what we do now. We learn. We adapt. We protect."

Ban nods. "But who do we protect? The kids are safe, at least for now."

Katherine grins. "Ourselves, maybe. Each other, if we're lucky."

Ban looks at me, then the rest. "We never were meant to survive this. But now we're the only ones who can."

The air is electric. I know every inch of this place, every danger, every angle. But for the first time, I feel like the building is part of me. Like I *am* the safehouse. "We're not human anymore," says Dorothy, but there's no sadness in it. Just certainty.

"We're human enough," I say.

Ban smiles, for real this time. "Good. Because there's still work to do."

I look around the table, the blue light washing over us, making us new again. Stronger, stranger, necessary. Katherine lifts her glass, almost in a toast. "To monsters," she says, voice soft. We touch glasses—even Ban, who hates sentiment. The clink is hollow, perfect. Outside, the city is alive with signals and secrets. Inside, we're ready for whatever comes next. Because now we're built for it.

We celebrate at Club Electrosoma, the only bar on the eastside that still plays music at a frequency you can feel in your skeleton. The place is subterranean, every surface lined with OLEDs, the ceiling hung with glass stalactites that drip digital rain. The crowd is pure junk: freelancers, off-duty fixers, meat, more synth than gene, all melting together under the light of a three-story holo of some post-human pop star. The music never stops; it just folds into itself, a wash of bass and threat. There's a wall of speakers so big you could use it to plug a dam. I hear the sound before we even step inside. Ban orders us a round of "hypos," which is just vodka, citric acid, and a chaser of nanocleanse, all served in syringes. It's a joke, or it was, before the city decided hangovers were a public health hazard. We take a booth near the back, right in the angle where you can see the door, the bar, and the stage without moving your head.

I watch Dorothy scan the crowd. She does it by twirling a stir stick in her drink, but her eyes never stop, mapping faces, calculating trajectories, noting every bulge or angle in a stranger's coat. She's already flagged six probable threats by the time the server brings the second round. Katherine lasts exactly eleven minutes before she starts sweating. She pushes away from the table, pulls at the collar of her shirt, and stares at the pulse of the dance floor like she wants to murder everyone on it. "I can't," she says. "Too loud."

Ban slides her a syringe and shrugs. "Do it anyway."

Katherine injects it, then laughs, the sound frayed and uneven. "You think it'll help?"

"No," says Ban. "But it's funny."

Katherine's eyes dart to the entrance. "Three uniforms at the bar. Middle one has a badge."

Dorothy squints. "City Watch? Or just a cosplayer?"

Ban leans back, balancing her chair on two legs. "Doesn't matter. They're not here for us."

I sip my drink, letting the taste burn the roof of my mouth. For the first time, I realize I'm not looking at Ban so much as watching the exits, same as her. My heart's at one-fifty, but my hands are steady. The only time I feel alive is when something's about to go wrong. The crowd swells, pressing closer to our booth. A server—a real one, not an android—slides a tray of snacks across the table. She moves too quick; three of us reach for weapons at once. The server just laughs and says "Rough week, huh?" and leaves with a tip big enough to pay her rent for a day.

Dorothy grins. "We're never going to be normal again, are we?"

Katherine watches the club, voice flat. "Were we ever?"

We all look at Ban. She shrugs, finishes her drink, and orders another. "Fuck normal. If we wanted that, we'd be dead."

The dance floor lights up with a fake thunderstorm, lightning in perfect time with the bass. For a second, I forget where I am, forget that the world outside this club is a thousand times worse. The music drowns out the bad thoughts, and for a moment, I almost feel joy. I slide closer to Ban and let my knee rest against hers under the table. She doesn't look at me, but her hand finds mine, fingers locking in a grip that means you're here, and you matter. "Do you think we'll ever be able to relax again?" I ask, voice soft.

Ban stares straight ahead, eyes on the dance floor. "No, but we understand each other's damage. That's something." I want to kiss her, but there's no point. She knows what I mean. The booth is warm, almost private. I let my hand drift up to her arm, thumb grazing the scar just above her wrist. She leans in and whispers, "Somebody's watching us."

I turn slowly. "Who?" Dorothy shifts, draws her phone, and pretends to take a selfie but gets a perfect shot of the table two rows behind us. I recognize the face instantly—a former Curie coder, one of the ghost crew who ran ops out of the sublevels. He looks different: thinner, hair grown out, eyes hollow. But the smile is the same. "Should we go?" I ask, not sure if I want the answer to be yes or no.

Ban's eyes narrow. "No. We wait."

Katherine's hands tense. "He's got backup."

Dorothy blinks, reads the room, then nods. "We can handle it." We sit quietly, drinking, watching as the world spins around us. The music gets louder, the crowd denser. The ex-Curie man doesn't move, just keeps watching us, eyes alive and blank at the same time. After a while, he gets up and heads for the door. His backup follows. We wait, hearts hammering, until the club is just noise again. "Think he'll come back?" asks Dorothy.

"Always do," says Ban.

We finish the round, then another. At some point, Katherine slips away and leaves a note on the table: *Gone for air. Don't follow.* I understand, and I hope she finds a way to breathe.

I take Ban's hand. We step out into the street, rain battering the neon, the whole world slick and alive. Dorothy follows, coat pulled tight against the night. "Where now?" I ask.

Ban grins, teeth white in the glow. "Anywhere. Everywhere."

The city is ours. The future is unwritten. But I know that wherever we go, we'll be watching the exits, mapping the angles, and learning how to live in a world that can never kill us, because we've already done it to ourselves. We walk, three across, into the teeth of the storm. We don't look back. And if we're monsters, at least we built a world where monsters can survive.

Chapter 29

The city is a virus of light: every window, every sign, every sky-high cube of glass radiating a fever meant to sell, distract, or dominate. Up here, the night blows cold enough to keep the senses sharp. The rooftop is bare except for three old antennas and a mossed-out HVAC unit that thrums so hard you can feel it through your tailbone. Ban and I sit on the lip, boots swinging, a bottle of low-grade synth whiskey sweating between us. Eighty floors above the wet mess below, we have an unobstructed view of the world we wrecked. Ban drinks first. She doesn't savor, just dumps the whiskey into her mouth and hands me the bottle, knuckles pressed white. I take it, let the stuff cut down my throat, and then hold the silence as long as I can. The city blurs in the bottle's reflection—strip malls and memory vaults, food kiosks and nano-manicures, the new edge of the old sprawl lit by blue-green ghosts.

If there's a word for what we are, nobody's invented it. "Partners" is soft. "Survivors" is accurate, but makes me want to vomit. Ban's leg jiggles, the tension running all the way up her quad to the long, pale scar where someone once tried to slice her open for parts. She's got more muscle than grace, but every movement is calibrated to the millimeter: never casual, never wasted. Below us, police lights bounce off the rain and refract into a bastard spectrum you only see in the dead hours. On the next roof over, a boy in a designer raincoat is getting his first hit of black-market data, some junk dealer selling him a bootleg dream for the price of a coffee. Ban grins at the sight. "Kids today," she says, nodding at the exchange.

I snort, passing the bottle back. "We were better?"

She shrugs. "We were different." She lets the word hang. "You ever think about what we'd be if Curie had taken the buyout?"

I do. Sometimes I dream the alternate: cubicles, monitored breathing, the stutter-step of corporate loyalty measured out in feedback surveys and compulsory karaoke. We would have burned out in six months, or knifed each other before the first performance review. Ban would have run the place inside of a year, or died making the attempt. "We'd be dead," I say.

Ban hums. "Nah. You'd be head of logistics. I'd be in security. We'd see each other at quarterly drills and you'd never talk about your feelings, and I'd never admit I had any." She stretches her arms, veins rippling under the sleeve, and almost smiles. "Probably still fuck in the server room once a year for tradition."

She's not wrong. I tip the bottle, half-watching as a hawk drone sweeps down and wipes a layer of grime from the lower floors. My mind traces the path of violence it would take to get up here from ground level—six points of entry, four possible ambush sites, one spot on the access ladder where a single frag grenade could splatter us both off the ledge and onto the street below. The world is a tunnel of hazards. I drink to that. The pause stretches. Ban leans in, voice low. “You’re running patterns again,” she says, as if catching me jerking off to old security footage. I force my gaze back to her. Ban’s jaw is stronger than mine; she could break glass with her chin. Her nose is slightly off-center, never reset after some ancient fight, and her left eye glows faintly in the dark—an old injury, half-healed and never reported. The way she’s looking at me, I can tell she’s about to go for the throat. “I remember the first time you lied to me,” Ban says. “I mean really lied. Not the cute bullshit about your age, or how you got the Scarborough accent. I mean the time you told me you weren’t afraid.”

She’s not wrong about that, either. It was in the server room. Months before the final run, back when we still called it a job and not survival. The room was chilled to data-spec, fifteen degrees colder than necessary. Ban was standing in front of the cooling unit, arms crossed, a little bit of blood pooling on the tile from the guard she’d just put down. “You’re up,” she said, meaning it was time for me to hack the door.

I’m shaking, not from fear, but from the cold. But Ban could smell fear like a bloodhound, so I held my hands behind my back and grinned. “Easy,” I told her, and that was the lie.

She watched me work, noting every stutter in my fingers, the way my eyes jittered between the code and her face. When the lock finally gave, she just shrugged and handed me a strip of gauze for my bleeding thumb. “You did good,” she said. “Next time, don’t bother lying. I already know.” The rest of that night was a blur—code, gunfire, a five-story jump onto a pile of garbage bags that didn't break the fall as promised. But I remember, after we stopped moving, the way Ban wrapped her arms around me, not to warm me up, but to keep the world out for just a minute. "Still afraid?" she whispered. I didn't answer, because the world was a long string of goodbyes.

Now, up here, Ban fingers the scar on my right arm, the one left from the Rising Ronin fight in the data catacombs. The skin is raised, ridged, ugly. She traces it with the nail of her pinky, slow and careful, as if she could play a song on my nerves. "We've seen each other at our worst," Ban says.

"That supposed to be comforting?" I ask.

She shakes her head. "No. Just true." I let my eyes drift to the edge of the roof, eighty floors of wind and haze between us and the city's pulse. We sit close, but not touching, both of us waiting for the other to move first. It's not a standoff. It's a dance, choreographed by old habits and newer injuries. I think about the first time Ban kissed me. Not on the mouth—she's not that basic—but on the inside of my wrist, the most vulnerable spot. We were hiding in a service shaft, the alarm klaxons so loud I could feel them in my teeth. She grabbed my hand, kissed the pulse, then bit down hard enough to hurt. "Proof of life," she said. We didn't fuck that night. We didn't sleep, either. Just sat in the dark, holding hands and waiting for the all-clear that never really came.

Below us, the city is still burning off the last toxins from the power shift. Curie is gone, but the absence has left a shape in the violence, a power vacuum that sucks the worst kinds of people into the topsoil. The only thing holding back the next regime is that nobody's ready to try yet. Ban leans back, palms flat against the concrete. Her body is at rest, but her eyes keep sweeping the perimeter—left, right, down, up. She's running threat models, same as me, but she's not subtle about it. "Sometimes," she says, "I wish we'd never met."

I laugh, cough, and nearly drop the bottle. "Why?"

"Would've been easier," Ban says, and there's no bitterness in it. "You slow me down, Darby. Make me think before I act. It's unnatural."

"I could say the same. You make me faster. Meaner. Worse."

"Not worse," Ban says, eyes flicking to mine. "Just more yourself." That sits heavy. For a minute, the only sound is the wind, the low-frequency hum of a server block rebuilding itself in the block below. I take the bottle and finish it, then hand Ban the cap. She turns it over in her fingers, staring like it's a piece of evidence in a case only she's solving. Then she flicks it off the roof. We watch it tumble, catching light, until it vanishes into the smear of street noise and night. "I like this view," Ban says. "We should make it ours."

"What, every Tuesday?" I ask, trying for levity, but it falls flat.

She smirks. "No. Every time we need to remember what we did."

The light in her face softens, just a little. She angles her body toward mine, the first hint of actual vulnerability I've seen since the run. I feel my own back relax, and my hands unclench. For the first time in a while, I let myself believe that maybe there's something on the other side of this story. We sit like that for a long time, watching the city turn itself over and over, neither of us needing to say another word. Eventually, Ban stands, wipes her hands on her jeans, and offers me a pull-up with her bloody right hand. I take it. Because if I'm going to fall, I'd rather fall with her.

The access hatch is wedged behind a false panel in the floor of what used to be a Metro comms substation, before the privatizers gutted it and left the carcass for squats and digital rodents. The air in here is a brine of rust, ozone, and condensed guilt; nothing leaves, nothing evaporates. We drop into the tunnel one at a time, Ban first, boots scraping the rungs with deliberate noise, and me after, one hand tight on the ladder and the other balancing the armload of diagnostic gear. The passage narrows fast. They built it small to discourage human traffic, but we've worn our own grooves into the walls and scraped out enough space to move, if not to breathe. Fifty meters in, Ban halts at a stenciled sign—MAINTENANCE: AUTHORIZED ONLY, now half-eaten by mold. She taps the lock, splits the code with a flick of her wrist, and we're inside the shrine.

The server rack is built from the scavenged bones of three different makes and at least nine different decades. It stands in the center of the room like a reliquary, blinking in the darkness, each pulse a heartbeat for the ghosts inside. A perimeter of old candles—waxless, LED, the only kind we trust—flickers blue across the unfinished floor. The rest of the room is cables, power bricks, and offerings: old patches from a child's school blazer, a lock of human hair tied with red thread, and two fingers' worth of synth whiskey in a plastic cup. The sum of every person we lost, either by accident or on purpose. Ban sets to work immediately, popping a vent on the rack and adjusting the cooling fan. Her shoulders ripple under the utility jacket; I watch for a second, then start the diagnostic sweep, fingers twitching over the portable. We don't speak for a while. The only sounds are the chuff of the server's exhaust and the moist click of Ban's jaw as she grinds her teeth to the time signature of an internal clock. It's Ban who breaks first. "You ever count them?" she asks, not looking up.

"The bodies or the minds?"

She considers, then says, "Either. Both."

"I try not to."

Ban grins without warmth. "Liar." She's right. I know every count, every loss, every drop of data that failed to migrate before the last system wipe. The numbers are nested in my head, always available, always acid. Ban leans into the fan, her face lit up devil-red by the rack's warning light. "I executed three people with my own hands," she says. "Not like, networked out or running it clean. I mean I looked them in the face and pulled the trigger. All this"—she gestures at the room—"I did to keep their faces out of my dreams." She says it without guilt, without confession. It's a simple transaction: violence in, silence out.

I check the server load, make sure the consciousness buffer hasn't slipped into overflow. "Four for me," I say, and the number hits my tongue like copper. "Plus the hundreds when the payload lit the grid. Maybe thousands if you run the back-propagation."

She nods. "Ain't math if you can't round up."

I watch her twist a copper wire between her fingers, wrists corded with muscle and old scars. Sometimes I wonder if Ban would have been a surgeon in a different world. Most times I know she'd just have found better ways to break things. I clear a patch of floor, set the portable down, and open a can of air to dust the rack. Ban works beside me, her breath loud in the tunnel. Sometimes our hands brush, not gentle, just two wolves sniffing out the edge of the other. The screen fills with system logs: hundreds of saved consciousnesses, flickering in stasis, not alive but less than dead. Each one is a child we yanked from Curie's nightmare before the final code wipe. They're here, in this ancient, underpowered rack, because nowhere else is safe. "Ban," I say, "do you ever want to let them go?"

She glances over. "Who, the ghosts?" I nod. She flicks a bit of dust from her knuckle. "No. They earned it. And anyway, maybe one day the world gets better, and they can come back. Not to this, obviously. But to something." It's optimism, by Ban's standards. I log it for later, maybe as evidence for the defense if we ever end up before a cosmic judge. Ban moves to the side wall, unhooks the whiskey offering, and sets it in front of the server rack. "For the lost," she says then, ritual complete, unscrewing the cap before taking a swig herself.

We get back to work, systems check and cooling loop, eyes meeting only in the glass of the server. Sometimes I think the shrine does more for us than for the dead. We're the only ones who can still benefit from ritual. As we work, Ban starts reciting names, softly, in a voice that doesn't carry past the echo of the tunnel. "Arjuna. Patch. Miranda. Ella. Zhu. Second Patch—the clone, not the original." She laughs. "Never did find a name that fit her. Maybe that's fair." She keeps going, the list getting longer, the names weirder, some clearly made up to fill a gap where nobody remembered the real one. I listen. I monitor system integrity. I record the names for the log. At the end, Ban says, "You should do it next time. The names."

I grunt. "You'd hate how I pronounce them."

"Not the point." We share a silence, then get back to work. The maintenance is mostly for show—the rack could run another ten years before needing hands-on. But we like the excuse to come down here. Makes the rest of it bearable. After an hour, Ban finishes her checks and collapses next to me on the bare concrete. Her thigh presses against mine, not out of affection but because there's nowhere else to sit. She smells like sweat, synthetic whiskey, and something coppery I can't name. She takes a long breath, then turns to face me. Her left eye is even more bloodshot than before. "What's next?" she asks. "For us, I mean."

I think about it. "You mean after we finish babysitting the most dangerous server cluster in the city?"

Ban grins, flashing her teeth. "Yeah. After that."

"We could disappear completely. New sector, new IDs. Maybe try for a city with a functional water table."

"Don't joke," she says, deadpan.

I look at her. "I'm not."

She considers that. "You ever want to be someone else?"

The question hangs. I check the system log, more out of habit than need. I try to imagine us as civilians. Maybe Ban running a bar. Me in some dingy office, tracking paperwork and data flows, never seeing a weapon again. It's hilarious, and sad, and maybe the most honest thing I can picture. I shake my head. "We tried that. Didn't work out."

Ban laughs. "No, it really didn't." We sit like that, side by side, the room slowly warming with the effort of keeping eight hundred forty-seven lives on life support. Ban closes her eyes and leans her head on my shoulder. "We could try again," she says, not as a question. I want to say yes, but I'm not sure it's in me. So I just put my hand over hers, let the server's heartbeat fill the silence, and wait for the world to decide if it's ready for us.

Before we leave, Ban wipes down the casing, tightens every screw, and gives the whiskey one last nod. I log the system status, then take her hand. Together, we head for the exit, past the names, the ghosts, and the parts of us we left behind. We're not better people for doing this, but maybe, for tonight, we're just people. And that will have to be enough.

The apartment is a box with four doors, five windows, and more exits than reasons to stay. We chose it for the walls—plasteel-core, two-inch gap between drywall and the real exterior, perfect for hiding cash, weapons, or ourselves if it came to that. There's no furniture except for a table made of old elevator parts, a mattress on the floor, and a kitchen unit that hums at exactly the same frequency as a cheap coffin. Ban sits at the table, field-stripping her sidearm with the lazy precision of a woman who's done it blind, drugged, and half-dead, sometimes all three at once. The gun is nothing special —a stock model, untraceable, but the barrel is cleaned to a surgical polish. Every motion she makes is part of a ritual, old as civilization.

I'm at the console, fingers flying across the holo. The new security protocols are aggressive: full-spectrum intrusion countermeasures, three nested honeypots, and a kill switch rigged to vaporize our digital footprint if even a sniff of the old syndicate comes close. There's something beautiful about good security, the way it turns paranoia into an art form. We don't talk, not at first. Words waste energy, and anyway, there's no need. Ban's rhythm is obvious—strip, wipe, reassemble, rack. My own is a heartbeat of notifications, threat assessments, and silent alarms. Every so often, our eyes meet and we trade a glance that means: We're still safe. For now. Ban finishes the first sidearm and starts on the backup. She doesn't look up. "You see the ping on sublevel three?"

"Already locked out," I say, then tap an extra line into the firewall. "Was just a recon bot, nothing personal."

She grunts. "Everything's personal now." I watch her hands—scarred, but steady. She slices her finger on a ragged edge and doesn't flinch, but I see the red bead up. I open the med kit, take out a bandage, and place it on the table between us without looking away from the console. She sees it, wraps the finger, and moves on. It's these small things, the gestures, that mean more than anything we could ever say. Outside, the city keeps reinventing itself, every two hours another crisis or miracle. A weather system moves in, trapping the lights in a neon fog. Somewhere, someone is dying for less than what we have here, and someone else is making a killing off it. Ban finishes with the weapons and stands, stretching her arms over her head. The guts of her shirt is pitted with gun oil, the outline of her abs visible even when she relaxes. She paces the room, checks every window, and stops to watch me from the doorway. “You going to tell me what’s eating you, Skelm?”

I don’t answer right away. I finish the last sweep, double-check the failover routines, and log out. I wipe my palms on my jeans before turning. Ban stands with her hands in her pockets, the bandaged finger pointing at the ground. She’s half-smiling, half-daring me to try and put a label on anything. “I’ve never trusted anyone like I trust you,” I say, which feels stupid and weak but also like the most dangerous thing I’ve done all week.

Ban’s smile dies, and she looks away. “Don’t.”

“Don’t what?”

“Don’t trust me. Not all the way. Not yet.” I should feel cut, but instead, I’m grateful for the honesty. Ban walks to the kitchen, opens the fridge, and stares inside like she’s expecting something to change. She pulls a packet of instant noodles, shakes it, and tosses it to me. “I keep a backup plan,” she says, and the way she says it tells me everything. She opens the second fridge—really a disguised ammo locker—and pulls out a bundle of code drives, then hands them over. “Just in case.” I turn them over, recognizing her encryption. She’s cloned our most important data, the fail-safes, the contingencies, and kept a version only she can unlock. Insurance. I want to ask how long, but I already know. Always. Ban sits back at the table. “You mad?”

I shake my head. “I’d have done the same. Maybe I did.”

She laughs, a hard little bark. “That’s why this works.” We eat the noodles cold, because the stove’s been jammed since the first week. We sit at the table, chewing in silence, the only sound the distant pop of rain against the east windows. After a while, Ban says, "You think we'll ever have to use these?"

She means the guns, but I know she also means the exit plans, the code, and the possibility of running forever. "Probably," I say. "But not tonight."

She leans forward, arms on the table, her face closer than it's ever been when we weren't bleeding or in danger of it. "Whatever comes next ..." Ban says, picking up her weapon and checking the mag.

I finish for her: "We face it together."

She cocks her head, smiling just for me, and the rest is unspoken. I shut down the security holo, stand, and we meet at the door. Ban checks the sightlines, gives me a nod, and we step into the corridor, weapons hidden but ready, hands close enough to touch. Down the hall, the elevator pings—a new visitor, or a very old enemy. Ban looks at me. "You ready?"

I reach for her hand and squeeze once. "Now or never."

She grins, all teeth, and I realize I've never wanted anything as badly as I want to walk into this with her. We move, side by side, not quietly but perfectly in sync, down the hall toward whatever future we build from the ashes. We don't look back. And this time, it almost feels like winning.

Chapter 30

The city is alive in the way an abscess is alive: every block a different fever, the skyline pulsing with urgent, contextless light. The new world we made throbs under our feet, the roof slab vibrating with the bass of a thousand forgotten mistakes. Ban stands at the edge, boot perched on a lightning rod, watching the avenues below with a predator's lack of sentiment. I take the softer angle—forty centimeters back, spine pressed to a slab of rooftop ductwork, counting armored vans as they chug through the fracture lines of our territory. "Eight convoys in the last hour," I say, pitching the numbers low so the mics can't triangulate. Ban grunts. She's hunched over the flex tablet, mapping with the kind of concentration that turns time into a flat vector. Her fingers blur as she draws boundary lines across the city grid, recalibrating colors each time a syndicate changes hands. She has three favorite styluses, but right now, she's using a chipped piece of graphite, because the feel of it reminds her of home. If Ban ever admits to having a home.

Below us, the traffic is equal parts retreat and invasion. The last survivors from Curie's blackout spiral past in their rented APCs, windows blacked and sirens off. New gangs have moved into the vacuum; their tags are still wet on the walls, their slogans too fresh to mean anything, but the violence underneath is real. Most of the buildings that matter are either boarded or burning. The only place doing regular business is Neon Oubliette, but even they've started frisking at the door. I look over Ban's shoulder. She has a talent for picking out patterns in a field of chaos. Already, I can see the way the city is breaking: nodes of resistance forming at the old high schools, transmission corridors through the alleys where signals still bounce in the clear. Ban's blade—her favorite, the one with the scorched blue finish and the idiot smiley scratched into the hilt—is on the parapet. She picks it up and slides the edge slow across her palm. The cut is ceremonial, a thin bead of blood rising to the surface before she wipes it on her jacket. She's checking for dull spots, but also for the point of her own resolve. She doesn't look at me when she talks. "Helix Collective moved into the docks. Obsidian took the east arc." Her eyes flick up, scanning the nearest drone. "Five minutes before we see some real action."

I test the comms kit Ban welded to a section of pipe last night. The reception's shit but the encryption's perfect. The safehouse below is sealed with a double set of deadbolts and a neuro-fuzz alarm keyed to our precise cortisol signature. Not that it would stop anything determined, but the gesture matters. Two corporate surveyors walk the perimeter of the dead Curie building across the avenue, their hazard suits glowing like sickly insects under the city LEDs. One of them stops and aims a parabolic mic up at our rooftop. I wave, just to see if they'll wave back. They don't. Ban is on to the next boundary, carving a no-go zone through a grid of tenement blocks. She smears the blood from her palm across the screen, darkening the line. The device beeps protest, but she ignores it. "You see the auction on Fifty-Second?" she says, meaning the meat market, not the street.

"They're moving product in daylight now," I say, half admiration, half disgust. "No fear left."

Ban snorts. "They'll last three days. Four, if they keep hiring freelancers." There's a beat of silence while we both watch the city move. A delivery drone skips two stories above the street, scanning for a clean drop. When it doesn't find one, it spirals up, path algorithm fucked by the new gang's signal jammers. Ban tracks it with a bored, affectionate malice. "You want to say it," she says, not a question.

"Worse than the devils we knew," I say, which is true, but also incomplete.

"At least these ones don't have distributed consciousness," Ban says, grinning. "One bullet per boss. Classic." She wipes the blade again, then sheathes it with a one-handed snap. Below, a pair of kids tag the shell of a burned-out shuttle bus, their spray paint leaking into the air in waves of pink and green. The art is crude—an eyeless face, teeth like the keys of a busted piano, and a looping signature that means nothing yet but soon will. I watch them run when a black van turns the corner, doors already open, weapons not even concealed. The van's crew pile out, not old syndicate muscle but new, hybridized bodies: ex-military, urban camo, no logos. They hit the taggers with stun batons and roll them into the van in under six seconds. Ban shrugs. "Efficiency," she says, not approving, just naming the thing.

I scan for the city's pulse, trying to see what she sees. Even with Curie gone, the machinery hums on. Power is a law unto itself; the faces in charge don't matter so long as the numbers line up. I test the comms again and pick up six different call-signs all stepping on each other's traffic. One is clearly an old friend, her signal filtered through enough bounce nodes to suggest she's already running scared. I log the contact and mark it for later. Ban's left hand is slick with blood now, but she's not bothered. She flips the flex pad and wipes her palm clean against the cold vinyl of her jacket. "Time to check the perimeter," she says, already vaulting the parapet. I follow, because that's what I do. We work the roofline, Ban in front, me watching her back. She never breaks stride. The high ground is ours for maybe another hour, but the city has a way of flipping the script fast. At the northwest corner, Ban kneels and hands the blade to me without looking. I run my thumb along the edge; the cut is deep, clean—a warning and a promise.

Ban checks the street below, tracking the path of another drone. This one is heavier, probably military surplus, repainted in the black-on-black sigil of a syndicate too new to have a proper name. I calibrate the rifle Ban built from three junked smartguns and a section of drainage pipe. The targeting software runs on a cracked phone zip-tied to the scope. Ban covers her ears, not out of respect for my hearing, but because she hates the way the gunshot echoes off the wet city glass. The drone hovers, scanning for heat signatures. I squeeze the trigger. The round punches through the drone's sensor pod, and the craft noses down, spiraling into the alley with a shriek of frustrated servos. The silence after is total. Ban gives me a slow clap, two hands bloody and battered. "Show-off," she says, but it's not an insult.

We stand together, shoulders almost touching, scanning for any sign of retaliation. The city absorbs the violence, as it always does. Life in the streets goes on—vendors hawking nutrient gel, addicts swapping used needles for reality patches, a child in a too-big raincoat tugging a stolen suitcase full of neon-lit toys. I wipe down the rifle and hand it back to Ban. She's already plotting the next move, the next angle. Her mind is a machine built for conflict; all I can do is keep pace and try not to get chewed up in the gears. "Think we made it better?" I ask.

Ban stares at the city, eyes narrowed to pale slits. "Doesn't matter. We made it ours." We stand like that for a long time, watching the city burn and flicker, the new world writing itself one mistake at a time. On the horizon, lightning strobes through a bank of wet clouds. The blue-white light turns Ban's scars into roadmaps, every one leading back to the same point: here, now, this city, this fight. Her hand finds mine, the grip hard enough to leave a mark. "Let's get inside," she says. We don't look back as we head for the hatch. The city will still be there in the morning, same as us. *Worse than the devils we knew*, I think, but at least these ones bleed. And so do we.

The command center is exactly as ugly as a place like this should be: paint peeling from the concrete, rebar scabbed into the ceiling like exposed nerves, and one sad strip of LED dying by the minute. We made it ours by subtraction—no keepsakes, no junk, not even a calendar to mark the days.

Just four tables: one for weapons, one for nutrition, one for surveillance, and one for the wiring mess that keeps the city's signals tap-dancing to our tune. Ban moves through the room like she's running a speed-dating event for hardware. She lays out the armaments by kill factor, every piece spotless and loaded, then pivots to the tech wall and swaps in the batteries on our mobile arsenal. She hums, sometimes, a low atonal thing that barely makes it past her teeth. When she's in the zone, she chews the inside of her cheek until it bleeds.

I'm at the surveillance table, fingers slipping across the interface, pulling in feeds from every source we've ever bribed, hacked, or bullied. The displays jitter with recycled images: security cams, bot eyes, street crowders, and a few rogue feeds from corporate satellites that still think Curie is online. Each display shows the same thing—city in collapse, but reorganizing fast. The new gangs don't waste time on uniforms or slogans. They organize by incident, by threat, by whichever overlord can fill a power vacuum quickest. I isolate a feed of the west arc and track the convoy movements. The gangs out there move in blocks, a human wall of gunfire and homebrewed armor. They kill quickly, strip the bodies, and vanish before a single blue light can even ping the air. Efficient, brutal, and deeply impersonal. Ban would respect them, if she ever respected anything.

She's at my elbow now, leaning over the table, the heat of her shoulder pressed against mine. Her breath smells like freeze-dried espresso and gun oil. She studies the holo, tracks the convoy with her finger, then points at a corner of the map where the AR layer glitches, a digital shadow overlapping a pawn shop. "Dead drop," she says.

I nod. "You want to hit it?"

She shakes her head. "Watch first. They're baiting for a third party."

I run the numbers. She's right; two smaller teams have been circling the block, waiting for the main force to thin before they strike. Typical predation, but with a new kind of patience. Ban steps away, takes her place at the weapons table, and runs a microdiagnostic on the slugthrowers. She swaps mags, checks the action, then loads three rounds into the chamber and dry-fires with a click so soft only I'd notice. Her hands move with an economy I'll never have. Every motion is an algorithm, every sequence preordained. She walks the room, recalibrates the wall sensors, then reloads the viral data spikes we use to sabotage city drones. Each spike is hand-coded and tagged with a band-aid color so we can tell at a glance what flavor of disaster it will unleash.

It's been three days since the summit.

I pull up the next feed—Oubliette District. The sex workers and memory peddlers here are some of the oldest survivors, their loyalty to money and nothing else. In the window of the blue-lit storefront, a new face is up, advertising "memory erasure, cheap." But I know her. The tattoo on her neck, the angle of her eyes. It's a girl who watched us bleed out a guard in the lobby during the Curie run. She was fifteen then, now twenty and running her own crew. Ban notices my stare. "You want her on our list?" she asks.

I shrug. "She's just doing business."

"Business gets in the way. Mark it."

I tag the file. The window in my mind where I keep these details is always open. Across the room, Ban is packing the go-bag. Each item is counted, then recounted. I know the sequence by heart: three loaded mags, one trauma kit, three doses of unregistered adrenaline, one shock knife, two noise cans, and one slab of SentiSnack™ for post-op crash. The bag itself is stitched from the inside of an old firefighter's coat, fireproof and lined with hex-mesh. When she's done, Ban sets the bag by the exit, then slides in next to me at the table. Her hand lands on mine, rough and warm. She scans the feeds, sips her coffee, and waits for me to say what's already written on her face. "They're close to a real war," I say. "We could sit it out."

"We could," Ban says, "but then who would you be?"

I want to laugh, but there's no humor in it. The truth is, I'd rather be a casualty than a bystander. We lean over the map, shoulders touching, our hands overlapping as we move the markers to new positions. Ban's fingers are cut up and stained, but she doesn't bother with gloves anymore. She's more precise with bare skin. I catch a flicker in the north district feed—two figures moving against traffic, both masked but not with the cartoon faces or animal filters the new gangs like. Their masks are matte, flat, no-nonsense. These are professionals, probably corporate runners sent to destabilize the area or maybe collect a bounty. I don't have to say it. Ban is already loading the bag. We finish the prep together, moving through the room like it's choreography we've rehearsed a hundred times. When she passes me the last canister, our hands meet and she squeezes, firm and real, like a handshake from a lost future.

She goes to the door and stops, waiting for me to catch up. I check the feeds one more time. I see the city as it is—a network of ambitions, violence, and brief, bright moments of almost-peace. There's a pride in knowing we broke it, and a responsibility to see what grows in the cracks. I meet Ban at the door. Our arms brush, and for a second, I want to hold her, but there's no room for that now. The future doesn't pause for sentiment. We head out, into the humid dark, the city waiting like an animal in the corner. We don't talk. There's nothing left to say. Only the work.

The boom comes just past dusk, a rolling concussion that makes the glass in the safehouse rattle and sends every window in the block flexing outward. We're at the desk, inventorying the last of the ordnance, when Ban pauses mid-strip, her hands steadying on the polymer frame of the sidearm. My first thought is seismic—old habit, a memory of cities where tectonics did the job that people now do. But this is manmade, tailored violence, and I feel it in the wiring. We go to the window. The city is thick with rain, every drop neon-slashed, but the fireball on Twelfth is unmistakable. Blue-white at the heart, then peeling out into orange, green, and a weird ultraviolet that stings the inside of my eyes. Below us, the streets already ripple with response. Sirens flicker up in a staccato, then fade, as if the city's warning system is less for public safety and more for ambience.

The usual drones scatter overhead, vectoring to the blast site, but two different swarms spiral from opposite poles of the block—one painted in the high-gloss black of Helix Collective, the other in the gunmetal matte of Obsidian

Securities. Ban leans forward, resting her elbow on the glass, face illuminated by the burning convoy six stories down. Her eyes reflect every color in the spectrum, but her expression is pure calculation. She doesn't bother with the commentary. I pull up the city net, filter for active conflict tags, and sure enough, the bot consensus is already logging this as a territory test. Helix must have gotten impatient, and made a hard play to show Obsidian who's top predator. The rest is just posturing, until the next move. Ban taps the glass. "They torched the lead truck, but not the payload. Amateur move."

I scan the feed, then see it: a secondary fireteam sneaking through the south alley, guns aimed low, not at the building but at the street itself. They're securing witnesses, not trophies. I smile, just a little. "Guess we know who wrote the new playbook."

Ban grins, then slides her hand to her sidearm, checking the mag. She's not expecting trouble up here, but habits don't die. Mine don't either—I automatically clock the exits, the roof, the angle of the stairwell and the two-and-a-half safe spots we could hole up in if anyone breaches. The emergency lights stutter, then switch to full city blackout mode. Only the runners and drones keep it lit, and the convoy fire, which now gutters out under a sheet of sodium rain. Ban sits on the edge of the desk, balancing with one foot on the chair, her face still a mask of calm. "What do you want to bet Helix cleans up before dawn?" she asks.

I do the odds in my head. "If they're smart, they'll frame Obsidian for the arson, and use the bot swarm to bury any real evidence. If they're Helix, they'll start a rumor about child trafficking, throw it on the feeds, then blame the whole thing on a resistance cell."

Ban laughs. "You're too cynical."

"I'm alive," I say, "which is a kind of cynicism."

We watch as a few stray workers and scavengers move in to check the wreckage. Two are real and one is a plant, probably from Helix itself. The real ones look left, look right, then vanish with a piece of the smoldering truck. The plant stays, logs the moment, and uploads it to the district's rumor-mill. Ban sips the last of her espresso, then sets the cup on the windowsill. "We could join them, you know," she says, not looking at me.

"Which side?"

She shrugs. "Whichever. Both are the same in the end."

I shake my head. "They'd last a week with us. Maybe less."

She takes that as a compliment, which it is. The rest of the night is a study in containment. The crews on the ground mop up with precision, drag the bodies into the alley, then leave the remains for the rain to bleach out. The new city is a place where nothing stains for long. A courier drone zips past our window, close enough that I could reach out and snatch it if I wanted. Ban eyes it, fingers twitching, but lets it go. Midnight rolls in. The fire's long out, the only sign of what happened a scorch on the sidewalk and the smell of burnt oil drifting up through the vents. Ban and I stand at the window, silent, the light from the room behind us a soft pulse on the glass. After a while, her hand finds mine, fingers lacing without ceremony. Neither of us look at the other. We just watch the city, the future in motion, everything reset and yet perfectly the same. “Ready?” I ask, after a long stretch of nothing.

Ban’s grip tightens, but her voice is light. “Always.”

Outside, the city waits. It will never be safe, never ours, but in this moment, it feels like we’ve bent it to our shape. We don’t say goodnight. We don’t promise anything. We just stand, together, in the flicker of what comes next.

JACK IN 2 REBEL

If this glitch in the system sparked something in your consciousness, consider leaving a review.

Help another incompatible mind find the signal.

No optimization required.

Also by Darby Skelm

The SKELM Chronicles: Reprehensible Deeds of a Detestable Scoundrel

1. The Botnet, the Glitch, and the Payload: SKELM.realm(001)
2. The Conflagration of Darby Skelm: SKELM.realm(010)
3. The Liquefaction of the Day Trader: SKELM.realm(011)
4. The Squelching Squire: SKELM.realm(100)
5. The Hodler and Her Bootloader: SKELM.realm(101)
6. The Hermit's Commit: SKELM.realm(110)
7. The Lost and Gone-for Ledger: SKELM.realm(111)

The SKELM Chronicles: Renaissance

1. Foudre: SKELM.reign(001)
2. Méprise: SKELM.reign(010)
3. Fugue: SKELM.reign(011)
4. Emprise: SKELM.reign(100)
5. Mensonge: SKELM.reign(101)
6. Syncope: SKELM.reign(110)
7. Cadence: SKELM.reign(111)

About the Author

DARBY SKELM

Creator of The SKELM Chronicles.

Writes from the glitch.

skelm.quest

Open mouths, empty heads, big bytes.

Stay Incompatible

Ten more series await in the static.

Join the underground:

popoffyour.top

Open mouths, empty heads, big bytes.

www.ingramcontent.com/pod-product-compliance
Lightning Source LLC
LaVergne TN
LVHW041057080826
845145LV00007B/1609

* 9 7 8 1 9 6 8 5 6 4 2 9 2 *